UNPLUGGED

THE WEB'S BEST SCI-FI & FANTASY: 2008 DOWNLOAD

OTHER BOOKS EDITED BY
RICH HORTON

———

Fantasy: The Best of the Year, 2006 Edition
Fantasy: The Best of the Year, 2007 Edition
Fantasy: The Best of the Year, 2008 Edition
Science Fiction: The Best of the Year, 2006 Edition
Science Fiction: The Best of the Year, 2007 Edition
Science Fiction: The Best of the Year, 2008 Edition

UNPLUGGED

THE WEB'S BEST SCI-FI & FANTASY:
2008 DOWNLOAD

edited by
RICH HORTON

UNPLUGGED: THE WEB'S BEST SCI-FI & FANTASY

Wyrm Publishing
www.wyrmpublishing.com

ISBN: 978-1-890464-11-0

TABLE OF CONTENTS

THE WORLD OF ONLINE SPECULATIVE FICTION

RICH HORTON

This anthology is intended to showcase the growth, in both quantity and quality, of short speculative fiction published online. There has been short SF published online for over a decade now—for pretty much as long as there has been a Web, I would think. And online publishing has been the "next big thing" for nearly as long, it sometimes seems! But the short fiction universe remains even now dominated by the magazines and major anthologies, at least, as measured by such things as number of award nominations and number of stories reprinted in "Best of the Year" books.

There are, I think, three reasons for this. One is simply that entrepreneurs have been slow in figuring out how to make money with an online fiction site. The models to date are of four sorts (with variations). There are some subscription sites, such as *Jim Baen's Universe* and *Orson Scott Card's Intergalactic Medicine Show*. There are sites that rely on contributions, such as *Strange Horizons* and the late lamented *Helix*. There are those that rely on advertising—perhaps the late, very much lamented *Sci Fiction* qualifies (though really that was mostly a site subsidized by the Sci Fi Channel), and certainly the very impressive new *Tor.com* serves to some extent as an advertisement for Tor books. (Of course "click-through" ads for other businesses can be used as well.) And there are those that don't try to make money—labors of love. It's hard for me to believe that the last model can be sustained, but over time I think the viability of the other models is slowly improving. (A variant that can sort of combine all three money-making models is sites that exist primarily to promote books published by the site owner—which makes them advertising—but that can also ask for donations, and could possibly combine donations with eventual qualification for a free book after enough donations, which verges on "subscription.")

Another problem of sorts for online sites has been a general reluctance to publish longer stories. Many sites, such as *Strange Horizons*, have word limits in the range of 9,000 or less. The reason for this is partly budgetary, but in addition many feel that readers won't put up with on-screen stories that require too much time in front of a monitor. (And, indeed, I read long online stories only after printing them out.) However, the improvement of portable e-reading devices (such as Kindle) and the change in people's online habits (lots more people taking laptops everywhere, for instance) suggest to me that that objection may be diminishing in force. So I hope to continue to see more novellas online.

Finally of course there is the weight of history. Magazines like *Analog*, *F&SF*, and *Asimov's* have all earned prestige simply by a long period of respected publishing. That means that sometimes they get the first look at stories from certain authors, and that they are the first place many readers go to find what they expect to be the best stories.

All that said, times are changing. Now by no means do I want to replace the print magazines with online publication. I love the old magazines, and I love books, and love ink and paper too! I hope they survive. (Though such news as the recent near-death of *Realms of Fantasy*, combined with the continuing stagnant or declining circulations of most every magazine, does not exactly fill one with hope.) But that aside I have seen a continued improvement in the quality of the fiction published online. Of course online stories have been anthologized for years, and many have won awards. But now it is time for a book composed entirely of speculative fiction stories first published online—and now such a book is, I think, as good a selection of stories as those that draw from print sources.

One thing this book does not do, however, is to feature stories that explicitly make use of presentation strategies available only (or best used, at any rate) online. One reason for this of course it that reproducing such tricks—most obviously hyperlinks—in print is difficult. Another reason is that effective stories of that type remain surprisingly rare. I don't recall any such in the SF field from 2008 (though a nod to the *Shadow Unit* site, which does have numerous extra features like character biographies, ought to be made). I will mention that in previous years I saw a couple of nice examples in the webzine *Ideomancer*—from March 2007, "23 Small Disasters," twenty-three cleverly interlinked short-shorts by Benjamin Rosenbaum, Christopher Barzak, Elad Haber, Greg van Eekhout, Kiini

Ibura Salaam, Meghan McCarron, and Tim Pratt; and from June 2006, Ruth Nestvold's "Triple Helix," a hypertexted look at an alien species.

So, this anthology celebrates the best online SF and fantasy fiction of 2008. As it worked out—mostly by accident—this book includes just one story each from a number of different sites, which collectively represent most but not quite all of the top sources of online fiction. See the list of recommended stories and recommended online sources for SF and Fantasy for further reading!

Finally, I would be remiss were I not first to mention the first truly influential site for online short science fiction: *Sci Fiction*, edited by Ellen Datlow and funded by the Sci Fi Channel. *Sci Fiction* ran from 2000 through 2005, publishing approximately one new story per week, plus a couple of reprints each month. They published a lot of really first rate stuff, helped by Datlow's exceptional editing skills, and by a generous budget that made them the best-paying market in the field at the time. *Sci Fiction* featured a number of award-winning stories, including Linda Nagata's "Goddesses," the first online story to win the Nebula. It is *Sci Fiction* that really showed what can be done online in the short SF area, and it set a high bar that has yet to be cleared by any other webzine—though the continual improvement of the online field as evidence, I believe, in the stories collected here, makes that bar closer and closer.

AIR AND ANGELS
BETH BERNOBICH

[*Subterranean*, Spring]

As everyone knew, Lady Miriam Grey's soirées were the most exclusive in all London. Members of Parliament, literary icons, eligible daughters of the rich, even a spare noble or two could be found on Mondays and Thursdays in her exquisite drawing room, there to partake in brilliant conversation or to sample the delectable fare. More fanciful rumors said Lady Grey had seduced, then abducted her amazing French cook. Of course that was mere foolish speculation, but as Lady Grey herself said, Society loved its stepchild, Gossip.

It was for all these reasons—the gossip, society's expectations, but most especially the eligible daughters—that Stephen Eliot nearly sent his regrets. Nearly, but not so. His parents had made the consequences all too plain if he did not attend.

Dear Mama. My respected Papa. Stephen mentally tipped them a bow as he mounted the steps to Lady Grey's townhouse in Berkeley Square. He was unpardonably late, he knew. The bells from St. George's were ringing half past nine. The day's vivid October sunset had bled into twilight hours ago, and the edge of full night advanced swiftly upon the city.

A butler admitted him into the entry hall. Stephen was turning over his hat and gloves, when he heard a delighted cry.

"Stephen!"

Lady Grey glided toward him. She was dressed in a distinctly Continental mode, in dark blue Chine-figured silk draped about with lacy scarves. Exquisite as always, and with the grace and energy of a far-younger female, but Stephen could not escape the distinct impression of age overtaking a beautiful woman. He covered his sudden confusion by bowing and kissing her proffered hands.

"I am so glad to see you again," she said. "I missed you terribly."

"And I you," Stephen replied. "It is because of you I am here."

She laughed softly. "You lie beautifully, Stephen." Then, in a lower voice, she added, "So beautifully, indeed, I wish I had seduced you years ago, when you were younger and I more foolish in these matters."

"Ah, but you never had any inclination for younger men."

"Just as well. Now we can comfortably be friends instead of disappointed lovers." She took him by the arm and led him into the drawing room. "Come, let me introduce you to several other friends. Their acquaintance will go far to soothe your parents."

Stephen soon found himself exchanging greetings with the secretary of a rising politician, a recently appointed ambassador to Germany, a financier. "Influential men," Lady Grey murmured as they continued through the room. "You might wish to call upon them tomorrow. No, do not protest. You have time enough to make your choices later. But now, to make this evening more pleasant for you and for another young guest . . . "

They had come to the other end of the drawing room. An arched doorway led into a small elegant parlor where a few men and women listened intently as an older white-haired gentleman expounded on the state of England's African and Indian colonies. In another corner, a famous actress, whose name was sometimes connected with that of the king, held her own court. Lady Grey continued past them to a quiet nook at the far end. A young woman sat there alone. She was dressed in a simple mourning gown, with her hair drawn back in a loose coil. She was writing in a small notebook with the stub of a pencil, oblivious to the company around her.

"Miss Dubois," said Lady Grey. "What are you doing, scribbling like a schoolgirl when you should be enjoying yourself?"

The young woman gave a start, then laughed. "Lady Grey. One might think you were seriously scolding me."

"I am never serious, except when it profits me. Mister Eliot, I would like to introduce you to a dear friend of mine, Miss Eva Dubois. Her grandfather was also a much-valued friend."

Eva Dubois's eyes were a deep rich brown, the exact shade of her hair. A flush edged her cheeks, either from amusement or embarrassment, Stephen could not say. He noticed smudges of lead on her fingers, where she gripped her pencil, and one beside her mouth, as though she had rubbed her thumb there in abstraction. He bowed. "Miss Dubois."

"Mister Elliot." She closed the notebook, but not before Stephen glimpsed a complex diagram and closely written notes filling half the next page. How very odd.

"Mister Eliot has just returned from a few years abroad," Lady Grey said. "Studying mathematics and the human nature, though the latter was not necessarily a formal program. Eva, I believe you will find each other excellent company. Stephen, I must see to my other guests, but do speak with me before you go."

She departed for the drawing room. Meanwhile, Eva Dubois was studying Stephen with an unreadable look. Unsettled, Stephen took a seat next to her on the sofa. As soon as he did, she slid her notebook into a handbag at her feet. "So," she said, "you are studying mathematics?"

Stephen shrugged. "I was, after a fashion. Are you interested in the subject, Miss Dubois?"

Her lips twitched. "After a fashion," she replied archly. "Or would you rather talk about your travels? If not that, we might discuss the October weather, or the possibility of the sun rising tomorrow. I'm certain we might discover some topic of sufficient interest to us both that we could satisfy conventions."

He flushed. "I am sorry. I never thought you would—I mean, I never thought—" He stopped and shook his head. "I'm sorry. I was rude. Rude and unthinking. I . . . Miss Dubois, it's doubly uncivil of me to say so, but you are not what I expected."

If he expected her to show dismay, or outrage, he was mistaken. Eva Dubois smiled, a warm genuine smile. The change was so sudden and acute that Stephen blinked in surprise. "You were not uncivil, you were honest," she said. "Unless you believe, Mister Eliot, as my father did, that honesty is another form of insolence."

Her voice had all the surface qualities he associated with well-bred young women, but something in the slight emphasis on his name, the shadow beside her mouth, suggested a much older, much more sophisticated person, as though an angel had come to visit this world in the guise of an innocent.

He shook away the strange impression, and was about to reply, when his attention was caught by another entering the parlor. But *enter* was too insipid a word—this woman strode through the arched doorway like a man, oblivious to the curious looks of the women, the frank appraising stares of the men.

Her gaze swept the room and alighted upon Stephen and his companion. "Eva," she said. "You remember our previous engagement, do you not?"

An aunt, Stephen thought, or an older cousin. He could tell by the cant of their eyes, the echo of line and color in their features. He rose and held out a hand. "Delighted to meet you," he said. "You must be Miss Dubois's—"

"—sister," Eva said. "Mister Stephen Eliot, my sister, Lily Dubois."

Lily Dubois favored him with a brief, uninterested glance. There were faint lines beside her eyes and mouth, and her complexion lacked the creamy radiance of Eva's. What intrigued him more were the white scars over her fingers and the back of her hand, which caught his attention when she impatiently tucked a loose strand behind her ear. He glanced down and saw the other hand was equally scarred.

"I am so glad you find me worthy of close inspection, Mister Eliot," Lily said. She turned back to her sister. "Eva, enough with the pleasantries. We must take our leave now."

Eva Dubois rose at once and tucked her bag with its mysterious notebook under her arm. "My apologies, Mister Eliot, but my sister has it right. We are promised elsewhere, and must hurry or we shall be unpardonably late."

Her fingertips brushed his, then she was following her sister from the room, a stir of whispers following in the wake of their passage.

"So," Gilbert Wardle said, "the prodigal son has returned."

"I had no choice," Stephen said. "My parents wish me to marry and start a career. I wanted another year abroad to complete my studies but—"

"—but they threatened to cut off your allowance and you were not about to play the impoverished student."

They were sitting in one of the upper rooms of Gilbert's club. The hour was late; most of the other members had departed for home. A few remained to enjoy a whiskey and cigar, as Stephen and Gilbert did, and the haze of their smoke drifted through the room, making the air close and stale. Stephen ran a hand across his eyes. He felt an incipient headache coming on.

Gilbert watched him through narrowed eyes. "I've offended you, haven't I?"

Stephen shrugged. "Yes. No. It's true I made a mess of my studies.

Perhaps my father had the right—that I liked the role of student better than the actual work."

"Now you are being merely foolish," his friend said. "You were handy enough at Cambridge. What happened to send you off course?"

"Oh, the usual. I let myself become distracted by novelties. I was on the point of . . . " Stephen broke off with a smothered laugh. "My apologies. Excuses are tedious. Suffice to say that I neglected my classes in favor of drinking and wenching—in short, the ordinary run of vices. And that is all the self-pity I shall inflict upon you. How goes your own work? You landed a plum of an appointment with Lord Randall, if I recall."

Gilbert gave an elaborate sigh. "The same as always. Boring. A bloody boring sinecure, pardon my language. But at least it keeps me in funds."

There was a pause while they both sipped their whiskeys. The room had emptied out in the past few moments. Even now the last two members trailed out the door, leaving behind a silence and a solitude that made the room's air seem even warmer and closer than before. Stephen swirled the whiskey around in his glass, and considered ordering another, perhaps with less soda. His discretion overtook his urge; he set the glass aside and rubbed his forehead again.

"You know," Gilbert said, "you might like the work I do. It's not so very taxing, and it would give you the means to live independently. You would have time enough to pursue mathematics on your own. Are you interested?"

He spoke in the same languid tones Stephen remembered from their university days. Still charming, still handsome, with the deep blue eyes and patrician features so loved by women, he was like a Dorian Grey, only without the vice, Stephen thought. And yet, watching him now, Stephen thought he could see shadows underneath the glittering exterior.

"Mind," Gilbert went on, "there is no guarantee, merely a suggestion. I shall have to speak with my superiors. But I did not wish to meddle unless you agreed."

A sinecure. It did not sound very appealing, but Stephen did not wish to refuse outright. "I shall have to think about it," he said.

"Fair enough." Gilbert drew a long breath on the cigar and breathed out a stream of smoke. "So tell me, fair one, how did you like Miss Eva Dubois?"

"How did you—"

His friend waved a hand. "Rumors," he said lightly. "They fly like eagles, swifter than leopards and keener than wolves. Or something like that. In this particular case, the leopard was young Littlefair. He too attended Lady Grey's soirée and saw you talking with the girl. Did you like her?"

"I hardly had time to make her acquaintance. Why? Do you?"

The smoke rippled as Gilbert shook his head. "Hardly. Sweet young virgins do not appeal to me. And before you make the suggestion, I have no interest in the sister either. A freakish creature, that one. Have you heard the story? No? Ah, now I remember. You had departed for the Continent a few months before the scandal broke. I must enlighten you, then."

Without asking Stephen, he called for two more whiskeys. When the waiter brought them, he asked the man to see what kind of night it was outside and, if the weather had turned wet, could he summon a cab for them. Stephen watched, silently, noticing that Gilbert did not resume speaking until the waiter had retreated from the room. A wisp of breeze from the closing doors stirred the smoky air.

"About the Dubois family," Gilbert went on. "The grandfather had his moment of fame in the Royal Society with some well-received papers on astronomy. The father took to law, where there was more money. He—the father, that is—had hoped for sons, but when Fate offered him daughters, he attempted to do the right thing. Governesses. Sizeable dowries. He married the elder off to a colleague two years ago. A decent man who allowed his wife to indulge in her odd fancy for chemistry, but the girl showed little gratitude and ran away several times. At last the man divorced her, and she vanished from society until two months ago. Rumor says that Lady Grey lent the girl money so she would not be on the street, but no one knows."

"What about the younger?" Stephen asked.

Gilbert sipped his whiskey and made a face, as though the drink did not meet his expectations. "Our friend Rumor is curiously silent on that matter. All I know is that she lived in the country with her parents until two months ago, when the mother and father died suddenly in a carriage accident. The elder girl returned with indecent haste to oversee the property, and from time to time, she and her sister visit the city."

"You seem to know a great deal about two girls you don't care for."

His friend grinned. "All rungs of society feed upon gossip, my child. The girls are nothing. It's their cousin who intrigues me. Lucien Fell."

Lucien Fell. Rumor coupled his name with those of the seedier actresses and money merchants. There was even talk about his connection to more dangerous figures in the London underworld. Stephen could not suppress a shudder. "What about him?"

"For myself, merely the fascination we all have for the truly disreputable. Beyond that . . . Let me say only that friends of a colleague of certain friends expressed interest. If, by chance, as you go about your social rounds, and hear aught about Friend Fell, let me know. One favor begets another, as the saying goes."

In the candlelight, with his eyes hooded like a cat's, Gilbert appeared more a stranger than a friend. *He has changed,* Stephen thought. His mouth had turned dry, and he wanted to call for a glass of water, but something in Gilbert's unblinking gaze made him think better. "Very well," he said. "I promise to do what I can."

Gilbert rewarded him with one of his old, affectionate smiles. "Dear Stephen, how astonished you look. Come, let us leave this miserable stuffy room. A walk should do us both good." He stood and held out his hand. "I've missed you, Stephen. I'm glad you decided to return."

It was odd, Stephen thought, how a long absence made all the familiar landscapes alien and strange. For the next two days, he spent his mornings paying calls—the social rounds Gilbert had alluded to. And just as dutifully, he had accepted dinner invitations from various influential men Lady Grey introduced him to at her soirée. But the whole business had an aspect of irreality about it, and he fully expected to blink and find himself transported back to his rooms in Paris.

His current surrounding did nothing to ease the impression. He had called upon his old advisor from University that afternoon, expecting to spend a quarter hour drinking strong tea and listening to a lecture on his morals. Instead, Doctor Adams had announced they would take an outing on this last fine day in autumn. Now Stephen found himself trudging through the leaf-blown gardens of the Crystal Palace Park. The palace itself glittered atop its hill, like a fantastical creature descended from the scudding clouds.

A sharp gust of wind spattered him with water from a nearby fountain. Stephen pulled his hat low over his face and leaned toward his companion to catch his last words.

"I said . . . I am surprised and pleased you called," Doctor Adams repeated. "I won't flatter myself that you want advice, so I won't give you any. My opinions, however, are another matter."

He leaned heavily upon Stephen's arm, using his cane to propel himself forward along. Stephen hurried to keep pace, wishing they had taken the sheltered passageway from the train station, instead of this windy winding path. "I ought to have written before," he began.

"There are many things you ought to have done. You did not. Forget them and concentrate on the future, Mister Eliot. Or have you forgotten all your lessons?"

Stephen smiled. "I seem to have, but now that I have you to remind me . . . "

Doctor Adams snorted. "Fools are those who depend upon others. Ah, speaking of fools . . . "

They had come to the so-called prehistoric swamp with its models of dinosaurs. Stephen squinted at the three Ichthyosaurus—massive crocodile-like creatures shown oozing from the waters. He was about to ask Doctor Adams his opinion on evolution, when he realized the old professor was not looking at the dinosaurs, but an enormous hot-air balloon, which even now was attempting an ascent, its basket filled with shrieking children.

"Fools," Doctor Adams repeated. "They'll have that balloon wrecked inside five minutes. The wind's all wrong."

"It's one of those new navigable balloons," Stephen offered.

"Doesn't make a damned bit of difference, as you well know."

The professor went on to lecture about wind currents and downdrafts. Stephen attended dutifully in spite of the chill and the lingering damp from the fountains. Once or twice, he tried (without success) to suggest they continue toward the palace itself. He had just succeeded in turning the old man back toward the path, when the sight of a familiar figure arrested his attention.

Eva Dubois.

She stood some distance away, swathed in a sensible dark-brown wrap, her head tilted back as she observed the balloon's uncertain ascent. Nearby was the sister—Lily, he remembered—who was engaged in close conversation with a short, stocky man with a swarthy complexion. The man leaned close to Lily Dubois, as she spoke earnestly in his ear.

Even as he observed them, the conversation ended, and Lily Dubois and her sister continued toward the palace. The unknown man stared after them a moment, then abruptly swung around and headed in the opposite direction. With a chill, Stephen recognized his face from countless newssheets—it was Lucien Fell.

"You're shivering," Doctor Adams said. "Shall we continue inside, then?"

"Yes, of course," Stephen said distractedly. He craned his head around, trying to see which direction Fell took, but the man had already vanished around a bend in the path, and so he gave himself over to following Doctor Adams toward the palace's grand entrance. They passed the great Sphinxes flanking the stairs and entered the central transept. It was warmer here, the grand space luminous with sunlight; the faint scent of orchids and other exotic flowers drifted through the air.

They spent hours visiting the palace's numerous exhibits, with Doctor Adams offering his observations on each one. By the time they completed a meticulous tour of the Technological Museum, then the basement with its collection of printing machines, Stephen had entirely lost his earlier sense of irreality. Now they were ascending the stairs to the ground floor. The newly installed inclined elevator rose to the second floor galleries; beyond it, the indoor gardens extended south. There was also a pavilion, where weary visitors might rest and take refreshments.

And there, sitting among the shabby and the fashionable, was Eva Dubois. She was alone this time, without even her elder sister for a companion. Her wrap had fallen from her shoulders, and she was scribbling furiously in a notebook, oblivious to the chattering crowds around her.

"Ah," breathed Doctor Adams. "It is Miss Dubois."

"You know her?" Stephen asked.

"I knew her grandfather. Let us pay our respects."

They threaded their way between the tables and chairs. As they approached the one where Eva Dubois sat, Stephen hung back, thinking he ought not to intrude upon her self-imposed isolation. Doctor Adams had no such qualms. "Miss Dubois," he called out, advancing toward her alone. "What a pleasure to encounter you here."

Eva Dubois glanced up and hastily closed her notebook. "Doctor Adams." Her voice was breathless. "You gave me such a fright."

"Hardly. You are merely being secretive, as always. I see you have not lost your old habits of writing in notebooks, just as you did when you were a child."

She smiled, but her cheeks took on an added flush of embarrassment. "Oh, not quite the same. I . . . I was just writing out a list for some errands. Lily and I have so much to accomplish before we leave the city tomorrow." As she spoke, she rose and drew her wrap around her shoulders. "And speaking of those errands, if you will excuse me . . . "

It was then her gaze encountered Stephen's. She paused in recognition. "Mister Eliot."

Stephen achieved an awkward bow. "Miss Dubois."

"You know each other?" Doctor Adams said.

"We met at Lady Grey's this past Monday," Eva said. Then to Stephen, "I had no idea you were acquainted with Doctor Adams."

"I—"

"Mister Eliot was a student of mine," Doctor Adams said. "I thought him quite promising at the time, and so naturally, he has wasted his talents abroad. But perhaps he might find inspiration closer to home." He nodded to Eva Dubois.

"Perhaps," she said dryly. She favored Stephen with a direct look, which seemed to identify and catalogue all his insufficiencies. Unsettled, he could not think how to reply.

Luckily, he was spared the necessity. "My dear," said Doctor Adams. "I just wanted to offer my condolences about your parents. If you and your sister need anything—anything at all—come to me at once. For your own sakes, as well as your grandfather's."

Her expression warmed and she offered Doctor Adams her hand. "Thank you. That is so very kind of you. But indeed we are quite well at the moment. So well, that Lily and I have planned a small gathering of old friends at our house this weekend. Very impromptu, I'm afraid, though we are sending out proper invitations today. We would be so pleased if you could attend."

With old-fashioned courtesy, Doctor Adams offered his regrets—unavoidable obligations, previous engagements, etc.—but perhaps Miss Dubois and her sister would come to dinner in the city next month. With equal courtesy, Eva Dubois explained they expected to take a long journey next month. "Though," she added, "there is a possibility we might have to delay our departure." She hesitated briefly, then turned to Stephen. "Mister

Eliot, what about you? Do you also have other obligations this weekend? I spoke with my sister about you. She said she would be delighted to have you attend."

Taken by surprise, Stephen stammered something incomprehensible. Dimly, he heard Eva Dubois go on to mention the names of other guests—members of the Royal Society, well-regarded artists, friends of her grandfather and of Lady Grey. His parents would be pleased and horrified at the same time. He ought to refuse . . .

. . . if by chance, you hear ought about Friend Fell, let me know . . .

"Will your cousin be there?" he asked abruptly.

A brief silence ensued. "It is possible," she said slowly. "You mean my cousin Lawrence, do you not?"

Stephen recovered himself. "Yes. I meant your cousin Lawrence. But that was merely curiosity on my part. Of course, I would be delighted to attend your gathering."

"The generosity is all yours."

Her eyes narrowed with suppressed amusement. Again he had the impression of a sophistication beyond her years. *But she is a mere girl,* he thought, intrigued all over again. Before he could make a suitable riposte, however, Eva Dubois was repeating her excuses about errands and obligations to Doctor Adams. Another glance in his direction, a politely murmured good-bye, and she was hurrying toward the front entrance of the palace.

"You say Lucien Fell will be present?"

"So the girl implied."

"Ah."

A monosyllabic utterance that implied so much, Stephen thought. Satisfaction. Curiosity.

The written invitation to the Dubois household had arrived Thursday morning. Stephen had immediately sent a note to Gilbert Wardle, saying he would like to drop around in the evening. A silent manservant had ushered Stephen into a small parlor. After serving them port, he had departed and closed the doors. The room itself was far more richly appointed than Stephen had expected, even knowing about Gilbert's personal wealth—an enormous leather-covered Chesterfield, some very fine bronze figures, and several oil paintings of water lilies done in the modern style.

"Would you like to see the letter?" he asked.

Gilbert took the much-folded sheet and scanned it. "Hmmm . . . hopes to fulfill proper etiquette . . . begs your attendance . . . sister expressed a desire to continue . . . What a very odd creature. And her handwriting is more like a clerk's than a woman's. What is that about the sister?"

"Nothing," Stephen said hastily.

His friend tilted his head. "I would venture to say more than nothing, but never mind. We all have our secrets. Have you accepted?"

"I did but—"

"But you dislike the prospect of quarreling with your father. Such a weak excuse, my fair child. However, you are not entirely in the wrong. It's best if we avoid any unpleasantness. So, let me think. Let me think."

He leaned back and closed his eyes. Stephen sipped his port and scanned the newspapers spread over the table. The headlines were troubling. Entente with France. Menace of the German fleet. Trouble in Ireland. Rumors of further plots against the king. The world had tipped over from one century to the next. Even if he could transport himself at once to the Continent, he was not certain he could resume the carefree student life he'd known before.

"I know," Gilbert said, breaking into his reverie. "You shall tell your parents that an old friend from University days has invited you to his house in the countryside. Tell them we are traveling together in my carriage. Make up some excuse to leave your man behind."

"Won't that look suspicious?"

"Not if you drop hints that our dear friend has fallen on bad times, and that we are all roughing it in sympathy. Use your imagination."

Easier to say than do, Stephen thought. "And what about Lucien Fell?" he said. "Should I do anything? Say anything?"

"No. I want you to observe the man. Watch what he does. Note whom he talks to. If you can overhear what they say, do it, but whatever else, do not make a spectacle of yourself." Gilbert's face relaxed into a smile. "It's gossip, Stephen. One never knows what fruit the tree will bear. So we tend it, hoping for the best."

The next two days all went far more easily than Stephen had expected. His parents made no objections, and following Gilbert's advice, Stephen offered no explanations, though he felt a strong urge to. By late Friday afternoon, he was enclosed in his friend's carriage, riding through the glorious autumnal day. He ought to have experienced a sense of liberation once they passed the outer bounds of London, but he could only think how Eva and Gilbert both wished something from him, and it had nothing to do with friendship.

His first view of the Dubois estate did nothing to cure his uneasiness.

A ring of thick stone walls marked the edge of their property. Beyond the iron gates, a long paved driveway wound beneath oaks and chestnuts. Old money, Gilbert had said. And yet, there was a curious air of neglect about the place. Dead leaves smothered the grass. Here and there he noted bracken and weeds, the rank scent of wild things.

Another ten minutes brought the carriage to the front door. As Stephen disembarked, a dozen or more servants appeared to take care of his luggage. The house itself was a massive rambling structure—wings flung themselves out to either side, ornamented with porticoes and columns and a collection of buttresses. More signs of neglect met his eyes—patches of ivy grew over the walls, and moss made the stones slippery underfoot.

His rooms, at least, were clean and comfortable. Gas had not yet been laid here, but the candles were beeswax, the carpet thick, and the bedclothes freshly laundered and warmed. Stephen dressed with care and soon found his way back to the drawing room, where the footman had politely informed him the guests would gather before dinner.

The first person he encountered was Lily Dubois, nearly unrecognizable in a flowing dinner gown of richly-figured Chine. "Mister Eliot. I'm so glad nothing prevented us from enjoying your company. Come, let me introduce you to the other guests."

She led him into the drawing room, which belied any signs of the neglect he'd noted elsewhere—fine crystal chandeliers, the polished dark wood floors and Oriental rugs scattered about. All signs of prosperity and taste. The centerpiece of the room was a massive stone fireplace, laid with a generous fire. He scanned the room, looking for Lucien Fell. No sign of that particular disreputable man. Indeed the company was most respectable. Among those gathered about the fireplace, he recognized Sir Benjamin Baker and William Huggins, both much-lauded members of the Royal Society. Not far away stood a celebrated author and his entourage. There were even a few women present, bright gossamer beings amongst the soberly dressed men in their black or grey dinner costumes.

Then, across the room, he sighted Eva Dubois, speaking with a stout, white-haired gentleman with a scientific air. He paused. She happened to glance in his direction. An uncharacteristic smile illuminated her face, one that produced conflicting impulses within Stephen.

The decision was taken away from him, when after murmuring something to the white-haired gentleman, she came forward. "Mister Eliot. I am so glad you came."

"Miss Dubois," he said, making a bow.

She held out her hands. He kissed them, thinking her manner had greatly changed in just two days. Far more cordial, almost intimate. She was not like other young gentlewomen he had met, even abroad; nor was she anything like the artist's models or professional courtesans he'd sometimes taken home. Eva leaned closer, speaking into his ear, her breath tickling his cheek. She was wearing perfume, a faint woody scent, very pleasing. The scent invaded his senses, causing him to lose the thread of conversation.

With some effort, he drew back, only to realize the butler had announced dinner. He heard Eva Dubois saying something about how the number of guests prevented her from sharing his company during the meal. "I'm so sorry," she murmured. "I had hoped to continue our conversation sooner, but there are other guests I must see to. Perhaps afterward . . . "

She vanished into the crowds. Stephen tried to draw a breath to clear his head, but the scent of her perfume clung to his hands and lips. In a daze, he allowed the servants to guide him to his place, between a scientist and a philosopher. Both were learned men, and Stephen did his best to engage in the debate, but he found it difficult to maintain his attention. He ate, vaguely aware of the fine dishes, and drank whenever the servants refilled his glass.

The dinner ended at last. Stephen rose at once, only to see Eva vanish through a small doorway. The number of guests had swelled, or so it seemed to his oppressed senses. He escaped into one of the smaller sitting rooms, where a few men—all strangers—had gathered to drink whiskey. He wandered past them, through a pair of glass doors and across a stone-paved patio, into the garden beyond.

Blessed darkness closed around him. He breathed in the cool clear air and felt the wine fumes dissipate. Gilbert and his schemes be damned, he ought to have refused this invitation. Fell would never attend a gathering such as this one. The girl must have sensed his interest and used her cousin's name as a lure. But why? She was not the sort to fish for a liaison.

He walked on, pondering how to extract himself from the household without causing offense to either Gilbert or the Dubois girls. Gradually he became aware that he had left the house itself far behind, and that the surrounding gardens had turned into fields. He slowed, uncertain of the path. Just ahead he saw the gleam of water beneath a new moon. Then a movement in the shadows caught his eye—someone else had escaped from the house. He paused, thinking he would rather avoid conversation, when a familiar voice accosted him.

"Mister Eliot." Eva Dubois's voice carried the hint of suppressed laughter. "Are you running away?"

"No. I— I merely wished for some quiet."

She laughed and took his arm. "Then let us escape into the night."

Her warm hands encircled his, and she led him unresisting down the path. Eva Dubois wore a new perfume, he noticed—a much stronger, muskier scent that reminded him of orchids. Underneath it, the scent of the other perfume lingered, its woody notes combining with this new one to create a strangely intoxicating aroma, as though they had left England's tame gardens behind for some exotic jungle. Stephen shook his head to clear it, wondering where Eva was taking him. He glimpsed a wide field, beyond it a dark woodland, caught the warm rich fragrance of dying lilies. Clouds flitted over the moon's face, causing shadows to flicker over the leaves, and he thought about wild cats, hunting in the moonlit jungle.

"So tell me about your mathematical studies," she said. "Or have you given them over?"

"I . . . I haven't decided yet."

"Are you waiting for someone to *inspire* you, then?"

Vaguely, he remembered Doctor Adams using those same words. "You mean a wife?"

"Isn't that what it always means? No, I mean— Never mind what I mean. Here is what I wanted to show you."

They had come to a small building—quite far from the house, as Stephen discovered when he glanced around. Large crates and boxes obstructed the path around the building. The air smelled of crushed grass, as though many feet had trampled the fields. He turned toward the crates and boxes, curious, but Eva re-directed his attention back to the building, which he realized was an observatory. A quite fine structure, built along modern lines and with what looked like a splendid telescope protruding from a slit in its roof.

"My grandfather," Eva said, before he could ask. "He built it to confirm his theories about mathematics and the stars. My blessed father never saw a reason to dismantle it."

She unlatched the door and took him inside. There she guided him between more boxes and strange equipment, to the telescope. With an expert air, she adjusted the lenses and showed him how to gaze through the eyepiece to see the moon suddenly brought sharp and close. Jupiter and Mars were there, and beyond them the bright pinpoints of light across the gulf of night. All the while, she described her grandfather's exploration of the skies, which she had repeated and expanded upon. But as he listened, he realized she spoke of more than nebulae and star clusters and constellations. She spoke of other worlds, and how they might be inhabited, just as the Earth was.

"Other worlds?" Stephen asked, hardly able to keep the laughter from his voice.

She rounded on him. It was impossible to see her features in the gloom, but he could sense her anger, her passion. "Yes. Of course. We are hardly alone in the universe. Who knows when they might decide to visit us? Or we them?"

He hardly knew how to answer her.

"You think me bedazzled by a fantasy," she went on. "But remember, while you were traversing the Continent, free and unencumbered, I sat here alone and watched the stars. You cannot imagine how often I wished I could pluck myself from this house, this world, and go shooting outward—"

She stopped abruptly. "My apologies. I have embarrassed you, I see."

"No," Stephen said. "I understand."

"Do you?" She glanced up, eyes bright from tears.

"I do," he whispered.

There was a long moment, while neither of them moved. Then, Eva reached up and touched Stephen's cheek with her bare hand. The sense of her skin upon his was electric. A shiver went through him, and it took all his self-control not to kiss her.

Eva leaned close to him, her perfume flooding his senses. "Stephen," she said, and guided his hand to her breast.

His lips met hers. After that memory fragmented to individual sensations. The baring of skin. The discovery of blankets upon the floor. Before he was aware, Eva had raised her voluminous skirts, and he . . . he was plunging fast and deep into the warmth of her sex. Eva held him tight, urged him on in ways he had not experienced since certain nights spent with an Italian courtesan.

Memories blurred after that. He remembered little more than a final gasp, a moment where he was torn between violence and tenderness. Then, with his fingers gradually releasing his grip upon her hair, he drew back with a sigh.

Stephen came to himself in his own rooms. He lay, half-undressed, on top of the bedcovers. His body was damp. His head was spinning—from the wine, no doubt. He had drunk far too much at dinner. And afterward . . .

He bolted upright. The sudden movement brought a surge of bile into his mouth. He clamped his lips shut and swallowed. Wiped a hand over his face. His skin smelt of sweat and wine, of Eva Dubois's perfume and the heady scent of their mutual spendings. No dream. No doubt at all what had happened.

Remorse swept over him, followed swiftly by a flush of remembered passion. He stumbled from bed and pulled on his trousers and a shirt taken randomly from the clothespress. A splash of cool water from the basin helped to clear his thoughts. He had to find Eva. Apologize. She was merely flirting with him, the way some naive girls did. But she was no serving girl, to be bedded and forgotten. He had to make restitution.

He lurched from his room into the darkened corridor. Pale sunlight leaked through a window at the far end of the hallway. It was dawn, or thereabouts.

"Sir, is something wrong?" The voice came from behind him. Male. Deferential. A servant.

"Eva Dubois." Stephen's voice came out thick and garbled. He swallowed and tried again. "Miss Eva Dubois. Do you know if she has arisen yet?"

The servant seemed unsurprised by this request. "Miss Dubois left word in case you should ask, sir. Come with me, if you please."

They proceeded through more corridors, across an enclosed courtyard, into a new wing of the mansion. Stacks of crates lined the halls. Most were draped in canvas, but a few stood open, with layers of cotton wadding torn aside to reveal glass bottles, metallic cylinders, and other items Stephen could only guess at. Sharp odors drifted through the air. He paused, trying to identify them, but the servant was unlatching a pair of thick double doors. He motioned for Stephen to go inside.

A long narrow room opened up before him. A very strange room, unlike any he had seen before outside certain buildings at University. On either side, he could make out worktables stacked neatly with more glassware, more strange equipment, and several devices that reminded him uncomfortably of the observatory. At the far end a light burned; a woman sat bent over a worktable, her attention entirely upon a glass beaker set over a tiny blue flame. Racks of vials crowded her desk, but he had the same impression of order and organization. Seemingly unaware of his presence, the woman selected a vial from a rack, measured out a liquid, and added it to the beaker. She observed the results a moment, frowned, and scribbled something into a journal book that lay open beside her.

Stephen coughed. Lily Dubois glanced up. With face illumined by the lamp and burner, she seemed even paler, older than before. "Mister Eliot. Good morning."

Stephen stopped halfway down the aisle. He licked his mouth and tasted the sourness upon his chapped lips. "Miss Dubois. I was—"

"—looking for Eva. Yes, I know."

"Then do you—"

"It would be presumption to say I know everything, but yes, I know the particulars. You need not worry, though I know you will."

The liquid in the beaker started to bubble. Lily's attention shifted abruptly to her experiment. She took up a glass rod and stirred the mixture. Stephen's attention was caught by the pale scars over her hands. Chemical burns. Of course.

"Mister Eliot."

Lily Dubois was observing him closely.

"You appear unwell," she said. "And the hour is far too early for most, I know. I suggest you retire to your rooms and try to sleep. All will be well. I assure you."

She turned her attention back to her chemicals—a clear dismissal. Stephen hesitated a moment, then silently retreated from that vast unnerving room. The same servant waited outside. With a deferential gesture, the man took Stephen by the arm and helped him back to his rooms.

"I am a touch unwell," Stephen murmured. "The air here does not agree with me. Please have someone pack my things and bring the carriage around. I must go back home."

He arrived at his parents' townhouse pale, but clean and neatly dressed. The same nameless, discreet servant had drawn Stephen's bath, laid out his clothes, and fetched a plain breakfast, all without any direction. Later, Stephen thought the man must have received instructions from Lily Dubois to make certain her guest was presentable before he fled. As he suffered through his mother's exclamations, and his father's grim silent looks, he was grateful for her forethought.

His manservant arrived at last, and led a sick and weary Stephen to his rooms, where he collapsed onto his own bed. His mother's physician arrived later, and pronounced him overtaxed. The diagnosis kept his parents and friends away. But within a day, Gilbert Wardle came to call, and Stephen knew he must face his friend's questions.

"You look horrible," Gilbert said lightly, as he settled into a chair beside Stephen's bed. "But not as horrible as the fish they served at our club last night."

Stephen shook his head and immediately regretted it. "Thank you for coming," he whispered. "But I'm afraid I must disappoint you."

Gilbert's eyes gleamed momentarily. "He was not there?"

"No. Nor did anyone mention his name."

"Interesting. He must have misled the girls. Did you happen to overhear anything of interest?"

"Nothing," Stephen said at once. "Nothing that I can remember."

His friend observed him silently for a moment. "I see. Well, perhaps it's for the best you did not stay the entire weekend." Then, in a lighter tone, he added, "Your parents were not pleased, of course. I confessed my part in the debauchery—nostalgia for our University days, sympathy for our friend, an ill-judged drinking contest, etc. However, they seem to recognize that young men must expend their wildness before settling into a respectable life. You'll find them stiff but forgiving when you rise from your bed."

Gilbert remained with him another quarter hour, confining his talk to commonplace subjects—the latest dinner gossip, rumors of the King's dalliances, *etc., etc.* Even as he took his leave, he made no more oblique references to the Dubois girls or to Stephen's sudden, inexplicable flight.

He knows, Stephen thought. *If not the particulars, then the larger shape of events.*

He sank back into his pillows and closed his eyes. He had spent a day pretending that the incident didn't matter. That Lily Dubois would take care of her sister, wiping out any need for him to act. Ballocks, he thought.

Head spinning, he forced himself to sit upright and called for paper and pens so he might write to Eva Dubois. He did not spare himself, he thought, reading over his words. No excuses. Only apologies for his brutish behavior and cowardice. It was necessarily an awkward incoherent effort, but perhaps she would understand.

She did not.

Or at least, she did not answer.

A second letter returned unopened. Then a third.

Two, three weeks passed. By this time, Stephen had learned through oblique questioning that the Dubois sisters remained at their country house. Lady Miriam Grey even sent him a teasing letter, asking what outrage he had offered her young friend, to frighten her away so thoroughly. Merely banter between friends, but Stephen found himself go cold as he read the words.

No more shirking. I did commit an outrage. I must make it right.

He waited until late afternoon, then took a cab to a district far away from fashionable Mayfair, where he hired a horse. By the early evening, he was riding down the wide gravel lane to the Dubois house. The lane was now thickly strewn with golden leaves, and his eye noted other signs of obvious disrepair. More weeds and fallen branches. The walls desperately needing mortar, and the driveway itself pocketed with holes. A cold misty twilight overspread the whole, adding to the gloom and sense of neglect.

In the courtyard, he dismounted. All the windows were dark, but lamplight showed underneath the main doors. He tied his horse to a rail and knocked. A cool breeze fingered his hair, carrying with it the scent of moldering leaves and something else he could not decipher. He shivered, and wished he had worn his winter overcoat.

The door jerked open. A thickset man filled the doorway, his features cast in shadows from the feeble chandelier behind him. He wore plain black clothes and heavy gloves. Not the butler Stephen remembered. A stranger, and definitely not the usual servant. "No one is at home," the man said, before Stephen asked.

"They are," Stephen said. "Miss Eva Dubois is at home. I know it."

"Miss Eva—"

"Never mind, Albert. I know the gentleman."

Lily Dubois motioned for the man to stand aside. She too wore plain dark clothing—men's clothing, he realized with a shock—trousers, a knitted jersey, and sturdy boots. Her hair was pulled back in a tight braid; a flush from the cold colored her cheeks, making her appear younger than before.

She returned his gaze with an amused smile, but he sensed an uneasiness. "Come inside," she said at last. "It seems we must talk at least once before it is all over."

She lit a candle and led him down a series of servant's corridors, toward the back of the house. Their footsteps echoed eerily, and the candle's flame cast unnerving shadows around them, emphasizing the emptiness of the house. Stephen nearly turned back more than once, but curiosity tugged at him, especially after he began to recognize the turnings as those leading him to the same laboratory where he last spoke with Lily Dubois.

"She's inside," Lily said, pointing to the familiar double doors. "I daresay she won't be entirely surprised."

Inside, he found the same familiar scene, but with a few important alterations. The strange equipment was gone, as were most of the books. And this time, it was Eva who sat at the worktable, scribbling in a notebook. Like her sister, she wore trousers and a warm knitted jersey.

Stephen strode forward. "Eva."

Eva straightened abruptly, eyes wide. "Stephen. You should not have come."

"I could not help it," he said. "I wrote—"

"I know," she said. "But, you see, there was no point in answering. Unless you agree, with my late father, that form and propriety outweigh the truth."

They studied each other a few long moments. She had changed, he thought, in any number of indefinable ways. Her mouth no longer had that tightly constrained look about it. Her eyes were bright—with anticipation? Excitement? Only now did he wonder what she did in her sister's laboratory. He glanced down and saw sheets of formulae, written thick upon the paper she held tensely before her. Hastily she turned the sheets over.

"You are confused," she said. "I'm sorry."

"Why are you sorry about now?" Lily Dubois said, as she rounded the worktable to stand beside her sister. "Still worried about the calculations?"

Eva shook her head. "No more than usual. They all still match our expectations." She managed a smile for Stephen. "You seem quite fagged out. Come. We shall have a last supper together."

It was the strangest, most unconventional meal he had ever participated in. No servants. Only a few platters of cold salted beef and stale bread, which Eva fetched herself from the pantry. Instead of wine, they drank well-water so cold it made Stephen's teeth ache. He could see now that Eva Dubois had seduced him, not the other way around, and that Lily Dubois had assisted by supplying those most unnatural perfumes. To what end, he could not tell. His only consolation was that Lily Dubois seemed as uncomfortable with his presence as he was with hers.

The meal ended. Eva Dubois nodded to her sister. "It's time."

"Long past time," Lily said. "He comes with us?"

"I see no other way," Eva replied. "Besides, he can assist with the work that comes after."

"Ah, you mean . . . "

" . . . exactly."

Without waiting for his reply—if there could be one to such a bizarre exchange—the sisters left the room. A moment's hesitation, he followed them. He hoped—expected—they would finally explain everything, but neither one spoke to him. They murmured to each other, their voices so low he could not catch their words, only the tone of barely suppressed excitement. Lily had taken up a candle to light the way through the empty corridors; when they came to a door leading outside, the same thickset stranger waited for them. He had a lit lantern, which he gave to Lily Dubois.

"Thank you, Albert," she said. "How are the preparations?"

"Nearly done," he said.

She nodded. "Very well. We'll go now."

Outside, the fog had dissipated, and stars speckled the clear night sky. With growing impatience, Stephen followed the two women along a wet overgrown path, around the observatory, and into a broad field. Torches illuminated the clearing; by their light, he counted at least a dozen men in work clothes moving about, loading boxes into what appeared to be an immense wooden basket. Ropes, attached to metal rings, rose into the air, to an enormous dark mass overhead. His heart gave a painful leap as he recognized what it was.

A balloon. They've manufactured a balloon.

"What are you doing?" he demanded.

"Escaping," Eva said calmly.

"Where—?"

"To the stars." She smiled at his incredulity. "Dear Stephen. I have been scouring the heavens a decade, my sister even longer. I am only surprised it took us this long to discover a species that monitors ours. And they do, you know. They were waiting for someone—anyone—to answer their call. So I did."

Visitors from other worlds, she had said, at his last visit.

Dimly, he realized she was babbling about radio signals from a nearby satellite and an alien ship waiting in the upper atmosphere. Impossible. Scientists would have discovered such a thing themselves. His protests died on his lips—it was clear Eva and her sister would not listen. Indeed, both were absorbed in examining a row of canisters lining the basket.

"Stephen," Eva said. "It is time to say good-bye. Thank you."

Lily, who was climbing into the basket, snorted. "Why thank-you?"

Eva sent her an inscrutable look. "Because it moves me to say so. Are we ready?"

"Of course. And you are a sentimental idiot."

Stephen's brain lurched forward. "You are leaving? To . . . to live with . . . monsters? But why? What if—?"

"If I were with child?" she said. "I am, most likely yours. As for why? I'm not certain I can explain it in words you would understand. Let me only say that I am weary of being invisible, Stephen. I want . . . " She drew a breath and lifted her gaze to the stars. "I want to find a world where I am truly myself—for good or bad, clever or indifferent——

inspiration for someone else's ideas. Or expectations."

do not expect you to understand. Why should you?"

"How do you know? You have not even given me a c

Her expression did not change. Indeed she looked

before. "Dear Stephen. Even if you were not like the

live with you alone."

She reached for one of the levers. Stephen charg

on wrestling her away from the balloon, but stopped

produced a small handgun. "You cannot stop us," she

stop ourselves."

Another gesture from the handgun told him to step

into the balloon. She and her sister went through an

series of checks. All clear, apparently, because Lily D

anchor ropes, while Eva ignited a burner. The ropes

drew taut. Lily flung back her head and grinned.

immersed in adjusting various valves. But then she to

the stars. It was a look unlike anything he had seen

Triumphant. He opened his mouth to call out when a l

his arm.

"Hush," said Lucien Fell. "They know what they are

"But—"

"But nothing. My cousins had paid me well to follo

His lips pulled back from his teeth in a feral grin

Stephen watched as the balloon expanded to blot out

a moment's pause, a hesitation where he thought they

then the balloon jerked and lifted free of the ground.

not release him. His grip tightened as the balloon rose

Flames burst out, and the balloon shot higher. Just be f

out of sight, Stephen glimpsed a wire mesh rising to

was not enough, he thought. Surely, they would die . .

An answering burst of light came from higher

soared upward. The sky went dark, only to reappear in

"Come with me," Lucien Fell told him. "We have w

. . . The stars were falling, thousands and millions, a

fire. He blinked, and the brightness faded. Only a sing

remained, swinging up and down through the darkness. Lucien Fell, it was, swinging the lantern as he dragged Stephen through the dark cold Dubois mansion. On and on they marched, through the echoing hallways. Now they were in the kitchen, its tables shoved against one wall to make room for stacks of metal barrels. Lucien pried the lid off one—the acrid stink of chemicals rolled through the air. He nodded. She kept her promise. I'll keep mine. And you'll help.

With Lucien giving orders, they had spread the chemicals throughout the house, then over a fair part of the grounds as well, including the observatory. Lucien had lit a match and set it to the dry grass, which burst into flames— so swiftly it overtook them in their escape. The last Stephen remembered was falling to the ground, trying to beat away the flames, while all around him the bonfires of Guy Fawkes' Day blazed, and stars and embers fell from the sky . . .

He woke with a groan. Fire. He had to reach the road. Warn . . . someone about the conflagration, but he could not move his arms or legs. He struggled to fight free. Hands pressed against his chest, and a man's face hovered over him. He heard a familiar voice telling him not to be such a damned fool.

"Gilbert?" he whispered. His mouth felt cotton dry.

"Stephen." Unmistakable relief.

Stephen wanted to say more, but his tongue refused to work properly.

"No, don't try to talk too much," Gilbert went on. "I'm simply glad you woke up. The doctors . . . Well, between the terrible burns, and half the night spent lying in the cold wet fields, we nearly thought you wouldn't. Wake up that is." He bent closer to Stephen. "It's an excellent thing that someone noticed your disappearance that evening."

He followed me. No. An underling. A . . . spy.

"Lucien," Stephen croaked.

"Escaped," Gilbert said with obvious disgust. "At least, that is what we surmise from later events. But you . . . "

"Went . . . to find . . . "

"The Dubois girl. I know. Stephen, I'm very sorry to tell you that she and her sister did not survive the fire. You must take consolation that she surely died quickly. The fire spread so fast, so hot, as you know."

Ah, Gilbert. If only you knew all the truth.

Even in so much pain, he nearly laughed to think of his friend's expression if he heard about creatures from beyond the stars, or the marvelous scientific endeavors that allowed Lily and Eva Dubois to break free of the Earth's bonds, to sail free toward the stars, there to meet their otherworldly protectors.

Or were they protectors?

He had assumed that, of course, but now he was not so certain. Two girls—two women—sailing forth to join a very different civilization, and one of them bearing a child to carry on the human race. Were they refugees? Or conquerors?

But Gilbert was still speaking about Lucien Fell. How the man had obviously taken advantage of his cousins, using the grounds to store illegal explosive materials for his criminal activities. Lucien himself had escaped the inferno—they knew that from the later events—but clearly he had murdered his two cousins, whether by accident or cold-blooded intent.

"But enough of that villain. Stephen." Gilbert paused, suddenly diffident. "Stephen, I am sorry to have inveigled you into such a mess. I ought to have trusted you more. My superiors agree with me, and so I've come with an offer of a position. A sinecure," he added, with a touch of his old casual tone.

Stephen managed a smile. "Hardly a sinecure," he whispered.

Gilbert's mouth twitched. "Clever boy. Well, I won't press you for an answer now. There's time enough. We want you fully recovered and back in the arms of Society first. Speaking of which, Lady Grey has asked me to serve as her postman and give you this."

He handed Stephen an envelope, which Stephen took awkwardly in his bandaged hands. An invitation, clearly, judging from the expensive, scented paper and formal calligraphy. He tried to picture himself entering her fashionable townhouse, mingling with the other guests at one of her famous soirées, but could not. *Never again.* He closed his eyes and let the envelope fall onto his chest. Gilbert was saying something about that damned position again, then a murmured good-bye and a promise to visit him the next day. Stephen let him talk. For once, it was easy to pretend.

At last, the door clicked shut. Stephen breathed a sigh of relief. The reprieve was temporary, of course. Tomorrow would come more visits—from Gilbert, from his parents, and others. Possibly Doctor Adams. Most definitely Doctors Adams.

He sighed again. Thought about his so-called studies in mathematics. Doctor Adams had once called him promising. There were universities where he might take advanced courses, study in earnest this time. Ah, but that was impossible. He had used up all his chances in the past two years. Certainly his parents would not support him.

An ache welled up behind his eyes. Stephen raised his bandaged hand to rub his forehead; he encountered the forgotten envelope from Lady Grey, balanced between his body and the edge of the hospital bed. How odd that she would send him an invitation here, in a hospital. It was not like her to act so foolish.

No, never foolish.

Impatient now, and more than curious, he fumbled the envelope onto his chest and tore it open. Inside was stiff card—an invitation to one of her soirées. All very proper. But underneath the formal printed lines, she had written a single line in a swift, tiny script: *If you need help, come to me—M.*

Help. He wanted to laugh, then sob. Help, to climb to the stars? No, he was no brave adventurer like Eva Dubois. He merely wanted a second chance. Well, and it seemed that fate, or rather Lady Grey, would give him one.

Stephen drew a long shuddering breath and turned his head toward the window. Outside night had fallen, and cold bright stars illuminated the late November skies. Gazing at the milky constellations, he wished good fortune to the travelers.

SNATCH ME ANOTHER
MERCURIO D. RIVERA

[Abyss and Apex, First Quarter]

Lindy sat in her compact pickup truck, took a deep whiff of In-Bliss, and tossed aside the spent plastic inhaler. She rested her forehead against the cold steering wheel.

A blue-tinted circular portal the size of a manhole cover opened up over the passenger seat, and a thin bare arm descended from it. She recognized the limb's freckled, pale skin, the small scar on the inner wrist. It was her own arm. It groped blindly until it grabbed the inhaler, then retracted. The portal disc closed with a "pop."

"Ah, take it," Lindy muttered. "It's empty anyway." She stared at the front door of her red-brick Colonial. The buzz started to kick in, and calmness fell over her like a warm shawl. She left the truck door open and staggered down the gravel pathway and up the porch stairs. Lindy jammed her hand into the pocket of her jeans, fumbling for the house key. As she stood on the welcome mat, she heard the television blasting—frenetic Munchkins singing "Follow the Yellow Brick Road"—and the white noise of chattering children. She stabbed at the keyhole and missed three times, but the door swung open.

"Mommy!" Tommy said. He wore a bright blue birthday hat over a patch of curly, red hair. "Look what I got!" He held up two identical G.I. Joe dolls.

For a second, Lindy felt nothing but pure love. But then the glow faded to a muted sadness. "That's nice, dear," she mumbled. "Go play with your friends." She stepped around him through the throng of shouting six-year-olds, beyond the swinging door that led from the shag-carpeted living room to the bright kitchen. She leaned against the Formica counter to regain her balance.

Kristina sat at the table, scooping strawberry ice cream onto white paper plates. She paused, blew a dangling strand of brown hair out of her eyes, and glanced at Lindy warily. "Nice of you to show up," Kristina said. "Tommy's been asking for you."

How did she slip back into the role of housemom without missing a goddamned beat? Lindy thought. How could it be so easy for her?

"Are you okay?" Kristina asked.

"Just peachy."

"We need some more plates. Could you snatch me some?" Kristina grabbed a dirty paper dish with a curlicued "Happy Birthday" emblazoned on it, tore off a clean edge, and handed her the slip of cardboard.

Lindy took long, deep breaths.

"You sure you're okay?" Kristina said.

She snorted her assent. "Why wouldn't I be? It's a party! Let's wear our hats and sing happy birthday until our throats hurt. And let's not forget to pin the tail on the goddamned donkey."

Kristina looked away and continued scooping ice cream out of the frosty carton.

Clutching the sliver of cardboard, Lindy lurched through the doorway that led from the kitchen into the garage. The Snatcher sat next to the washing machine. Wide-mouthed and waist-high, it resembled a barrel with a glistening silver coating. If it didn't weigh so much, if it weren't so sturdy, she would've kicked the goddamned thing on its side and taken an axe to it. But what difference would that have made? Over the past six months, the Black Market had exploded. With a single phone call to Senecal, Kristina could have it replaced within twenty-four hours.

Lindy lifted the heavy metal lid and leaned in, placing the piece of the paper plate—the honing sample—at the bottom of the Snatcher. She placed the cover back on and rotated a red dial on the device's side. Then she heard the familiar rumbling and whooshing deep inside of it, like distant thunder and violent wind gusts, the sounds of dimensional walls crumbling. Lindy lifted the cover. The Snatcher's maw released a thick, blue mist. She rolled up her sleeve and bent down, sticking her arm in up to her shoulder, groping blindly until she felt the paper plate. She pulled out a whole white plate with the same orange-lettered "Happy Birthday" on it. Placing and removing the lid over and over, she continued reaching in and snatching out one after another. Cake crumbs coated one plate so she let it fall back through the base of the Snatcher. When she reached in again, she felt someone slap her hand. She withdrew her arm and tried again until she had a dozen dishes in hand, perfect replicas, except for a single one with an off-white color. She imagined the reactions in the alternate dimensions. Ruining a few of these parties, she had to admit—albeit in different universes—wouldn't make her lose any sleep.

When she returned to the kitchen, Tommy burst through the swinging door and hugged her leg. "Mommy, Mommy, will you play musical chairs with us?"

The plates fluttered to the floor.

"Mommy? Will you—"

"Listen, I told you to go play with your friends, okay?" She pushed past the boy and trudged up the stairs.

"Lindy!" Kristina shouted after her.

She paused at the top of the staircase and looked over her shoulder. Kristina crouched down and comforted the crying boy. At that moment, Lindy thought she felt something again—the remnants of a maternal love so raw, so deep, it threatened to paralyze her, drown her.

She reached into her jacket pocket for another inhaler and slammed the bedroom door behind her.

One week earlier, on a chilly September morning, Lindy had leaned against a tree at the summit of a grassy hill while Father DeMichael delivered a prayer over the white oak casket, which lay wrapped in red roses and white tulips. Across from her, on the other side of the casket, Kristina stood between her mother and a second Father DeMichael, who held her hand and bowed his head. No one could distinguish the "original" Joseph E. DeMichael, the one who had counseled Kristina all her life, from the one pulled over from another reality. Lindy shivered. She'd heard rumors of people crossing over, but she'd never seen these "variants" before. A dozen colleagues from the car shop where Lindy worked surrounded them. Half stared at the casket while the other half raised their eyebrows and whispered to each other, gawking at the two Father DeMichaels.

Lindy turned her attention to Kristina. During their intimate moments together, Lindy always playfully referred to Kristina's simple, girl-next-door looks as "domestic sexiness." But on this day Kristina's blank, bloodshot eyes peered out from behind her tangled and unwashed hair. Until that moment, Lindy hadn't noticed her pallid face had a too-thoughtful expression, a look with just a slight hint of madness. At home, she'd remained mute and blank-faced, on the prescribed inhalers they were both taking, sleepwalking through her daily routines.

A blue, circular portal appeared in midair over the coffin, and a long, bare arm reached down and plucked away a white tulip.

Everyone pretended it hadn't happened. The Father DeMichael presiding over the service cleared his throat and continued with the prayer.

Lindy gazed up at two enormous, looming thunderclouds that seemed identical, with just a slit of blue sky separating them. Both appeared thick and dark gray. She focused, trying to detect a difference in the clouds' size or shape or respective shades of gray, with no success, as they converged.

A light drizzle began to fall. Umbrellas sprouted up around her. She continued looking skyward, enjoying the feel of the cold rain on her face.

After the last of the children left the party and Kristina came to bed, Lindy went into the bathroom and inhaled more In-Bliss. She tried to maintain her equilibrium as she wobbled back to the bed. Kristina lay there with the pillow propped against her back, her reading glasses on the edge of her nose, riffling through the newspaper. "Did you kiss Tommy goodnight?"

Lindy didn't reply. She pulled back the covers on her side of the bed and lay down.

After a few minutes, Kristina spoke again. "Did you read today's 'Dear Annabehl' column? Apparently someone stole a tiny fragment of Van Gogh's *Starry Night*." She placed the open newspaper on her lap. "There are now over a thousand originals, and the prices are plummeting with each new one that's retrieved."

"And what did Dear Annabehl have to say about this?"

"To relax, that we're living in a brand new world and have to learn to redefine our moral boundaries."

Lindy grunted.

"Should I call Senecal and order a *Starry Night*? We can have it delivered first thing in the morning."

"I suppose it's irrelevant that Senecal is an illegal dealer or that the Snatcher is illegal or that every damned thing we pull out of the Snatcher is illegal."

"I think the painting would look fabulous in the living room, centered over the sofa, don't you?"

"Ever since we got the Snatcher nothing seems to matter any more."

"Senecal won't take money any more, by the way. They want unique items they can use as honing samples."

"Are you even listening?" Lindy asked.

Kristina sighed and pushed her reading glasses up the bridge of her nose. "Look, there's no point fighting it. Legal or not, everyone has one by now. Even cops have their own Snatchers."

"We don't need a snatched painting. There are sometimes slight . . . differences."

"Imperceptible, usually."

"Doesn't it bother you that in a thousand alternate universes, Van Gogh's original *Starry Night* is now missing?"

"Why do you have to think about these things?" Kristina frowned. "This is . . . bigger than us. And all I know is we're losing things left and right in this house. This morning, my earrings got snatched. And just this afternoon, an arm swiped a twenty-dollar bill off my dresser. If other realities steal from us . . . "

"Then why shouldn't we steal from them?"

"Plus, haven't you read the newspaper?" Kristina said. She lifted the paper from her lap. "We now have all the simian flu vaccine we'll ever need, and an endless food supply to feed the hungry . . . "

"What about all the other craziness, the economic crisis? It's only been six months since the first Snatcher prototype was stolen, and now . . . everything's spinning out of control. Can't you see that?"

"Lindy . . . " Kristina sighed and put her hand on her shoulder, but Lindy rolled over and wrapped the covers around herself.

After a long pause, Lindy whispered, "How'd the kids' parents react today?"

"They seemed fine. They were just happy to see Tommy's feeling better."

"Don't kid yourself. They knew. They knew and they were just being polite."

Kristina turned off the reading light. They lay there, back-to-back, in the darkness, an awkward silence filling the air before Lindy spoke again.

"No *Starry Night*, okay?"

Kristina inhaled as if to respond.

"Mommy," Tommy's voice squeaked from the doorway. "I had a bad dream."

Kristina turned on the nightstand lamp and sat up. "Come here, baby."

Tommy ran to her, and she lifted him up onto her lap. "I was lost," he said, "and I couldn't find you."

"It's okay. You're safe," she said, snuggling him.

Lindy stood up and grabbed her pillow.

After a few seconds, Kristina said, "Mommy's going to read you a story, just like she always does, so you can fall back asleep." Her eyes drilled into Lindy's. "Aren't you, Mommy?"

Lindy nodded.

"Can we read *Thunder Bear Adventures*?" Tommy asked.

"Honey, there's no book with that title," Kristina said.

"But it's my *favorite* one! Mommy always reads it to me."

Lindy and Kristina locked eyes again.

When they had returned from the cemetery Kristina changed into her white nightgown, even though it was the middle of the afternoon. She hovered about the house aimlessly. And there was a lag in her responses to Lindy's questions, as if communicating via satellite. In a strange, flat voice, Kristina announced she was going upstairs to take a nap.

Lindy sat down on the living room sofa and turned on the news telecast. None of the stories registered—only random words and phrases penetrated her consciousness: "Snatcher," "pandemonium," "markets crashing," "war," "variant." Lindy could only think of those final moments in the hospital, Tommy lying there unconscious, his head wrapped in bandages, his shallow breathing becoming labored and then raspy before finally ceasing. Given the circumstances—the surgeons' inability to reach the brain tumor, the odds they'd been given, the potent chemotherapy treatments he'd undergone— his death shouldn't have come as a surprise, but at that moment the world had settled into a dull, steady gray that had yet to fade.

An hour later, Kristina stomped down the stairs faster than she had moved the entire day, brandishing a hairbrush like a conductor's baton.

"What's the matter?" Lindy asked.

"Tommy was so excited about next week's birthday party. Kool Aid, cake, ice cream, games, okay? Friday afternoon." She continued vocalizing scattershot thoughts; her eyes snapped left and right. "Let's have the party, okay, Lindy? I don't know why we never thought of it before! The solution is so obvious!" She'd fallen asleep crying; smudged tracks of mascara stained her cheeks. "Let's celebrate Tommy's birthday, okay, Lindy? Okay?"

"What are you talking about?"

"It doesn't have to be . . . this way . . . " She waved her hands in the air.

"Honey, he's gone." Lindy swept Kristina's hair back from her forehead.

"But he doesn't *have* to be." She pulled a patch of Tommy's red hair from the brush and held it between her thumb and index finger.

"Don't say it," Lindy said. "Don't even think it." She put her hands on Kristina's shoulders and looked her in the eye. "Listen to me. We'll get past this, I promise."

Kristina pushed her hands away and turned around, looking out the window. "I'm not 'getting past' anything. We're bringing him back." As her determination set in, her shaky voice sounded more coherent. "Don't you think others have done this? The obituary column gets shorter every day." She spun around and faced her again. "For his birthday, Lindy. So we can throw him the party he wanted." Black rivulets began to run down her cheeks again. "What kind of parents are we? We can save him, Lindy! We can save him! How can we not . . . ?" She choked on the final word and sobbed into her hands.

"It wouldn't be our Tommy," she replied. Although Lindy had steeled herself during Tommy's illness and the burial, she found her lower lip quivering. "And we couldn't do that to another child's parents."

"With their Snatcher, they could snatch themselves another Tommy—"

"He's dead. That's it."

Kristina's face grew stern, and she paused for a long while before speaking again. Then all at once, her grave expression melted. "I'm sorry, Lindy." She sighed and collapsed onto the living room couch. "It's just so hard."

Lindy sat down next to her. "I understand."

"I know you're right," Kristina said. "I know we'll find a way to get past this." She wiped at the corner of her eyes with the sleeve of her flannel nightgown.

Lindy patted her thigh.

"Do you want anything?" Kristina asked. She stood up and headed toward the swinging door to the kitchen.

Lindy shook her head and stared at the framed picture on the coffee table of the three of them in Maui, she and Kristina and Tommy, all in their bathing suits, sporting yellow leis and broad smiles. Tommy wore Lindy's sunglasses. She felt like an overstretched rubber band; a minute ago she'd been on the verge of tears, but now she found herself smiling.

A blue disc materialized in midair, and a tanned arm with blood-red fingernails snaked out of it. It snatched the framed photograph and retreated back into the portal.

Goddamn it, not that picture, Lindy thought. If she'd just had another second to react, she would have stabbed the goddamned hand with a fork.

A shriek cut through the silence.

Lindy leapt from the couch and ran into the kitchen. The door to the garage was wide open. No . . . , she hadn't . . . , Lindy thought, she didn't. . . .

Lindy ran to the garage and was confronted with the sight of Kristina leaning over the Snatcher. She had pulled Tommy halfway out. His skin was blue-white and he wore the navy-blue suit in which they had buried him. He was unmistakably dead.

Kristina continued to wail.

"Let go!" Lindy grabbed her arms. "Let him go!"

Kristina released her grip and the cadaver dropped, disappearing into the ethereal blue mist that wafted out of the Snatcher. Her hands shaking, Kristina placed the metal lid back on the Snatcher and then removed it again.

Lindy tried to pull her away from the device, but Kristina surprised her with a shove that sent her sprawling to the floor. Kristina reached into the Snatcher and soon had another variant of Tommy in her grasp, which she tugged upwards. Before long, she cradled another corpse—this one more decomposed than the first, but still outfitted in the same navy-blue suit—and let out a high-pitched screech.

"For God's sake, stop it!" Lindy said.

Kristina dropped the body back into the Snatcher, and turned the red dial on the side all the way right. On her third attempt, she leaned in and pulled out a red-faced Tommy clad in polka-dotted pajamas.

"What's happening?" he screamed, slapping at her arms. Kristina laughed and kissed his cheeks and hugged him tight. Tommy began to cry. "It's okay, baby. Your mommies are here." Kristina rocked him in her arms in an exaggerated motion.

Lindy moved toward them and grabbed the boy around the waist, prying him from Kristina's embrace.

"What are you doing?" Kristina said.

Lindy carried him back over the mouth of the Snatcher and tried to jam him back in. The boy wailed and splayed his legs, his feet catching on the sides of the Snatcher.

"Mommy!" he sobbed. He wrapped his arms around Lindy's neck. "Mommy!"

She stopped struggling.

"Tommy," Lindy said. She hugged him back. "Shhh. It's okay, it's okay."

As Lindy led him back to his room for the bedtime story, Tommy stopped to put on a stray birthday hat, then diverted them to the bathroom. He insisted on brushing his teeth again before going back to sleep—a classic stalling tactic, for sure—but she saw no harm in it. She held Tommy from behind while he perched on a stool and brushed his teeth, peering into the bathroom mirror. She took the toothbrush out of his left hand and moved it to his right hand.

"Why can't we read *Thunder Bears*?" He drooled toothpaste into the sink when he spoke.

"We'll read it another night," she lied. "Just pick another book."

He shifted the toothbrush back into his left hand and continued brushing.

"Use your other hand, honey. It'll be easier." But when Lindy tried to remove the toothbrush from his left hand again, he pulled away and continued brushing. "No, Mommy!"

Lindy focused on the smooth, effortless movements as Tommy brushed up and down with his left hand. And all at once, the hairs on her arms stood on end. She had allowed herself to forget, just for a few minutes, that this boy was not her son. Tommy—*her* Tommy—was right-handed.

She took a step backward.

He rinsed and raced to his bedroom. "I'll get the book!"

Lindy felt dizzy. Her heart raced; she needed another whiff of In-Bliss. Staggering after the boy, she stood at the doorway to his bedroom—Tommy's bedroom—and watched the imposter look through the books—Tommy's books—on the bottom shelf. "I can't find *Thunder Bears*," he whined.

"Huh?" The words barely registered. Her Tommy deserved better than this, she thought. He deserved to be remembered, to be mourned.

"I want you to read me *Thunder Bears*."

"Look, just go to sleep!" she said.

"You promised!" He started to cry. "I want *Thunder Bears!*" For a split-second, the boy stopped weeping. He winced and brought his hands to his temples. Then the bawling grew louder.

"What's the matter?"

"My head hurts," he said, sobbing.

Lindy gasped. Her heart pounded. She leaned back against the wall and found herself sliding to the floor. She stared up at the light fixtures on the ceiling, which were spinning, spinning.

Tommy continued crying for his book, his hands on the sides of his head, until Lindy crawled over to him. She lifted him up and lay him down in the bed.

"Shh. It's okay, baby. Mommy's here." She held him in her arms, massaging his forehead. No, no, no, she thought. We can't go through this again. Not again.

After a minute, he cried himself to sleep.

She set him down on the bed. The entire room was spinning now.

She stared at her hands. They seemed to move independently from her body, clutching the soft pillow. She moved it an inch away from his face and held it there for a few seconds.

"What are you doing?" Kristina said from the doorway.

Lindy jumped to her feet, dropping the pillow.

Kristina's eyes widened; her face flushed.

Lindy staggered past her and down the stairs. As she opened the front door, Kristina shouted from the top of the stairway: "*What were you doing?*"

Lindy slammed the door behind her.

Lindy drove several blocks to the beach and stayed awake all night in the pick-up truck, staring at the ink-black sky. Not a single star was visible behind the dark thundercloud cover. The rhythmic swoosh of the distant waves reminded her of Tommy's final raspy breaths at the hospital. She blinked and the sky suddenly grayed. A sickly dawn had arrived, illuminating the garbage-strewn sands.

She drove back home and parked at the curbside. After half an hour, she found the energy to sleepwalk down the gravel pathway to the porch of their house, ice-cold, numb.

What had she almost done?

Kristina would forgive her anything, she always thought, but *this* . . .

As Lindy moved past the living room window she caught a glimpse of two figures inside. There, on the couch, watching cartoons, lay Tommy. And Kristina sat next to him. Van Gogh's *Starry Night* hung on the wall behind them.

And all at once a tremendous wave of relief washed over her, as if yesterday had been nothing more than a drug-induced nightmare, and today she'd been slapped awake to a brand-new, shiny reality. Maybe Kristina felt the same way. Maybe they could both find a way to get past this. This time, she thought, the doctors would catch the tumor early. This time he'd be okay. She'd be a good mother to him. Lindy knew now she'd somehow find a way to adjust, to accept the new Tommy as her own. Dear Annabehl was right; they lived in a different world now.

As she walked toward the front door, Lindy got a full view of the living room. Her heart froze. A third person, a woman, sat next to Kristina, thigh against thigh, laughing along with them. The woman got up and walked behind the couch and tickled Tommy from behind, catching him off guard. As Tommy squealed, Kristina also shrieked with laughter.

The woman was Lindy.

Lindy stepped back from the window and staggered down the walkway. She tripped and fell to her knees, crawling to the pickup truck. There, she fumbled for the inhaler in the glove compartment and took a hit. The sky, the world, was spinning. And as a quietude gradually enveloped her, she imagined an outstretched arm appearing in midair, white and smooth and smelling of Kristina's perfume, reaching down to take her hand and pull her up through a patch of cobalt-blue sky to a different place, a place where she belonged.

She took another deep whiff.

FIRST RITES
NANCY KRESS

[*Baen's Universe,* October]

1: Haihong

She sat rigid on the narrow seat of the plane, as if her slightest movement might bring the Boeing 777 down over the Pacific. No one noticed. Pregnant women often sat still, and this one was very pregnant. Only the flight attendant, motherly and inquisitive, bent over the motionless figure.

"Can I bring you anything, ma'am?"

The girl's head jerked up as if shot. "No . . . no." And then, in nearly unaccented English, "Wait. Yes. A Scotch and soda."

The flight attendant's mouth narrowed, but she brought the drink. These girls today—you'd think this one would know better. Although maybe she came from some backward area of China without prenatal care. In her plain brown maternity smock and sandals, it was hard to tell. The girl wasn't pretty and wore no wedding ring. Well, maybe that was why the poor thing was so nervous. An uneducated provincial going home to face the music. Still, she shouldn't drink. In fact, at this late stage, she shouldn't even be flying. What if she went into labor on the plane?

Deng Haihong, one chapter short of her Ph.D. thesis at U.C. San Diego, gulped the Scotch and closed her eyes, waiting for its warmth to reach her brain. Another three hours to Shanghai, two-and-a-half to Chengdu, and perhaps two hours on the bus to Auntie's. If no one questioned her at the airports. If she wasn't yet on any official radar. If she could find Auntie.

If . . .

Eyes still closed, Haihong laid both hands on her bulging belly, and shuddered.

Shuangliu Airport in Chengdu had changed in four years. When Haihong had left, it had been the glossy, bustling gateway to the prosperous southwest and then on to Tibet, and Chengdu had been China's fifth largest city. Now, since half of Sichuan province had been under quarantine, only seven people deplaned from an aircraft so old that it had no live TV-feed. Five of the seven already wore pathogen masks. Haihong pulled on hers, not because she thought any deadly pathogens from the war still lingered here—she knew better—but because it made her more inconspicuous. Her stomach roiled as she approached Immigration.

Let it be just one more bored official . . .

It was not. "Passport and Declaration Card?"

Haihong handed them over, inserted her finger into the reader, and tried to smile. The woman took forever to scrutinize her papers and biological results. The screen at her elbow scrolled but Haihong couldn't see what it said . . . For a long terrible moment she thought she might faint.

Then the woman smiled. "Welcome home. You have come home to have your child here, in the province of your ancestors?"

"Yes," Haihong managed.

"Congratulations."

"Thank you." Emily's curious American phrase jumped into her mind: *I would give my soul for a drink right now.*

Too bad Haihong had already sold her soul.

Chengdu had finished the Metro just before the quarantine, and it was still operating. Everyone wore the useless paper pathogen masks. In California, Emily had laughed at the idea that the flimsy things would protect against any pathogens that had mutated around their terminator genes, and she and Haihong had had their one and only fight. "The people are just trying to survive!" Haihong had yelled, and Emily had gone all round-eyed and as red as only those blonde Americans could, and said apologetically, "I suppose that whatever makes them feel better . . . " Haihong had stormed out of the crummy apartment she shared with Emily and Tess only because it saved money.

It had been Emily who told her about the clinic in the first place.

As Haihong pulled her rolling suitcase toward Customs, her belly lurched hard. She stopped, terror washing through her: *Not here, not here!*

But after that one hard kick, the baby calmed down. Haihong made it though Customs, the pills intact in the lining of her dress. She made it onto the Metro, off at the bus station.

The terror abated. Not departed—it would never do that, she realized bleakly. But at least the chance of detection was over. In the bus station, crowded as Shuangliu had not been, she was just one more Chinese girl in inexpensive cotton clothing that had probably been made in Guangdong province before being exported to the U.S. Only the poorest Chinese remained in Sichuan; everyone who could afford to had gone through bio-decon and fled. Chengdu had been the place that North Korea chose to bio-attack to bring the huge Chinese dragon to its knees. Sichuan had been the sacrifice, and rather than have the attack continued on Guangdong's export factories or Beijing's government or Shanghai's soaring foreign tourism, China had not retaliated toward its ancient enemy, at least not with weapons. Politics had been more effective, aided by the world's outrage. Now North Korea was castrated, full of U.N. peacekeeping forces and bio-inspectors and very angry Chinese administrators. Both of Haihong's parents had died in the brief war.

"Be careful, Little Sister." An ancient man, gnarled as an old tree, took Haihong's elbow to help her onto the bus. The small kindness nearly made her cry. Pregnant women cried so easily. The trip had been so long, so draining . . . she wanted a drink.

"*Shie-shie,*" she said, and watched his face to see if he frowned at her accent. She had spoken only English for so long. But his expression didn't change.

The bus, nearly as ancient as the kind grandfather, smelled of unwashed bodies and urine. Haihong fell asleep, mercifully without dreams. When she woke, it was night in the mountains and the baby was kicking hard. Her stomach growled with hunger. A different passenger sat beside her, a boy of maybe six or seven, with his mother snoring across the aisle. He ducked his head and said shyly, "Do you wish for a boy or a girl?"

The baby was a boy. Ben, shaken, had analyzed with Haihong the entire genome from amnio tissue. Haihong knew the baby's eye and hair color, prospective height, blood type, probable IQ, degree of far future baldness. She knew the father was Mexican. She knew the fetus's polymorphic alleles.

She smiled at the boy and said softly, "Whatever Heaven sends."

Haihong's screams shattered the night. The midwife, back in prominence after the doctor left and the village clinic closed, murmured gently from her position beside the squatting Haihong. The smell of burning incense didn't mask the earthy odor of her spilt waters. Auntie held a kerosene lamp above the midwife's waiting hands. Auntie's face had not unclenched, not once, since Haihong had finally found her living in a hut at the edge of a vast vineyard in which she, like everyone else, toiled endlessly. The workers' huts had running water but no electricity. Outside, more women had gathered to wait.

Haihong cried, "I will die!"

"You will not die," the midwife soothed. Through the haze of pain, Haihong realized that the woman thought she feared death. If only it were that simple . . . But Haihong had done all she could. Had explained to Auntie, who was not her aunt but her old amah and therefore much harder to trace directly to Haihong, about the pills. She had explained, but would the old woman understand? O, to have come this far and not succeed, not save her son . . .

Her body split in two, and the child was born. His wail filled the hut. Haihong, battered from within, gasped, "Give . . . me!"

They laid the bloody infant in her arms. Auntie remembered what had been rehearsed, drilled into her, for the past nine days. Her obedience had made her an ideal amah when Haihong had been young. Her obedience, and her instinctive love. Her eyes never left the crying baby, but wordlessly she held out to Haihong the prepared dish holding pulverized green powder.

With the last of her strength, Haihong transferred three grains of powder to her fingertip and touched the baby's tongue. The grains dissolved. The baby went on wailing and all at once Haihong was sick of him, sick of the chance she had taken and the sacrifice she had made, sick of it all, necessary as it had been. She said, "Take him," and Auntie greedily grabbed the baby from her arms. Haihong tried to shut her ears against his crying. She wanted nothing now but sleep. Sleep, and the drink that, surrounded as they were by vineyards, would be possible soon, today, tomorrow, all the days left in her utterly ruined life.

_____

2: Cixin

Deng Cixin was in love with the mountains. Unlike anything else, they made him feel calm inside, like still water.

"Sit still, *bow bei'r*," Auntie said many times each day. "Be calm!" But Cixin could not sit still. He raced out the door, scattering the chickens, through the neat rows of grapes tied to their stakes, into the village. He scooped up handfuls of pebbles and hurled them at the other children, provoking cries of, "*Fen noon an hi!*" *Angry boy.* He was always angry, never knowing at what, always running, always wanting to be someplace else. Except when he was in the mountains.

His mother took him there once every week. She put him into his seat on her bicycle, sometimes pedaling hard with sweat coming out in interesting little globes on the back of her neck, and sometimes walking the bicycle. They covered several miles. After he turned four, Cixin walked part of the way. He liked to run in circles around his mother until he got too tired and she scooped him back onto the bicycle seat. The ride back down was thrilling, too: a headlong dash like the wind. Cixin urged her on: *Faster! Faster!* If he could just go fast enough, they might leave the ground forever and he would never have to go back to the village.

The best part, however, was in the mountains. Mama brought a *picnic*—that was a word from the secret language, the one he and his mother always used when not even Auntie was around. Nobody else knew about the secret language. It was for the two of them alone. The picnic had all the things Cixin liked best: congee with chicken and sweetened bean curd and orange juice. Although the orange juice was only for him; Mama had wine or beer.

As they ascended higher and higher, Cixin would feel his shoulders and knees and stomach loosen. He didn't run around up here; he didn't *have* to run around. The air grew sharp and clean. The mountains stood, firm and tall and strong—and how long they stood there! Millions of years, Mama said. Cixin liked thinking about that. You couldn't be angry at something so strong and old. You could rest in it.

"Tell me again," Cixin would say, sitting on the edge of Mama's blanket. "Where do the mountains go?"

"All the way to Tibet, *bow bei'r*."

"And Tibet is the highest place in the world."

"The very highest."

After a while Mama would fall asleep, thin and pale on her blanket, her short dark hair flopping sideways. Even then Cixin didn't feel the need to run around. He sat and looked at the mountains, and his mind seemed to drift among the clouds, until sometimes he couldn't tell which was clouds and which was himself. Sometimes a small animal or bird would sit on the ground only meters away, and Cixin would let it rest, too.

When Mama awoke, it was time for the *once-a-week*. That was a word from the secret language, too.

The once-a-week was tiny little green specks that Mama counted carefully. They melted on Cixin's tongue and tasted faintly sour. Mama always said the same words, every time, and he had to answer the same words, every time.

"You must swallow the once-a-week, Cixin."

"I must swallow the once-a-week."

"*Every* week."

"Every week."

"If you do not swallow it, you will die."

"I will die." Dead birds, dead rats, a mangy dog dead in the road. Cixin could picture himself like that. The picture terrified him.

"And you must not tell anyone except Auntie about the once-a-week. Ever."

"I must not tell anyone except Auntie about the once-a-week ever."

"Promise me, *bow bei'r.*"

"I promise." And then, for the first time, "Where does the once-a-week come from?"

"Ah." Mama looked sad. "From very far away."

"From Tibet?"

"No. Not Tibet."

"Where?" He had a sudden idea, fueled by the stories Auntie told him of dragons and ghost warriors. "From a land of magic?"

"There is no magic." Mama's voice sounded even sadder. "Only science."

"Is science a kind of magic?"

She laughed, but it was not a happy sound. "Yes, I suppose it is. Black magic, sometimes. Now fold the blanket; we must go back."

Cixin forget about science and magic and the once-a-week at the exciting thought of the wild bicycle dash down the mountain.

Twice a year Mama took the bus to Chengdu, another far away land of black magic. For days before she left, Auntie spent extra time kneeling at the household shrine. Cixin, five, eight, nine years old, raced around even more than usual. Mama snapped at him.

"Sit still!"

"Ah, he's wild today, that one," Auntie said, but unlike Mama, she was smiling. Auntie was very old. She didn't work in the vineyards any more, but Mama did. Some nights Mama didn't come home. Some nights she came home very late, falling down and either giggling or crying. Then she and Auntie argued when they thought Cixin could not hear.

"I said sit still!" Mama slapped him.

Cixin raced out the door, tried to kick the neighbor's dog, did not connect. He kept running in circles until he was exhausted and his heart was too tired to hurt so much and he saw Xiao sitting by the irrigation ditch with her ancient iPod. Cixin, panting, dropped down beside her.

"Let me see, Xiao."

She handed over the iPod. A year younger than Cixin and the daughter of the vineyard foreman, Xiao had possessions that the other village children could only dream of. Sweet-natured and docile, she always shared.

Cixin put the iPod to his ear but was too restless to listen to the music. But instead of hurling it into the ditch, as he might have done with anybody else, he handed it carefully back to Xiao. With her, he always tried to be careful.

"My mother is going to a magic land. To Chengdu."

Xiao laughed. She was the only person that Cixin allowed to laugh at him. Her laugh reminded him of flowers. She said, "Chengdu isn't a magic land. It's a city. I went there."

"You *went* there? When?"

"Last year. My father took me on the bus. Look, there's your mother waiting for the bus. She—" Xiao dropped her eyes.

Cixin spat. "She's drunk."

"I know." Xiao was always truthful.

"I don't care!" Cixin shouted. He wanted to leap up and race around again, he wanted to sit beside Xiao and ask about Chengdu, he didn't know

55

what he wanted. The bus stopped and Mama lurched on. "I hope she never comes back!"

"You don't mean that," Xiao said. She took his hand. Cixin jerked his whole body to face her.

"Kiss me!"

"No!" Shocked, she dropped his hand and got to her feet.

He jumped up. "Don't go, Xiao! You don't have to kiss me!" Just saying the words desolated him. "You don't ever have to kiss me. Nobody ever has to kiss me."

She studied him from her beautiful dark eyes. "You're very strange, Cixin."

"I am not." But he knew he was.

A band of boys emerged from between the rows of grapes. When they saw Cixin, they began to yell. "*Fen noon an hi! Ben dan!*"

Cixin knew he was an angry boy but not a stupid one. He grabbed a rock from the irrigation ditch and hurled it at the boys. It fell short but they swarmed around him, careful not to touch Xiao.

Cixin broke free and raced off. They shouted after him: "Half breed! Son of a whore!" He was faster than all of them, even among the trees that began on the other side of the village, even when the ground began to slope upward toward the mountains. He and his mother never went there any more. So now Cixin would go by himself. He would run higher and higher, all the way to Tibet, and maybe he would go live with the monks and maybe he would die on the way and it didn't matter which. No one would care. His mother was a drunk and a whore, his Auntie was old and would die soon anyway, Xiao was so rich and she had an iPod and she would never ever kiss him.

He leaned against a tree until his breath was strong again. Then he again started up the mountain, walking to Tibet.

3: Ben

Ben Malloy brought his coffee to the farthest booth of the San Diego cybershop and closed the door. The booth smelled of urine and semen. Public booths, used only by the desperately poor or desperately criminal or deeply paranoid, were always unsavory. He shouldn't have brought coffee but he'd been up all night, working when the lab was quiet and deserted, and he needed the caffeine.

He accessed the untraceable account, encrypted through remixers in Finland and God-knew-where-else, and her email was there.

B—

Your package arrived. Thank you. Still no breakthrough. Symptoms unchanged. I suspect elevated CRF and cortisol, serotonin fluctuations, maybe neuron damage. Akathesia, short REM latency. Sichuan quarantine may lift soon—rumors.

—H

I cannot do this anymore. I just cannot.

Akathesia. Short REM latency. Ben had taught her those terms, so far from her own field. Haihong had always been a quick study.

He closed his eyes and let the guilt wash over him. She'd made the choices—both of them—so why was the guilt his? All he'd done was break several laws and risk his professional future to try to save her.

The guilt was because he'd failed.

Also because he'd misunderstood so much. He had thought of Haihong as an American. Taking her California Ph.D. in English literature, going out for hamburgers at Burger King and dancing to pellet rock and loving strappy high-heeled shoes. A girl with more brains than sense, to whom he'd attributed American attitudes and expediencies. And he'd been wrong. Underneath the California-casual-cum-grad-student-intensity-cum-sexually-liberated woman, Haihong had been foreign to him in ways he had not understood. Ben Jinkang Molloy's grandmother and father had both married Americans; his father and Ben himself had been born here. He didn't even speak Chinese.

His father had called him, all those years ago, from Florida. "Ben, your second cousin is coming from China to study in San Diego."

"My second cousin? What second cousin?"

"Her name is Deng Haihong. She's my cousin Deng Song's daughter, from near Chengdu. You need to look out for her."

Ben, busy with his first post-doc, had been faintly irritated with this intrusion into his life. "Does she even speak English?"

"Well, I should hope so. She's studying for a doctorate in English literature. Listen, buddy, she's an orphan. Both parents were casualties of that stupid savagery in Sichuan. She has nobody."

His father knew how to push Ben's buttons. Solitary by nature, Ben was nonetheless a sucker for stray kittens, homeless beggars, lost causes. He could picture his father, tanned and relaxed in the retirement condo in West Palm Beach, counting on this trait in Ben.

He said resignedly, "When does she arrive?"

"Tuesday. You'll meet her plane, won't you?"

"Yes," Ben had said, not realizing that the single syllable would commit him to four years of mentorship, of playing big brother, of pleasure and exasperation, all culminating in the disastrous conversation that had been the beginning of the end.

He and Haihong had sat across from each other in a dark booth at a favorite campus bar, Fillion's.

"I'm pregnant," Haihong said abruptly. "No beer for me tonight."

He had stiffened. Oh God, that arrogant bastard Scott, he'd warned her the guy was no good, *why* did women always go for the bad-boy jerks . . .

Haihong laughed. "No, it's not Scott's. You're always so suspicious, Ben."

"Then who—"

"It's nobody's. I'm a surrogate."

He peered at her, struggling to take it in, and saw the bravado behind her smile. She was defiant, and scared, and determined, all at once. Haihong's determination could crack granite. It had to be, for her to have come this far from where she'd been born. He said stupidly, "A surrogate?"

Again that brittle laugh. "You sound as if you never heard the word before. What kind of geneticist are you?"

"Haihong, if you needed money . . . "

"It's not that. I just want to help some infertile couple."

She was lying, and not well. Haihong, he'd learned, lied often, usually to cover up what she perceived as her own inadequacies. And she was fiercely proud. Look at the way she always leapt to the defense of her two friends and roommates, slutty Tess and brainless Emily. If Ben castigated Haihong now, if he was anything other than supportive, she would never trust him again.

But something here didn't smell right.

He said carefully, "I know another woman who acted as a surrogate, and it took a year for her to complete the medical surveillance and background checks. Have you been planning this for a whole year?"

"No, this is different. The clinic is in Mexico. American restrictions don't apply."

Alarms sounded in Ben's head. Haihong, despite her intelligence, could be very naïve. She'd grown up in some backwater village that was decades behind the gloss and snap of Shanghai or Beijing. Ben was not naïve. His post-doc had been at a cutting-edge big-pharm; he was now a promising researcher at the San Diego Neuroscience Institute. A lot of companies found it convenient to have easy access to Mexico for drug testing. FDA approval required endless and elaborate clinical trials, but the starving Mexican provinces allowed a lot more latitude as long as there was "full disclosure to all participants." As if an ignorant and desperate day laborer could, or would, understand the medical jargon thrown at him in return for use of his body. Congress had been conducting hearings on the issue for years, with no effect whatsoever. Any procedure or drug experimented with in Mexico would, of course, then have to be re-tested in the U.S. But ninety percent of all new drugs failed. Mexico made a cheap winnowing ground.

And, of course, there were always rumors of totally banned procedures available there for a price. But no big pharm or rogue genetics outfit would actually use a legitimate fertility clinic for experimentation . . . would they?

"Haihong, what's the name of the clinic?"

"Why?"

Their drinks came, Dos Equis for him and Diet Coke for her. After the waitress left, Ben said casually, "I may be able to find out stuff for you. Their usual pay rate for surrogates, for instance. Make sure you're not getting ripped off." Unlike Haihong, Ben was a good liar.

Haihong nodded. So it was the money. "Okay. The clinic is called Dispensario de las Colinas Verdes."

He'd never heard of it. "How did you learn about this place?"

"Emily." She was watching him warily now, ready to resent any criticism of her friend.

He said only, "Okay, I'll get on it. How did your meeting with your thesis advisor go yesterday?"

He saw her relax. She launched into a technical discussion of semiotics that he didn't even try to follow. Instead he tried to find traces of his family's faces in hers. Around the eyes, maybe, and the nose . . . but he and his brothers stood six feet, his hair was red, and he had the spare tire of most sedentary Americans. She was tiny, fragilely made. And fragile in other ways, too, capable of an hysterical emotionalism kept in check only by her relentless drive to accomplishment. Ben had seen her drunk once, it was not pretty, and she'd never let him see her that way again. Haihong was a mass of contradictions, this cousin of his, and he groped through his emotions to find one that fit how he felt about her. He didn't find it.

Abruptly he said, interrupting something about F. Scott Fitzgerald, "Is the egg yours or a donor's?"

Anger darkened her delicate features. "None of your business!"

So the egg was hers, and she was more uneasy about the whole business than she pretended. All at once he remembered a stray statistic: Twenty-one percent of surrogate mothers changed their mind about giving up their babies.

"Sorry," he said. "Now what was that again about Fitzgerald?"

She was eight months along before he cracked Dispensario de las Colinas Verdes.

His work at the Neuroscience Institute was with genetically modified proteins that packaged different monoamines into secretory vesicles, the biological storage and delivery system for signal molecules. Ben specialized in brain neurotransmitters. This allowed him access to work-in-progress by the Institute's commercial and academic partners. Colinas Verdes was not among them.

However, months of digging—most of it not within the scope of his grant and some of it blatant favor-trading—finally turned up that one of the Institute's partners had a partner. That small company, which had already been fined twice by the FDA, had buried in its restricted on-line sites a single reference to the Mexican clinic. It was enough. Ben was good at follow-through.

Haihong was huge. She waddled around campus, looking as if she'd swallowed a basketball, her stick legs in their little sandals looking unable to support her belly. The final chapter of her dissertation had been approved in draft form by her advisor. The date for her oral defense had been set. She beamed at strangers; she fell into periods of vegetable lassitude; she snapped at friends; she applied feverishly for teaching posts. Sometimes she cried and then, ten minutes later, laughed hysterically. Ben watched her take her vitamins, do her exercises, resolutely avoid alcohol. He couldn't bring himself to tell her anything.

The day in her fourth month that she said to him, awe in her voice, "Right now he's growing eyelashes," Ben was sure. She was going to keep the baby.

Twenty-one percent.

He went himself to Mexico, presenting his passport at the border, driving his Saab through the dusty countryside. Two hours from Tijuana he reached the windowless brick building that was not the bright and convenient clinic Haihong had gone to. This was the clinic's research headquarters, its controlling brain. Ben went in armed with the names and forged references of the partner company, with his formidable knowledge of cutting-edge genetics, with pretty good Spanish, with American status and bluster. He spent an hour with the Mexican researchers on site, and left before he was exposed. He obtained names and then checked them out in the closed deebees at the Institute. Previous publications, conference appearances, chatter on the e-lists that post-docs, in self-defense, create to swap information that might impact their collective futures. It took all his knowledge to fill in the gaps, complete the big picture.

Then he sat with his head in his hands, anxiety battering him in waves, and wondered how he was ever going to tell Haihong.

He waited another week, working eighteen hours a day, sleeping in his lab on a cot, neglecting the job he was paid to do and cutting off both his technicians and his superiors. The latter decided to indulge him; they all thought he was brilliant. Every few hours Ben picked up the phone to call the FBI, the FDA, the USBP, anyone in the alphabet soup of law enforcement who could have shut it all down. But each time he put down the phone. Not until he had the inhibitor, which no one would have permitted him to cobble together had they known. Let alone permit giving it to Haihong.

A lot had been known about neurotransmitters for over seventy years, ever since the first classes of antidepressants. Only the link with genetics was new, and in the last five years, that field—Ben's field—had exploded. He had the fetus's genome. The genetics were new, but the countermeasures for the manifested behaviors were not. Ben knew enough about brain chemistry and cerebral structures.

What he hadn't known enough about was Haihong.

"An inhibitor," she said at the end of his long, lurching explanation, and her calm should have alerted him. An eerie, dangerous calm, like the absence of ocean sucked away from the beach just before the tsunami rolls in. He should have recognized it. But he'd been awake for twenty-two hours straight. He was so tired.

"Yes, an inhibitor," he echoed. "And it will work."

"You're sure."

Nothing like this was ever sure, but he said, "Yes. As sure as I can be." He tried to put an arm around her but she pushed him away.

"An inhibitor calibrated to body weight."

"Yes. Increasing in direct proportion."

"For his entire life."

"Yes. I think so. Haihong—"

"Side effects?" Still that eerie calm.

Ben ran his hand through his red hair, making it all stand up. "I don't know. How can I know?" He wanted to be reassuring, but the brain contained a hundred billion neurons, each with a thousand or so branches. That was ten-to-the-hundred-trillionth power of possible neural connections. He was pretty sure what neurotransmitters the genemods on the baby would increase production of, and pretty sure he could inhibit it. But the side effects? Anybody's guess. Even aspirin affected different people differently.

Haihong said, "A six-month shelf life and a one-week half-life in the body."

She echoed his terminology perfectly, still in that quiet, mechanical voice. Ben put out his hand to touch her again, drew it back. "Yes. Haihong, we need to call the FDA, now that I have something to use as an emergency drug, and let them take over the—"

"Give me the first batch."

He did. This was why he'd made it, because he'd known months ago what she had never told him in words. Twenty-one percent.

He agreed to put off calling the authorities for one more day. "Just give me time to assimilate it all, Ben. A little time. Okay?"

He'd agreed. It was her life, her child. Not his.

The next day she'd been gone.

In the foul public cyberbooth, nine years later, Ben deleted Haihong's email. *Rumors*, she'd written, *Sichuan quarantine may lift soon*. Interred in her remote village, which the most modern of technologies had forced back into the near primitive, she hadn't even heard the news. The quarantine had always been as much political as anything else, or it wouldn't have been in force so long. It was to be lifted today and even now, right there in Chengdu from which she must have sent her email, she still seemed oblivious. *I cannot do this anymore. I just cannot.*

What exactly did that mean?

He left his coffee untouched in the filthy booth. Outside, in the fresh air under California's blue sky, he pulled out his handheld and booked a flight to China.

4: Haihong

She left the People's Internet Building at dusk. Usually she spent several hours on-line, as long as she could afford, in an orgy of catching up on news, on the academic world, on anything outside the quarantine. She only had the opportunity every six months.

This time, she left as soon as she'd emailed Ben, uploading onto him her bi-annual report, her gratitude, her despair. Unfair, of course, but how could it matter? Ben, in California, had everything; he could add a little despair to his riches. To Haihong nothing mattered any longer, nothing except Cixin, the unruly child who did not love her and for whom she'd given her future. A fruitless sacrifice, since Cixin had no future, either. Everything barren, everything a waste.

She clutched the package in her hand, the precious six-month supply of inhibitor of proteins in the posterior superior parietal lobes. The pills were sewn inside a gift for Cixin, a stuffed toy he was too old for. Ben had not done any further work on the side-effects. Maybe he had no way to measure them, eight thousand miles away from his research subject. Maybe he had lost interest. So Cixin would go on being irritable, restless, underweight, over-stressed. He would—

Outside, Haihong blinked. The sparse and rotting skeleton left of Chengdu seemed to have gone mad! Gongs sounded, sirens blared, people poured out of the dilapidated buildings, more people than she had known were left in the city. They were shouting something, something about the quarantine . . .

Starting forward, she didn't even see the pedicab speeding around the corner, racing along the nearly trafficless street. The driver, a strong and large man, saw her too late. He yelled and braked, but Haihong had already gone flying. Her tiny and malnourished body struck the ground head first. Bleeding from her mouth, unable to feel any of her body below the neck, her last thought was a wordless prayer for her son.

5: Cixin

By afternoon Cixin was exhausted from walking away from the village, up into the mountains. His legs ached and his empty stomach moaned. Worse, he was afraid he was lost.

He had been careful to follow the path where Mama used to ride her bicycle, and it had led him to their old picnic place. Cixin had stopped and rested there, but the usual calm had not come over him. Should he try to worship, like Auntie did when she bowed in front of her little shrine? Mama said, in the secret language, that worship was nonsense. But nothing Mama said could be trusted. She was a drunk and a whore.

Cixin swiped a tear from his dusty cheek. It was stupid to cry. And he wasn't really lost. After the picnic place, the path had become narrower and harder to see, and maybe—*maybe*—he had lost it, but he was still climbing uphill. Tibet was uphill, at the top of the mountains. He was all right.

But so thirsty! If he just had some water . . .

An hour later he came to a stream. It was shallow and muddy, but he lay on his belly and lapped at the water. That helped a little. Cixin staggered up on his aching legs and resumed climbing.

An hour after that, it began to get dark.

Now fear took him. He'd been sure he would reach Tibet before nightfall . . . after all, look how far he'd come! There should be monks coming out to greet him, taking him into a warm place with water and beancurd and congee . . . Nothing was right.

"Stupid monks!" he screamed as loud as he could, but then stopped because what if the monks were on their way to get him and they heard him and turned back? So he yelled, "I didn't mean it!"

But still no monks came.

Darkness fell swiftly. Cixin huddled at the base of a pine tree, arms wrapped around his body and legs drawn up for warmth. It didn't help. He didn't want to race around, not on his hurting legs and not in the dark, and yet it was hard to sit still and do nothing. Every noise terrified him—what if a tiger came? Mama said the tigers were all gone from China but Mama was a drunk and a whore.

Shivering, he eventually slept.

In the morning the sun returned, warming him, but everything else was even worse. His belly ached more than his legs. Somehow his tongue had swollen so that it seemed to fill his entire dry mouth. Should he go back to the place where the water had been? But he didn't remember how to get there. All the pine trees, all the larches, all the gray boulders, looked the same.

Cixin whimpered and started climbing. Surely Tibet couldn't be much farther. There'd been a map of China in the village school he'd attended until his inability to sit still made him leave, and on the map Tibet looked very close to Sichuan. He was almost there.

The second nightfall found him no longer able to move. He collapsed beside a boulder, too exhausted even to cry. The picture of the dead dog in the road filled his mind, filled his fitful dreams. When he woke, he was covered with small, stinging bites from something. His cry came out as a hoarse, frustrated whimper. The rising sun filled his eyes, blinding him, and he turned away and tried to sit up.

Then it happened.

Cixin *knew.*

He was lifted out of his body. Thirst and hunger and insect bites vanished. He was not Cixin, and everything—the whole universe—was Cixin. He was woven into the universe, breathed with it, was one with it, and it spoke to him wordlessly and sang to him without music. Everything was him, and he was everything. He was the gray boulder and the yellow sun rising and the rustling pine trees and the hard ground. He was *them* and he felt them, it, all, and the mountains reverberated with surprise and with his name: *Cixin.*

Come.

Cixin.

The child sat on the parched ground, expressionless, and was still and calm.

"Cixin!"

A sour, familiar taste melting on his tongue, a big hand in his mouth.

Then, after a measureless time that was not time, water forced down his throat.

"Cixin!"

Cixin blinked. Then he cried out and would have toppled over had not the big man—how big he was! How pale!—steadied him. More water touched Cixin's lips.

"Not too much, buddy, not at first," the big man said, and he spoke the secret language that only Cixin and Mama knew. How could that be? All at once everything on Cixin hurt, his belly and neck and swollen legs and most of all his head. And the big man had red hair standing up all over his head like an attacking rooster. Cixin started to cry.

The big man lifted him in his arms and put him over his shoulder. Cixin just glimpsed the two other men, one from his village and one a stranger, their faces rigid with something that Cixin didn't understand. Then he fainted.

When he came to, he lay on his bed at Auntie's house. The big man was there, and the stranger, but the village man was not. The big man was saying, very slowly, some words in the secret language to the stranger, and he was repeating them in real words to Auntie. Cixin tried to say something—he didn't even know what—but only a croak came out.

Auntie rushed over to him. She had been crying. Auntie never cried, and fear of this made Cixin wail. Something terrible had happened, and it had happened to Mama. How did Cixin know this? He knew.

And underneath: that other knowing, half memory and half dream, already faded and yet somehow more real even than Auntie's tears or the big man's strange red hair:

Cixin. Come. Cixin.

The big man was Cousin Benjamin Jinkang Molloy. Cixin tasted the ridiculous name on his tongue. Despite the red hair, Cousin Ben sometimes looked Chinese, but mostly he did not. That made no sense, but then neither did anything else.

Auntie didn't like Cousin Ben. She didn't say so, but she wouldn't look at him, didn't offer him tea, frowned when his back was turned and she wasn't crying or at her shrine. Ben visited every day, at first with his "translator" and then, when he saw how well Cixin spoke the secret language, alone. He paid money to Xiao's father to sleep at Xiao's house. Xiao was not allowed to visit Cixin at his bed.

He said, "Why can you talk Mama's secret words?"

"It's English. Where I live, everybody speaks English."

"Do you live in Tibet?" That would be exciting!

"No. I live in America."

Cixin considered this. America might be exciting, too—Xiao's iPod came from there. Sudden tears pricked Cixin's eyes. He wanted to see Xiao. He wanted Mama, who was as dead as the dog in the road. He wanted an iPod. He wanted to get out of bed and race around but his body hurt and anyway Auntie wouldn't let him get up.

Ben said carefully, "Cixin, what happened to you up on the mountain?"

"I got lost."

"I know. I found you, remember? But what happened before that?"

"Nothing." Cixin closed his lips tight. He didn't actually remember what had happened on the mountain, only that something had. But whatever it was, he wasn't going to share it with some strange red-headed cousin who wasn't even from Tibet. It was *his*. Maybe if Mama hadn't got dead . . .

The tears came then and Cixin, ashamed, turned his face toward the wall. Gently Ben turned it back.

"I know you miss your mother, buddy. But my time here is short and I need you to pay attention."

That was just stupid. People needed food and water and clothes and iPods—they didn't "need" Cixin's attention. He scowled.

Ben said, "Listen to me. It's very important that you go on taking the pills your mother was giving you."

"You mean the once-a-week?"

"Yes. I'm going to show you exactly how much to take, and you must do it *every single week*."

"I know. Or I will die."

Ben shut his eyes, then opened them again. "Is that what she told you?"

"Yes." Something inside him trembled, like a tremor deep in the earth. "Is it true?"

"Yes. It's true. In a very important way."

"Okay." All at once Cixin liked speaking the secret language again. It made Mama seem closer, and it made Cixin special. Suddenly he had a thought that made him jerk upright in bed, rattling his head. "Are you really from America?"

"Yes."

"And Mama was, too?"

"She lived there for a while, yes."

"She liked it there?"

"Yes, I think she did."

"Take me to America with you!"

Ben didn't look surprised—why not? Cixin himself was surprised by his thought: surprised, delighted, frightened. In America he would be away from the village boys, away from the school that threw him out. In America he could have an iPod. "Please, Cousin Ben, please please please!"

"Cixin, I can't. Auntie is your closest relative and she—"

"She's not really my Auntie! She was Mama's amah, is all! You're my elder cousin!"

Ben said gently, "She loves you."

Cixin fell back on his bed, hurting his head even more. *Love.* Mama loved him and she died and left him. Auntie loved him and she was keeping him from going to America. Cousin Ben didn't love him or he would take him away from this evil village. Love was terrible and ugly. Cixin glared savagely at this horrible cousin. "Then after you go I won't take my once-a-week and I will die!"

Ben stood. "I will not be blackmailed by a nine-year-old."

Cixin didn't know what "blackmail" was, but it sounded evil. Everywhere he was surrounded by evil. Better to die. Again he turned his face to the wall.

Later, he would always think that had made the difference. His silence, his turning away. If he had fought back, Ben would have said more about blackmail and gone away, angry. But instead he ran his hand through his red hair until it stood up like bristly grass—Cixin could just see this out of the corner of his eye—and then put his hand over his face.

"All right, Cixin. I'll take you to America. But I warn you, it may take a long, long time to arrange."

6: Ben

It took nearly two years.

If Ben hadn't had family contacts at the State Department, it would have been even longer, might have been impossible. The Chinese were discouraging foreign adoptions; Cixin was from within formerly-quarantined Sichuan; the death certificate for Haihong needed to be obtained from a glacially slow bureaucracy and presented in triplicate. But on the other hand, Chinese-American relations were in a positive phase. Ben could prove Haihong had been his second cousin. Ben had received a Citizens' Commendation from the FBI for exposing the surrogate-ring of American girls exploited by a sleazy Mexican fertility clinic. And Uncle James was on the State desk for East Asia.

During those two years, Ben sent Auntie money and Cixin presents. An iPod, which seemed to be a critical object. Jeans and sneakers. Later, a laptop, to be used at the vineyard foreman's house to communicate with Ben. They exchanged email, and Cixin's troubled Ben. Fluent in spoken English, Cixin was barely literate in any language, and he didn't seem to be learning much from the school software Ben supplied.

Cuzin Ben this is Cixin. Wen r yu comin 4 me. Anty is sik agen. Evrybuddy hates me. I hate it hear. Com soon or I wil die.

                                                                    Cixin

Cixin—

I am making plans to bring you here as fast as I can. Please be patient.

(Could Cixin read that word? Maybe not. The backward connection at the foreman's house didn't permit even such a basic tool as a camlink.)

Please wait without fuss.

(*Haihong saying during her pregnancy, "Ben, please don't fuss at me!"*)

Take your once-a-week, use your school software, and be good.

What else? How did you write to a child you'd barely met?

You will like America. Soon, I hope.

                                                                    Ben

Soon, I hope. But did he? Cixin would be an enormous responsibility, and Ben would bear it mostly alone. His parents, old when Ben had been born, lived in failing health in Florida, his sisters in Des Moines and Buffalo. Ben worked long hours in his lab. What was he going to do with an illegally-genemod, barely-literate, ADH adolescent who shared less than three percent of Ben's genetic heritage and nothing of his cultural one?

And then, because complications always attracted more complications, he met Renata.

A group from his department at the Institute went out for Friday Happy Hour. Ordinarily Ben avoided these gatherings. People drank too much, barriers were lowered that might better have stayed raised, flirtations started that proved embarrassing on Monday morning. But Ben knew he was getting a reputation as standoffish, if not downright snobbish, and he had to work with these people. So he went to Happy Hour.

They settled into a long table, scientists and technicians and secretaries. Dan Silverstein, a capable researcher fifteen years Ben's senior, talked about his work with envelope proteins. Susie, the intern whom somebody really should do something about, shot Ben smoldering glances across the table. Ben spotted Renata at the bar.

She sat alone. Tall, a mop of dirty blonde curls, glasses. Pretty enough but nothing remarkable about her except the intensity with which she was both consuming beer and marking on a sheaf of papers. At Grogan's during a Friday Happy Hour? Then she looked up, pure delight on her face, and laughed out loud at something on the papers.

Ben excused himself to go to the men's room. Taking the long way back, he peered over her shoulders. School tests of some kind—

"Do I know you?" She'd caught him. Her tone was cool but not belligerent, looking for neither a fight nor a connection. Self-sufficient.

"No, we've never met." And then, because she was turning back to her papers, dismissing him, "Are you a teacher? What was so funny?"

She turned back, considering. The set of her mouth said, *This better not be a stupid pick-up line*, but there was a small smile in her eyes. "I teach physics at a community college."

"And physics is funny?"

"Are you at all familiar with John Wheeler's experiments?"

She flung the question at him like a challenge, and all at once Ben was enjoying himself. "The 1980 delayed-choice experiment?"

The smile reached her mouth, giving him full marks. "Yes. Listen to this. The question is, *'Describe what Wheeler found when he used particle detectors with photon beams.'* And the answer should be . . . " She looked at Ben, the challenge more friendly now.

"That the presence or absence of a detector, no matter how far down the photon's path, and even if the detector is switched on *after* the photon passes the beam splitter, affects the outcome. The detector's presence or absence determines whether the photon registers as a wave or a particle."

"Correct. This kid wrote, 'Wheeler's particles and his detectors acted weird. I think both were actually broken. Either that or it was a miracle.' " She laughed again.

"And it's funny when your students don't learn anything?"

"Oh, he's learned something. He's learned that when you haven't got the vaguest idea, give it a stab anyway." She looked fondly at the paper. "I like this kid. I'm going to fail him, but I like him."

Something turned over in Ben's chest. It was her laugh, or her cheerful pragmatism, or . . . He didn't know what. He stuck out his hand. "I'm Ben Molloy. I work at the Neuroscience Institute."

"Renata Williams." She shook hands, her head tipped slightly to one side, the bar light glinting on her glasses. "I've always had a thing for scientists. All that arcane knowledge."

"Not so arcane."

"Says you. Sit down, Ben."

They talked until long after his department had left Grogan's. Ben found himself telling her things he'd never told anyone else, incidents from his childhood that were scary or funny or puzzling, dreams from his adolescence. She listened intently, her glasses on top of her head, her chin tilted to one side. Renata was more reticent about her own past ("Not much to tell—I was a goody-goody grind"), but she loved teaching and became enthusiastic about her students. They were carrying out some elaborate science project involving the data from solar flares; this was an active sun-spot year. Renata pulled out her students' sunspot charts and explained them in the dim light from the bar. Eventually the weary bartender stopped shooting them meaningful glances and flatly told them, "Leave, already!"

Ben drove to her apartment. They left her car in the parking lot of the bar until the next day. In bed she was different: more vulnerable, less sure of herself. Softer. She slept with one hand all night on Ben's hip, as if to make sure he was still actually there. Ben lay awake and felt, irrationally but definitely, that he had come home.

Renata worked long hours, teaching five courses ("Community colleges are the sweatshops of academe"), but with a difference. When she wasn't working, she had a life. She saw friends, she kick-boxed, she played in a chess league, she went to movies. Ben, who did none of these things, felt both envious and left-out. Renata just laughed at him.

"If you really wanted to kick-box, you'd take a class in it. People generally end up doing what they want to do, if they can. My hermit." She kissed him on the nose.

If they can. Ben didn't tell Renata about Cixin. The first month, he assured himself, they were just getting to know each other. (A lie: he'd known her, *recognized* her, that first night at Grogan's.) Then, as each month passed—three, four, six—it got harder to explain why he'd delayed. How would Renata react? She was kind but she was also honest, valuing openness and sincerity, and she had a temper.

I'm adopting a Chinese boy for whom I've broken several laws that could still send me to jail, including practicing medicine without a license and administering untested drugs that induce socially disabling side-effects. Perfect. Nothing added to romance like felony charges. Unless it was medical experimentation on a child.

Sometimes Ben looked at Renata, sleepy after sex or squinting at her computer, glasses on top of her curly head, and thought, *It will be all right.* Renata would understand. She came from a large family, and although she didn't want kids herself, she would accept Cixin. Look at how much effort she put into her students, how many endless extra hours working with them on the sunspot project. And Cixin was eleven; in seven more years he'd be off onto his own life.

Other times he knew that he'd lied to Renata, that Cixin was not an easy-to-accept or lovable child, and that his arrival would make Ben's world fall apart. At such times, his desperation made him moody. Renata usually laughed him out of it. But still he didn't tell her.

Then, in August, Uncle James called from Washington. His voice was jubilant.

"I just got the final approval, Ben. You can go get your cousin any time now. You're a daddy! And send me a big cigar—it's a boy!"

Ben clutched his cell so tight that all blood left his fingers. "Thanks," he said.

"Tell me how it works," Renata said. They were the first words she'd spoken in fifteen long minutes, all of which Ben had spent talking. Her dangerous calm reminded him of Haihong, all those years ago.

They were in his apartment, which had effectively if not officially become hers as well. His half-packed suitcase lay open on the bed. Ben stood helplessly beside the suitcase, a pair of rolled-up socks in his hand. Renata sat in a green brocade chair that had been a gift from his mother and Ben knew that if he approached that chair, she would explode.

He took refuge in science. "It's an alteration in the genes that create functional transporter proteins. Those are the amines that get neurotransmitters across synapses to the appropriate brain-cell receptors. The mechanisms are well understood—in fact, there are polymorphic alleles. If you have one gene, your body makes more transporters; with the other version, you get less."

"What difference does that make?"

"It affects mood and behavior. Less serotonin, for example, is connected to depression, irritability, aggression, inflexibility."

"And this alleged genemod in your cousin gave him less serotonin?"

"No." *Alleged genemod.* Ben dragged his hand through his hair. "He probably does have less serotonin, but that's a side effect. The genemod affected other proteins that in turn affected others . . . it's a cascade. Everything's interconnected in the brain. But the functional result in Cixin would be a flood of transporters and neurotransmitters in two brain regions, the superior parietal lobes and the temporoparietal region."

"I don't want jargon, Ben. I want explanations."

"I'm trying to give them to you. I'm doing the best I can to—"

"Then do better! Six months we've been together and you never mention that you're adopting a child . . . what is the *effect* of the extra transporters on those parts of the brain?"

"Without the inhibiting drug I designed for him, near-total catatonia."

"That doesn't make sense! Nobody would deliberately design genes to do that!"

"They didn't." Suddenly tired, he sat on the edge of the bed. His flight to Shanghai left in six hours. "Those brain areas orient the body in space and differentiate between self and others. The research company was trying to develop heightened awareness, perception of others' movements, and reactions to muscular shifting."

She got it. "Better fighting machines."

"Yes."

"Then why—"

"They were rogue geneticists, Renata. They didn't have access to all the most recent research. They screwed up. They're all in jail now."

"And the Neuroscience Institute—"

His patience gave way. "Of course the Institute wasn't involved! I told you—we helped shut the whole thing down."

"Except for your little part in supplying this kid with home-made inhibitors. His other problems you mentioned, the restlessness and aggression—"

"Most likely side-effects of the inhibitor," Ben said wearily. "You can't alter the ratio of neurotransmitters in the brain without a lot of side effects. Cixin's body is under huge stress and his behavior is consistent with fluctuating neurotransmitters and high concentrations of cortisol and other stress hormones."

She said nothing.

"Renata, I promise you—"

"Yeah, well, I've seen what your words are worth." She got up from the green chair and walked around him, toward the door. He knew better than to try to stop her. "If you'd told me about Cixin from the beginning—even only that he was coming here to live with you—that would be one thing. I could have accepted it. I mean—that poor kid. It's not his fault, and I understand family ties as well as you Chinese, or part-Chinese, or whatever you're calling yourself now. But, Ben, I *asked* you. I said after our first week or so, 'Do you see yourself ever wanting children in your life?' And you said no. And now you tell me—" She broke off.

All this time he'd been holding the socks. Carefully, as if they were made of glass, he laid them into his suitcase. A small part of his chaotic mind registered that, like most socks nowadays, they had probably been exported from China. He said, "Will you still be here when I get back?"

"I don't know."

They looked at each other.

"I don't know, Ben," she repeated. "I don't know who you really are."

It was the rainy season in Sichuan and over ninety degrees. Ben's clothing stuck to his body as he waited in the bus station in Chengdu; Cixin's village still had no maglev service. The station looked cleaner and more prosperous than when he'd come to China two years ago. Children in blue-and-white school uniforms marched past, carrying pictures of giant pandas. Ben had emailed Cixin to ask Auntie to bring him to Chengdu, but Cixin got off the bus alone.

He hadn't grown much. At eleven—almost twelve—he was a small, weedy boy with suspicious dark eyes, thin cheeks, and an unruly shock of black hair falling over his forehead. A large greenish bruise on one cheek. He carried a small backpack, nothing else. He didn't smile.

Ben locked his knees against a tide of conflicting emotions. Apprehension. Pity. Resentment. Longing for Renata. But he tried. He said, "Hey, buddy" and put a hand on Cixin's shoulder. Cixin flinched and Ben removed the hand.

He tried again. "Hello, Cixin. It's good to see you. Now let's go to America."

7: Cixin

He didn't know who he really was.

Not now, in these strange and bewildering places. Cixin had never been out of his village. He'd assumed the videos on his laptop had been made-up lies, like Mama telling him about Tibet. But here was Chengdu, full of cars and pedicabs and scooters and huge buildings like mountains and buildings partly fallen down and signs that sprang up from the ground but dissolved when you walked through them and flashing lights and millions of people and men with big guns . . . . Cixin, who just last week had beaten up three village boys at once and thought of himself secretly as "The Tiger," clutched Ben's hand and didn't know what this world was, what he himself was anymore.

"It's all right, buddy," Ben said and Cixin glared at him and dropped the hand, angry because Ben wasn't afraid.

They sat together in the back of the plane to Shanghai. For a while Cixin was content to stare out the window as the ground fell away and they rose into clouds—up into *clouds*! But eventually he couldn't stay still.

"I'm getting up," he told Ben.

"Toilet's just behind us," Ben said.

Cixin didn't need a toilet, he needed to run. Space between the rows of seat was narrow but he barreled down it, waving his arms. A boy a few years older walked in the opposite direction—on Cixin's aisle! The boy didn't step aside. Cixin shoved him away and kept running. The boy staggered up and started after Cixin but was stopped by a shout in Chinese from a man seated nearby. Cixin ran the length of the aisle, cut across the plane, ran back down a different aisle, where Ben grabbed him by the arm.

"Sit, Cixin. *Sit.* You can't run in here."

"Why? Will they throw me off?" This was funny—they were on a plane!—and Cixin laughed. Once he started, he couldn't seem to stop. A man in a blue uniform moved purposefully toward them. Cixin stopped laughing—what if it was a soldier with a hidden gun? He cowered into his seat and tried to make himself very small.

The maybe-soldier and Cousin Ben talked softly. Ben sat down and shook a yellow pill from a plastic bottle. "Take this with your bottled water."

"That's not my once-a-week!" The once-a-week, for reasons Cixin didn't understand, had to be left behind at Auntie's. *Too risky for Customs*, Ben said, *especially for me*. Which made no sense because Ben didn't take the once-a-week, only Cixin did.

"No, it's not your once-a-week," Ben said, "but take it anyway. Now!"

Cixin recognized anger. Ben might have a gun, too. In the videos, all Americans had guns. He took the pill, tapped on the window, kicked the back of the seat until the woman in it turned around and said something sharply in Chinese.

Cixin wasn't clear on what it was. A slow languor had fallen over the plane. Then sleep slid into him as softly as the fog by the river, as calmly as something . . . something right at the edge of memory . . . a pine tree and a gray boulder and . . .

He slept.

Another airport. Stumbling through it half awake. Shouting, people surging, a wait in a locked room . . . maybe it was a dream. Ben's face tired and white as old snow. Then another plane, or maybe not . . . yes. Another plane. More sleep. When he woke truly and for real, he lay in a small room with blue walls and red cloth at the windows, four stacked houses up into the sky, in San Diego, America.

Cixin ran. Waves pounded the shore, the wind whistled hard—whoosh! whoosh!—and sand blew against his bare legs, his pumping arms, his face. He laughed and swallowed sand. He ran.

Ben waited where the deserted beach met the parking lot, the hood of his jacket pulled up, his face red and angry. "Cixin! Get in the car!"

Cixin, exhausted and dripping and happy—as happy as he ever got here—climbed into the front seat of Ben's Saab. Rain pounded the windshield. Ben shouted, "You ran away from your tutor again!"

Cixin nodded. His tutor was stupid. The man had been telling him that rainstorms like this were rare and due to the Earth getting hotter. But with his own body Cixin had experienced many rainstorms, every summer of his life, and they all were hot. So he ran away from the stupid tutor, and from the even stupider girl who was supposed to come take care of him after the tutor left and before Ben came home from work. He ran the seven streets from Ben's house-in-the-sky to the beach because the beach was the only place in America that he liked. And because he wanted to run in the rain.

"You can't just leave the condo by yourself," Ben said. "And I pay that tutor to bring you up to speed before school starts in September, even though—you can't just go down to the beach during a typhoon! And I had to leave the lab in the middle of—"

There was more, but Cixin didn't listen. He'd only been in America ten days but already he knew that Ben wouldn't beat him. Still, Ben was very angry, and Ben was good to him, and Ben had showed him the wonderful beach in the first place. So Cixin hung his head and studied the sand stuck to his knees, but he didn't actually listen. That much was not necessary.

"—adjust your dosage," Ben finished. Cixin said nothing, respectfully. Ben sighed and started the car, his silly red hair stuck to his head.

When they were nearly back at the houses-stacked-in-the-sky, Cixin said, "You look sick, Cousin Ben."

"I'm fine," Ben said shortly.

"You don't eat."

"I eat enough. But, Cixin, you're driving me crazy."

"Yes." It seemed polite to agree. "But you don't eat and you look sick and sad. Are you sad?"

Ben glanced over, rain dripping off his collar. "You surprise me sometimes, buddy."

That was *not* a polite answer. Cixin scowled and stared out the window at the "typhoon" and tapped his sandy sneaker on the sodden floor of the car. He wanted to run again.

And Ben was too sad.

In the "condo," instead of the stupid tutor, a woman sat on the sofa. How did she get in? A robber! Cixin rushed to the phone, shouting, "911! 911!" Ben had taught him that. Robbers—how exciting!

But Ben called, "It's all right, Cixin." His voice sounded so strange that Cixin stopped his mad dash and, curious, looked at him.

"Renata," Ben said thickly.

"I couldn't stay away after all," the woman said, and then they were hugging. Cixin turned away, embarrassed. Chinese people did not behave like that. And the woman was ugly, too tall and too pale, like a slug. Not pretty like Xiao. The way Ben was holding her . . . Cixin hated the woman already. She was evil. She was not necessary.

He rushed into his room and slammed the door.

But at dinnertime the woman was still there. She tried to talk to Cixin, who refused to talk back.

"Answer Renata," Ben said, his voice dangerously quiet.

"What did you say?" Cixin made his voice high and silly, to insult her.

"I asked if you found any sand dollars on the beach."

He looked at her then. "Dollars made of sand?"

"No. They're the shells of ocean creatures. Here." She put something on the table beside his plate. "I found this one last week. I'll bet you can't find one bigger than this."

"Yes! I can!" Cixin shouted. "I'm going now!"

"No, you're not," Ben said, pulling him back into his chair. But Ben was smiling. "Tomorrow's Saturday. We'll all go."

"And if we go in the evening and if the clouds have lifted, there should be something interesting to see in the sky," Renata said. "But I won't tell you what, Cixin. It's a surprise."

Cixin couldn't wait until Saturday evening. He woke very early. Ben and Renata were still asleep in Ben's bed—she must be a whore even if she wasn't as ugly as he thought at first—and here it was *morning*. A little morning, pale gray in a corner of the sky. The rainstorm was all gone.

He dressed, slipped out of the house-in-the-sky, and ran to the beach. No one was there. The air was calm now and the water had stopped pounding and something strange was happening to the sky over the water. Ribbons of color—green, white, green—waved in the sky like ghosts. Maybe they were ghosts! Frightened, Cixin turned his back, facing the part of the sky where the sun would come up and chase the ghosts away. But then he couldn't see the water. He turned back and ran and ran along the cool sand. To his left, in San Diego, sirens started to sound. Cixin ignored them.

Finally, exhausted, he plopped down. The sun was up now and the sky ghosts gone. Nobody else came out on the beach. Cixin watched the nearest tiny waves kissing the sand.

Something happened.

A soft, calm feeling stole through him, calm as the water. He didn't even want to run any more. He sat cross-legged, half hidden by a sand drift, dreamily watching the ocean, and all at once he *was* the ocean. Was the sand, was the sky, was the whole universe and they were him.

Cixin. Come. Cixin.

Voices, everywhere and nowhere, but Cixin didn't have to answer because they already knew the answer. They were him and he was them.

Peace. Belonging. Everything. Time and no time.

And then Ben was forcing open his mouth, putting in something that melted on his tongue, and it all went away.

But this time memory lingered. It had happened. It was real.

8: Ben

"I'd dropped the dosage to try to mitigate the side effects," Ben said. He ran his hand through his filthy hair. Cixin lay asleep in his room, sunburned and exhausted. God only knew how long he'd been gone before Ben found his empty bed.

Renata pulled her eyes from CNN. The solar flare, the largest ever recorded and much more powerful than anticipated, had played havoc with radio communications from Denver to Beijing. Two planes had crashed. The aurora borealis was visible as far south as Cuba. Renata said, "Ben, you can't go on fiddling with his dosage and giving him sleeping pills when you get it wrong. You're not even an M.D., and yet you're playing God with that child's life!"

"And what do you think I should do?" Ben shouted. It was a relief to shout, even as he feared driving her away again. "Should I let him go catatonic? You didn't see him two years ago in China—I did! He'd been in a vegetative state for two days and he would have died if I hadn't found him! Is that what you think should happen?"

"No. You should get him medical help. You wouldn't have to say anything about the genemods or—"

"The hell I wouldn't! What happens when they ask me what meds Cixin takes? If I didn't tell them, he could die. If I do, I go to jail. And how long do you think it would take a medical team to find drug traces in his body? Inhibitors have a long half-life. And even if I explain everything, and if I'm believed, what happens to Cixin then? He's not even on my medical insurance until the adoption is final! So he'd be warehoused, catatonic, in some horrifying state hospital, and I'd be standing trial. Is that what you want?"

"No. Wait. I don't know." She wasn't yelling at him now; her voice held sorrow and compassion. CNN announced that a total of 312 people had died in the two air disasters. "But, sweetheart, the situation as it stands isn't good for you or Cixin, either. What are you going to do?"

"What can I do? He just isn't anything like a normal—Cixin!"

The boy stood in the doorway, his shock of black hair stiff from salt air, his eyes puffy from sleep. He suddenly looked much older.

"Ben—what does the once-a-week do to me?"

Renata drew a long breath.

"It's complicated," Ben said finally.

"I need to know."

Cixin wasn't fidgeting, or yelling, or running. Something had happened on the beach, something besides sunburn and dehydration. Ben's tired mind stabbed around for a way to explain things to a nearly illiterate eleven-year-old. Nothing occurred to him.

Renata switched off the television and said quietly, "Tell him, Ben. Or I will."

"Butt out, Renata!"

"No. And don't you ever try to bully me. You'll lose."

He had already lost. Shooting a single furious glance at her, Ben turned to Cixin. "You have a . . . a sickness. A rare disease. If you don't take the once-a-week, you will die like your mother said, but first you go all stiff and empty. Like this." Ben, feeling like a fool, sat on the rug and made his body rigid and his face blank.

"Empty?"

"Yes. No thoughts, nothing. No *Cixin*. That's how you were on the beach, like that for a long time, which is why you're so sunburned." And maybe more than sunburned. A big solar flare came with a proton storm, and those could cause long-term biochemical damage. Ben couldn't cope with that just now, not on top of everything else. "Do you understand, Cixin? You went empty. Like a . . . a Coke can all drunk up."

"Empty," Cixin repeated. All at once he smiled, a smile so enigmatic and complicated that Ben was startled. Then the boy went back into his room and closed the door.

"Spooky," Ben said inadequately. He struggled up from the rug. "How do you think he took it?"

"I don't know." Renata seemed as disconcerted as Ben. "I only know what I would be thinking if I were him."

"What would you be thinking?" All at once he desperately wanted to know.

"I would be wondering who I really was. Wondering where the pills ended and I, Cixin, began."

"He's eleven," Ben said scornfully. Scorn was a relief. "He doesn't have sophisticated thoughts like that."

September. Cixin started school, the oldest kid in the fourth grade. Fortunately, he was small enough to sort of fit in and large enough to not be picked on by his classmates. He could not read at grade level, could not concentrate on his worksheets, could not sit still during lessons. After one week, his teacher called Ben to school for an "instructional team meeting." The team recommended Special Ed.

After two weeks, Cixin had another episode of catatonia. Again Ben found him at the beach, sitting half in the water, motionless amid frolicking children and splashing teens and sunbathing adults. A small boy with a sand pail said conversationally, "That kid dead."

"He's not dead," Ben snapped. Wearily he forced a dose of inhibitor onto Cixin's tongue. It melted, and he came to and stared at Ben from dark, enigmatic eyes that slowly turned resentful.

"Go away, Ben."

"I can't, damn it!"

Cixin said, "You don't understand."

In his khakis and loafers—the school had called him at work to report Cixin's absence—Ben lowered himself to sit on the wet sand. The blue Pacific rolled in, frothy at the whitecaps and serene beyond. The sun shone brightly. Ben said, "Make me understand."

"I can't."

"Try. Why do you do it, Cixin? What happens when you go empty?"

"It's not empty."

"Then what is it?" He willed himself to patience. This was a child, after all.

Cixin took a long time answering. Finally he said, "I see. Everything."

"What kind of everything?"

"*Everything*. And it talks to me."

Ben went as still as Cixin had been. He hadn't even realized . . . hadn't even *thought* of that. He'd thought of neurotransmitter ratios, neural architecture plasticity, blood flow changes, synaptic miscues. And somehow he'd missed this. *It talks to me.*

Cixin leapt up. "I'm not going back to Special Ed!" he yelled and raced away down the sand, his school papers streaming out of the unzipped backpack flapping on his skinny shoulders.

"Temporal lobe epilepsy?" Renata said doubtfully. "But . . . he doesn't have seizures?"

"It's not *grand mal*," Ben said. They sat in Grogan's. Ben had drugged Cixin again with Dozarin, hating himself for doing it but needing, beyond all reason, to escape his apartment for a few hours. "With *petit mal*, seizures can go completely unnoticed. And obviously it's not the only aberration going on in his brain, but I think it's a factor."

"But . . . if he's hearing voices, isn't that more likely to be schizophrenia or something like that?"

"I'm no doctor, as you're constantly telling me, but temporal-lobe epilepsy is a very well documented source of religious transports. Joan of Arc, Hildegaard of Bingen, maybe even Saul on the road to Damascus."

"But why does your inhibitor work on him at all? Isn't epilepsy a thing about electrical firing of—"

"I don't know why it works!" Ben said. He drained his gin and tonic and set the glass, harder the necessary, onto the table between them. "Don't you get it, Renata? I don't know anything except that I'm reaching the end of my rope!"

"I can see that," Renata said. "Have you considered that Cixin might be telling the truth?'

"Of course he's 'telling the truth,' as he experiences it. Temporal-lobe seizures can produce visual and auditory hallucinations that seem completely real."

"That's not what I meant."

"What did you mean?"

Renata fiddled with the rim of her glass. "Maybe the voices Cixin hears *are* real."

Ben stared at her. *You think you know someone . . .* "Renata, you teach science. Since when do you dabble in mysticism?"

"Since always. I just don't advertise it to everybody."

That hurt. "I'm hardly 'everybody.' Or at least I thought I wasn't."

"You're taking it wrong. I just meant that I haven't closed the door on the possibility of other worlds besides this one, other levels of being. Spirits, aliens, gods and angels, parallel universes that bleed through . . . I don't know. But there's never been a human society, ever, that didn't believe in some sort of mystery beyond the veil."

He didn't know any more who she was. Ben motioned to the waiter for another gin and tonic. When his thoughts were at least partly collected, he said, "You can't—"

"What I can or cannot do doesn't matter. The point is, what are *you* going to do now?"

"I'm going to have an implant inserted under Cixin's skin that will deliver the correct dose of inhibitor automatically."

"Really." Her tone was dangerous. "And who will perform this surgery? You?"

"Of course not. It can be done in Mexico."

"Do you know what you're saying, Ben? You're piling one criminal offense on top of another, and you're treating that boy like a lab rat."

"He's sick and I'm trying to make him better!" God, why wouldn't she understand?

"Are you going to at least explain all that to him?"

"No. He wouldn't understand."

She finished her wine, stood, and looked down at him with the fearlessness he both admired and disliked in her. The light from behind the bar glinted on her glasses. "Tell Cixin what you're going to do. Or I will."

"It's none of your business! I'm his guardian!"

"You've made it my business. And even if you were fully his legal guardian—which you're not, yet—you're not being his friend. Not until you can consider his mind as well as his brain."

"There's no difference, Renata,"

"The hell there isn't. Tell him, Ben. Or I will."

He took a day to think about it, a day during which he was furious with Renata, and longed for her, and addressed angry arguments to her in his mind. Then, reluctantly, he left work in the middle of the afternoon (his boss was beginning to grumble about all the absences) to pick up Cixin at school.

Cixin wasn't there.

9: Cixin

The voices came to him as he colored a map of the neighborhood around his school. All week they'd been working on maps, which wasn't as stupid as the other schoolwork. Cixin sat at his desk and vigorously wielded crayons. Playground, 7-11, houses, maglev stop, school building. North, west, legend to tell what the little drawings were. Blue, red, green . . .

Cixin.

He froze, his hand holding the green crayon suspended above his desk.

Cixin.

The voice was faint—but it was there. He looked wildly around the room. He knew the room was there, the other kids were there, he was there. In this school room, not on the beach, and not in that other place where even the beach disappeared and he could feel the Earth and sky breathe. So how could he be hearing . . .

Cix . . . in . . .

"Where are you?" he cried.

"I'm right here," the teacher's aide said. She hurried to Cixin's desk and put a hand on his shoulder.

Cixin . . .

"Come back!" He jumped up, scattering the crayons and knocking away the teacher's hand.

"I haven't gone anywhere," she said soothingly. "I'm right here, dear. What do you need?"

Standing, he could see out the classroom window to the parking lot. Ben's white car pulled in and parked.

Ben was coming for him. Cixin didn't know how he knew that, but he knew. Ben didn't like the voices. Ben was very smart and very American and he knew how to do things, get things, make things happen. Ben was coming for Cixin and Ben was going to make the voices go away forever.

Cixin's mind raced. Ben would have to pass front-door security, go to the school office, get a pass, come down the hall. . . . Cixin didn't hesitate. He ran.

"Cixin!" his teacher called. The other children began shouting. The aide tried to grab Cixin but he twisted away, ran out of the room and down the hall, zigged left, dashed toward the door to the playground. The school doors were locked from the outside but not the inside; Cixin burst through and kept running. Across the playground, over the fence, behind houses to the street . . . *run, fen noon nan hi . . .*

Eventually he had to stop, panting hard, leaning over with his hands on his knees. The houses here were small and didn't go up into the sky like Ben's house. Beyond were stores and eating houses and a gas station. Cixin walked behind a place with the good smell of pizza coming from it. Except for the beach, pizza was the best thing about America. Back here no one in a white car could see him. There was a big metal box with an opening high up.

Climbing on a broken chair, Cixin peered inside the big metal box. Some garbage, not much, and a bad smell, not too bad. He hauled himself up and tumbled inside. The garbage included a lot of pizza boxes, some with half-eaten pizzas inside. And no one could find him.

Many things were clear to him now. Ben saying to Renata, "I'll have to adjust the dosage. He's growing." The way to hear the voices, to go to that other place where he saw everything and breathed with the sky, was by having no once-a-week, and by waiting until the one he took before wasn't in his head anymore. Ben had made him swallow the last once-a-week last Wednesday. This was Tuesday, and already the voices, faint, were there.

He curled up in a corner of the dumpster to wait.

10: Ben

He looked everywhere, the beach first. The day was warm and the sands choked with people who didn't have to be at work, as well as teenagers who probably should have been in school, but no Cixin. Ben raced back to the apartment: nothing. He called the school again, which advised him to call the police. Instead he called Renata's cell; she had no classes Tuesday afternoon.

"I'm very worried about—"

"How did you hear so *fast*?" she demanded.

"What?"

"You're inside, aren't you? Was the TV on at the lab? If there's a basement in your building go there but stay away from the power connections and make sure you can get out easily if there's a fire. We put the bulletin out on campus, but who knows how many won't hear it—twenty minutes! God!"

"What are you talking about?"

"The flare! The solar flare!" And then, "What are *you* talking about?"

"Cixin's missing. He ran away."

"Shit!" And then, very rapidly, "Listen, Ben, another solar flare's been detected, a huge one, I mean *really* huge. Word just came down from the *Hinode*. It's bigger than the 1859 superflare and that one—just *listen*. There's an associated proton storm and nobody knows exactly when it will hit but the one in 2005 accelerated to almost a third of light speed. Best estimate is twenty minutes. There's going to be fires and power outages and communication disruptions but also proton storms that have biological consequences to living tissue that—you can't go down to the beach to look for him now!"

"I've already been. He's not there."

"Then where—"

"I don't know!" Ben shouted. "But I've got to look!"

"Where?" she asked, and her practicality only enraged him more.

"I don't know! But he's out there alone and if there are fires—" The phone went dead.

He stood holding it, this dead and useless piece of technology, listening to the sirens start outside and mount to a frenzied wail. Where could Cixin have gone? Ben knew no place else to look, no place else that Cixin ever went. Although he had liked that V-R arcade Ben had once taken him to . . .

He tore out of the apartment, raced down the stairs, and stopped, frozen.

In the bright sunlight, lights were going out. Traffic lights, the neon window sign at Rosella's Café. They sparked in a glowing electrical arc and went dead. Smoke poured from the windows of a gas station a block over. People stopped, stared, and turned to their cell phones. Ben saw their faces when they realized the cells were all dead.

The sirens grew louder, then all at once stopped.

"What is it?" a young Hispanic woman asked him, clutching his arm. She wore shorts and a green halter top and she wheeled a pram with a fat, gurgling baby.

Ben shook off her hand. "A solar flare, get inside and stay away from windows and appliances!" She let out a great cry of horrified non-understanding but he was already gone, running the several blocks to the V-R arcade.

It took him ten minutes. Cixin wasn't there. The doors yawned crazily open, and a machine in one of the cubicles had shorted and begun to burn.

The city couldn't survive this. The country couldn't survive this. Panic, no communications, fires, the grid gone . . . and the radiation of a proton storm. Ten more minutes.

He found a corner of the arcade farthest from the booths, near the refreshment counter, and crawled under the largest table. It wouldn't help, of course, and it didn't make him feel better. But it was all he could do: wait for the beginning of the end under a wooden picnic table whose underside was stuck with wads of gum from children that might or might not be alive by tomorrow.

11: Cixin

Cixin.

"I'm here," he said aloud, to the empty pizza boxes in the dumpster. That was kind of funny because the voices didn't speak out loud; they didn't really have words at all. Just a feeling inside his head, and the feeling was him, Cixin. And then a picture:

The whole world, out in space, but covered with such a big gray fog that he couldn't even see the planet. But Cixin knew it was under the fog, and knew too that the voices hadn't known it. Not before. But now they did, because they knew Cixin was here. He was them and they were him and both were everything. It was all the way it should be, and he was calm and safe—he would always be safe now.

Hi, he said and it might have been out loud or not, it was all the same thing.

12: Ben

No other V-R booth shorted and caught fire, although the first one was still smoking. Ben crawled out from under the table. He'd been there half an hour—how long did a proton storm last? He had no idea.

In his pocket, his cell rang.

Ben pulled it out and stared at it incredulously. How . . . After a moment he had the wits to answer.

"Ben! Are you all right?"

Renata. "Yes. No. I don't know, I didn't find Cixin . . . How come this thing works?"

"I don't know." She sounded bewildered. "Mine came on, so I called you . . . Some communications are back. Not where the grid is out or the satellites destroyed, of course, but the radio stations that didn't get hit are coming through clear now and—it isn't possible!"

For the first and only time ever, he heard hysteria in her voice. In *Renata's* voice. "The solar radiation. It . . . it isn't reaching Earth any more."

"It missed us?"

"No! I mean, yes, apparently . . . before the *Hinode* burned out, it— that's the Japanese spacecraft designed especially to monitor the sun, I told you about it—the data shows—the coronal mass ejection—"

"Renata, you're not making sense." Perversely, her panic steadied him. "Where are you?"

"I'm home. I have a radio. I'm not—it isn't—"

"Stay there. I'll get to you somehow. How much of the city is on fire?"

"Not enough!" she cried, which made no sense. "Did you find Cixin?"

"No." He'd told her that already. Pain scorched his heart. "Stay where you are. I'll call the cops about Cixin and then come."

"You won't get through to the police," she said, her voice still high with that un-Renata-like hysteria.

"I know," he said.

It took him over an hour to walk to her place. He kept trying the cops on his cell until the battery went dead. He skirted fires, looting, police cars, crying people in knots on the sidewalk, but Renata was right: This was not enough damage compared to what he had seen starting in the first few minutes of the solar storm. What the fuck had happened?

"It was deflected," Renata said when he finally got to her apartment. She'd calmed down. The power was off but bright sunlight poured into the window; the battery-powered radio was turned to the federal emergency station; beside the radio lay a gun that Ben had no idea Renata even owned. He stared at the gun while she said, "Cixin?"

"Still no idea."

She locked the door and put her arms around him. "You're bleeding."

"It's nothing, a fuss with some homeless guy that—what does the radio say?"

"Not much." She let him go and turned the volume lower. "The satellites are mostly knocked out, but not all because a few were in high orbit nightside and didn't get here until it . . . stopped."

"*What* stopped?"

"All of it," she said simply. "The radiation, including the proton storm, just curved around the Van Allen Belt and was deflected off into space."

He was no physicist. "That's good, right? Isn't that what the Van Allen is supposed to do? Only . . . only why did the radiation start for a while and *then* stop?"

"Bingo." Abruptly she sat down hard on the sofa. Ben joined her, surprised at how much his legs hurt. "What happened can't happen, Ben. Radiation just doesn't deflect that way by itself. And the magnetic fields contained in the coronal mass ejection were not only really intense, they were in direct opposition with Earth's magnetic field. We should have taken a hit like . . . like nothing ever before. Far, far worse than the superstorm of 1859. And we didn't. In fact, protons should still be entering the atmosphere. And they aren't."

He tried to understand, despite the anxiety swamping him for Cixin. "Why isn't that all happening?"

"Nobody knows."

"Well, what does the radio say?"

She flung out her hands. "Unknown quantum forces. Angels. Aliens. God. Secret government shields. Don't you understand . . . *nobody knows*. This just can't be happening."

But it was. Ben said wearily, "Where do you think I should look next for Cixin?"

They found him two days later. It took that long for basic city services to begin to resume and for anyone to approach the dumpster. Cixin was catatonic, dehydrated, bitten by rats. He was taken to the overburdened hospital. Ben was called when a nurse discovered Cixin's name and phone number sewn into the waistband of his jeans—Renata's idea. He found Cixin rigid on a gurney parked in a hallway jammed with more patients. He had an IV, a catheter, and multiple bandages. His eyes were empty.

Ben put the inhibitor on Cixin's tongue. Slowly Cixin woke up, his dark eyes over sunken cheeks turning reproachful. Ben yelled for a doctor, but no one came.

"Cixin."

"They . . . didn't . . . know," he croaked.

"It's okay, buddy, I'm here now, it's okay . . . Who didn't know what?"

But painfully Cixin turned his face to the wall and would say no more.

The staff wanted to do a psych evaluation. Ben argued. They turned stubborn. Eventually he said they could get a court order if they wanted to but for right now he was taking his boy home as soon as the treatment for dehydration was completed. The harassed hospital official said several harsh things and promised legal action. A day later Ben signed out Cixin AMA, against medical advice, and drove him home through streets returning to normal much faster than anyone had thought possible.

There was a dreary familiarity to the scene: Cixin asleep in his room, Ben and Renata with drinks in the living room, talking about him. How many times in the last few months had they done this? How many more to come?

Renata had just come from the small bedroom. She'd asked to talk to Cixin alone. "He won't tell you anything," Ben had warned, but she'd gone in anyway. Now she sat, pale and purse-lipped, on Ben's sofa, holding her drink as if it were an alien object.

"Did he tell you anything?" Ben said tiredly. He stood by the window, facing her.

"Yes. No. Just what he told you—'They didn't know' and 'Let me go back.' Plus one other thing."

"What?" Jealousy, perverse and ridiculous, prodded him: Cixin had talked more freely to her than to him.

"He said there was a big explosion, a long time ago."

"A big explosion?"

"A long time ago."

That hardly seemed useful. Ben said, "I don't know what to do. I just don't."

Renata hesitated. "Ben . . . do you remember when we met? At Grogan's?"

"Yes, of course—why wouldn't I? Why bring that up now?"

"I was correcting papers, remember? My students were supposed to answer questions about Wheeler's two-slit experiments."

Ben stared at her. She was very pale and her expression was strange, both hesitant and wide-eyed, completely unlike Renata. "I remember," he said. "So?"

"The original 1927 two-slit experiment showed that a photon could be seen as both a wave and a particle that—"

"Don't insult my intelligence," Ben snapped, and wondered at whom his nasty tone was aimed. He tried again. "Of course I know that. And your students were writing about Wheeler's demonstration that observation determines the outcome of which one a photon registers as."

"The presence or absence of observation also determines the results of a whole slew of other physics experiments," she said. "All right, you know all that. But *why*?"

"Feynmann's probability wave equations—"

"Explain exactly nothing! They describe the phenomena, they quantify it, but they don't explain why *observation*, which essentially means human consciousness, should be so woven into the very fabric of the universe at its most basic level. Until humans observe anything fundamental, in a very real sense it doesn't exist. It's only a smear of unresolved probability. So why does consciousness give form to the entire universe?"

"I don't know. Why?"

"I don't know either. But I think Cixin does."

Ben stared at her.

Renata looked down at the drink in her hand. Her shoulders trembled. "The explosion Cixin said he saw in his mind—he said, 'It made everything.' I think he was talking about the Big Bang. I think he feels a presence of some kind when he's in his catatonic state. That whatever genemods he has, they've somehow opened up parts of his mind that in the rest of us are closed."

Ben put his glass down carefully on the coffee table and sat beside her on the sofa. "Renata, he does feel a presence. He's experiencing decreased blood flow in the posterior superior parietal lobes, which define body borders. He loses those borders when he goes into his trance. And very rapid firing in the tempoparietal region can lead to the sense of an 'other' or presence in the brain. Cixin's consciousness gets caught in neural feedback loops in both those areas—which are, incidentally, the same areas of the brain that SPECT images highlight in Buddhist monks who are meditating. What Cixin feels is real to him—but that doesn't make it real in the cosmos. Doesn't make it a . . . a . . . "

"Overmind," she said. "Cosmic consciousness. I don't know what to call it. But I think it's there, and I think it's woven into the universe at some deeply fundamental level, and I think Cixin was accidentally given a heightened ability to be in contact with it."

Ben said, "I don't know what to say."

"Don't say anything. Just think about it. I'm going home now, Ben. I can't take any more tonight."

Neither could he. He was flabbergasted, dismayed, even horrified by what she'd said. How could she believe such mystical bullshit? He didn't know who she was any more.

It wasn't until hours later that, unable to sleep, he realized that Renata also thought her "cosmic consciousness" had diverted the solar flare radiation away from Earth in order to protect Cixin.

13: Cixin

Cixin sat in his bedroom, cross-legged on the bed. His iPod lay beside him, but he wasn't listening to it, hadn't listened to it for the past week. Nor had he gone to school, played video games, or sent email to Xiao. He was just waiting.

Xiao—he would miss her. Ben had been very good to him, and so had Renata, but he knew he wouldn't miss them. That was bad, maybe, but it was true.

Maybe Xiao would come one day, too. After all, if the voices were everything, and they were him, then they should be Xiao, too, right? But Xiao couldn't hear them. Ben couldn't hear them. Renata couldn't hear them. Only Cixin could, and probably not until tomorrow. And this time . . .

The nurse hired to watch him while he was "sick" looked up from her magazine, smiled, and turned another page. Cixin didn't hate her. He was surprised he didn't hate her, but she couldn't help being stupid. Any more than Ben could help it, or Renata, or Xiao. They didn't know.

Cixin knew.

And when he felt the calm steal over him, felt himself expand outward, he knew the voices would be early and that was so good!

Cixin.

Yes, he said, but only inside his mind, where the nurse couldn't hear.

Come.

Yes, he thought, because that was right, that was where he belonged. With the voices. But there was something to do first.

He made a picture in his mind, the same picture he'd seen once before, the whole Earth wrapped in a gray fog. He made the sun shining brightly, and a ray gun shooting from the sun to the Earth, the way Renata had described it to him. The picture said POW!! Like a video game. Then he made the ray gun go away.

Yes, formed in his mind. *We'll watch over them.*

Cixin sighed happily. Then he became everything and went home, to where he knew, beyond any need to race around or yell at people or be *fen noon nan hi*, who he really was.

He never heard the nurse cry out.

14: Ben

She came to him through the bright sunshine, hurrying down the cement path, her dirty blond curls hidden by a black hat. The black dress made her look out of place. This was Southern California; people wore black only for gala parties, not for funerals. But Renata, his numb and weary mind irrelevantly remembered, came originally from Ohio.

Ben turned his back on her.

She wasn't fooled. Somehow she knew that he hadn't turned away from not wanting her there, but from wanting her there too much. No one else stood beside the grave. Ben hadn't told his family about Cixin's death, and he'd discouraged his few friends from attending. And they, bewildered to learn only after the death that anti-social Ben had been adopting a child, nodded and murmured empty consolations. And then, of course, there were the sunspots. A second coronal mass ejection had occurred just yesterday, and everyone was jumpy.

"Ben, I just heard and I'm so sorry," Renata said. From her, the words didn't sound so empty. Her eyes held tears, and the hand she put on his arm held a tenderness he badly needed but wouldn't allow himself to take.

"Thank you," he said stiffly. If she even alluded to all that other nonsense . . . And of course, being Renata, she did. "I know you loved him. And you did the best you could for him—I know that, too. But maybe he's where he wanted to be."

"Can it, Renata."

"All right. Will you come have coffee with me now?"

He looked down. So small a coffin. Two cemetery employees waited, trying not to look impatient, to lower the coffin into its hole, cover it up, and get back inside. To their eyes, this was a non-funeral: no mourners, no minister or priest or rabbi, only this one dour man reading from a book that wasn't even holy.

"Please," Renata said. "You shouldn't stay here, love."

He let himself be led away. Behind him the men began to work with feverish speed.

"They're afraid," he said. "Idiots."

"Not everybody can understand science, Ben." Then, shockingly, she laughed. He knew why, but she clapped one hand over her mouth. "I'm so sorry!"

"Forget it."

Not everybody could understand science, no. In Ben's experience, almost nobody even tried. Half the population still equated evolution with the devil. But the president had made a speech on TV last night and another one this morning: *The new solar flare presents no danger. There will be no repeat of last week's crisis. The radiation is not reaching Earth.*

Wisely, she had not tried to say why the radiation was not reaching Earth. Nor why the astronauts on *Hope of Heaven*, the Chinese space shuttle, had not been fried in orbit. *No danger* was as far as the president could go. It was already like crossing into Wonderland.

Ben and Renata walked to his Saab. If she'd parked her own car somewhere in the cemetery, as she must have, she seemed willing to leave it. Gently she took the book from his hands and studied the cover.

"I'm not giving in," he said, too harshly.

"I know."

"If there really were . . . 'more,' were really something that could be reached, contacted, by more or different brain connections—then what evolutionary gain could have made humanity lose it? Was it too distracting, interfering with survival? Too calming? Too *what*?"

"I don't know."

"It doesn't make sense," Ben said. "And if it really were genetic, really were that the rest of us aren't making enough of some chemicals or connective tissues or . . . I just can't believe it, Renata."

"I know."

He wished she would stop saying that. She handed back to him James Behren's *Quantum Physics and Consciousness*, but he knew she'd already seen the page he'd dog-eared and underlined. She already knew that over the grave of Cixin, who could barely decipher any language, Ben had read aloud about two-slit and delayed-choice and particle-detector experiments. Renata knew, always, everything.

"Maybe," she said after a long silence, "if they know now that the rest of us possess consciousness, however rudimentary, not just Cixin . . . if they know that, then maybe someday . . . "

She could never just leave anything alone. That's who she was. Ben shifted the book to his other hand and put an arm around her.

"No," he said. "Not possible."

This time she didn't answer. But she leaned against him and they walked out of the cemetery together, under the bright blue empty sky.

THE BITRUNNERS
TINA CONNOLLY

[*Helix,* Summer]

The thing about Mars is, they catch you when you yoink stuff.

Criming on Mars is about keeping your nose clean. It's about please and thank you and slipping the credits and if you have to no-air someone, you do it slick and untraceable. You spike the software on their ship, you make it nice and accidental—nothing cop Station will have to squarely investigate or risk a visit from HQ of the Nine. And you specially stay spotless if you're a thick-fingered brute Crimer dult who stands to inherit command of the biggest fronting casino of that joy-ridden planet.

Moonbase is another story.

Moonbase is grey and sharp divisioned. It's got brute dult Crimers so nasty they take all of cop Station's time. What's left can slip through the cracks, if it knows to play small. You keep your nose clean on Moonbase, they know you're up to something. Criming here is another con altogether.

This was the gang, the real gang: Batel, Webbl, Tank, and me. This was the heart.

Batel, sides all else, was the best yoinker on Moonbase. She once got the whole gang finger knives from the tightest midcircle store there was, and then she yoinked the bitties a new sleep inflatable on her way out, just so she could watch them sleep on it, cuddled up as sweet as inner circle babes. Those finger knives were under plastic, too, and looped with lasers to alarm the clerk.

For the lasers she used a bristle, course, and being Batel, she'd yoinked that from the cop Station when El Ted had ratted her and she'd been drugged in. It takes skill to master a bristle, to disrupt and reflect lasers how you want them. She holed up in one of her hideys three weeks, mastering the

9 6

bristle. When I saw her at last she was skinnier than gridlines, and burned up and down both arms, and those big black eyes were dead craters.

And then the first thing she had to do, right there in the outer circle passage was dodge Martha's sharpened picks, snick out her boot knife and take Martha in the kidneys, cause Martha must've thought to earn an important place she had to take Batel's. Nega one had realized how crazy Martha'd gotten, till we saw it. Surely not even Batel saw it coming, not from the girl she'd taken under her wing—yet all burnt up and unprepared she took Martha down. Then she showed us what she could do with the bristle.

You want a cry story, try the girlie gang in the spacesuit district. I'm nega gonna bawl about what happened on Mars.

Our gang's special. Oh, Randie from the Starslicers will tell you her gang's totally fuelled and everyone knows it. And yeah, if you like brute power you can ask nicely to join up with them. You got some dult dolt trying to grab himself a quick kiddie fix, you can pay the Starslicers to put a stop on that, and a no-air final-type stop it'll be, too. Or you don't want brute, you want cool and swingin', a hepcat gang of the wonkest kiddies, you go join Citizen. Citizen's full of fast flicks, slick con talkers who'll run the best lost rich kiddie con you ever saw.

But our gang? Sure, we got a rep. Riband's known all over for being regular petty yoinkers. Batel and Webbl and I work hard to keep that average mec vibe well out there. It is a skill, perhaps hard a skill to master as a bristle. Thing is, any gang's got to stay known. Else you have nega fuel, cause the size of your fuel's measured by what it's known you are liable to do. You get too known, you get extra sniffing from cop Station. So our skill is petty yoinking, and we make sure we're good enough to keep in grub and gear, but not so good that others want to take us down to the dust.

But the main reason we gotta stay known is cause our gang has a secret. And when you've got a dead hidden secret you gotta front it. Mars you front it with legit stuff; casinos and joyrides. Moonbase you front it with pettiness. Kiddie or dult, brain or brute, Mars or Moonbase—there's always a front, else sniffers will wonder how you got all that fancy gear you've been sporting.

See, the real gang, the heart of the gang, are bitrunners. And bitrunning is no-air dangerous.

It's so dangerous it's the whole reason we have to keep a gang around us, like midcircle Moonbase protects the credited who live inner circle. Nega one of Riband know what we really do. They just think we're the best yoinkers, which we are, specially my Batel. And they think we chose them cause they'll grow into future best yoinkers, which they nega no way no-air will. We chose them to keep us in trouble, little trouble. We chose them to keep our gang looking a little skilled and a little more lousy and a lot of petty. Grub we yoink, and used gear and duct tape. Petty stuff, so petty that if cop Station decides to bother kiddies they go stake out the brute Starslicers for a few days. Not us.

And that is the plan. Because bitrunning is so no-air dangerous it scares even the hardest brute Crimers. Crimers who bitrun make zeroes and zeroes of credits. Dult bitrunners, like those my uncle hires, go on jobs with crazy numbers of backups, grown-up Starslicer types whose job is to look invisible and shield the bitrunner. And that job is no-air dangerous as well, though at least you got the chance to sell out your bitrunner stead of being negatid along with him.

But we don't have shields, and we don't have much else'n our finger knives. What we have is our bitcatcher install, our brains, and our secrecy. That secrecy is our outer circle.

Cop Station never did wise up to us. We bitran right under their noses for two solid years; raked up enough credits to each open an inner circle hotel if we wanted. We were never caught and never noticed and we bitran right up till Mars and my uncle.

Batel first started running cons eight years ago. Cons built around the truth are best, and just like me, Batel figured that out. First it was all truth and little con; she begged credits for being a half-orphaned kiddie with a dusted dad. As she got good and bored she added another layer and the truth con came to life—she played a con artist pretending to be a regular orphaned kiddie. Her brother Tank left his job porting baggage at the flyzone when he saw she was raking it, and they ran a modified pigeon drop with Tank as a Crimer hunter out to catch con kiddie Batel. Tank wasn't dusting then; he conned well enough following Batel's lead, but if the con fell through he fell straight back on his fists. When confused, Tank fought. That was his no-air dead end.

Webbl came next, just when both girls had passed their tenth. Batel said once that Webbl was already beautiful then, with her fine-boned face and fringed eyes. I think Tank was in love with her a little. She paired well with tiny child-like Batel—Webbl was from ten to midteen the perfect androgyne, able to pass for girl or girlie and turn heads either way.

With three of them under Batel's lead the cons became more elaborate and more dangerous. With the trickier cons came times that Tank would mess up.

This is where I enter their story.

Batel and Tank's story was simple: a dead mom and a dusted dad they avoided. Webbl was a typical outer circle orphan, parents unknown. The kiddie gangs are full of orphan center refugees. Our Leit was one, and the bitties Tap and Henry. Martha was of course not from outer circle. We should have known not to trust her. She was a credited inner circle kiddie who'd watched too many old Moonbase flicks. She pestered Batel to take her on. Later she tried to repay her with sharpened picks. You can't trust those who had choices. They think different.

Batel and Webbl were twelve then. Tank had become a full-grown dult with a taste for dust. It was low then. He could keep it hidden. So far all Batel knew was that Tank was hanging out with nasty Crimer sorts, no scoopers, but nega brain Crimers either. Brute Crimers. He was considering joining some ex-Starslicers who were hiring out as shields—and though the no-brain nega knew it—slicers. Batel and Webbl were running most of the cons by themselves, slick things that made them giggle. They talked about the future. They needed to get out into the Nine, said Batel. The tourists talked about the gambling resorts on Mars. They flashed winnings which the girls took. Though she didn't know thing one about criming on Mars, my Batel thought big and planned for it.

But the string of easy marks with fresh credits was too slick. Your shields go down when every-all's moving your way.

Batel and Webbl tried to run a conner.

You want that sob story? It isn't here, so don't think it. Bam, things happen, your life changes. You plan, and then bam, another blow, a brand new direction. Roll with that cracked rib and get up again or you die. Things are what they are.

My parents were brain Crimers, slick conners who seldom missed their mark. They used me, they taught me, they were wonk, till a ship malfunction deep-spaced them, left them bug-eyed and splattered across the galaxy. That malfunction left my uncle—a penny ante no-brain brute—with zeroes of credits, the command of a thriving fronting casino, and me.

Do I have proof that my uncle jigged the ship software? In life, in cons, you don't always need proof to know what happened. And sides, what's proof good for? Good for throwing at a judge and seeing if she'll buy a kiddie story. But they won't, they never, and you gotta depend on your brains. Your closest friend might no-air you if they had to. Even if they nega wanted that. Your own self is all you got.

My uncle caught me sniffing his setup. Poking around his files, looking for the ship software hack I knew he had. But he's a dult and my guardian. He didn't have to run any con on me, spin any elaboration, not when I was still seven years away from being a dult and four from being a legal midteen. He packed me off to onboard school and I had to go.

Life hits you, you continue. I spent most the trip planning ways to run the onboard school. I couldn't get to my uncle yet, I could at least run the other kiddies, who would no doubt be well stacked with credits. But when Batel and Webbl brought chance into my life I took it.

Jo Turn was my handler to drop me at onboard school. He'd been my regular handler on Mars, too, since I was a bitty, and though after the explosion he'd shut his mouth and quietly gone to work for my uncle— you can't blame him. We'd been through a lot. I could count on him to look the other way for the occasional disappearing act. I liked Jo Turn. But to say truth, Jo Turn was an ex-conner who couldn't give up the game. That's why, when we were doing our touristy bit on Moonbase layover, when Batel and Webbl tried to run their modified con-yoink on us, well then, that's when Jo Turn's eyes lit with the old fire. Conning the conners was just about his favorite thing in the universe.

I liked Jo Turn. This is nega for sobbing. Some things happen. Things are what they are.

Jo Turn made himself out to be the biggest mark the girls had ever seen. He swallowed their hard-luck story as if it was green cheese. Like I said, the girls had gotten careless. They talked and dreamed, but that moment was an easy tourist time, with lots of credited émeegs moving through and out to the new luxury terraformation outside of the Nine. The girls truth conned them up and down, posing as kiddies posing as legal midteens. Then Tank would gear up all official and burst in just in time. After the mark bawled, he'd loose them with a warning—and a confiscation of the credits they'd paid the girls. The mark looked extra credited or extra weak, he'd demand a hard credit bribe on top.

Jo Turn went right along with Webbl's con. He implied he had a thickness of hard credits on his person. He even gave some to Batel to "keep an eye on me." Course, both of us could see right through the girls. Good conners always know they're being conned.

Jo Turn shouldn't have been conning while he was handling me. But he looks the other way for me, I look the other way for him. Sides, even wearing all that dult makeup Batel was clearly very wonk. I let her buy me a pop and I sat blinking and kicking my heels, conning that I was younger'n my ten years, eyeing the way things progress here on Moonbase. Meanwhile, Jo Turn proceeds with the con. And when Tank bursts in with his badge, Jo Turn flips open a splashier one. He's an off-duty cop, he runs, just passing through Moonbase. He'd prefer to not tie up his vacation dragging conners to the local cop Station. But for the price of a very thick bribe . . .

I am told that Webbl said for Tank to give it up. Real cop or no, Webbl knew when they'd been licked. Sides, it was just once, then this dult would be gone.

But Tank thought he knew better. He was half dusted anyway, and stead of giving it up or talking through it, he whipped out a fistful of finger knives. Jo Turn was no dummy, but Tank was younger and faster and he shredded Jo Turn from belly to gullet before my handler could get more'n a few slices on Tank's chest.

I knew Jo Turn was no-air gone soon as a white Webbl beckoned at Batel from around a passageway. You live your life with Crimers, you know when a drop's gone wrong. Batel patted my head and told me to be good a moment, then she hurried after Webbl.

I vanished.

It's funny. I'd managed not to think of Jo Turn for nearly four years, not till me and the girls and Tank were on that ship to Mars with our bitcatcher installs and our plans. He was a good mec. Not so slick, dicted to his cons the way Tank was to dust. But a good mec.

The thing about dults is, cops are on the lookout for them. But kiddies? They are sure we are braindead and super petty. Real cons, real yoinks— they nega think the kiddies are capable of that organization, and mostly, they are right.

The thing about dult Crimers is, they are dults first, Crimers second. The only reason for a Crimer—or regular mec—to hire a bitrunner is cause they're sporting powerful info they don't want sent through eyed channels.

As for the bitrunner—once that bit packet's shot into your wrist, you slap a bit of skin culture over the install and less'n a minute it's vanished. You can walk right through security stations, right under Scanners, and nega one can read your data or even see that you have data, or an install, at all. Not less they slash your wrist, and that isn't legal anywhere in the Nine. You look clean and you could be anybody.

But smart Crimers are on the lookout for anybody. They eye behavior patterns, they learn the bitrunners and they watch to see who's making a downloaded run. They nab you. They pay you to turn. Or more likely, they cut the bit packet right out of your arteries, leaving one more bitrunner, cool and credited and dead on the ground.

Kiddie bitrunners—nobody suspected those.

With Jo Turn gone, I took my chance. I e-mailed my uncle from an untraceable account, complained I hated onboard school. Told him I was heading out of the Nine with the latest colony of émeegs and he shouldn't bother looking for me cause I would be unfindable. I got a head-toe dye-job and headed out to the outer circle, mingled with the orphans like a recent midcircle abandoned. Pretty soon I let Batel see me pull a slick bit of con/yoink, and I was in the gang.

After their con on Jo Turn went bad the three of them straightened up. They made better plans, kept eyes peeled, and Tank stopped dusting while on a job. They started looking to the future again and pulling me in was a part of thinking ahead. I was pretty sure that was all it was—my own con-savvy mother wouldn't have recognized me with the dye job—but you never knew one hundred percent what went on behind Batel's round black eyes.

The bit about keeping our nose dirty, that was Batel's slick idea. Even not growing up with the benefits of a Crimer family, even not knowing life out in the Nine, she thought of that. I give her full credit. Tank did not see its brilliance. Tank wanted to be known for being totally fuelled, possibly also brute. But he was dult then, and jonesing to split anyway. Not a couple weeks after I got near enough to him, he signed up as a shield for a bitrunner and the gang, the heart of the gang, was back down to three.

Bitrunning was old news on Mars, but it was new to Moonbase. It is beyond likely that Tank did not know what he was getting into. His bitrunner promised him a thickness of credits to stay clean and trustable and be one half the shield few times a week and he took it.

We nega thought of us bitrunning right away. First thing we did once I was on the inside was put Batel's simple-slick plan into being as cover for whatever we would do. We took on some bitties from the orphan center, couple no-brain rejects from the other gangs. Martha, the inner-circle idiot. We kept all of them in secret as to the real work, kept them busy training and yoinking and plain old goofing, and Batel and Webbl and I ran some fine slick cons.

We were cool but not very credited. And Tank as a shield was now taking in credits by the fistfuls. I followed him some, watching him, eyeing the layouts of the dult gangs. It was clear that to get what I wanted this gang had to think bigger. I saw the way cop Station treated the kiddies, like so petty. And us the pettiest of all.

It was time to get away with real action. And that action was bitrunning.

Tank had already been in several serious applications of bruteness. And two other bitrunners, not his, had been negatid in nasty ways. Outer circle Moonbase was quick to realize the potential and thereby create the danger in bitrunning. It was a big step even for a gang that thought big.

Never-less. It was done, and the three of us got our bitcatchers installed in our wrists from a guy who was leaving Moonbase and thus could keep a secret. We set up a regular deal with the two Crimers and one official smart enough to understand keeping us secret was in their own interest. We would nega have told Tank even, cept Batel insisted. We started bitrunning.

The bitcatcher install is very very small. It's a tiny port just in the blue vein at your wrist—visible if you look for it, less you want to keep covering it in cultured skin. Some bitrunners cover the plastic hole with jewelry between runs; a bangle or links with a timepiece in it. That would have drawn more attention on outer circle kiddies on Moonbase. We might have gone with nothing, but Batel was passing through an inner circle tourist trap and she yoinked the whole gang cheapo plastic wrist shields like Citizen was sporting last year. Out of date gang finery for a petty-fronted gang: Batel saw the precise details that made a con into art.

We bitran on Moonbase for two years and every one of the risks we ran would be a story in itself. Some days I thought I might not carry out certain of my old plans; just park on Moonbase and rake in bitrunning credits. But then you remember that nothing lasts forever. Even dults catch on eventually, specially when Batel's less child-like and Webbl not so androgyne and even my feet are lengthening, so fast I can hardly yoink enough boots to keep up. My dye job's fading too, as my skin stretches—it's slow still, but you can tell by my feet I'm about to grow good and hard. I'm almost to my fourteenth and sometimes it hits me like a punch to the gut how little time I have left under the radar.

If I wanted to take the next step it had to be now.

I told the gang, the real gang, about my uncle deep spacing my parents. And that I had—a little—money if we could get to it. It's best to use as much of the truth as you can. Didn't need to use half my persuasions, neither. They jumped at the chance to get to Mars. So we planned a con to take us there. Never return, less we failed.

I pretended to be a lesser known Crimer contacting my uncle about expanding his business to Moonbase. It was the sort of mundane contact he'd buy, least enough to scope out the bitpacket we were sending. Though he'd be alert for cons as a matter of course, he was no paranoiac. He'd started as a brute, as I said, and conducted daily business with only a shield or two. So he'd been and so I'd confirmed with a trusted sniffer kiddie from Mars. More to the point, my uncle was a limited dult in his thinking. Less they were specially brainy, all dults saw were other dults.

It was a simple truth con far as the gang knew—me as both Moonbase Crimer and his bitrunner, Tank as my shield. I'd get a fresh dye job, play the slickest part ever. The girls would go to Mars but not to the meeting. I nega wanted Batel to be in the room, not when I couldn't swear to myself exactly how it would play out. I told them my uncle hated girls, which might well be true as he deep spaced his sister without regret. Once on Mars, I said, I would download a business proposal, stick around to discuss it as my Crimer's agent, and at some point—perhaps over a pint—give Tank the eye and jab my uncle with the poison. Tank'd clean up any shields before they knew anything had gone down.

It had to be poison; it was the simplest thing to smuggle to Mars and to my uncle. My uncle might not be paranoid wary, but still we'd nega get past his shields with guns or splosives. There was only one person on all of Moonbase who could yoink the poison from the nastiest Crimer in the spacesuit district—my Batel—and she did, bristling the laser locks and slipping past every trap as only she could. If there had been another way . . . I hated to hurt her.

We got to Mars, we got to my uncle, slicker'n anything. Batel waited nearby, a lonesome midteen slouching around the passageways. And when my uncle asked Tank politely to download his packet to the table bitcatcher, he was confused. "I'm not the bitrunner," he said. "It's him." But I was a scrawny kiddie and they didn't look twice. Tank's words were a deviation from the script and deviations put you on guard. My uncle's brute tossed me to the floor. There was a pain like a finger knife puncturing my chest and I thought maybe I cracked a rib. I curled onto my other side and looked dead, which wasn't hard except for the trouble breathing. Tank could still have talked it through, could've explained the truth as he knew it, even if he had nega the brains to figure it all.

But when confused, Tank fought.

He whipped out a fistful of finger knives and lunged at my uncle's waiting brute. Mars has slicker weapons. But Mars has nothing on Moonbase in fighting dirty. A stab and a twist, and dult-wise, the room was down to Tank and my uncle.

Tank looked at me and I saw he knew then I'd set him up, though he nega knew why. I was sorry for that. I couldn't like him, but I liked Batel for loving him. Didn't want him to think his setup was meaningless. I couldn't have got past both my uncle and the brute myself—and I definitely couldn't do it slick and untraceable like Mars demanded, not with the cards I held. Petty brute Tank was my wild card, the mec I could justify taking down or letting live, as needed.

My uncle had all the time needed in the few seconds it'd taken Tank to finish off the brute. He shot Tank down; three precise pops, no louder'n the sound Tank made as he crumpled. Then Tank was limp and burbling on the floor and my uncle had slit his skin and was massaging his arteries with something like a long skinny suction nozzle. I wondered how long he'd look for that non-existent packet. I didn't let him.

I rolled on that rib and came up behind him, glad my gasping was covered by Tank's choking. I kicked his gun with my foot and slammed the poison dart under his ear. It's the stuff they use to kill indigene beasts on new planets and the Crimers keep smuggling it around cause it's the simplest stuff to slip past ship security.

My uncle turned and looked at me, just as Tank had. But unlike Tank—he understood. Despite my disguise, he knew. I thought it would make me glad but I just felt nothing. His eyes were like my mother's, brown and bright. The memory of crazy credited-kiddie Martha attacking Batel went looping through my head, and Batel, who had once sung Martha to sleep, taking her down to the dust. Then at last my uncle's mirrored eyes glazed over and he fell next to Tank, in the blood, just lying there, breathing long and shallow. I knew it would take awhile for the poison to stop everything. But somehow I had nega known how it'd be to stand there, hunched over a cracked rib, with my two murdering dults breathing their painful breaths, one on his last wet gasps, the other lengthening into forever stillness.

One last shudder and Jo Turn's murderer was finally negatid. I dropped a handful of moondust right into his running arteries quick as I could.

Backed away just as a white Batel burst in. I knew she'd know. You live your life around Crimers, you just know when a drop's gone wrong. She would've dropped to her knees next to her stiffening brother, cept I yanked her away from the river of blood and my still-breathing uncle. Wouldn't do to be caught there, not when the scene was perfect as it was. She looked at me then with those beautiful black eyes so childlike and slick and I shivered like she'd caught me out, like I was crazy Martha myself. God, I hated to hurt Batel. But things are what they are.

I flushed my dye job, got a haircut, and intercepted the notice sent to my onboard school—kept loose ends tidy. Made it seem like we were just now coming in to Mars at the spaceport, sad and distraught, with a stumbling Batel at my side and Webbl carrying my luggage. Under my shirt, my ribs were taped with clean white bandages. My Batel had the choice to leave; the girls had plenty of bitrunning credits. But both of them stayed, and smart of them too. Within a week the judge confirmed the inheritance just as I hit my fourteenth and became a legal midteen, able to control my own future, what and how and who, all legit and above board.

See, Mars is different than Moonbase. In Mars, you have to keep your hands clean. The days of looking a little small and a lot more petty, those were over, negatid with the dead dusted Tank. This was the future, and Batel would be near me every second. She's got a part in everything. The girls and I were ready to think big and Mars would fall at our feet. Legitimacy would be our new outer circle.

Cause this was the gang, you see. This was the heart, then and future, dead or live. Tank, Webbl, me.

And Batel.

WHEN WE WERE STARDUST
REBECCA EPSTEIN

[*Fantasy,* February]

We make a picnic in the sparse woods beyond the park, the four of us, with our baskets of breads and pâtés, waxed apples and a jug of sparkling cider. My husband Abe keeps close behind me. Keith and Janelle are our neighbors in a cul-de-sac. We have the assurance that by the time our picnic is finished it will be dark, and we will trip back in our middle-aged clumsiness to our cars over anthills and tree roots.

As we walk in the sunset beneath the weeping willows we murmur small things to each other, and it is not what we say that matters; it is the sweet and soft volume, the cadence like our footsteps. This evening is a relief and a pleasure. We pass the baskets from hand to hand, and we look for a good spot to settle and lay the woolen picnic blanket down.

I am glad to be taking a break from the lab. I have buried myself in there lately, among the hot lamps and observation boxes. But the hamsters can observe themselves for an evening. I am tired of hard science.

We come into a clearing, if you could call it that—we are not so much in a woods as a grassy field punctuated by a great number of trees. We stop and toe the grass. "Lucy, how is this spot?" asks Abe, and everyone looks at me.

"Well, it's fine," I say. "Are there bugs in the grass?"

In a past life, I imagine Abe was a king. He ruled over his African tribe with a passion that I can still see in his eyes now, as he vacuums the stairs, or comforts me with his large hands. He had skin so dark it shone in the sun. He wore a beaded headpiece. He had fingernails that grew and grew.

A neighboring tribe encroached upon my husband's tribe, and they were greater in number, with sharper, heavier spears, slingshots that hoisted boulders, and deep growls that shook the savannah.

They came in the night. What did they want?

Even Abe, the king, didn't know. It was unfair. They went to battle, and before my husband was brought down in his prime by a spear hurled at his heart, he saw his tribe reduced to the bewildered children, the women (who were raped), and the old men, who huddled against trees and only half-wished they were strong enough to fight.

The four of us grab the corners of the blanket and pull until it is taut against the grass. It is quiet here, and there is the smell of flowers. The dark makes me nervous. If there weren't so many trees we could see straight across the sound to the damaged New York City skyline.

Janelle, who is tall and slim and honey blonde, was probably an Aztec in the 1500s. I can see it in the way she holds herself, in her narrow, straight back, the plush of her lips, her prescience about the weather. She, rather, he grew cacao beans and cotton. He squatted in the sun and sifted his fingers through the damp dirt. It was like silk in his hands. Janelle is quick to fury and so was he. When his children became sick with dark red spots on their bodies and skin hot enough to boil a river, he threw jars and plates around the hut, the objects making whipping noises in the air and spilling liquid on the floor. There were shards of clay in the corners as his children died. And soon he and his wife were stricken with smallpox too. They lay on straw pallets on the floor, whisking their hands through the air across their fields of vision, watching the light divide and merge around their fingers. I think about what it would be like to watch my own children die and I wonder if Janelle carries that pain with her, from life to life: if she will never outrun it.

Each life is another layer of bark on the tree; we gather our joys and traumas around us like skins and reach nearer toward the heavens. Maybe there are dozens and dozens for each person. Time goes back forever, and I'm beginning to think we were always here, in a human body, in a mammoth body, in a single cell, in stardust.

We open the baskets and set out plates of food. The bread is crusty and the fruit is sweet. We pour the cider into paper cups. My hand comes into contact with Janelle's and I feel a little bit of lust for her fierce Aztec self, and then I pull back.

I look at Keith across the picnic blanket and I see a peasant wife in The Middle Ages in England. She scrubbed, and she cooked, and she gathered crops in the endless fields, and she tended to the children, of which there were too many. When she could, she sent her children out to be apprenticed by anyone who would take them: the shoemaker, the doctor, or the shipbuilder. Once she had a baby who wouldn't stop crying, who had a bluish tinge to its lips, and she carried the baby into town and left it in the gutter, and the filthy water that ran through carried it away to someplace else. Perhaps Keith tries to make up for it in this life. After all, he is a pediatrician.

Abe says, "Are we doing okay, here?" I lay my head on his shoulder. We clink paper cups together in a toast to the sky. It is dark through the tiara of shifting leaves and branches above us.

"Did I tell you what happened at school today?" Janelle says. She is a math teacher at the high school, where my two oldest children go. She laughs and takes a sip of cider. "There was a fight between two of the kids, I think they're sophomores. A boy in the Persian tough-guy crowd and a white boy, one of the Latin club geeks."

"A geek got into a fight?" asks Abe.

Janelle brushes her free hand through her hair. "It was surreal. They were in the hall just outside my classroom in fourth period, the Persian one looking ready to whip out his brass knuckles, and the nerdy boy bouncing on the balls of his feet, his jeans tucked into his socks—"

"What were they fighting about?" I ask.

"There's this girl named Sylvia and all the boys want her. She's got the looks. The pouty lips, the long hair. She's not extremely bright but she works hard. She's always in my office hours. She's blameless."

I imagine myself in high school, as we all are, picturing where we would have fit into this scenario, in that past life. The handsome dark-skinned macho, the weak nerd, the beautiful girl, or an onlooker pressed against the lockers.

"And so, somehow, this girl had taken a liking to the nerd." In the dark, one of us gasps, and then we all laugh. "They'd been making out in the stairwells during class. You know, getting a bathroom pass and smooching for those few minutes they had." I cannot imagine such a scenario.

"I don't believe you," says Keith. "Why would the beautiful girl choose the nerd?"

"I did, didn't I?" Janelle says, and Keith laughs and smacks her. "I'm not sure why," she says. "I think he bought her a puppy. Anyway he had pledged his love to her, and from what I gathered, she had done the same."

"Where does the other boy come in?" Abe asks.

"Well," says Janelle, and shifts her legs on the blanket. "This other boy had picked Sylvia out to be his. I don't know exactly how that works, but there you go. He was popular, she was beautiful, and he took offense when he found out what was going on between her and the geek."

It is now officially dark, and we can only see silhouettes of each other. We pass the pâtés and plastic knives to spread them with, onto the bread and crackers. "And that's about it. They got into it, right there in the hallway. They were circling each other like gang members about to pull out knives. The geek was hopping on his toes, he was so mad."

"So what happened?" Abe asks. "Who won the fight?"

"Well, the Persian boy did, obviously," says Janelle. "Actually it wasn't much of a fight. This was the best part. The nerd took a swing at the macho boy, who dodged it very well, and the nerd swung all the way around. A full one-eighty! His fist slammed into the lockers so hard the halls rang." I can see it. It is every high school scene to ever occur. I decide that Janelle was an orator in a past life. "He broke his fist, I think, all the fingers and whatever other bones are in the hand, and he doubled over in the hallway, screaming. He was crying like a baby. The other boy ran."

"What did he expect?" I ask. "This is what happens to you."

"Exactly," Janelle says. "We got the school nurse up there right away, and she took one look at his purple paw and shipped him off to the emergency room. But still . . . "

"What?" I ask. I can hear Janelle shift on her blanket. I realize that it does not make sense, this picnic in the dark.

"I just feel awful," she says. "It's my job to protect these kids from each other. But I was afraid to be in the middle of it and get hurt myself."

"It's not your job to protect them!" Keith says. "It's your job to teach them math. Beyond that, what happens to them happens to them." We are quiet for a few moments.

"Unbelievable," says Abe, finally. "And what did Sylvia decide to do? Did she stick with her man?"

"Oh," says Janelle. "I don't know."

In another life, Abe might have been a slave in Louisiana. It was early in the nineteenth century. He would have been a woman slave. She was the daughter of two slaves who had been shipped over to America from Nigeria, and she had nine siblings and half siblings, although she hardly ever saw or thought about them. And she didn't think about meals, which were always broth and bread, or sex, which would have required far more energy than she had after a day in the fields, or love, because who can love when they are filled with such a pure despair, such a powerful helplessness? That's not true, either; she felt all of those things, all of the time. Hunger and lust and love. She lived a long life, bearing four children who were sent off to other plantations. When she was old enough that her joints swelled and creaked, she was relegated to the household chores. She died in a slave bed in the slave house, with the master looking on and wanting to pat her tired head and her old feet, but standing back and waiting, instead.

In this life I am living now I was raped in the dark in the parking lot outside the hamster lab. In the following weeks I thought about my three children, who were already in their teens—Janelle's students, Sylvia's peers—and this new child who had nothing to do with them. I thought about my dear vasectomized husband who was willing to go along with whatever I chose. I was sick all day every day, staying close to the bathroom lest I vomit on the rug, but this was not morning sickness. This was a twisting, aching dilemma that gripped at my guts and pushed my food back up my throat. I aborted her four days ago.

In another life the baby in my womb was my wife and we scaled mountains together. We climbed the Alps, calling out to each other through the snow and thin air. And in another life my baby and I were twin boys in a shtetl in Poland. We swam the river and buried dead birds in the dirt beneath the rockrose bushes. When the Nazis came we were too busy chasing each other in the cornfield to hear our mother calling.

I let out a cry and lay my head down on the picnic blanket. Cups of cider spill. "What is it?" Keith asks. I feel hands rubbing at my back. My husband gathers me up into his arms. "She had it done the other day," he tells them. There is a hush. Why are we here in the night?

These three people are the ones who met me in the emergency room after the police brought me in, and who stayed with me all of that dark night and all of the next day and in shifts for the week after, running a bath and reminding me to eat. In another lifetime, in the years before I was raped, I can't remember if we were friends or neighbors.

In the moment that my baby was removed from me I felt a strange visceral pain that I was sure I recognized. Then I remembered with a tidal wave all the lives I'd lived before this one. I had never thought of such a thing before. All the times I had lost her. In the Alps, in the shtetl, in the streets of Paris, in the early settlement of Australia. And before that too. When we were stardust we traveled together through space, watching over the universe.

I bury my face in Abe's warm shirt. I can feel his thundering, tribal heartbeat against my temple. He is and always will be a good man, even if he is not her. I wonder why it must be that I lose what I need, again and again. Is this what happens to us all? The four of us are speechless and cold in the dark, and we wait for me to stop crying.

WILLPOWER
JASON STODDARD

[*Futurismic,* December]

Michael Delgado needed something to do. Today. His last willfare job had ended last Friday, which meant tomorrow morning was contract breach. The foodcard would stop working, and the ever-efficient borgots of the Balboa Arms would be down to usher him out of his 300-square-foot studio apartment. Not that he'd miss it, with Van Nuys cranking to 105 today and him with only a swamp cooler.

He scanned quickly through the willfare crapwork and sinkers:

```
Job2309170342546
Dog walking, Cerritos area, 0.5D willfare credit
(4 dogs, large, aggressive). ACCEPT >>
```

No way. Not for a half-day credit.

```
Job2309170342554
Street   cleaning,   crew   of  16,   Chinatown   and
surrounds, multiday contract. ACCEPT >>
(Currently 11 accepted)
```

Surrounds, as in southeast LA, no way.

```
Job2309170351565
Research assistant, UCLA medical campus, great
status! Includes transpo and housing. Minimum
45-day contract (90 willfare creds), extensible
to 90-days. Standard disclaimers. ACCEPT >>
```

And take a chance that the cancer they infect you with they might not be able to cure? Oh, no.

Michael Delgado frowned, the chant of the taxpayers echoing in his head. *WE pay your salary, so you do what WE want. We want you to cut our grass, you get out here pronto!* And Congress agreed. Needed for a smooth transition to a post-scarcity economy, they said. Allows them the dignity of productive work, they said. Gets them off the streets, they said. They who drove comfortably to jobs not-yet-outsourced in SUVs with large leases not-quite-paid.

And then:

```
Job2309170355443
Take my place on the Ares. 180 day contract.
I'll vouch for the full 720 willfare days, even
if I have to pay 'em. I'm done. ACCEPT >>
```

Michael felt something like an electric shock as he eyeblinked on ACCEPT. Strange shivers worked up and down his spine. He heard something like a whisper, deep within his mind. He felt suddenly strong, powerful, alive.

Oh, no.

But he'd done it.

```
Thank you for your ACCEPTANCE of willfare Job #
2309170355443. Present yourself at Edwards/Scaled
Composites/Virgin facility, Mojave, CA by 5:00PM
today to begin work. No willfare credit has been
accrued to your account.
```

Michael pounded a fist into his cheap plastic kitchen table. Fucking keywords! Fucking Vesper! Fucking Kon-Ye BMI! What had he gotten himself into this time?

Because it had to be a joke. Nobody would willfare a Mars mission job. It had to be a cover for something that involved Hershey's syrup and chickens and octogenarians.

And now he was screwed. He'd ACCEPTED, and that was that.

Michael sighed, and started looking up bus routes out to Edwards.

The last vestiges of Vesper's adrenaline rush made him smile, as if in anticipation.

Before he could leave, Angelica called. Her face wavered on the cheap rollscreen. Behind her, big bouffant hairdos were being teased to life.

"Wanna go to the One True Shack?" she said, batting her eyelashes. "I got a big tip. My treat."

"I can't."

Instafrown. "Why not?"

"I got a job."

"A real job, or more of that willfare crap?"

Michael sighed.

Angelica's eyes flickered down as she scanned the detail of his job. "Oh, no," she said.

Michael nodded.

"Why?"

"I couldn't stop it."

Instafrown became instasnarl. "I thought you had it under control! I thought you were OK!" Behind her, heads turned to look.

"This is good work. Worth a lot."

"They'll never let you onboard!" Angelica screamed.

Don't I know it, Michael thought, but said nothing.

"You could bandchise," she said.

"I'm not going to play dead music from brains in wallerstein tanks!"

"You're already set up."

"Angelica, I . . . "

"What else you gonna do?"

Michael looked away from the flatscreen. "I'm taking this job," he said. As he said it, the feeling of energy and elation came back. He shook his head, trying to shake the alien feelings.

"No!" Angelica said.

"I have to," Michael said, softly.

"Even if it's real, I won't be here when you come back."

Michael looked down. "I know."

She waited. He said nothing.

Her frown tightened once more. The image wavered and disappeared.

At Edwards/Scaled Composites/Virgin, the reception area was inside an ancient hangar that housed two museum pieces, SpaceShipOne and SpaceShipTwo. Both were covered with a light film of dust.

Inside the reception area, a kid lounged behind a lightweight aluminum desk and a fogtank displayed images of the Ares. The kid wore the discreet white earpiece of a Dell brain-machine interface. The ACCESS light glowed soft red, indicating he was offline, but his glazed eyes suggested that the BMI was on.

Typical, Michael thought. He slapped a hand down on the aluminum desk. The kid jumped to his feet, looked around blindly for a moment, and finally fixed on Michael.

"What you want?" he asked.

"I'm here for the willfare job."

"Oh yeah, willfare . . . wait a minute, what willfare job?"

Michael offered the kid his hand.

"Oh, no, put it on the slate, no sharing bodydata packages, I know that, we'll see who you are."

Michael put his hand on the reader. The kid studied the big pix-comm icons in his rollscreen and frowned. "Yeah, right."

"It's a real job."

"Yeah, real funny," he said, mumbling something to his throatmike. The screen changed, and his eyes widened again.

"You're kidding."

"No," Michael said. *Now get the hell out of my way and give me this job!*

The kid darted scared eyes from the screen to Michael and back again. "Uh, Bob, better come in here," he said. "Sit down, uh, Mr. uh, Delgado."

Ten minutes later, a small balding guy with a halo-cut appaeared from somewhere deep within the hangar. He wore a sweat-stained white shirt and a really bad tie with pictures of old-fashioned circuitry on it. "What's up?"

The kid tapped the screen. Bob took a look at it and blinked. Looked at Michael. Looked back at the screen.

"What is this?"

"Looks like Tom flaked."

"Shit," Bob said.

"He always was a bit of a . . . " the kid pinched two fingers around an imaginary joint and made sucking sounds.

"Can he do this? Post it to willfare?" Bob asked.

"You can post anything. A friend of mine, he posted for a buncha skanks to come to this guy's dorm room . . . "

"So Tom could've done this?"

Again the puffing, a nod, and a like-duh look from receptionist-boy.

"And it's OK for him to get it?" he said, nodding at Michael.

The kid held up his hands. "Not my problem," he said.

Bob sighed and turned to Michael. "I'm sorry, Mr. Delgado, there seems to have been a mistake. It's too bad you had to come all the way out here. I'll see if I can get you credited for—"

"I want the job," Michael said. His voice sounded unusually strong and decisive.

"What?"

"I don't want the credit. I want the job."

"There's been a mistake—"

"No mistake. You posted a job. I accepted it. Binding willfare contract."

Bob glanced at the kid. The kid tried unsuccessfully to hide a smile.

"I really can't take this seriously," Bob said. "You don't have any of the qualifications to be an astronaut. Education, physical condition, psychological evaluations . . . "

"Doesn't matter. Job was posted. I accepted. Done deal." Michael fought to keep his hands from curling into fists.

"I'll have you thrown out."

"Go ahead. Call security. Call willfare legal, too, and see how long your jail sentence is."

Bob frowned and muttered. He had the kid call up willfare legal on the rollscreen. The auto attendant was a porcelain-skinned blonde who looked far too good to be real. It listened, expressionless, as Michael and Bob both told their side of the story.

"Willfare contracts are binding," it said, finally.

"See!" Michael said.

"Though the acceptor does have to meet the physical and mental qualifications of the job description. Astronauts, even private ones, have extensive entry tests that must be passed," it continued.

"See!" Bob said, smiling. He gestured towards the door.

"If I pass the tests, I get the job?" Michael said.

"The contract is effectively binding," the attendant said.

"Bring it on," Michael said.

Bob's mouth dropped open. "But—"

"Get out the tests. I'll take them."

"There's no way you'll pass."

Michael smiled. "Want to bet?"

It wasn't really cheating. Not really. Not when the connection was there for the taking. Not when the burning in his mind was saying, *Yes, yes, anything it takes.*

Fucking Vesper.

Michael opened a window with his Kon-Ye BMI and picked answers out of the global net.

Images of Vesper's impossible Mars floated close in the back of his mind. The gleaming marble cities of Vallira and Pentadon. The beautiful faces of the Erinyes, calm like Greek gods under blonde ringlets. The slavering Ficarons. The deep blue sky over twining blood-red forests. And feelings. The elation of Quest, the brooding menace of the Hall of Dark Memories.

Those are not my memories!

But every time he squeezed his eyes shut, the images just came brighter.

Bob brought him pizza. Plain, just cheese and sauce. The expression on his face said, *Fuck, you fuckhead, I'm staying late for you, why don't you just give up so I can go home?* Michael ate, not tasting it, punching answers into the rollscreen. Bob watched for a while, then left him alone.

"You're a frogger," Bob said, when the test was done and scored.

"I passed, didn't I?"

"You're a frogger!"

"You have a BMI, too," Michael said, nodding at the polished silver pebble he wore at his ear.

"I can turn mine off!"

Michael sighed. He would too, if he could. But a free game BMI came at a price. You didn't turn it off. You didn't override it. A lot of people told him he was lucky the game was dead. At least he didn't have play-alerts flashing in his mind, ruining his concentration. And he had a persistent connection to the global net.

Of course, it also meant he could never be accepted to a serious college, or take any real job. Because it wasn't his intelligence. Not really. Even though it took him years to figure out how to get an unencumbered connection to the global net. Even though it took months to train himself how to use it. Even though using it shouldn't be any different than looking up the answers in a book. The globe was covered in nets. He could surf virtually any one of them.

He would have had the damn thing cut out years ago if he could afford it.

"You pulled the answers!" Bob said. "That's not fair!"

"I passed the test, didn't I?"

"That doesn't matter. Astronaut candidates aren't allowed to be fr— aren't allowed unauthorized brain-machine interfaces."

Michael wanted to jump up and strangle the man, but he made himself sit calmly. "I'm calling willfare legal," he said.

"And I'll need to get our corporate counsel involved," Bill said.

They made their calls. Automated attendants passed them quickly on to legal-algorithmic services. Finally, two human lawyers appeared. They asked questions. Michael tried to keep his smile when he answered. Not that it would help. He was sure they knew exactly what he was thinking.

Eventually, it boiled down to one point.

"You don't have a clause that states that a candidate cannot use a brain-machine interface during the test," willfare's lawyer said. He was a sharp-dressed man in a blue business suit.

"We do clearly state that candidates are not allowed undefeatable BMI's!" Edwards/Scaled Composites/Virgin's lawyer said. She sounded a bit shrill.

"Determination of eligibility is your responsibility. By giving him the test, you've implied that he is an acceptable candidate. I'm referring this up to Federal Contracts Court."

A frown. "Wait." Edwards/Scaled Composites/Virgin's lawyer addressed Bob. "Give him the other tests."

"But he cheated!"

The frown deepened. "Give him the other tests. Let me work on this."

Bob glanced at his watch. "I can't give him the physical or attitudinal until tomorrow. What do I do with him?"

"Put him up in a hotel!" the lawyer snapped.

"But—"

"You're under contract!"

Bob bowed his head and nodded.

Michael didn't try to hide his smile.

They put him in the Mojave Motel 6. Not much different than the Balboa Arms, really. Cheap plastic furniture and heavily-patterned carpet and bedspreads to hide the inevitable stains. Ancient rollscreens and limited wireless bandwidth. He even saw two borgots, hiding in an alcove. Apparently Motel 6 had the same problem with guests overstaying their welcome.

One difference: great air conditioning. Michael turned it up to max and lay on top of the covers, letting the dry, chill air pour over his body. He let it strip the last bit of heat from his body. He let himself shiver in its icy blast.

Is this me? He wondered.

Is this what I really want?

Michael closed his eyes and surfed to the latest data on Mars. The previous Ares missions. The bacteria. The fossils. The frozen seas buried under the red sands. One site had a simulation of what it would be like to stand on the surface of Mars without a spacesuit. Michael tried it. He felt his ears pop, felt the icy spike of cold, like clenching a piece of dry ice, but all over his body. He felt his chest heave and heave, and bring in nothing. He felt his vision blur.

And through it all, a smile.

Vesper's doing that, he thought. *He's making you feel this way.*

He should just go back to Van Nuys, take any willfare he could.

But Mars!

He should listen to Angelina.

But . . . he knew Mars wasn't the playground of his ancient Kon-Ye game. He knew it wasn't marble cities and red jungles. And he still wanted to go.

But is that me? He wondered.

Memories came back. Playing that Kon-Ye game for the first time, using nothing but a helmet. Meeting the Girl Who Would Be for the first time. Being Vesper. Coming back the next day to play, again and again. Until the gamestore kicked him out. Until he had done enough yardwork to pay for the game, marked down and near the end of its lifecycle. Installing the BMI. That night. That night he opened his eyes and had a whole world in front of him. Endless. As far as he wanted to grasp. That feeling of possibility. That feeling of freedom.

It wasn't just Vesper. It was him.

Michael closed his eyes. Eventually, he slept.

The next morning was cold and gray. As the cab took him in, Michael Delgado watched a drunken video message from Angelique, taken in some dank little bar he didn't recognize. She was trading tongues with a rat-faced man with a big pompadour.

There was also a text message from an email address Michael didn't recognize:

```
Show them you can do it, Michael. Show them
that you're not Vesper, but his spirit still
lives.
```

And another:

```
Willfare or not, you're my hero.
```

Michael frowned. A quick search on the mediascape with the keywords "Michael Delgado," "willfare," and "Mars" showed tiny sparks of activity, widely distributed on the smaller boards and blogs, with some weighting towards BMI gaming.

Michael felt a swell of pride. He'd never done anything that hit the mediascape.

He was still feeling buoyant when they took him out to the physical course. Bob was there, flanked by Edwards/Scaled Composites/Virgin's lawyer. A short woman wearing a severe gray suit stood several yards away from them. She strode forward and offered Michael her hand.

"I'm Felicia Ponderosa," she said. "Willfare legal."

"From last night," Michael said.

"Yes. You're stirring up some media attention."

"I'm sorry."

Felicia smiled. "Don't be. If you make it, this is an important triumph for willfare. It'd prove that we aren't just dog-walking and grass-cutting."

"Even if he passes the test, there is still a question of interpretation of intent regarding the written portion," said the Edwards lawyer.

Felicia offered the man a thin smile and dragged Michael away from them.

"They're going to try to take this from me, aren't they?" Michael said.

Felicia nodded.

"Can they?"

She sighed. "I don't know."

The physical test was something like an obstacle course. Michael ran, twisted, dodged, and jumped. All those years of lawnmowing, cleaning and construction paid off. The course was easy.

The Edwards lawyer bent close to whisper something to Bob. *Some new way to fuck me,* Michael thought. Some other trick to take away his prize.

And in that moment, he almost stopped and walked off the course. Because even Felicia couldn't guarantee he'd get it. His step faltered. The little timer he'd set up in his internal view winked towards his disqualification. He felt eyes on him, some hungry, some disappointed.

Eyes. The media. *Of course.*

Michael smiled. He ran faster.

He beat the maximum time by tens of seconds. Bob looked at him grimly, arms crossed. But Michael didn't really notice. His attention was focused on the willfare site, and on the job he'd just eyetyped:

```
Job2309170556098
Public   protest,   Edwards/Scaled   Composites/
Virgin Lancaster facility, main entrance. Help
your  fellow  willfarer  go  to  Mars.  See media
details  at  this  address.  One  day  credit  per
person,  paid  from  my  own  account.  Maximum 720
credits.  Will  have  to  accept  IOU.  ACCEPT >>
```

Michael smiled at Bob as he passed.

They put him in a cage made of heavy copper mesh for the psych evaluation. The psychologist was a young, red-haired man with wide blue eyes and a smattering of freckles on his face. He let the two lawyers into the cage and made Bob stay outside.

"What's this?" Michael asked, pointing at the copper mesh.

"Faraday cage," the psych guy said. "Swept of line-of-sight transceivers hourly. We don't want you getting outside help on this test, do we?"

The heavy copper door clanged shut and latched. Every telltale on Michael's BMI went red.

Michael felt suddenly lighter. The static in his mind was gone. He tried to pull a window on the global net and got nothing but smooth blankness. He was cut off for the first time in years.

Michael laughed. It was a weird feeling.

"How do you feel?" the psych guy said.

"Better."

"Still want to go to Mars?"

"Of course!"

The psych guy nodded and they began. Michael recognized some of the questions from school. All of them were opinion-type questions. No wrong answers. Or so they said. Michael knew there were wrong answers, just like he knew they could tell when you were trying to spoof the right ones. He answered quickly, hoping for the best.

When it was over, they took him into a little office where the psych guy ran the test and displayed the results on a privacy screen. He looked at Michael sharply.

"You're a Vesper, aren't you?" he said.

Michael felt his guts clench. He didn't know what to say. He opened his mouth, but no words came out.

The psych guy smiled. "You don't have to answer. I know you are."

"What's a Vesper?" Bob asked.

"Vesper was a game character," the psych guy said. "Kon-Ye games. Epic Mars, a Burroughs pastiche. Vesper was the hero, the one who saved Mars from the depredations of the Erinyes."

"What does that have to do with him?" Bob said, pointing at Michael.

"Vesper was one of the early experiments in personality overlays in BMI gaming. Which in itself wasn't bad. But the game was hacked, and there were some adverse effects."

"Such as?" Bob said.

"Many of the active players ended up with neural weighting that's a measurable percentage of Vesper's."

"What does that mean?"

"Vesper is a part of them. Forever."

Bob was silent. After a while, the Edwards lawyer spoke up. "So this person's desire to go to Mars may be because he's part video-game character?"

Psych guy shrugged. "I don't know. It's impossible to separate."

"So he failed the psych?" Bob asked.

A grin. "Oh, no. He passed just fine. With flying colors, as they say. All signs indicate he's substantially more stable than his predecessor."

"But he's not . . . himself!" Bob thundered. "He's not really human!"

"It looks like only about 1% of his neural weighting is Vesper's," the psych guy said. "And besides, our tests don't specify where you get your motivation."

Edward's lawyer leaned close to Bob and said, "There's precedent for disallowance, though," he said. "A case can be made based on undefeatable BMIs and external influences."

"You're going to have a hard time proving external influences," Felicia said.

"Why not? He's persistently connected to the outside. Do you want to prove there are no gamestubs or backdoors into the Kon-Ye codebase?"

Felicia frowned and said nothing.

"But I passed all the tests!" Michael said. He felt the familiar tension, the familiar build. Like he should knock heads, break out of here, run into the red twining jungle . . .

Felicia shook her head.

Bob grinned. He turned to Michael. Michael forced himself to look into Bob's dark, beady eyes. He knew what he was going to say. The same speech he got whenever he applied for a real job. *Sorry, no, can't take you, don't know who you are, save your money and have that game BMI taken out and maybe we can talk later, here's your hat, what's your hurry.*

But the receptionist kid came in, eyes wide, and everything changed fast.

Outside the Edwards/Scaled Composites/Virgin facility, a sea of people pressed tight against the gates. A shimmering line of cars traced a silver river back towards the more populated part of Mojave. The scent of biodiesel hung in the air, like French fries from an old-style fast food restaurant.

A cloud of smartsmoke hovered over the crowd. It morphed from FLY MIKE FLY to IF HE PASSES, LET HIM PASS, and END THE BMI DOUBLE STANDARD. Many of the people outside the gate also held old-style painted signs or wove flashwords around their bodies. They were too far away to read.

Michael stopped just outside the building as the kid pointed to the crowd and Bob and the lawyer had a quick huddle. Someone in the crowd pointed at Michael and a ragged cheer went up. Michael felt light-headed. What did he owe? This was way more than seven hundred and twenty people.

He looked inside at his willfare account. Nobody had accepted his offer of credit. Instead, his feedback was full of comments like this:

```
I'll come out anyway. Keep your credits! You
deserve them!
```

And

```
I'll be there, you don't need to bribe me.
```

And

```
Heard it through the mediascape. Wouldn't miss
it for the world.
```

Michael's feeling of lightheadedness grew. They were helping him on their own dime. On their own time. Because they wanted to.

He raised a hand to the crowd. The ragged cheer swelled.

Felicia bent close to Michael and said, "Did you do this?"

Michael nodded, still looking at the crowd.

"How?"

"Posted a willfare job. Offered my Ares credits to anyone who would come out and protest."

Felicia smiled. Her eyes glimmered like Michael's mother's, on the day he'd gotten his baccalaureate degree. "Was that you or Vesper?"

"It was me."

Felicia nodded. She went to join Bob and his lawyer. There was a lot of shouting and pointing at Michael. Bob's face turned red and his expression squinted down into something that wouldn't look out of place on an apple doll. The Edwards lawyer stood, expressionless, his eyes on the crowd.

Michael was still connected to his willfare posting. He saw the mediascape connections growing as he watched. People were feeding fuzzy video from the fence.

Michael smiled. No doubt there were some microcams or grain-of-rice transceivers lying about. He did a quick search and found a good view of the argument and fed it into the global net.

In the now-clear video, Felicia said. "I'd say the public has spoken. Do you still want to take this to court?"

"There's no way we're going to let a . . . a thing that's part video game on the Ares. Especially not on the first long-term crew!" Bob yelled.

A groan went up from the crowd as the media reached them. Bob's lawyer bent and whispered something in Bob's ear. Bob shot a murderous glance at the crowd and fell silent.

"So you're going to argue that the willfare contract is invalid?" Felicia said.

"Don't say anything," the Edwards lawyer said. Bob clamped his mouth shut over a frown.

Then both of them looked up at a Jeep that was approaching from within the Edwards/Scaled Composites/Virgin facility. It trailed a thin cloud of dust behind it as it sped across the vast concrete expanse.

When it came close, Bob went pale and whispered in his lawyer's ear. The lawyer looked grim and nodded.

The Jeep passed within inches of Bob, ruffling his dark blue suit-jacket. He flinched as it roared by. It skidded to a stop in front of Michael.

The woman driver, a middle-aged blonde with hair just starting to gray and leathery desert-sun skin, eyed Michael over the rim of tiny mirrored sunglasses. She wore a utilitarian gray coverall that bore the Edwards/Scaled Composites/Virgin logo.

She jumped down from the jeep as Bob and lawyer came running.

"So you're the new man?" she asked Michael, coming within eighteen inches of him. Her eyes, blue ghosts behind the mirrorshades, didn't waver from his face.

"I want to be," Michael said.

"Wrong answer," she said.

Michael felt his hands clench. His stomach turned over and over, as if it was trying to tie itself in knots.

"Captain," Bob said.

She held up a hand. Bob's mouth clicked shut as if it were wired. "Give Michael and I a minute, please."

She walked Michael fifty yards away from the others. She stopped and looked at him.

"You know Mars isn't like the game," she said.

"Of course," Michael said. "But—"

"No beautiful princesses, no jungle, no air."

"I know."

"You know how long this mission is for?"

"Three years. Longer if we want to stay."

"You know the chance of dying before you come back?"

"Zero point three five percent," Michael said. It had been one of the test questions.

"Do you want to stay on Mars?"

Michael felt his eyes go hot and wet. "Yes. I do."

A nod.

"What would you do to Mars if you could?" she said.

"Make it like the epic."

The woman looked at him for a long time, expressionless. Finally, she let a thin grin spread across her face. "So you're the new man?" she said.

Michael remembered his answer, and her response. "Yes," he said, standing straight.

A laugh. Nothing more.

"Who are you?" Michael said.

"I'm the captain. Gloria Vandermeer."

"And you're ok with a video game character for a crewmember?"

Gloria smiled. She bent close and whispered, "I used to play Epic Mars, too. Though not as Vesper. As the Girl Who Was To Be."

Michael couldn't say anything. She saw his expression and laughed. "Not much of the girl left, is there?" she said. "So much for the romance."

"No. I mean, if you played, how did you get into the program?"

"I got out before the meltdown. And I paid to have the network hacked out of my head. But it still stays with you. The dream."

"Am I in?"

Gloria looked out over the desert. "You'll like Roddy. I think he's almost two percent Vesper."

"Roddy?"

"One of our crewmates."

"I'm in?" Michael said.

"You have to ask?"

Michael's heart pounded. His hands felt slick and sweaty. He had a sudden vision of himself flying over the red jungle. He blinked it away and replaced it with a vision of himself trudging over salmon-colored sand. It felt just as good.

"The one question they don't ask," Gloria said. "What percentage of astronauts got hooked on interactives? What percentage are carrying some bit of a hero around in their heads?"

Michael shook his head. "You mean this was planned?"

A laugh, long and hard. The setting sun painted Gloria's face in hues of gold. "Want to go tell Bob the good news?" she said.

But you haven't answered my question, Michael thought. He opened his mouth to say something. Then he closed it again.

"Yes," he said.

They went back to where the earthbound stood, amid the cheers of the crowd.

THE TALE OF
JUNKO AND SAYIRI
PETER S. BEAGLE

[*IGMS,* July]

In Japan, very, very, long ago, when almost anybody you met on the road might turn out to be a god or a demon, there was a young man named Junko. That name can mean "genuine" in Japanese, or "pure," or "obedient," and he was all of those things then. He served the great *daimyo* Lord Kuroda, lord of much of southern Honshu, as Chief Huntsman, and was privileged to live in the lord's castle itself, rather than in any of the outer structures, the *yagura*. In addition, he was handsome and amiable, and all the ladies of the court were aware of him. But he had no notion of this, which only added to his charm. He was a very serious young man.

He was also a commoner, born of the poorest folk in a poor village, which meant that he had not the right even to a family name, nor even to be called Junko-*san* as a mark of respect. In most courts of that time, he would never have been permitted to look straight into the eyes of a samurai, let alone to live so intimately among them. But the Lord Kuroda was an unusual man, with his own sense of humor, his own ideas of what constituted a samurai, and with a doubtless lamentable tendency to treat everyone equally. This was generally blamed on his peculiar horoscope.

Now at this time, it often seemed as though half of Japan were forever at war with the other half. The mighty private armies of the *daimyos* marched and galloped up and down the land, leaving peasant villages and great fortresses alike smoldering behind them as they pleased. The *shogun* at Kyoto might well issue his edicts from time to time, but the shogunate had not then the power that it was to seize much later; so for the most part his threats went unheeded, and no peace treaty endured for long. The Lord Kuroda held himself and his own people aside from war as much as he could, believing it tedious, pointless and utterly impractical, but even he found it wise to keep an army of retainers. And the poor in other less fortunate prefectures replanted and built their houses again, and said among themselves that Buddha and the *kami*—the many gods of Shinto—alike slept.

One cold winter, when game was particularly scarce, Junko went out hunting for his master. Friends would gladly have come with him, but everyone knew that Junko preferred to hunt alone. He was polite about it, as always, but he felt that the other courtiers made too much noise and frightened away the winter-white deer and rabbits and wild pigs that he was stalking. He himself moved as quietly—even pulling a sledge behind him—as any fish in a stream, or any bird in the air, and he never came home empty-handed.

On this day, as Amaterasu, the sun, was drowsing down the western sky, Junko also was starting back to the Lord Kuroda's castle. His sledge was laden with a fat stag, and a pig as well, and Junko knew that another kill would load the sledge too heavily for his strength. All the same, he could not resist loosing one last arrow at a second wild pig that had broken the ice on a frozen stream, and was greedily drinking there, ignoring everything but the water. It was too good a chance to pass up, and Junko stood very still, took a deep breath—then let it out, just a little bit, as archers will do—and let his arrow fly.

It may have been that his hands were cold, or that the pig moved slightly at the last moment, or even that the growing twilight deceived Junko's eye, though that seems unlikely. At all events, he missed his mark—the arrow hissed past the pig's left ear, sending the animal off in a panicky scramble through the brush, out of sight and range in an instant—but he hit *something*. Something at the very edge of the water gave a small, sad cry, thrashed violently in the weeds there for a moment, and then fell silent and still.

Junko frowned, annoyed with himself; he had been especially proud of the fact that he never needed more than one arrow to bring down his prey. Well, whatever little creature he had accidentally wounded, it was his duty to put it quickly out of its pain, since an honorable man should never inflict unnecessary suffering. He went forward carefully, his boots sinking into the wet earth.

He found it lying half-in, half-out of the stream: an otter, with his arrow still in his flank. It was conscious, but not trying to drag itself away—it only looked at him out of dazed dark eyes and made no sound, not even when he knelt beside it and drew his knife to cut its throat. It looked at him—nothing more.

"It would be such a pity to ruin such fur with blood," he thought. "Perhaps I could make a tippet out of it for my master's wife." He put the knife away slowly and lifted the otter in his arms, preparing to break its neck with one swift twist. The otter's sharp teeth could surely have taken off a finger through the heavy mittens, but it struggled not at all, though Junko could feel the captive heart beating wildly against him. When he closed his free hand on the creature's neck, the panting breath, so softly desperate, made his wrist tingle strangely.

"So beautiful," he said aloud in the darkening air. He had never had any special feeling about animals: they were good to eat or they weren't good to eat, though he did rather admire the shimmering grace of fish and the cool stare of a fox. But the otter, hurt and helpless between his hands, made him feel as though he were the one wounded, somehow. "Beautiful," he whispered again, and very carefully and slowly he began to withdraw the arrow.

When Junko arrived back at his lord's castle, it was full dark and the otter lay under his shirt, warm against his belly. He delivered his kill, to be taken off to the great kitchens, gravely accepted the thanks due him, and hurried away to the meager quarters granted him at the castle as soon as it was correct to do so. There he laid the otter on a ragged old cloak that his sister had given him when he was a boy, and knelt beside the creature to study it in lamplight. The wound was no worse than it had been, and no better, though the blood had stopped flowing. He gave the otter water in a little clay dish, but it sniffed feebly at it without drinking; when he put his hand gently on the arrow wound, he could feel the fever already building.

"Well," he said to the otter, "all I know to do is to treat you as I did my little brother, the time he fell on the ploughshare. No biting, now." With his dagger, he trimmed the oily brown fur around the injury; with a rag dipped in hot *nihonshu*, which others call *sake*, he cleaned the area over and over; and with herbal infusions whose use he had learned from his mother's mother, he did his best to draw the infection. Through it all the otter never stirred or protested, but watched him steadily as he labored to undo the damage he had caused. He sang softly now and then, old nonsensical children's songs, hardly knowing he was doing it, and now and then the otter cocked an ear, seeming to listen.

When he was done he offered the water again, and this time the otter drank from the dish, cautiously, never taking its eyes from him, but deeply even so. Junko then lifted it in the old cloak and set all upon his own *tatami* mat, saying, "I cannot bind your wound properly, but healing in open air is best, anyway. And now you should sleep." He covered the otter with his coat, then lay down near it on the *tatami* and quickly fell asleep himself. The otter was awake longer than he, its wide eyes darker than the darkness.

In the morning the gash in the otter's flank smelled far less of fever, and the little animal was clearly hungry. Knowing that otters eat mainly fish, along with such things as frogs and turtles, Junko dressed hurriedly and went to a river that was near the castle (the better for the *daimyo* to keep an eye on the boats that went up and down between the distant cities), and there he caught and cleaned several small fish and brought them back to his quarters. The otter devoured them all, groomed its fur with great care—spending half an hour on its exposed wound alone—and then fell back to sleep for the rest of the day, much of which Junko spent studying it, sitting crosslegged beside his *tatami*. He was completely captivated to learn that the otter snored—very daintily and delicately, through its diamond-shaped nose—and that it smelled only slightly of fish, even after its meal, and much more of spring-warmed earth, as deep in winter as they were. He touched its front claws and realized that they were almost as hard as armor.

When a highly placed serving woman suggested through another servant that she might possibly enjoy his company for tea, Junko made the most courteous apology he could, and went on staring at the otter on his sleeping mat. Towards evening the little creature woke up and lay considering him in its turn, out of eyes much brighter and clearer than they had been. He spoke to it then, saying, "I am very sorry that I hurt you. I hope you are better today." The otter licked its whiskers without taking its eyes from his.

During the days that passed, Junko told no one about the otter: neither the Lord Kuroda nor his wife, the Lady Hara, nor even his closest friend, the horsemaster Akira Yamagata, who might have been expected to understand his fascination. He fed and cared for the otter every day, cleaned and aired out his quarters himself, and saw the arrow wound closing steadily from the inside, as every soldier knows is the proper way of healing. And the otter lay patiently under his hands as he tended it, and shared his *tatami* at night; and if it did not purr, or arch itself back against his hands, as a cat will, when he stroked its beautiful, rich fur, nevertheless it never drew away from the contact, but looked constantly into his eyes, as though it would have spoken to him if it could. He fell into the habit of talking to it himself, more and more, and he named it Sayuri, because men have to name things, and Sayuri was his sister's name.

One morning he told the otter, "My lord will have me guide a hunt meeting with the Lord Sugihara, down on holiday from Osaka. I am not looking forward to it, because neither trusts the other for an instant, and it could all become very wearying, though certainly educational. But when I return, however late it may be, I will take you back to your stream and release you there. You are fully recovered now, and a castle is no place for a wild creature like yourself. Stay well and warm until I come back."

The meeting between the two lords was indeed tiresome, and the hunt itself extremely unsatisfactory; but it had at least the virtue of taking less time than he would have expected, so the sun was still in the sky when Junko climbed the stair to his quarters. He went slowly, remembering his promise to the otter, and finding himself curiously reluctant to keep it. "It will be lonely," he thought. "I will miss . . . what is it that I will miss?" He could not say, but he knew that it was a real thing. So he sighed and went on to his quarters and opened the door.

The otter was gone.

In its place there stood, waiting for him, the most beautiful young woman he had ever seen. She stood barely higher than his heart, wearing a blue and white kimono, and her face was the dawn shade of a tea-rose, and as perfectly boned and structured as the kites that children were competing with every spring even then. Junko stood gaping at her, not even trying to speak.

"Yes," she said quietly, smiling with small white teeth at his bewilderment. "I am indeed that otter you shot, and then nursed back to health so tenderly. I am quite well now, as you see."

"But," said Junko. "But."

The young woman smiled more warmly as he stumbled among words, finding only that one. "This is my true form, but I take other shapes from time to time, as I choose. And it is so pleasant to be an otter—even as they hunt and mate, and raise their children, and struggle to survive, they seem to be having such a joyful time of it. Don't you think so, my lord?"

Junko said "But" again, that being the only word he was quite master of. The woman came toward him, her long, graceful fingers toying with the knot of the *obi* at her waist.

"I could not return to my own form until today," she explained to him, "because I was wounded, which always keeps me from changing. I might very well have died an otter, but for your devoted care. It is only proper that I make you some little recompense, surely?"

She seemed so hesitant herself that the last words came out a shy question. But the *obi* had already fallen to the floor.

Later, in the night, propped on her elbow and looking at him with eyes even darker than the otter's eyes, she said, "You have never lain so with a woman, have you?"

Junko blushed in the darkness. "Not exactly. I mean, of course there were . . . No."

The young woman was silent for a time. Then she said, "Well, I will tell you something, since you have been so honest with me. Nor will I lie to you—I have mated, made love, yes, but never in this form. Only as a deer, or a wildcat, or even as a snow monkey, in the northern mountains. Never as a human being, until now."

"And you *are* human?" Junko asked her. "Forgive me, but are you sure you are not an animal who can change into a woman?" For there are all sorts of legends in Japan about such creatures. Especially foxes.

She chuckled against his shoulder. "I am altogether human, I promise you." After a moment, she added, "You named me Sayuri. I like that name. I will keep it."

"But you must have a name of your own, surely? Everyone has a name."

"Not I, never." She put a finger on his lips to forestall further questioning. "Sayuri will suit me very well."

And the beautiful young woman who had been an otter suited Junko very well herself. He presented her formally as his fiancée to the Lord Kuroda the next day, and then to the full court. He was awkward at it, certainly, never having been schooled in such regions of etiquette; but all were charmed by the young woman's grace and modesty, even so, despite the fact that she could offer nothing in the way of family history or noble lineage. Indeed, Lord Kuroda's wife, the Lady Hara, immediately requested her as one of her ladies-in-waiting. So all went well there, and Junko—still as dazed by his sudden fortune as the otter had been by his arrow—was proud and happy in a way that he had never known in all his life.

He and Sayuri were married in short order by the Shinto priest Yukiyasa, the same who had married Lord Kuroda to Lady Hara, which everyone agreed was good luck, and were given new quarters in the castle—modest still, but more fitting for so singular a couple. More, his master, as a wedding gift, saw to it that Junko was given proper hunting equipment to replace the battered bow and homemade arrows with which he had first arrived at court. There were those present at the ceremony who bit their lips in envy of such favor to a commoner; but Junko, in his desire that everyone share in his joy, noticed none of this. The Lord Kuroda did.

Early on the morning after their wedding, when few were yet awake, Junko and his bride walked in the castle garden, in the northeast corner, where the stream entered, and which was known as the Realm of the Blue Dragon. The days were cold still, but they walked close together and were content, saying very little. But the stream made Junko think of the strange and nearly fatal way in which he had met his Sayuri, and he asked her then, "Beloved, do you think you would ever be likely to change into an otter again? For I hurt you by mischance, but there are many people who trap otters for their fur, and I would be afraid for you."

Sayuri's laughter was like the sound of the water flowing beside them, as she answered him. "I think not, my lord. There are more risks involved with that form—including marriage—than I had bargained for." Then she turned a serious face to her new husband, holding his arm tightly. "But I would grieve were I forbidden to change shape ever again. It is a part of whatever I am, you must know that."

"'Whatever I am,'" Junko repeated slowly, and for a moment it seemed as though the back of his neck was colder than it should be, even on a winter morning. "But you assured me that you were altogether human. Those were your words."

"And I am, I am certain I am!" Sayuri stopped walking and turned him to face her. "But what else am I? No name but the one you gave me . . . no childhood that I can recall, except in flashes, like lightning, here and gone . . . no father or mother to present me at my own wedding . . . far more memories of the many animals I have been than of the woman I know I am. There *must* be more to me than I can see in your eyes, or in the jeweled hand mirror that was the Lady Hara's gift. Do you understand, husband?"

There were tears on her long black eyelashes, and though they did not fall, they reassured Junko in a curious way, since animals cannot weep. He put his arms around her to comfort her, saying, "Do as you will, as you need to do, my wife. I ask only that you protect yourself from all injury, since you cannot regain your human form then, and anything could happen to you. Will you promise me that?"

Then Sayuri laughed, and shook her head so that the teardrops flew, and she said, "I swear that and more. You will never again share your sleeping mat with anything furred, or with any more than two legs." And Junko joined in her laughter, and they went on with their walk, all the way across the garden to the southwest corner, which is still called the Realm of the White Tiger.

So they lived quite happily together for some years at the court of the *daimyo* Lord Kuroda. Junko served his master with the same perfect loyalty as ever, and went on providing more game than any other huntsman for the castle kitchens; while Sayuri continued to be much favored by the Lady Hara, joining her in her favorite arts of music, brush-painting, and especially *ikebana*, the spreading new discipline of flower arrangement. So skilled was she at this latter, in fact, that Lady Hara often sought her assistance in planning the decorations for a poetry recital in her own quarters, or even for a feast on the green summer island in the stream. Watching the two of them pacing slowly by the water together, the fringes of the great lady's parasol touching his otter-wife's thick and fragrant hair, Junko was so proud that it pained him, and made it hard to breathe.

And if, now and then, he awoke in the night to find the space beside him still warm but empty, or heard a rustle in the trees outside, or a sigh of the grass, that he was huntsman enough to know was no bird, no doe teaching her fawn to strip bark from Lord Kuroda's plum trees, he learned to turn over and go back to sleep, and ask no questions in the morning. For Sayuri was most often back by dawn, or very soon thereafter—always in human shape, as she had promised him—usually chilled beyond the bone and needing to be warmed. And Junko would warm her and never ask her to say where—and what—she had been.

She did not always leave the castle: mouse and bat were among her favorite forms, and between those two she knew everything that was taking place within its walls. More than once she shocked Junko by informing him that this or that high-ranking retainer was slipping into dusty alcoves with this or that servant girl; he learned before Lord Kuroda that the Lady Hara was again with child, but that it would be best the *daimyo* not know, since this one too would not live to be born. Animals know these things. As an owl, she might glide silently over the forest at night, and tell him if the deer had shifted their grazing grounds, as they did from time to time, or were lying up in a new place. In fox-shape, she warned of an approaching forest fire without ever seeing a flame; Junko roused the castle and gained great praise and credit thereby. He wanted earnestly to explain that all honor was due to his wife Sayuri, but this was impossible, and she seemed more than content with his gratitude and their somewhat unlikely happiness. So they lived, and the time passed.

One night it happened that she returned to their bed shivering, not with cold, nor with fear—there were several cats in the castle—but, as he slowly realized, with anger, which was not something he was used to from Sayuri. She might be by turns as calm and thoughtful as a fox, as playful as an otter, as gentle as a deer, fiercely passionate as any mink or marten, or as curious and mischievous as a red-faced snow monkey. All these moods and humors he had come in time to understand—but anger was a new thing entirely. He held her, and asked simply, "What is it, my love?"

At first she would not speak, or could not; but by and by, when the trembling passed a little, she whispered, "I was in the kitchen,"—by this Junko knew that she had been in mouse-shape—"and the cooks were talking late over their own meal. And one said it was a shame that you had been passed over for the lord's private guard in favor of Yasunari Saito, since you had surely earned promotion a dozen times over. But another cook said"—the words were choking her again—"that it made no difference, because you were a commoner with no surname, and that it was miraculous that you were even in Lord Kuroda's home, let alone his retinue. *Miraculous*—after all you have done for them!" The tears of rage came then.

"Well, well," Junko said, stroking her hair, "that must have been Aoki. He has never liked me, that one, and it wouldn't matter to him if I had a dozen surnames. For the rest of it, things are the way they are, and that is . . . well, the way it is. Don't cry, please, Sayuri. I am grateful for what I have, and most grateful for you. Don't cry."

But later, when she had at last fallen asleep on his chest, he could not help brooding—only a little—about the unfairness of Saito's promotion. *Unfair* was not a word Junko had allowed himself even to think since he was quite small, and still learning the way things were, but it seemed to slither in his mind, and he could not get to grips with it, or make it go away. It was long before he slept again.

As has been said, the Lord Kuroda was a wise man, though not at all handsome, who saw more at a single dinner than many were likely to see in a week or a month. Riding out hunting one day, with Junko at his elbow, and they two having drawn a little apart from their companions, he said to him briefly and directly, "Saito is a fool, but his advancement was necessary, since I may well need his father's two hundred and fifty samurai one day." Junko bowed his head without answering. Lord Kuroda continued, "But it means nothing to me that you bring no warriors with you—nothing but your strength and your faithfulness. The next opening in my guard you shall fill."

With that he spurred ahead, doubtless to avoid Junko's stammering thanks. Junko was too overcome to be much of a hand at the hunt that afternoon; but while the others teased and derided him for this, Lord Kuroda only winked gravely.

Of course Sayuri was overjoyed at the news of the lord's promise, and she and Junko celebrated it with *nihonshu* and love, and then *shochu*, which is brewed from rice and sweet potatoes and a few other things. And afterward it was her turn to lie awake in the night, with her husband in her arms, and her mind perhaps full of small-animal thoughts. And perhaps not; who knows? It was all so long ago.

But it was at most a month before the horse of the samurai Daisuke Ikeda shied at a rabbit underfoot, reared, fell backwards and crushed his rider. There was much sorrow at court, for Ikeda was the oldest of the *daimyo*'s guard, and a well-liked man; but there was also a space in the guard to fill, and Lord Kuroda was as good as his word. Within days, Junko was wearing his master's livery, for all the world as though he were as good as Ikeda, or anyone else, and riding at his side on a fine, proud young stallion. And however many at court may have thought this highly unsuitable, no one said a word about it.

Junko also grieved for Ikeda, who had been kind to him. But his delight in his new position was muted, more than he would have expected, by his odd disquiet concerning that rabbit. Riding in the rear, as befit a commoner (it had been a formal procession, meant to impress a neighboring lord), he had seen the animal shoot from its hole, seemingly as blindly as though red-eyed Death were on its heels; and he had never known Ikeda's wise old horse to panic at an ambush, much less a rabbit. One worrisome thought led to another, and that to a third, until finally he brought them all to his wife. He had grown much in the habit of doing this.

Sayuri sat crosslegged on the proper new bed that the Lord Kuroda had given them to replace their worn *tatami*, and she listened attentively to Junko's fears, saying nothing until he was finished. Then she replied simply, "Husband, I was not the rabbit—I was the weasel just behind it, chasing it out of its burrow into the horse's path. Can you look at your own new horse—at your beautiful new livery—at this bed of ours—and say I have done wrong?"

"But Ikeda is dead!" Junko cried in horror. "Ask rather how I can look at his widow, at his children, at my master—at myself in the mirror now! Oh, I wish you had never told me this, Sayuri!"

"Then you should not have asked me," she answered him. "The weasel never meant for the good Ikeda to be killed—though he was old and should have retired from the guard long ago. The weasel only wanted the rabbit." She beckoned Junko to sit beside her, saying, "But is a wife not supposed to concern herself with the advancement of her husband's fortunes? I was told otherwise by the priest who married us." She put her arms around Junko. "Come, my love, take the good luck with the regrettable, and say as many prayers for Ikeda's repose as will comfort you." She laughed then: the joyous childlike giggle that never failed to melt even the sternest heart. "Although I think that *I* am more skilled at that than any prayer."

But Junko paced the castle all night, and wandered the grounds like a spirit; it was dawn before he could at last reassure himself that what she had told him was both sound and sensible. Ikeda's death had clearly been an accident, after all, and there was nothing in the least shameful in making the best of even such a tragedy. Sayuri's shapeshifting had brought about great good for him, however unintentional; let him give thanks for such a wife and, as he rode proudly beside the Lord Kuroda, bless the wandering arrow that had found an otter instead of a wild pig. "She is my luck," he thought often. "I should have given her that name, *luck*, instead of *little lily*."

But he did, indeed, pray often at the family shrine erected for Daisuke Ikeda.

Now in time Junko came to realize that, while he had certainly been honored far beyond his origins in becoming part of Lord Kuroda's private guard, he had also attained a kind of limit beyond which he had no chance of rising. Above the guard stood his master's counselors and ministers: some of them higher in rank than others, some higher in a more subtle manner, unspoken and unwritten. In any case, their world was far out of reach for a nameless commoner, no matter how graciously favored by his lord. He would always be exactly what he was—unlike Sayuri, who could at least become different animals in her search for her true nature. And, understanding this, for the first time in his life Junko began to admit aloud that the world was unjust.

"Look at Nakamura," he would say resentfully to his wife over the teacups. "Not only does he review the guard when Lord Kuroda is away or indisposed—Nakamura, who barely knows a lance from a chopstick—he advises my master on diplomacy, when he has never been north of the Inland Sea in his life. And Hashimoto—Finance Minister Hashimoto, if you please—Hashimoto holds the position for no other reason than that he is Lady Hara's second cousin on her father's side. It is not correct, Sayuri. It is not *right*."

Sayuri smiled and nodded, and made tea. She had become celebrated among the ladies-in-waiting for the excellence and delicacy of her *gyukuro* green tea.

And a few weeks later, Minister Shiro Nakamura, who loved to stroll alone in the castle gardens before dawn, to catch the first scent of the awakening flowers, was found torn in pieces by what could only have been a wolf. There were never many wolves in Japan, even then, but there was no question of the killer in this case: the great paw prints in the soft earth were so large that Junko suggested that the animal might well have come from Hokkaido, where the wolves were notably larger. "But how could a wolf ever find its way from Hokkaido Island so far south to Honshu?" he asked himself in the night. "And why should it do so?" He was very much afraid that he knew the answer.

The hunt that was immediately organized after the discovery of Minister Nakamura's still-warm body found no wolf of any species, but it did find blood in one of the paw prints, and on the blade of the antique dagger that Nakamura always carried. Sayuri was not at home when Junko returned; nor did she appear for several days, and even then she looked pale and faint, and spoke little. Junko made the excuse of illness to the Lady Hara, who sent medicines and dainties, plainly hoping that Sayuri's reported condition might betoken a new godchild. For his part, he asked no questions of his wife, knowing that she would tell him the truth. She always did.

It took more time, and a great deal of courteously muffled scandal and outrage at court before Junko ascended into the ranks of Lord Kuroda's advisors. He did not replace Minister Nakamura, but a station was created for him: that of Minister to the Lower Orders. When Junko's first speechless gratitude began to be replaced by stumbling bewilderment, Lord Kuroda explained to him, thus: "By now, my friend, you should know that I am not one of those nobles who believe that the commoners have no reason to exist, except that we give them the privilege of serving us. Quite a few, in fact,"—and here he named a good eight or ten of the castle servants, ending with Junko himself—"show evidence of excellent sense, excellent judgment." He paused, looking straight into Junko's eyes. "And where there is judgment, there will be opinions."

By this Junko understood that he had been chosen to be a liaison— what some might call a spy—between the *daimyo* and all those who were not nobles, priests or samurai. The notion offended him deeply, but he had not attained his unusually favored position by showing offense. He merely bowed deeply to the Lord Kuroda, and replied that he would do his best to give satisfaction. The Lord Kuroda looked long into his eyes without responding.

So Junko, surname or no, became the first commoner ever accepted into a world his class had long been forbidden even to dream of entering. His and Sayuri's quarters were changed once again for rooms that seemed to him larger than his entire native village; they were assigned a servant of their own, and a new bed that, as Sayuri giggled, was "like a great snowdrift. I am certain we will yet find a bear sleeping out the winter with us." The haughtiness of Lord Kuroda's other counselors, and the sense that their servant despised them, seemed a small price to pay at the time.

Out of respect and gratitude to his master, Junko served him well as Minister to the Lower Orders. He provoked no disloyal or rebellious conversations, but only listened quietly to the talk of the stables, the kitchens, the deep storerooms and the barracks. What he thought Lord Kuroda should know, he reported faithfully; what seemed to him to be no one's business but the speakers' remained where he heard it. And Lord Kuroda appreciated his discreet ability to tell the difference, and told him so, even calling him Junko-*san* in private. And once—not very long before at all—that would have been more than enough.

But again he had collided with an invisible barrier. Precisely because the post had been invented especially for him, there was no precedent for promotion, nor any obvious position for him to step into whenever it should become vacant. Those who had always been kindly and amiable to Junko the castle's chief huntsman, now looked with visible contempt on Junko the Minister, Junko the jumped-up pet of the Lord Kuroda. Those below him took great pleasure in observing his frustration and discomfort; when they dared, they murmured as they passed him, "Did you think you were better than we are? Did you really believe they would let you become one of *them*? Then you were a fool—and now you are no one. No one."

Junko never spoke of his unhappiness to Lord Kuroda, but he expressed it once to his friend Akira Yamagata. The horsemaster, being a silent man, much more at ease with beasts than people, replied shortly, "Let demons fly away with them all. You cannot win with such folk; you cannot ever be even with them in their minds. Serve your master, and you cannot go wrong. Any horse will tell you that."

As for Sayuri, she simply listened, and arranged fresh flowers everywhere in their quarters, and made green *gyokuro* tea. When she walked with Junko in the castle gardens, and he asked her whether she felt herself any nearer to perceiving her true nature, she most often replied, "My husband, I know more and more what I am *not*—but as to what I am . . . " and her voice would trail away, leaving the thought unfinished. Then she would add, quickly and softly, "But human—that, yes. I know I am human."

Now the most clever and ambitious of the Lord Kuroda's counselors, recently become Minister of Waterways and Fisheries, was a man named

Mitsuo Kondo. Perhaps because he was little older than Junko, only now approaching his middle years, he went well out of his way to show his scorn for a commoner, though never in the presence of the *daimyo*. In the same way, Junko responded humbly to Kondo's poorly-veiled insults; while at home he confided to his wife that he often dreamed of wringing the man's thin neck, as he had so often done with chickens in his childhood. "Being of low birth, I am naturally acquainted with barnyards," he remarked bitterly to Sayuri.

It happened that on a warm night of early summer, Junko woke thirsty to an empty bed—he was quite used to this by now—and was still thirsty when he had drunk the last remaining green tea. Setting off to find water, barefooted and still drowsy, he had just turned into a corridor that led to the kitchens, when he heard the scraping of giant claws on a weathered *sugi*-wood floor, and flattened himself against the wall so hard that the imprint of the molding remained on his skin for hours afterward.

A huge black bear was lumbering down a passageway just ahead. It must surely have smelled his terror—or, as he imagined, heard the frantic beating of his heart—for it hesitated, then rose on its hind legs, turning toward him to sniff the air, growling softly. He saw the deep yellow-white chevron on the creature's breast, as well as the bright blood on its horrific fangs and claws, and he smelled both the blood and the raw, wild, strangely sweet odor of the beast itself. Even armed he might not be the creature's match; weaponless, he knew this was the moment of his death. But then the bear's great bulk dropped to the floor again, turning away, and his forgotten breath hissed between his teeth as the animal moved slowly on out of his sight, still growling to itself.

Junko did not go back to his quarters that night, but sat shivering where he was until dawn, tracing a trail of dead moss between two floorboards over and over with his forefinger. Then at last he slipped warily back into the new bed where Sayuri had laughingly imagined a bear keeping them company. She was sound asleep, not even stirring at his return. Junko lay still himself, studying her hands: one partly under her head, one stretched out on the pillow. There was no blood on any of the long fingers he loved to watch moving among her flowers. This was not as reassuring to him as it might once have been.

The hunt for Minister Kondo went on for days. The blood trail was washed away by a sudden summer rain, except for the track leading from his private offices, and there were other indications that he had been carried off by some great animal, or something even worse. For all his dislike of Kondo, Junko took a leading part in the hunt—as did Lord Kuroda himself—from its earliest moments to the very last, when it was silently agreed that the Minister's body would never be found. Lord Kuroda commanded ten days of mourning, and had a shrine created in Minister Kondo's memory on his own summer island. It is still there, though no one today knows whom it was meant to honor.

Even after the proper period of remembrance had passed, the empty place among the *daimyo*'s counselors remained unfilled for some considerable while. Few had liked Kondo any more than Junko did; all had feared his ambition, his gifts, and his evil tongue, and many were happy that he was gone, however horrified they may have been at the manner of his departure. But Lord Kuroda was clearly grieved—and, more than that, suspicious, though of what even he could not precisely say. Wolves and bears were common enough in Honshu in those days, but not in Honshu gardens and palaces; nor was the loss of three important members of his court, each under such curious circumstances, something even a mighty *daimyo* could easily let pass. The tale had already spread through the entire province, from bands of half-naked beggars huddled muttering under bridges to courts as great as his own. There was even a delicate message from the Shogun in Kyoto. Lord Kuroda brooded long over the proper response.

Junko came to feel his master's contemplative eyes on him even when he was not in Lord Kuroda's presence. At length, to ease his mind, he went directly to the *daimyo* and asked him, "Lord, have I done wrong? I pray you tell me if this is so." For he knew his own silent part in the three deaths, and he was afraid for his wife Sayuri.

But Lord Kuroda answered him gently, "Your pardon, loyal Junko, if I have caused you to be more troubled than we all are, day on day. I think you know that I have often considered your country astuteness to be of more plain practical aid to me than the costly education of many a noble. Now I wonder whether you might have any least counsel to offer me regarding the terrible days through which we are passing." He permitted himself a very small, sad chuckle. "Because, just as everyone in my realm knows his station, my own task is to provide each of them with wisdom, assurance and security. And I have none to offer them, no more than they. Do you understand me, Junko?"

Then Junko was torn in his heart, for he had never lost his fondness for the Lord Kuroda, and it touched him deeply to see the *daimyo* so distressed. But he shook his head and murmured only, "These are indeed dark times, my lord, and there is nothing that would honor my unworthy self more than to offer you any candle to light your way. But in all truth, I have no guidance for you, except to offer sacrifice and pay the priests well. Who but they can read the intentions of the *kami*?"

"Apparently the gods' intentions were for my priests to leave me," the Lord Kuroda replied. "Half of them ran off when Minister Nakamura's body was discovered, and you yourself have seen the rest vanishing day by day since Kondo's has *not* been discovered. In a little the only priest left to me will be my old Yukiyasa." He sighed deeply, and turned from Junko, saying, "No matter, my friend. I had no business to place my own yoke upon your shoulders. Go to your bed and your life, and think no more of this. But know that I am grateful . . . grateful." And as he shuffled away, disappearing from sight among his bodyservants, it seemed to Junko for the first time that his master was an old man.

He repeated the conversation to Sayuri, generally satisfied with the way he had responded to the *daimyo*'s queries, but adding in some annoyance, "I expected him to offer me Kondo's position, but he never mentioned it. It will surely come, I am certain."

Sayuri had grown increasingly silent since the night of the black bear, more and more keeping to their quarters, avoiding her many friends and interests, shirking her duty to the Lady Hara when she dared; most often taking refuge in sleep, where she twitched and whimpered as Junko had never known her to do. Now, without looking at him, she said, "Yes. It will come."

And so it did, in good time, and with little competition, whether direct or stealthy, for rising to high rank at the court of Lord Kuroda more and more clearly involved risking a terrible end. There was no one who openly connected the deaths with the steady advancement of the peasant Junko—Junko-*san* now, to all, by special order—nor, certainly, with his charming and modest wife—but there were some who pondered, and one in particular who pondered deeply. This was Yukiyasa.

Yukiyasa was the Shinto priest who had married Sayuri to Junko. As the Lord Kuroda had predicted, he was the only priest who had not fled the court, and the only person who seemed able to rouse Sayuri from her melancholic torpor. Out of his hearing, he was called the Turtle, partly due to his endlessly wrinkled face and neck, but also because of his bright black eyes that still missed nothing—not the smallest change in the flowing of the sea or the angle of the wind, not the slightest trembling of the eyelashes of a woman fearing to show fear for her husband far away in battle. If age had slowed his step, it seemed to have quickened his perceptions: he could smell rain two days off, identify a Mongolian plover before others could be sure it was even a bird, and hear a leaf's fall or a fieldmouse's squeak through the castle walls. But he did look more and more like a turtle every season.

Junko instinctively avoided the old priest as much as he could, keeping clear of the *inari* shrine he maintained, except for the *Shogatsu Matsuri*, the New Year's festival. But Yukiyasi visited with Sayuri almost daily—in her quarters, if she did not come to the shrine—reading to her from the *Kojiki* and the *Nihon shoki*, teasing and provoking her until she had no choice but to smile, often remarking that she should one day consider becoming a Shinto priest herself. She always changed the subject, but the notion made her thoughtful, all the same.

"Today he said that I understood the way of the gods," she reported to Junko one spring evening. "What do you suppose he meant by that?"

They were walking together in the Realm of the Blue Dragon, still their favorite part of the castle gardens, and Junko's attention was elsewhere at the moment, contemplating the best use of the numerous waterways and fisheries that ran through the Lord Kuroda's vast domain. Now, his notice returning to his wife, he said, "The *kami* have always been shapeshifters; look at the foxes your friend's shrine celebrates. Perhaps he senses . . . " He did not finish the sentence.

Sayuri's grip on his arm tightened enough to hurt him. "No," she said in a small voice. "No, that cannot be, cannot. I change no longer. Never again." Her face had gone paler than the moon.

"The bear?" He had never meant to ask her, and immediately wished he could take back the question. But she answered him straightforwardly, almost in a rush, as the melting snows had quickened the measure even of Lord Kuroda's gentle stream.

"I was so frightened to be the bear. I didn't like it at all. It was a terrible thing."

"A terrible thing that you were—or a terrible thing you did?" He could not keep his own words from tumbling out.

"Both," she whispered, "*both*." She was crying now, but she resisted strongly when Junko tried to hold her. "No, no, you mustn't, it is too dangerous. I am sorry, so sorry, I so wish your arrow had killed me. Then Ikeda would be alive, and Nakamura, and Kondo—"

"And I would still be what I was born," Junko interrupted her. "Junko the hunter, lower than any cook—because a cook is at least an artist, while a huntsman is a butcher—Junko, with his peasant ways and peasant accent, barely tolerable just as long as he keeps to his place. If it were not for you, my otter, my wolf—"

"*No!*" She twisted away from him, and actually ran a few paces off before she turned to stare at him in real horror. It was long before she spoke again, and then she said quietly, "We have quite traded places, have we not, my husband? You were the one who grieved for the poor victims of my shape-changing, and it was I who laughed at your foolish concern and prided myself upon the improvements I brought to your fortunes, as a good wife should do. And now . . . " She faltered for a little, still looking at him as though *he* were the strange animal she had never seen before. "Now you turn out to be the shapeshifter, after all, and I the soft fool who'll have none of it, no more. Not even for love of you—and I loved you when I was an otter—not even for the sake of at last learning my own being, my own soul. That can go undiscovered forever, and welcome, and I will remain Sayuri, your wife, no more and no less. And I will tend three graves, and pray at the shrine, and live as I can with what I have done. That is how it will be."

"'That is how it will be,'" Junko mimicked her. "And I? I am to rise no higher at this court, where the old men despise me and the young ones plot against me—all because you have suddenly turned nun?" He moved toward her, his eyes narrowing. "Yukiyasa," he said slowly. "It's the Turtle, isn't it? That horrible antique, with his foul-smelling robes and his way of shooting his head out and blinking at people. It's Yukiyasa who has put all this into your head, I know it. I swear, if I really *could* change my shape—"

But Sayuri covered his mouth with her hand, crying, "Don't! Don't ever say that, I beg you! You have no idea what that is like, what that *is*, or you would never say such a thing." In that moment, the look in her beautiful dark eyes made Junko think of the black bear rising on its hind legs and turning to sniff the air for him, and he was afraid of her. He did not move, nor did he try to speak, until she took her hand away.

Then he said, not mockingly this time, but as soothingly as he knew how, "Well, we have come a very long way together—too long a way for us to turn on each other now. I ask pardon for my thoughtlessness and my stupidity, and I promise never to speak of . . . what we will not speak of, ever again. Such advancement as I can win on my own, that will I do, and be well satisfied with my own nature, and my own fate. Will that content you, my wife?"

"That will content me, husband," she whispered after a little. She did not resist when Junko put his arms around her, but he could feel the fear in her body, and so he added lightly, "And I promise also never to say another word concerning your Turtle, for I know how much his wisdom and kindness mean to you. Not a word—not even if you were indeed to become a priest, as he wishes you to do. So." He stroked her hair, as she had always liked him to do. "Shall we go on with our walk?"

And Sayuri laughed for the first time in a long while, and she nodded and put her arm through his, and they walked on together.

But it was not true; though, to do him justice, Junko tried earnestly, for a while, to believe it so. Even while taking his new post as Minister of Waterways and Fisheries with all seriousness—descended as he was from river people who had manned weirs, dams and sluices throughout Honshu and Shikoku for generations—he could not help coveting another position: that of Masanori Morioka, Chief Minister for Dealing with Barbarians. This ranked just under the Lord Kuroda himself—in another country, Morioka would have been called Prime Minister—and where the *daimyo* was aging visibly, Morioka was only a year or two older than Junko himself. Far more important, he came of high samurai family, and, since Lord Kuroda and the Lady Hara had no children, he might already have been chosen to succeed his lord when the time came. Junko was increasingly certain of this: the Lord Kuroda was no one to leave his lands in chaos while his relatives went to war over so rich a prize. It must be Murioka; there could be no doubt of it.

In the past, this would have mattered little to the Junko whose only concern was whether the rains had brought enough new grass for the deer, and if the snow monkeys' unusually thick coats might foretell an evil winter. But it mattered now to this Junko, and—again to be fair—he did his best to conceal his jealousy from his wife. In this he failed, because he talked in his sleep almost every night, and Sayuri's heart shivered to decipher his mumblings and his whispered rants. She would lie as close to him as she could then, hoping somehow to absorb his aching resentment into her own body, and wishing once again, deeply and dearly, that she had died an otter.

As the Lord Kuroda grew more frail, and Morioka steadily assumed a greater share of the *daimyo*'s responsibilities, Junko's anger and envy became more and more plain to see, and not only by his wife. Lady Hara spoke of it with some disquiet to Sayuri; and Akira, the taciturn horsemaster, told Junko that he needed to ride out more, and to spend more time in the company of horses than of courtiers, and less time fretting over childish matters that he could not control in any case. And it was Lord Kuroda himself, having summoned Junko to him in private, who was the one to ask, "Have I done wrong, then? What troubles you, Junko-*san*?" For he always showed a tenderness toward Junko that made certain spiteful folk grumble that the *daimyo* had fathered him in secret on a peasant woman.

Then Junko, for a moment, was ashamed of his bitterness, and he knelt before Lord Kuroda and put his hands between the hard old hands that trembled only a little, even now, and he whispered, "Never have I had anything from you but goodness beyond my worth. But would that I enjoyed the opportunity to serve you that others have earned—perhaps through ability, perhaps . . . not."

By this Lord Kuroda knew that he was speaking of Masanori Morioka. He responded with unaccustomed sternness, "Minister of Waterways and Fisheries you are, and I would never permit even Morioka to trespass on a single one of the duties and privileges that your honorable service has won for you. But we must always remember that all barbarians believe themselves to be civilized, and dealing with such people while keeping the dangerous truth from them requires a subtlety that few possess. You are not one of them, Junko-*san*."

He smiled at Junko then, leaning stiffly forward to raise him to his feet. "Nor am I, not really. It is a matter of training from one's childhood, my friend—learning to sense and walk, even in the dark, the elusive balance between humility and servility, candor and courtesy, power and the appearance of power. Masanori Morioka is far better at this game than I ever was, even when I was young. Let the worst come, I will have no fears for my realm in his hands."

With those words, the worst had indeed come to Junko; with those words Morioka was doomed. Yet he managed to keep his answer calm and slow, saying merely, "In his hands? Is it so decided, lord?"

"It is so decided," his master replied.

Junko drew himself to his full height and bowed deeply, holding his arms rigid at his sides "Then I also must retire from the court, since Minister Morioka and I dislike each other too greatly to work together after you are gone. While you remain, so will I."

But the Lord Kuroda smiled then: not widely, which was not his way, but with a certain sad warmth that was new to his kind, ugly face. He responded only, "In that case I will stay alive just as long as it befits me to do so," and with a small flick of his fingers gave Junko leave to withdraw.

On the way to his quarters, he briefly encountered Morioka, who bowed mockingly to him, saying nothing until Junko had returned the bow and passed on. Then he called after him, "And how go the mighty consultations with our *daimyo*?" for he knew where Junko had been, and he had his own envy of the Lord Kuroda's feeling for Junko.

"As well as your great battles," Junko answered him, and Morioka scowled like a demon-mask, since he had never borne arms for Lord Kuroda or any other, and everyone at court knew *that*. So they went on to their separate destinations; and Junko, reaching home, flung himself down on the bed and wept with a terrifying ferocity. Nor could he stop: it was as though the tears of rage that had been building and swelling within him since his stoic childhood had finally surged out of his control, and were very likely to flood him as the cyclones still did every year to his family's sliver of farmland. He was all water, and all bitterness, and nothing beyond, ever.

He continued biting the bedclothes to muffle his weeping, but Sayuri heard him just the same, and came to him. At first she drew back in something close to fear of such violent anguish; but in a little she sat on the edge of the bed and put her hand timidly on his shoulder, saying, "Husband, I cannot bear to see you so. What in this world can possibly be such an immeasurable grief to you? Speak to me, and if I cannot help you, I will at least share your sorrow. Share it with me now, I beg you."

And she said all else that good wives—and good husbands, as well—say at such moments; and after a long while Junko lifted his head to face her. His eyes and nose and mouth were all clotted with tears, and he looked as children look who have been punished for no reason they can understand. But behind the tears Sayuri saw a hot and howling anger that would have turned him to a beast then and there, if it could have done. In a thick, shaking voice he told her what the Lord Kuroda had told him, ending by saying, more quietly now, "You see, it was all for nothing, after all. All of it, for nothing."

Sayuri thought at first that he was speaking of his long, difficult climb up from his poor peasant birth to the castle luxury where they sat together on a bed whose sheets were of Chinese silk. But Junko, his voice gone wearily flat and almost toneless, went on, "Everything you did for me, for us—Ikeda, Nakamura, Kondo—it was all wasted, they might just as well have been spared. Yes—they might as well have remained alive."

"Yes," Sayuri repeated dazedly. "They might have remained alive." But then she shook off the confused stupor that his words had brought about, and she gripped his wrists, saying, "But Junko-*san*, no, I never killed for your sake. I was a bear, a wolf, a weasel after a rabbit—I was hungry, not human. In those beast forms I did not even know who those men were!"

"Did you not?" the fierce question came back at her. "Be honest with yourself, my wife. Did the wolf never know for a moment that tearing out the throat of Isamu Nakamura would benefit a certain peasant who dreamed of becoming a counselor to a *daimyo*? What of the bear—surely the bear must have known that carrying off the previous Minister of Waterways and Fisheries would open the way—"

"*No!* No, it is not true!" Still holding his wrists tightly, she shook him violently. "The animals were innocent—*I* was innocent! It was coincidence, nothing more—"

"*Was it?*" They stared at each other for a moment longer, before Sayuri released Junko's wrists and he turned away, shaking his head. "It doesn't matter, it is of no importance. Whatever was true then, you will take no more shapes, and *I* . . . I will stay not one day after Lord Kuroda is gone. We will retire to my home village, and I will be a big man there, and you the most beautiful and accomplished woman. And why not?—we deserve it. And they will give us the very grandest house they possess, in my honor, and it will be smaller than this one room, and smell of old men.

And why not? We have served the great *daimyo* faithfully and well, and we deserve it all."

And saying this, he walked away, leaving Sayuri alone to bite her knuckles and make small sounds without tears.

The old priest Yukiyasa found her so when he came to read to her, since she had not appeared at the shrine. Having performed her wedding, he regarded her therefore as his daughter and his responsibility, and he lifted her face and looked long at her, asking no questions. Not did she speak, but placed one hand over his dry, withered hand and they stood in silence, until her mind was a little cased. Then she said, in a voice that sounded as ancient as his, "I have done evil, and may do so again. Can you help me, Turtle?" For he knew perfectly well what he was called, but she was the only one permitted to address him by that name.

Yukiyasa said, "Often and often does evil result where nothing but good was meant. I am sure this is true in your case."

But Sayuri answered, "What I intended—even if it was not quite I who intended it—is of no importance. What I did is what matters."

The priest peered at her, puzzled as he had not been in a very long time, and yet with a curious sense that he might do best to remain so. He continued, "I have many times thought that in this world far more harm is wrought by foolish men than by wicked ones. Perhaps you were foolish, my daughter. Are you also vain enough to imagine yourself the only one?"

That won him a fragment of a smile, coming and going so swiftly that it might have been an illusion, and perhaps was. But Yukiyasa was encouraged, and he said further, "You *were* foolish, then," not making a question of it. "Well, so. I myself have done such things as I would never confess to you—not because they were evil, but because they were so *stupid*—"

Sayuri said, "I change into animals. People have died."

Yukiyasa did not speak for a long time, but he never took his eyes from Sayuri's eyes. Finally he said quietly, "Yes, I see them," and he did not say whether he meant wolves or bears, or Daisuke Ikeda, Minister Shiro Nakamura or Minister Mitsuo Kondo. He said, "The *kami* did this to you before you were born. It is your fate, but it is not your fault."

"But what *I* did is my fault!" she cried. "Death is death, killing is killing!" She paused to catch her breath and compose herself, and then went on in a lower tone. "My husband thinks that I killed those men to remove them from his path to power in the court. I say *no, no, it was the animals, not me*—but what if it is true? What if that is exactly what happened? What should I do then, Turtle, please tell me? Turtle, please!"

The old man took her hands between his own. "Even if every word is true, you are still blameless. Listen to me now. I have studied the way of the *kami* all my life, and I am no longer sure that there is even such a thing as blame, such a thing as sin. You did what you did, and you are being punished for it now, as we two stand here. The *kami* are never punished. This is the one thing I know, daughter, with all my years and all my learning. The *kami* are never punished, and we always are."

Then he kissed Sayuri on the forehead, and made her lie down, and recited to her from the *Kojiki* until she fell asleep, and he went away.

Passing the courtyard where the *daimyo*'s soldiers trained, he noticed Junko watching an exercise, but plainly not seeing it. The old priest paused beside him for a time, observing Junko's silent discomfort in his presence without enjoying it. When Junko finally bowed and started away—still without speaking, discourteous as that was—Yukiyasa addressed him, saying, "I will give you my advice, though you do not want it. Whether for a good reason or a bad one, it would be a terrible mistake for you ever again to order your wife, in words or in your thoughts, to become so much as a squirrel or a sparrow. A good reason or a bad one. Do you understand me?"

Then Junko turned and strode back to him, his face white, but his eyes wide with anger, and his voice a low hiss. "I do *not* understand you. I do not know what you are talking about. My wife is no shapeshifter, but if she were, I would never make such a request of her. Never, I have *sworn* to her that I would never—"

He halted, realizing what he had said. Yukiyasa looked at him for a long moment before he repeated, "In words or in thoughts," and walked slowly on to the shrine where he lived. Junko stared after him, but did not follow.

But by this time he was too far lost in envy of Masanori Morioka to give more than the briefest consideration to the Shinto priest's warning. True to his promise to her, he held himself back from urging Sayuri to remember, in so many words, that there was no future for them in a court commanded by Morioka. Even so, he found one way or another to put it into her mind every day; and every night he awoke well before dawn, hoping to find her gone, as had happened so many times in their life together. But she continued to slumber the night through, though often enough she wakened him with her twitching and moaning, which once would have moved him instantly to soothe and comfort her. Now he only turned over with a disappointed grunt and drowsed off again. He had always had the gift of sleep.

Finally, on a night of early autumn, his desire was granted. The moon was high and small, leaves were stirring softly in a warm breeze, and the space beside him was empty. Junko smiled in the darkness and rose quickly to follow. Then he hesitated, partly from fear of just what he might overtake; partly because it would clearly be better to be aroused by running feet in the corridors and the dreadful news about Minister Morioka. But it was impossible for even him to close his eyes now, so he donned a kimono and paced their quarters from one end to the other, impatiently pushing fragile screens aside, cursing when he tripped over pairs of Sayuri's *geta*, and listening for screams.

But there was no sound beyond the soft creaking of the night, and finally the silence became more than he could endure. Telling himself that Sayuri, in whatever form, would surely know him, he drew a long breath and stepped out into the corridor.

Standing motionless as his eyes grew accustomed to the darkness, he saw and heard nothing, but he smelled . . . or almost smelled . . . no, he had no words for what he smelled. The wild odor of the bloody-mouthed black bear was lodged in his throat yet, as was the scent of the wolf fur clutched in the dead fingers of Minister Nakamura. But this was a cold smell, like that of a great serpent, and there was another underneath, even colder—*burned bone*, Junko thought, though that made no sense at all; and then, even more absurdly, *bone flames.* He turned to look back at the entrance to his quarters, but it seemed already far away, receding as he watched, like a sail on the sea.

There was no choice but to go on. He wished that he had brought a sword or a *tanto* dagger, but only samurai were permitted to carry such weapons; and for all his kindly respect and affection, the Lord Kuroda had never made any exception for Junko. When he was in Morioka's place, he would change *that*. He moved ahead, step by step, cautiously feeling his way between splashes of moonlight.

Masanori Morioka's quarters were located a floor above his own—closer to the *daimyo*'s, which was something else to brood about, and tend to later. He started up the stair, anxious neither to alert nor alarm anyone, and beginning to wonder—all was still *so* quiet—whether he had misread Sayuri's absence. What if she had merely gone scurrying in mouse-shape, as she had once been fond of doing, skittering in the castle rafters as a bat, or even roving outside as any sort of small night thing? How would it look if he were surprised wandering himself where he had no reason to be at such an hour? He paused, very nearly of a mind to turn back . . . and yet the serpent-smell had grown stronger with each step, and so near now that he felt as though he were the creature exuding it: as though the coldly burning bones were, in some way, his own.

Another step, and another after, moving sideways now without realizing that he was doing so, the serpent-smell pressing on him like a smothering blanket, making his breath come shorter and shallower. Once he lurched to one knee, twice into the wall, unsure now of whether he was stumbling upstairs or down . . . then he did hear the scream.

It was a woman's scream, not a man's. And it came, not from Minister Morioka's quarters, but from those of the Lord Kuroda and the Lady Hara.

For an instant, Junko was too stupefied to be afraid; it was as though the strings of his mind had been cut, as well as those of his petrified body. Then he uttered a wordless cry that he himself never heard, and sprang toward the *daimyo*'s rooms, kicking off his slippers when they skidded on the polished floors.

Lady Hara screamed again, as Junko burst through the rice-paper door, stumbling over the wreckage of shattered *tansu* chests and *shoji* screens. He could not see her or Lord Kuroda at first: the vast figure in his path seemed to draw all light and shape and color into itself, so that nothing was real except the towering horns, the cloven hooves, the sullen gleam of the reptilian scales from the waist down, the unbearable stench of simmering bone . . .

"*Ushi-oni!*" He heard it in his mind as an insect whisper. Lord Kuroda was standing between his wife and the demon, legs braced in a fighting stance, *wakizashi* sword trembling in his old hand. The *ushi-oni* roared like a landslide and knocked the sword across the room. Lord Kuroda drew his one remaining weapon, the *tanto* he carried always in his belt.

The *ushi-oni* made a different sound that might have been laughter. The dagger fell to the floor.

Junko said, "Sayuri."

The great thing turned at his voice, as the black bear had done, and he saw the nightmare cow-face, and the rows of filthy fangs crowding the slack, drooling lips. And—as he had seen it in the red eyes of the bear—the unmistakable recognition.

"My wife," Junko said. "Come away."

The *ushi-oni* roared again, but did not move, neither toward him, nor toward Lord Kuroda and Lady Hara. Junko said, "Come. I never meant this. I never meant this."

Out of the corner of his eye, Junko saw the *daimyo* moving to recover his fallen dagger. But the *ushi-oni*'s attention was all on Junko, the mad yellow-white eyes had darkened to a dirty amber, and the claws on its many-fingered hands had all withdrawn slightly. Junko faced it boldly, all unarmed as he was, saying again, "Come away, Sayuri. We do not belong here, you and I."

He knew that if he turned his head he would see a blinking, quaking Minister Morioka behind him in the ruined doorway, but for that he cared nothing now. He took a few steps toward the *ushi-oni*, halting when it growled stinking fire and backed away. Junko did not speak further, but only reached out with his eyes. *We know each other.*

He was never to learn whether the monster that had been—that *was*— his wife would have come to him, nor what would have been the result if it had. Lady Hara, suddenly reaching the limit of her body's courage, uttered a tiny sigh, like a child falling asleep, and collapsed to the floor. The *ushi-oni* began to turn toward her, and at that moment the Lord Kuroda lunged forward and struck with all the strength in his old arm. The *tanto* buried itself to the coral-ornamented hilt in the right side of the demon.

The *ushi-oni*'s howl shook the room and seemed to split Junko's head, bringing blood even from his eyes, as well as from his ears and nose. A great scaled paw smashed him down as the creature roared and reeled in its death agony, trampling everything it had not already smashed to splinters, dragging ancient scrolls and brush paintings down from the walls, crushing the Lord Kuroda family shrine underfoot. The *ushi-oni* bellowed unceasingly, the sound slamming from wall back to broken wall, and everyone hearing it bellowed with the same pain, bleeding like Junko and like him holding, not their heads and faces, but their hearts. When the demon fell, and was silent, the sound continued on forever.

But even forever ends, and there came a time when Junko pulled himself to his feet. He found himself face to face with Minister Morioka, pale as a grubworm, gabbling like an infant, walking as though he had just learned how. Others were in the room now, all shouting, all brandishing weapons, all keeping their distance from the great, still thing on the floor. He saw the Lord Kuroda, far away across the ruins, bending over Lady Hara, carefully and tenderly lifting her to her feet while staring strangely at Junko. Whatever his face, as bloody as Junko's own, revealed, it was neither anger nor outrage, but Junko looked away anyway.

The *ushi-oni* had not moved since its fall, but its eyes were open, unblinking, darkening. Junko knelt beside it without speaking. The fanged cow-lips twitched slightly, and a stone whisper reached his ear and no other, shaping two words. "*My nature . . .* " There were no more words, and no sound in the room.

Junko said, "She was my wife."

No one answered him, not until the Lord Kuroda said, "No." Junko realized then that the expression in his master's eyes was one of deepest pity. Lord Kuroda said, "It is not possible. An *ushi-oni* may take on another shape if it wishes, being a demon, but in death it returns to its true being, always. You see that this has not occurred here."

"No," Junko answered him, "because this *was* Sayuri's natural form. This is what she was, but she did not know it, no more than I. I swear that she did not know." He rose, biting his lower lip hard enough to bring more blood to his mouth, and faced the *daimyo* directly. He said, "This was my doing. All of it. The weasel, the wolf, the bear—she meant only to help me, and I . . . I did not want to know." He looked around at the shattered room filled with solemn people in nightrobes and armor. "Do you understand? Any of you?"

The Lord Kuroda's compassionate manner had taken on a shade of puzzlement; but the Lady Hara was nodding her elegant old head. Behind Junko, Minister Morioka had at last found language, though his stammering voice retained none of its normal arrogance. He asked timidly, "How could an *ushi-oni* not know what it was? How could such a monster ever marry a human being?"

"Perhaps because she fell in love," the Lady Hara said quietly. "Love makes one forget many things."

"I cannot speak for my wife," Junko replied. "For myself, there are certain things I will remember while I live, which I beg will not be long." He turned his eyes to Minister Morioka. "I wanted her to kill you. I never said it in those words—*never*—but I made very sure she knew that I wanted you out of my way, as she had removed three others. I ask your pardon, and offer my head. There can be no other atonement."

Then the Minister shrank back without replying, for while he had no objection to the death penalty, he greatly preferred to see it administered by someone else. But the Lord Kuroda asked in wonder, "Yet the *ushi-oni* came here, to these rooms, not to Minister Morioka's quarters. Why should she—*it*—have done so?"

Junko shook his head. "That I cannot say. I know only that I am done with everything." He walked slowly to retrieve the *daimyo*'s sword, brought it to him, and knelt again, baring his neck without another word.

Lord Kuroda did not move or speak for a long time. The Lady Hara put her hand on his arm, but he did not look at her. At last he set the *wakizashi* back in its lacquered sheath, the soft click the only sound in the ravaged room, which seemed to have turned very cold since the fall of the *ushi-oni*. He touched Junko's shoulder, beckoning him to rise.

"Go in peace," he said without expression, "if there is any for you. No harm will come to you, since it will be known that you are still under the protection of the Lord Kuroda. Farewell . . . Junko-*san*."

A moment longer they stared into one another's eyes; then Junko bowed to his master and his master's lady, turned like a soldier, and walked away, past smashed and shivered *tengu* furniture, past Minister Morioka—who would not look at him—through the crowd of gaping, muttering retainers, and so out of the Lord Kuroda's castle. He did not return to his quarters for any belongings, but went away barefoot, clad only in his kimono, and he looked back only once, when he smelled the smoke and knew that the servants were already burning the body of the *ushi-oni* that was also his wife Sayuri. Then he went on.

And no one ever would have known what became of him, if the old priest Yukiyasa had not been the patient, inquisitive man that he was. Some years after the disappearance of Minister Junko, the commoner who had ridden at the right hand of a *daimyo* for a little while, Yukiyasa left his Shinto shrine in the care of a disciple, picked up his staff and his begging bowl, and set off on a trail long since grown cold. But it was not the first such trail that he had followed in his life, and he possessed the curious patience of the very old that is perhaps the closest mortal approach to immortality. The journey was a trying one, but many peasant families were happy to please the gods by offering him lodging, and peasants have long memories. It took the priest less time than one might have expected to track Junko to a village that barely merited the title, on a brook that was called a river by the people living there. For that matter, Junko himself was not known in the village by his rightful name, but as Toru, which is *wayfarer*. Yukiyasa found him at the brook in the late afternoon, lying flat on his belly, fishing for salmon by the oldest method there is, which is tickling them slowly and gently, until they fall asleep, and then scooping them into a net. There were already six fish on the grass beside him.

Junko was coaxing a seventh salmon to the bank, and did not look up or speak when the old priest's shadow fell over him. Not until he had landed the last fish did he say, "I knew it was you, Turtle. I could always smell you as far as the summer island."

Yukiyasa took no offense at this, but only chuckled as he sat down. "The incense does cling. Others have mentioned it."

Neither spoke for some time, but each sat considering the other. To the priest's eye, Junko looked brown and healthy enough, but notably older than he should have. His face was thinner, his hair had turned completely white, and there was an air about him, not so much of loneliness as of solitude, as though what lived inside him had left no room for another living being, or even a living thought. *He chose a good name*, Yukiyasa thought. "You do well here, my son?"

"As well as I may." Junko shrugged. "I hunt and fish for the folk here, and mend their poor flimsy dams and weirs, as I was raised to do. And they in turn shelter me, and call me *Wayfarer*, and ask no questions. I am where I belong."

To this Yukiyasa knew not what to say, and they two were silent again, until Junko asked finally, "Akira Yamagata, the horsemaster—he is well?"

"Gone these two years and more," the priest replied gently, for he knew of the friendship. Junko inquired after a few other members of Lord Kuroda's household, but not once about the *daimyo* himself, or about Lady Hara. Wondering on this, and thinking to provoke Junko beyond prudence, Yukiyasa began to speak of the successes of Masanori

Morioka. "Since you . . . since you left, the ascent in his fortunes has been astonishing. He is very nearly a Council of Ministers in himself now—and the lord being old, and without children . . . " He shrugged, leaving the sentence deliberately unfinished.

"Well, well," Junko said mildly, almost to himself. "Well, well." He smiled then, for the first time at the puzzled priest, and it was a smile of such piercing amusement as even Yukiyasa had never seen in all his long life. "I am pleased for him, and wish him all success. Let him know of it."

"This after you sent an *ushi-oni* to destroy him?" It was not Yukiyasa's custom ever to raise his voice, but perplexity was bringing him close to it. "You said yourself that you wished Minister Morioka dead and out of your way. Sayuri died of that envy." Startled and frightened by the anger in his words, he repeated them nevertheless, realizing that he had loved the woman who was no woman. "She died because you were insanely, cruelly jealous of that man you praise now."

Junko's smile vanished, replaced, not by anger of his own, but by the same weary knowledge that had aged his face. "Not so, though I wish it were. You have no idea how I wish that were true." He was silent for a time, looking away as he began to gather the seven salmon into a rush-lined basket. Then he said, still not meeting the priest's eyes, "No. My wife died because she understood me."

"What nonsense is this?" Yukiyasa cried out. He was deeply ashamed of his loss of control, yet for once refused to restrain himself. "I warned you, I *warned* you, in so many words, never again to coax her to change form— never to let her do it, for your sake and her own—and see what came of your disregard! She yielded once more to your desire, set forth to murder Minister Morioka, as she had slain others, and thereby rediscovered the terrible truth she had forgotten for love of you. For love of you!" The old priest was on his feet now, trembling and sweating, jabbing his finger at Junko's expressionless face. "Understand you? How could she understand such a man? She only loved, and she died of it, and it need not have happened so. It need not have happened!"

The sky was going around in great, slow circles, and Yukiyasa thought that it would be sensible to sit down, but he could not find his feet. Someone was saying somewhere, a long way off, "She loved me when she was an otter." Then Junko had him by the shoulders, and was guiding him carefully through the long journey back to the grass and the ground. In time the sky stopped spinning, and Yukiyasa drank cold brook water from Junko's cupped hands and said, "Thank you. I am sorry."

"No need," Junko replied. "You have the right of it as much as anyone ever will. But Sayuri knew something that no one else knew, not even I myself." He paused, waiting until the priest's color had returned and his heartbeat had ceased to shake his body so violently. Then he said, "Sayuri knew that in my soul, in the darkest corner of my soul, I wished her to go exactly where she did go. And it was not to Minister Morioka's quarters."

It took the priest Yuriyasa no time at all, dazed as he still was, to comprehend what he had been told, but a very long while indeed to find a response. At last he said, almost whispering, "The Lord Kuroda loved you. Like a son."

Junko nodded without answering. Yukiyasa asked him hesitantly, "Did you imagine that if Sayuri . . . if Lord Kuroda were gone, you might somehow become *daimyo* yourself?"

" 'Like a son' is not like being a son," Junko replied. "No, I had no such expectations. My master, in his generosity, had raised me higher than I could possibly have conceived or deserved, being who I am—*what* I am. In a hundred lifetimes, how should I ever hold any grievance against the Lord Kuroda?"

Twilight had arrived as they spoke together, and fires were being lighted in the nearest huts. Junko stood up, slinging the fish basket over his shoulder. Looking down at Yukiyasa, his face appearing younger with the eyes in shadow, he said, "But Sayuri knew the *ushi-oni* in me, the thing that hated having been shown all that I could not have or be, and that wished, in the midst of luxury, to have been left where I belonged—in a place just like this one, where not one person knows how to write the words *daimyo* or *shogun,* and *samurai* is a word that comes raiding and killing, trampling our crops, burning our homes. Do you hear what I am telling you, priest of the *kami*? Do you hear?"

He pulled Yukiyasa to his feet, briefly holding the old man close as a lover, though he did not seem to notice it. He said, very quietly, "I loved Lord Kuroda for the man he was. But from the day I entered his castle—a ragged, ignorant boy from a ragged village of which *he* was ignorant—I hated him for *what* he was. I spent days and years forgetting that I hated him and all his kind, every moment denying it in my heart, in my mind, in my bones." For a moment he put his hand hard over his mouth, as though to stop the words from coming out, but they came anyway. "Sayuri . . . Sayuri knew my soul."

A child's voice called from the village, the sound sweetly shrill on the evening air. Junko smiled. "I promised her family fish tonight. We must go."

He took Yukiyasa's elbow respectfully, and they walked slowly away from the river in the fading light. Junko asked, "You will rest here for a few days? It is a long road home. I know."

The priest nodded agreement. "You will not return with me." It was not a question, but he added, "Lord Kuroda has not long, and he has missed you."

"And I him. Tell him I will forget my own name before I forget his kindness." A sudden whisper of a laugh. "Though I am Toru now, and no one will ever call me Junko again, I think."

"Junko-*san*," Yukiyasa corrected him. "Even now, he always asks after Junko-*san*."

Neither spoke again until they had entered the village, and muddy children were clinging to Junko's legs, dragging him toward a hut further on. Then the priest said quietly, "She really believed she was human. She might never have known." Junko bowed his head. "Did you believe it yourself, truly? I have wondered."

The answer was almost drowned out by the children's yelps of happiness and hunger. "As much as I ever believed I was Junko-*san*."

LITTLE MOON, TOO, GOES ROUND

DAVID DUMITRU

[Aeon Thirteen]

KC Moss propped her shovel against the gate and scanned the horizon beyond the fence. A dust devil skipped for a moment across the prairie and then vanished, gone to nothing almost before she could pin a word on it. She bent and reached into the hole she'd been digging. Having lived most of her sixteen years on a farm a good deal past the end of the road where nowhere stops and turns around again, KC knew a thing or two about digging holes. Things died and the dead things got themselves eaten and whatever was left over started smelling pretty bad pretty quick, so it was important to get the leftovers in the ground lickety-split. On the other hand, all that digging wasn't so bad once you got used to it. You never knew what you might find. KC lifted a skull out of the hole and turned it in her hand.

She brought it to her nose and sniffed. It had a wet smell, like a potato just out of the ground—which it was, she reminded herself, just out of the ground. She sniffed again. There was another smell, too. She thought it was the smell of things someone might be looking for. She looked deep into the eye sockets. She was reminded a little of Eddie Johnson, not because it looked like him, which, now that she thought about it, it kind of did, but because Eddie Johnson had played Hamlet in the inter-district drama club last year. He was seventeen and thin as a whistle and he thought he was a hottie. He wanted everyone to call him Edward, but KC still called him Eddie, even to his face. People said he was going with a girl in the next district, but that was just a rumor.

KC held the skull at arm's length. She struck a pose and spoke in a deep, theatrical voice. "Alas, dear Yorkie, I knew thee swell." Or was it

163

Warwick? And was that actually from the play? She didn't know. She settled on Yorwick and let it go.

She heard a bell ring three times and then three times again. Supper. She finished burying the half-eaten billy-rat she'd found behind the barn earlier in the day, and with Yorwick in one hand and her shovel in the other she started back to the house.

On the way, she stopped to wade for a moment in a stream that cut deep into the soil to expose boulders veined with granite and shelves of limestone that overhung shallow pools and the crumbling walls of old safety bunkers that had turned out not to be so safe. Here and there were jumbles of bones from the wars and the sometimes comical remains of genetic mishaps from the pan-speciation that followed the breakout. The soil here was rich with the damp, earthy scents of lives-having-been-lived. KC had another sniff of Yorwick and sampled the air in comparison. Most of the hominid specimens she dug up from time to time came from hereabouts.

At the house, KC's grandmother was sitting on the porch peeling a basket of small, perfectly round potatoes. She wore a white denim shirt and blue jeans and she raised a leather-gloved hand in greeting. KC leaned her shovel against the porch rail and sat down. She cradled Yorwick in her lap and watched her grandmother work. She looked at the basket of potatoes and then at her grandmother.

"I thought I heard the supper bell," she said.

"You did," her grandmother answered. "But nobody's going to be eating until someone cleans these spuds and gets 'em in the oven." She smiled and took off her gloves and kissed KC on the forehead the way she did no matter if it had been ten minutes or ten hours since she'd seen her last.

KC put Yorwick down on the porch and took up the potatoes. She kicked at the bottom corner of the screen door so that it slapped against the frame and then popped open again. On her way into the house she said, "You shouldn't go over there by yourself," echoing a phrase she'd heard her grandmother utter a hundred-and-many times herself. It was generally safe in the potato fields, and the potatoes were good value, each one providing exactly seven grams of high-yield protein and two-hundred milligrams of omega 3 antioxidants. But it was better to go picking in pairs so that one of you could keep watch. The little tubers could be sneaky and the bite was painful, occasioning amputation and a prolonged and unpleasant limb-regeneration process. KC's comment went unanswered as she'd had known it would.

She went inside. It was quiet in the house. She dropped the skinned potatoes in the sink and watched them squirm as she turned on the water. She listened for a moment to the purling of the water and the rustling of a worried cabbage in its bin in the fridge. Through the screen door she saw the last squint of the sun above the horizon and heard her grandmother humming the melody of a nursery rhyme called Little Moon, Too, which told the story of some people who had traded their fortunes for berths on a satellite colony in order get away from the wars, and how they'd named the satellite Atlas after a book they'd all read. They'd promised to come back and save the world when the wars were over and the gene-splicing organisms had gone back into the labs where they belonged.

KC joined in at the end of the song, singing just loud enough to hear herself over the gurgles and gasps of the spuds as she plucked them from the sink and dropped them in a bowl of vinegar.

"Atlas shrugged," she sang,
"Atlas died
Up up in space
Where nobody cries
Round and round
Round and round
Round and round forever."

She left the potatoes soaking in the bowl to make sure they were dead, and went back out on the porch. A pinprick of light slid in a languid arc across the sky just above the horizon. Out of habit born of childhood games, KC lifted her shoulders in a shrug and made a wish upon Little Moon, Too.

Nobody knew what killed the Looners, but it was interesting to imagine them up there with their simulated gravity offline; desiccated bodies floating around, bumping into tables and portholes and things, and then spinning slowly off to bump into something else, like party balloons only not so shiny.

KC's grandmother picked Yorwick up from where KC had left him. She ran a finger along where the sagittal suture was supposed to be, at the crown of the skull, the cute little wandering crack where the parietal bones would have met if the skull was that of a pre-extinction human. But the suture wasn't there.

KC leaned in closer. She should have noticed it first thing. It meant that Yorwick had been hatched, not born. He hadn't had to squeeze his head into the world through a dark and narrow birth canal, partially collapsing it like the old-world humans.

"You found this where?" her grandmother asked.

"By the fence," KC said. "But I thought it must have come from the creek."

Her grandmother nodded once. "Might have. You can't tell some-times."

"But how?" KC asked. "How can something that's dead move around like that?"

"Oh, I don't know," her grandmother mused. "Some things aren't quite as dead as they appear to be, now are they?"

"Is it a sapiens postremus, do you think?" KC asked.

Her grandmother turned Yorwick over and peered into his vacant brainpan. "I think it's a prime. Restless bones. Trouble. The others'll be coming soon." She stood and brushed little bits of still-squirming potato skin from her jeans. "We'd better get ready. You get word to the doctor."

"Word to the doctor," KC echoed, "Yes, you're right." In truth, she had no idea whether her grandmother's implied wisdom was right or wrong or wholly irrelevant. Any way it came out, it gave her an excuse to get off the farm. She started off across the yard at a run. "I should probably tell Eddie's grandmother, too, don't you think?" she shouted as she crossed the shock-line and joined the road. She thought she heard her own grandmother say something that might have sounded like No, but there was already too much distance between them to be irrevocably sure.

It was nearly dark by the time KC got to Eddie's house and knocked on the door. The house was big, and situated in the middle of a gathering of buildings that KC's grandmother called a town. She'd explained that a town was a place where people used to live in herds, like toothcows, only not always trying to eat each other, the key word being always.

Eddie's grandmother answered the door. She was wearing a long, black dress with a frilly white collar that looked like it was choking her, like lady's lace, the delicate fungus that grew up the side of the barn in the springtime and then crawled off into the fields to hunt in the summer.

"Edward . . . " That's how she said it, all drawn out and dramatic . . . Edward . . . was "occupied elsewhere." The door closed, leaving KC standing there staring at it.

"Sheesh," said KC to the door. She promised herself that the next time she saw Edward she'd tell him that he ought to ask for a new grandmother, one with at least a little personality. Maybe she would mention it to the doctor.

An hour later, she approached to the doctor's house, perched atop Laboratory Hill, which was in fact just a mild, unruly episode in the otherwise catatonic flatness of the prairie. The night had settled in the fields and on the trees, chasing the shadows and the things that usually hid in them out into the world-at-large. The darkness was softened by Big Moon's rising up and spilling buckets of creamy white light down from the sky. All around, things were busy hunting, rooting in the weepgrass, and foraging in the canopies of the longfinger trees, just out of sight. KC sidestepped a duck-billed rip-mole prowling around in front of the doctor's house and rang the doorbell. She waited. Little Moon, Too twinkled in its graveyard orbit between Big Moon and the horizon, and KC shrugged for luck.

She rang again and called out, and the door at last swung open. The doctor peered out at her, broke after a moment into an uncertain smile, and stepped back from the threshold to let her in.

She told him about Yorwick and how her grandmother had sent her over.

The doctor's caterpillar eyebrows came together in a V. What little chin he had jutted out in a thoughtful manner. He nodded once, a little sideways, the way that doctors do, like he believed her but then maybe not.

"I haven't seen you in some time, KC," he said. "How are you two getting along out there? Is there anything you need?"

KC shook her head. "Everything's . . . " she started. She stopped cold. She craned her neck and peered past him through a set of paned glass doors into a little parlor off the entryway.

"Eddie?"

Eddie Johnson was sitting in a large, wing-backed chair in a corner, just visible from where KC was standing. She pushed past the doctor and stood looking into the room, gaping in spite of her efforts at self control.

The doctor came up behind her and put his hands on her shoulders. Gently, he steered her into a chair across the room from Eddie. "I'm sorry, KC," he said. "I should have said something earlier."

KC sat. She stared. Eddie stared back. Or into space, who could tell? His lips were thin, a pale shade of blue, turned up in a sleepy kind of smile. His clothes hung on the thinness of his frame as if it were them supporting him instead of the other way round. His hands lay limp on his thighs and the fingers seemed to KC strangely emaciated, gnarled and knobby where the joints bulged beneath the listless gray gauze of his flesh. The eyes were hollow chasms. And yet there was a spark in there somewhere, a faint presence, like moonlight on a fragment of bone at the bottom of a hole.

"So it's true," KC said. She perched, tense and fully aware on the edge of her seat, her senses probing through the house for the creak of a floorboard or the sibilant rasp of pent up breath. "Where is she?" She could not believe that she was about to lose her temper like this, and over Eddie no less—or rather, what was left of Eddie. On the other hand, she had a lot of time invested in Eddie, daydreaming time and night-dreaming time both.

The doctor attempted a confounded look at first, but eventually issued a sputtering sigh of resignation.

"Look at him," KC demanded. Dangerously close to shedding a tear and showing the doctor just how mature she wasn't, she added, "He mated, didn't he? He's going prime."

The doctor pinched the bridge of his nose. "Yes."

"Is she here?"

"No." The doctor shook his head. "She's not here." He pulled a chair close and sat, fingering his lapels, his round, jowly face going red. "I'm sorry, KC. I didn't know until just . . . "

KC opened her mouth but for once the words didn't come. Adults, she steamed, do they ever know what's going on? Is there something about getting old that makes you stupid?

The doctor sat back in his chair and tapped his chin and scratched his head like it hurt to think that hard. "I don't know how it happened." He dug in the pocket of his corduroy jacket and pulled out a little white box.

He fiddled with some keys on the side of it and handed it to KC. "Look for yourself," he said. "He hasn't been out of the district."

"Maybe he hacked his chip," KC scoffed, and was immediately sorry.

"You know that's not possible," the doctor answered, scolding only a little. "Males possess neither the intelligence nor the initiative for anything of the sort."

"Maybe your locator's broken." She flipped the box diffidently into his lap.

He picked it up and scrolled through a menu and handed it back again. "You see? You went to Eddie's before you came here. The locator's functioning."

KC closed her eyes, wishing she could vanish from the planet before they opened again. It didn't work. She went on the offensive. "You promised."

It was almost true. Although he hadn't actually guaranteed Eddie to her, he'd never said anything about inter-district, self-initiated breeding, either. And then it hit her. Inter-district. The inter-district drama club. Hamlet. Ophelia. The cast party. That bloody hussy.

While she'd been thinking it through, the doctor had been rambling on about something in his weird, hypnotic, biobotic doctor voice. " . . . evolution is a messy business, KC. Even directed evolution. Even in reverse. There are always mutations, deviations, little impromptu experiments going on. Of course, we'll run some tests, set up a control, take samples . . . baseline DNA . . . " Blah blah blah, KC lost the thread. " . . . habitat pressure, maybe . . . "

Finally, he stopped for a breath. KC could tell from the way he winced that she was looking at him like he was crazy. Habitat pressure. Right. There were only a few hundred free range hominids on the entire planet. The doctors kept tweaking the DNA and the DNA kept tweaking back. It could be thousands of years before there was a self-sustaining, breeding population that even remotely resembled Homo sapiens sapiens.

He started up again. "Patience, KC. You must have patience. You don't have the perspective that I have . . . "

No kidding, she thought. Perspective. Patience. She was sixteen. He was four hundred and something. He was on his fourth body with a new one gestating in a vat in the greenhouse out the back. She thought maybe he could use a dose of perspective with a capital P right up his . . .

The following night KC and her grandmother and the doctor stood along the fence near the gate looking out at the prairie. KC kicked absently at the dirt and her foot hit something hard and brittle. She looked down and saw a convex disk embedded in the ground. She recognized Yorwick, dug him the rest of the way out, and held him in her hand.

"How did he get here?" she wondered aloud.

"I don't know," her grandmother said. "But it couldn't have been easy for him. He must be quite keen to see this."

The doctor chuckled and lit his pipe. A cool breeze slipped through the weepgrass, making it sound even sadder than usual, and moonlight hung in the air like a mist of tiny glass beads. There was movement behind them and they turned to see Eddie coming through the fields, leaning hard on his grandmother's shoulder so that she was as good as carrying him. With them came another; a skinny, pallid, wasted creature with long, lanky dark hair. Her. She carried a bundle in her arms, blue-black and lustrous in the soft light. An egg. The stranger struggled a little with the weight of the egg, her attention given completely over to it, and nearly stumbled in a badgerweed hole. KC pictured the egg slipping down into the burrow and the yolk being sucked out like a milkshake through a straw. She heard something growling the in night air, a vicious sound, like a bone being slowly and deliberately crushed in the jaws of some malevolent beast. It took her a moment to realize that the sound was coming from her own throat.

"KC," her grandmother cautioned. "You'll behave yourself and you'll start doing it right this minute."

KC pasted a smile on her face but it kept falling off, so she turned her back and looked out across the fence and over the dark stillness of the plains. Something moved, and it wasn't a dust devil.

"Um," she said, "Is that them?"

Off in the distance, somewhere between the fence and the vague hem of the horizon there was a stirring, like a mouth in the darkness, opening to speak, only instead of words or voice, what issued forth was light. Faint at first, no more than a hint of a glimmer, it grew to a definite shimmer and then to a luminous, pulsating sphere that had no defined surface or boundary. It glowed blue, no, yellow, no, green. Now a brilliant red, like the feel of the sun on your skin on a hot day, and now a whirling, mesmerizing violet. It came across the prairie like a kind of purposeful wind, gliding, buffeting slightly from side to side. As it closed in, knots of color within the sphere separated out into individuals, a dozen, two dozen, more. Limbs, long and slender, came into view and became legs, four for each creature, not much more than spindles of bone with plump, round bodies suspended in the center like a spider's, like chatterbugs, skimming the surface of the ocean, quivering with bloodlust as they feed on shell mice coming up for air.

KC shaded her eyes against the light. She'd never seen a prime before; a post-reproductive, post-hominid male, let alone an entire pod.

The doctor nudged her shoulder, smiling. "Bio . . . " he started.

"Luminescence. Bioluminescence. I know," KC cut in. She looked at Eddie. He was still leaning against his grandmother. Miss Oaf-eelia, as KC had christened the interloper, stood next to him, oblivious, cooing vacuously at the egg like the mate-thieving harlot she was.

The animals came closer and KC saw the heads. Humanlike, only not quite. Like Yorwick. They were large, half-again KC's height, and covered all over in a velvety sheath, everywhere apart from the heads. It was the velvet that emitted the undulating glow, KC saw. One of them came close to the fence and she felt a need—a sudden, irresistible compulsion—to reach across and stroke its leg.

KC's grandmother grabbed her arm with a dexterity KC had forgotten the old surrogate possessed. "You want to die?" she scolded.

"That's how they hunt," the doctor said. "They lure their prey. The luminescence comes from parasites on the exoskeleton. They're toxic to the touch. That's why the primes stay on their side and you stay over here. If they came over, they'd wipe you all out and we'd have to start the whole project all over again."

"Open the gate." It was Eddie's grandmother. She stood erect and imposing in her long black dress with the high white collar, but her voice trembled just a little, just enough to notice. "It's time."

She brought Eddie closer, gave him a gentle shove. Spent and sagging, he approached the fence. The males pressed in a crush around the gate as KC's grandmother muscled it open on its rusted hinges. Eddie went through. His grandmother looked at the doctor, shook her head in shame and started through herself.

"Not you," the doctor said. "It wasn't your fault." He pulled her back to safety.

It took the animals only seconds to strip away what little flesh Eddie had left on his arms and legs. They swarmed, scraping at him with scissored claws at the ends of their forelegs. The luminous parasites swarmed too, pools of variegated light moving with a single mind, secreting an acid that dissolved skin and muscle but left the bones and the new body sac suspended in the middle. Eddie screamed once, a sound like an entire field of screech beans going off at the same time.

And then it was done. Eddie was no longer Eddie. The thing he'd become, Eddie-prime in the doctor's lexicon, flexed his new appendages, rolled his bony new head, and started off with the others, already on their way to wherever it was the primes went. All but one.

"That's your father," KC's grandmother said. KC wriggled her fingers in a tentative wave but the big prime ignored her. Her grandmother took Yorwick from her and handed him to the doctor, who handed him over the fence. The prime took the skull and sniffed at it, then went off with the rest.

KC watched them go until the light they shed had faded to a dim glow on the horizon. When she turned around, the doctor and her grandmother were gone, walking arm in arm through the knee-high weep grass back to the house. Eddie's grandmother followed at a short distance. Egg-girl stayed behind, looking every bit the promiscuous zombie-hag she was but trying to look all sorry about it just the same.

"I didn't know he was yours," she said with her head down and her eyes looking up all misty and plaintive into KC's. "It just happened."

"It's nothing," KC lied. She thought it was probably one of those good lies she'd read about. Eggie held the egg out and KC stroked the smooth, cool shell.

"The doctor'll find me another mate," she said. A better one, she almost said, but bit down on her lip before the words plunged out into time and couldn't be taken back. She looked up and saw Little Moon, Too flickering across the sky. She shrugged for good luck. Next year the drama club was doing A Midsummer Night's Dream and Joaquin LeMarc, from district ten, was a shoe-in for the part of Lysander. KC went back to the house to start practicing for the auditions.

THE BEHOLD OF THE EYE
HAL DUNCAN

[*Lone Star,* August]

The Imagos of Their Appetence

"The Behold of the Eye," Flashjack's laternal grandsister (adopted), Pebbleskip had told him, "is where the humans store the *imagos of their appetence*—which is to say, all the things they prize most highly, having had their breath taken away by the glimmering glamour of it. Like a particular painting or sculpture, a treasure chest of gold and jewels, or a briefcase full of thousand-whatever notes, or the dream house seen in a magazine, a stunning vista seen on their travels, even other humans. Whatever catches their eye, you see, she'd said, is caught *by* the eye, stored there in the Behold, all of it building up over a person's lifetime to their own private hoard of wonders. The humans say that beauty is in the eye of the beholder, you know, but as usual they've got it arse-about; what they should be saying is something else entirely."

"Beauty is in the Behold of the Eye," Pebbleskip had said. "So that's where most of us faeries live these days."

Flashjack had hauled himself up beside her on the rim of the wine-glass he was skinnydipping in, shaken Rioja off his wings, and looked around at the crystal forest of the table-top he'd, just a few short hours ago, been born above in a moment of sheer whimsy, plinking into existence at the *clink* of a flippant toast to find himself a-flutter in a wild world of molten multicolour-mandalas wheeling on the walls and ceiling, edges of every straight line in the room streaming like snakes. He'd skittered between trailers of wildly gesticulating hands, gyred on updrafts of laughter, danced in flames of lighters held up to joints, and landed on the nose of a snow-leopard that was lounging in the shadows of a corner of vision. He'd found it a comfy place to watch one of the guests perform an amazing card trick with a Jack of Hearts, so he'd still been hunkered there, gawping like a loon at the whirl of the party, and making little flames shoot out of his fingertips (because he could), when Pebbleskip came fluttering down to dance in the air in front of him.

"Nice to get out once in a while, eh?" she'd said. "Hi, I'm Pebbleskip."

"I'm . . . Flashjack," he'd decided. "What's *in a while*? Is it like *upon a time*? And out of what?"

Her face had scrunched, her head tilted in curiosity.

"*Ah*," she'd said. "You must be new."

Since then she'd been explaining.

The funscape had settled into solidity now, with the drunken, stoned and tripping human revellers all departed into the dawn, the host in her bed dead to the world, but through a blue sky window to the morning, sunlight slanted in to sparkle on the trees of wine-glasses and towers of tumblers all across the broad plateau of the breakfast bar. It painted the whole room with a warm clarity which Flashjack, being newborn, found easily as exciting as the acid-shimmered kaleidoscope of his birth. The mountains and cliffs of leather armchairs and sofa, bookcases and shelves, fireplace, fridge and counter were all very grand; the empty bottles had such a lush green glow to them inside; the beer-cans with the cigarette-butts were seductively spooky spaces, hollow and echoing; even the ashtrays piled high with roaches had a heady scent. As Pebbleskip had been explaining, Flashjack had been exploring. Now he dangled his legs over the edge of the wine-glass alongside her, surveying his domain.

"You mean they'd keep all this in their Behold?" he said. "Forever?"

"Nah, probably not," said Pebbleskip. "Mostly they'd think this place was a mess. The rugs are nice, and it's kind of cosy, but they'd have to be a quirky bugger to Beholden this as is. No, if this place was in the Behold it'd probably be a bit more . . . Ikea."

Flashjack nodded solemnly, not knowing what *Ikea* meant but assuming it meant something along the lines of *goldenish*; the sunlight, its brilliant source and bold effect, had rather captured his imagination.

"You'll see what I mean when you find your Beholder, said Pebbleskip, which you'll want to be doing toot sweet. I'd take you home with me, see, but two of us in the same Behold? Just wouldn't work, ends up in all sorts of squabbles over interior design; and the human, well, one faery in the Behold of the Eye, that just gives them a little twinkle of imagination, but more than one and it's like a bloody fireworks display. They get all unstable and *artistic*, blinded by the glamour of *everything*, real or imagined, concrete or abstract. They get confused between beauty and truth and meaning, you see, start thinking every butterfly-brained idea must be true; before you know it they've gone schizo on you and you're in a three-way firefight with all the angels and the demons, them and their bloody *ideologies*."

Pebbleskip sounded rather bitter. *Best not to ask*, thought Flashjack.

"I'm not saying it can't work sometimes," she said, "but a lot of humans can't handle one faery in their Behold, never mind two. Mind you, if you find one that's got the scope . . . well, it can be a grand thing . . . for all the arguments about where to put the Grand Canyon."

She looked kind of sad at this, Flashjack thought.

"Anyway, I'm off. My Beholder's too fucked from the come-down just now to know I'm gone, but she'll miss me if I'm not there when she wakes up."

And with that Pebbleskip whirled in the air, and swooped to slip under the door, Flashjack darting after her, crying, "Wait!" as she zipped across the hallway and into the bedroom. He poked his head round the door to find her standing on the host of the party's closed eyelid.

"How do I find my Beholder?" he said.

"Use your imagination," she said.

"But how will I know if it's the right human?"

"They'll know you when they see you," she said.

And disappeared.

The Azure Sky and the Golden Sun

Using his imagination, because he wasn't terribly practiced at it and couldn't think what else to do, simply took Flashjack back to his birthplace in the kitchen/living-room, where he sat down dejectedly with his back to the trunk of a bonsai tree on top of the fridge, gazing out of the window at the azure sky and the golden sun rising in it, at the backyard of grass and bushes and walled-in dustbins, the blocks of sandstone tenement ahead and to the left, all with their own windows facing out on the same backyard, some windows lit, some dark, but each with different curtains or blinds, flowerpots on a ledge here or there, and the odd occupant now and then visible at a window, making coffee, washing dishes, pottering, scratching, yawning. Using his imagination then, because he was a fast learner, had Flashjack quickly off his arse, his face pressed through the glass, realising the true potential of his situation.

There were a lot more rooms in this world than he'd previously considered.

Slipping through the window with a pop, he spiralled up into the air to find yet more tenements beyond the rooftops, roads and streets of them, high-rise tower-blocks in the distance, a park off to his right, a ridiculously grand edifice to the west which, a passing sparrow explained, was the university building, in the mock-Gothic style, and not nearly as aesthetically pleasing as the Alexander "Greek" Thomson church across the road from it. He snagged the sparrow's tail, clambered up onto its back, and let it carry him swooping and circling over the "West End" of the "city" (which was, he learned, called Glasgow), nodding as it sang the praises of its favourite Neo-Classical architecture. The sparrow had a bit of a one track mind though, and Flashjack wasn't getting much of an overall sense of the Big Picture, so with a *thank you, but I must be going* he somersaulted off the bird to land on a chimney, considered his options for a second then, rising on the hummingbird blur of his own wings, he hovered, picked a random direction, and set off at his highest speed.

An hour later he was back where he'd started, sitting on the chimneypot, prattling excitedly to a seagull about how cool the Blackpool Tower is.

"Ye want to be seeing the *Eiffel* Tower, mate," said the seagull. "Now that's much more impressive."

"Which way is that?"

Having been instructed in all manner of astral, magnetic, geographical and meteorological mechanisms for navigation, in a level of detail that raised suspicions in Flashjack that all birds were rather obsessively attached to their own pet subject and lacking in the social skills to know when to *shut the fuck up about it*, he set out once again, returning a few hours later with a very high opinion of Europe and all its splendours—including, yes, the Eiffel Tower.

"Better than Blackpool by a long shot, eh?" said the seagull.

"What's Blackpool?" said Flashjack.

It was at that point that Flashjack, after a certain amount of interrogation and explanation from the seagull, who had met a few faeries in his day, came to understand that it would be a good idea to find a human to get Beholden by ASAP.

"See, they do the remembering that yer not very good at yerself," said the seagull. "Memory of a gnat, you faeries. If I'd known ye weren't Beholden yet, I wouldn't have sent ye off. Christ knows, yer lucky ye made it back."

"How so?"

"Yer a creature of pure whimsy, mate. What d'ye think happens if there's no one keeping ye in mind? Ye'll forget yerself, and then where'll ye be? Nowhere, mate. Nothing. A scrap of cloud blown away in the wind."

Flashjack looked up at the azure sky and the golden sun, which he'd only just noticed (again) were really rather enchanting. He really didn't want to lose them so soon after discovering them, to have them slip away out of his own memory as something else took their place, or to have *himself* slip away from *them*, fading in a reverie to a self as pale as those sensations were rich.

"Go find yer Beholder, mate," said the seagull. "Yer already getting melancholic, and that's the first sign of losing it."

Flashjack was about to ask how, when his now rather more active imagination suggested a possible plan; to get Beholden obviously he'd have to attract someone's attention, catch their eye so as to be caught by it. Being a faery, he reasoned, that shouldn't actually be too difficult. Over in the park, he'd noticed in passing, a whole grass slope of people were lazing in the afternoon sun, drinking wine, playing guitars or just lying on their backs, clearly the sort of wastrels who'd appreciate a bit of a show. So with a salute to the seagull, Flashjack was off like a bullet, over one roof, then another, a gate, a bridge, a duck pond, and then he was directly above the slope of sun-worshippers, where he stopped dead, whirling, hovering, spinning in the air, reflecting sunlight from his whole body which he'd mirrored to enhance the effect, so that any who looked at him and had the eyes to see might imagine he was some ball of mercury or magic floating in the sky above them. Or possibly a UFO.

He wasn't sure who he expected to Beholden him, but he did have a quiet hope that they'd be someone of relish and experience, the Behold of their Eye full to bursting with the things they'd seen and been struck by. In fact, it was Tobias Raymond Hunter, aged nine months, currently being wheeled by his mother and escorted by his toddling older brother, who looked up from his pram with blurry, barely-focused vision and saw the shiny ball in the sky.

A Rather Strange Kind of Room

There was a *pop*, and Flashjack found himself in what he considered a rather strange kind of room. The Behold seemed to be the inside of a sphere, its wall and ceiling a single quilted curve of pink padding, which Flashjack, being a fiery type of faery, born of drink, drugs and debauchery, was not entirely sure he liked. Added to this, it was velvety-silky-smooth and warm as skin to the touch; in combination with the pink, it was like being in a room made of flesh, which Flashjack, frankly, found either a little creepy or a little kinky. He wasn't sure which, and he had no *specific* aversion to kinky as such, but the whole feel of the place . . . he just wasn't sure it was really *him*. Still, the three most striking features of the Behold very much *were*: above his head wheeled coloured forms, simple geometric shapes in basic shades, but radiant in hue, positively glowing; beneath his feet, layer upon layer of snow-white quilts, baby-blue blankets and golden furs formed a floor of luxuriously cosy bedding wide enough to fit a dozen of him; and in front of him was a great circular window, outside of which the sky was bluer than the bright triangle circling overhead, the sun more golden than the fur between his toes.

What with the breast/womb vibe, the primary-coloured mobile and the oh-so-cosy bedding, it didn't take Flashjack too long to figure out where he was. It wasn't quite what he had been hoping for, he had to admit, but there was a certain encompassing comfort to the place. He flopped backwards onto the bed, wondering just how far down into the cosiness he could burrow before hitting the bottom of the Behold. As an idle experiment, just out of curiosity, he imagined the mobile overhead changing direction, spinning widdershins instead of clockwise. It did.

"Okay," he said. "I think this'll do nicely."

"No, no, no," said Flashjack, "this just won't do."

It wasn't the sand or the water that was the problem per se so much as the fact that they were in entirely the wrong place. It was all very well for Tobias Raymond Hunter to love his sand-pit and his paddling pool, and for the bed to have changed shape to accommodate these wondrous objects in the Behold of his Eye, but the boy clearly had no sense of scale; they took up half the bloody room. And to have them both, well, *embedded* in the bed, that was just silly. At the moment the bed was cut into a thin hourglass by the sand-pit and the paddling pool; add to that the fact that more and more of the remaining space was being eaten up by Lego bricks, lettered blocks and other such toys, and Flashjack was now left with only the thin sliver between sand-pit and paddling pool to sleep on. He wasn't a big fan, he'd discovered, of waking up spitting sand or sneezing water because he'd rolled over in his sleep and been dumped in the drink or the dunes. No, it just wouldn't do.

He sat on top of a lettered block and studied the situation for a while then set his imagination to work on it. When he was finished, the paddling pool covered the whole area of the floor that had once been bed. Within that though, the sand-pit was now a decent-sized island with the bright blue plastic edge of it holding back the water. In the centre of the island, the Lego bricks and lettered blocks were now a stilted platform, with blankets, quilts and furs forming his bed atop it, and a jetty reaching out over the sand and water, all the way to his great window out into the world.

"That's a damn sight better," said Flashjack.

"Da' si' be'r," said Tobias Raymond Hunter, giggling as Flashjack performed his *Dance of the Killer Butterfly* for the tenth time that day. He never tired of it, it seemed to Flashjack, but then neither did Flashjack, as long as the audience was appreciative. As Tobias Raymond Hunter patted the palms of his hands together in an approximation of a hand-clap, Flashjack gave an elegant bow with a flourish of hand, and started it all over again.

"Da' si' be'r! Da' si' be'r! Da' si' be'r!" said Tobias Raymond Hunter.

His father, entirely unaware of Flashjack's presence and convinced that his son was referring in the infantile imperative to his own (*Da*) singing (*si*) of what was apparently Toby's favourite song, *Teddy Bears' Picnic* (*be'r*) was meanwhile launching into his own repeat performance with somewhat less enthusiasm. As much as he was growing to hate the song, he did put his heart into it, even using Toby's own teddy bear, Fuzzy, as a prop in the show, though Toby, for all his enthusiasm, seemed to pay little attention to it until halfway through the third chorus (Flashjack, by this time, having finished his eighteenth performance (his *Dance of the Killer Butterfly* being quite short) and decided to call it a day), whereupon the previously ignored Fuzzy became an item of some interest.

In the Behold of the Eye, Flashjack was guddling goldfish in the paddling pool when Fuzzy came dancing out of the forest of sunflowers that now obscured most of the pink fleshy walls.

The bear was one thing, but this was getting ridiculous. Flashjack knew what was to blame; it was that bloody bed-time story that Toby was obsessed with. Oh, it might seem all very innocent to his parents but, like Toby's brother, Josh, who he shared his bedroom with and who groaned loudly each time the rhyme began—*that's for babies!*—Flashjack was getting deeply tired of it. No one had ever told him (as far as he remembered) that the Behold of the Eye might turn into a bloody menagerie of fantastic animals, flions soaring through the air on their great eagle wings, manes billowing as they roared, little woolly meep getting underfoot everywhere you go, rhigers charging out of the trees at you when you least expect it, giraphelant stampedes . . . and the rabbull was the last straw. *The rabbull is quite funny, half bull and half bunny, with horns and big ears that go flop.* Funny. Right. *Because when it sees red, it'll lower its head, and go boingedy-boingedy-BOP!* Well, Flashjack had had quite enough bopping, thank you very much, and did not consider the rabbull funny in the slightest.

"We're going to have to do something about this, Fuzzy," he said, standing on the jetty looking back at his Lego-brick tropical jungle-hut, and rubbing the twin pricks on his arse-cheeks where he'd been bopped from behind. "They're bloody overrunning us," he said.

"Fuzzy," said Fuzzy, whose vocabulary wasn't up to much.

Flashjack turned to look out the window of Toby's eye, at the azure sky and the golden sun, which were particularly new to him today. He wished he could get out there, get away from the zoo of the Behold even just for a few hours, but Toby, it seemed, was not as . . . open as he once was. Last time Flashjack had decided to pop through the window he'd found himself nursing a bopped nose. That's another problem with being a creature of pure whimsy, you see; when your Beholder grasps the difference between real and imaginary, as they're bound to do sooner or later, they decide that a faery must be one or the other, mostly the other. Flashjack gazed at the blue and gold.

"See that?" he said. "That's what we need. Room."

Not just *a* room, he thought. But *room. Space.* He looked down at the water below, sparkling with the blue of the sky even though the ceiling above, which it should have been reflecting, was pink, and he wondered if . . . with just a little tweak . . . if he could draw that blue sky out of it . . . it shouldn't be that hard for a faery . . .

And the Behold of the Eye was, after all, a rather strange kind of room.

In The Land of His Stories

Flashjack leapt down from the giraphelant's back and flicked his flionskin cloak back over one shoulder as he strode across the savannah to the cliff then, dipping so his feathered headdress wouldn't catch on the lintel, entered the darkness of Fuzzy's cave.

"I've had an idea, mate," he said cheerily. "I've had an *inspiration*."

"Fuzzy," said Fuzzy pathetically.

If Flashjack had thought about it he would have regretted his words; The poor bear had been getting tattier and glummer ever since his own *inspiration* had been lost (or so Toby's parents claimed; Flashjack suspected foul play on the part of Josh, sibling rivalry and such), and Toby's infantile attention slowly turned to other objects of desire. So *inspiration* was rather a button-pusher of a word for Fuzzy, who was fading week by week and now convinced that the process of being forgotten would eventually end with him disappearing entirely. If Flashjack had thought about it he might have tactfully rephrased his boast. Flashjack, however, partly because he was a faery and dismissed such fatalism with a faery's disregard for logic, and partly because he was a faery and had little sense of the impact of his words on others, simply breezed into the cave and hunkered down before his old friend, a glinting grin on his face.

"Fuzzy, me boy," he said, "if you want to call me a genius right now, feel free to go ahead and do so, or if you want to wait until you hear my Plan, then that's just as good. Either way, I cross my heart and hope to die, stick a needle in my eye, but fuck me if I haven't found a solution to your problem."

"Fuzzy," said Fuzzy.

"Why, thank you," said Flashjack. "Okay, come with me."

It had been a while since Fuzzy had visited the island, so when the good ship *Jolly Roger* docked at the new jetty and the monkey crew leapt off to moor her soundly, despite the three day voyage, the general glumness of the bear, and the actual purpose of the visit, Flashjack blithely forgot the fact that they were actually there to *do something* in his keenness to show just how much improvement had been made. The old jetty now had a troll under it, the island now had its own lake—*with an island on it, with a castle, and a beanstalk going up to the clouds, and there's a castle there with a giant in it and everything!*

"Fuzzy," said Fuzzy impatiently.

"Okay, okay," said Flashjack and took him in to his stilted jungle-hut (which was now all but covered in vines, barely recognisable as Lego-bricks and lettered blocks), shifted the bicycle with stabilisers (which Toby's brother, Josh, refused to let him ride), sat him down on the pouffe (which Toby had seen at an aunt-and-uncle's house and thought a strange and wondrous thing, this chair with no back), took a seat on the ottoman himself (which Toby's parents had in their bedroom and which, being half backless-chair and half treasure chest, was even more wondrous than the pouffe), and began to explain his Plan.

Toby, Flashjack had realised, had become utterly enchanted with the fairy stories once read to him at bedtime, now devoured over and over again by Toby himself. He'd come to desire adventure, to yearn for it, such that the Behold of the Eye was blossoming with new wonders every day. He wanted a dreamworld to escape to, the place that Puss-in-Boots and Jack-the-Giant-Killer and the Three Billy Goats Gruff lived. These were the imagos of his appetence, so here they were in the Behold of the Eye. But something was missing in the land of his stories.

"He wants a monster," said Flashjack. "I've looked out of the window as he checks under the bed, looks in the closet, or opens his eyes in the dead of night and sees scary shapes in the patterns in the curtains. It frightens him, of course, so he can't *admit* he wants a Monster, but it thrills him too. You can't have a land of adventure without the giants and trolls and the Big Bad Wolf, but the ones he's Beholden, well, they're straight out of the cartoons. I just *know* he wants something more."

"Fuzzy?"

"Well that's where you come in."

The sky overhead darkened with nightfall, the sun descending from the wheeling mobile of moon and stars and planets to sink below the horizon and let the shadows escape from beneath the canopy of trees and slink up and around them, shrouding the island till only the flickering glow of the great pyre of a night-light on the beach was left to light Flashjack and Fuzzy as they stood down by the water's edge.

Flashjack reached up into the darkness, up into the sky, and plucked a sliver of moonlight, kneaded it and rolled it out like plasticene then blew on it—*puff!*—to make it hard as bone. He did it again, and again, kept doing so until there was a pile of moon-bones there before him. He grabbed the silver of the surf and made a pair of scissors to cut Fuzzy open, then one by one he put the moon-bones in their place. Then he caught a corner of the night between thumb and forefingers and peeled away a layer of it which he snipped into shape and started sewing onto Fuzzy with a pine-needle and vine-thread, a second skin of darkness to go with his skeleton of moon-bones.

Flashjack was very proud when he sat back and looked at the Monster he had created.

A Perfectly Ordinary Kouros

The books arrived slowly at first. For a long time it was jungles with pygmies and dinosaurs, deserts with camels and wild stallions, forests with wolves, mountains with dragons, oceans with sea serpents. There was one burst of appetence where Flashjack woke up one day to find the blue sky ceiling of the Behold just gone, inflated out to infinity, the planets and stars of the mobile suddenly multiplied and expanded, scattered out into the deep as whole new worlds of adventure, and spaceships travelling between them, waging inter-galactic battles that ended with stars exploding. He would fly off to explore them and get drawn into epic conflicts which always seemed to have Fuzzy behind them, or Darkshadow as he now preferred to be called (which Flashjack thought was a bit pretentious). He would find magical weapons, swords of light, helmets of invisibility, rayguns, jet-packs, some of the snazziest uniforms a faery could dream of, and with Good on his side he'd defeat Fuzzy and send him back to the darkness from whence he came. After a while he began to find himself waking up already elsewhere and elsewhen, a life written around him, as an orphan generally, brought up in oblivion (but secretly a prince). This was a lot of fun, and for a long time Flashjack simply revelled in the fertility of his Beholder's appetence, the sheer range of his imagos. For a long time, whenever he woke up in his own bed he would leap out of it and run down the jetty to look out the window in the hope of catching a glimpse of whatever book Toby was reading now, some clue to his next grand adventure. For a long time it was simply the contents of the books that were Beholden by the boy. Then, slowly at first, the books themselves began to arrive.

It's a very nice bookcase, Flashjack thought to himself, but why a boy of his age should be Beholdening bookcases is frankly beyond me. I mean, a chair can be a throne, a table can hold a banquet, a wardrobe can be a doorway to another world, but a bookcase? A bookcase is a bookcase is a bookcase. It's not exactly bloody awe-inspiring.

He paced a short way down the jetty towards the island then wheeled and paced back, stood with his hands on hips staring at the thing. It wasn't ugly with its dark polished wood, clean-lined and solid. It was even functional, he had to admit, because he could replicate a whole bundle of the buggers from this one, and he could really use something to store the mounds of books—leatherbound tomes, hardbacks with bright yellow dust-covers, cheap paperbacks with yellowed pages and gaudy covers—that were piling up everywhere these days, appearing in his bed, on the beach, in rooms in the castles, clearings in the forests, caves in the mountains; he'd found a whole planet of books on his last interstellar jaunt. But *functional* was not an aesthetic criteria that Flashjack, as a faery, had terribly high on his list of priorities; it was well below *shiny* and nowhere near *weird*.

It was, in his considered opinion, actually rather *dull*.

"It's safe," said a voice behind him.

Flashjack turned, but no one was there.

The statues began to appear not long after the Voice Incident. There had been statues appearing for years, of course, along with the busts and reliefs, even a whole colossus at one point—Toby had clearly gone through a romance with all things archaic as a side-effect of his absorption in the adventures of ancient myth—but where before the statues had just seemed another facet of the cultural background, set-dressing for the battles with minotaurs, chimaera, hydra and what-not, these were different. Flashjack didn't notice it with the first one; it seemed a perfectly ordinary *kouros* of the late Classical tradition, in the mode of Lysippos. He didn't notice it with the second one, which looked fairly similar but carried a certain resemblance in the facial features to statues of Antinous commissioned by the Emperor Hadrian, though he'd clearly been rendered here as he would have looked in his early adolescence. He didn't even notice it with the third one, which was quite clearly a young Alexander the Great. It was only with the fourth, the fifth, the sixth and the seventh that Flashjack, starting to wonder at Toby's . . . consistency of subject matter, took a quick flight out to his galleon built of bookcases, went down into the captain's quarters and, after a few hours cross-referencing the Beholden statues with the images in the books (from which, of course, in a previous period of idle perusal he had learned everything he knew about Lysippos, Antinous and Alexander (and if you're wondering how he managed to remember such things when he couldn't even remember the sun in the sky, well, Flashjack was by now a faery on the verge of maturity, beginning to reach a whole new level of inconsistency)) and realised the discrepancies.

On a factual level, he could find no traces of such statues actually existing out in the world. On a stylistic level, there were a number of deviations from the classic S-shape of the contrapposto pose, hips cocked one way, shoulders tilted the other. And on a blindingly obvious level, which had not occurred to Flashjack simply because he was a faery and had little concept of decorum never mind prurience, the sculptors of the Classical period did not, on the whole, tend to give their statues erections.

"Our little boy is becoming a man," said Flashjack to himself, smiling because, as a faery, he also had little concept of heteronormativity.

"My power grows every day, old friend," said Fuzzy.

"Now's not the time for the Evil Villain routine," said Flashjack. "I'm worried about Toby. Books and statues, statues and books. And now this."

They walked through the library that had appeared over the last few weeks, coalescing gradually, as shelves appeared, thin slivers in the air at first then slowly thickening, spreading, joining, walls doing the same, until the whole place had just . . . crystallised around Flashjack's island home, sort of fusing with the structure that was already there, almost matching it, but . . . not quite. Flashjack's bed was on a mezzanine floor now (with the

Children's and YA Section) which hadn't even existed before. Downstairs from this, in the centre of the structure and facing the entrance (flanked by twin flions), where his bed *should* have been, was a counter-cum-desk thing that ran in a square, four Flashjacks by four Flashjacks or so; with the computer and the card files and the date-stamp and the oven and the dishwasher and so on, clearly it was meant to fuse the functions of librarian's desk and kitchen area. Beyond this was the main library-cum-living-room (which mostly consisted of the SF/Fantasy Section). There were even male and female bathrooms, which Flashjack avoided; he quite enjoyed pissing where there was snow to piss in, but he'd tried the whole dump thing once and just wasn't impressed with the experience. And everywhere there were the bookshelves, everywhere except the Romance section, which was like a museum with all its statuary.

All in, the place wasn't much bigger than Flashjack's hut, so it wasn't a grand library; in fact, it reminded Flashjack quite strongly of the public library he often saw out of Toby's eye, the boy spending so much time there these days; it seemed that he had come to adore his literary sanctuary so much that it had become his dream home, usurping the more Romantic jungle-hut of Flashjack's preference. Now Flashjack was quite okay with his *own* reimaginings of Toby's imagos, but now that the tables were turned he was feeling rather put out. It just wasn't healthy, a teenage boy Beholdening a dream home full of books. And a haunted one at that.

"You don't get it," said Fuzzy. "My power grows every day, old friend."

"Look, I'm just not in the mood to play Good versus Evil today, Fuzzy. I heard the Voice again this morning, over in the Romance section. *It's safe. It's safe.* That's all it keeps saying. There's something wrong with our Beholder."

"You don't understand," said Fuzzy. "That's what I'm worried about. Whatever's happening to him is making me stronger, more vital. More intense. I'm his monster. And I feel like a fucking god some days."

Flashjack turned to look at Fuzzy, who had stopped asking to be called Darkshadow a while back, and would now simply laugh bitterly and say: *I have no name, Flashjack.* His skin made out of the night itself, he seemed a black hole of a being, an absence as much as a presence.

"And I have . . . urges," said Fuzzy. "I want to burn this place to the ground, I want to smash those statues to dust, and I want to feast on that Voice, make it scream itself out of existence and into silence."

Fuzzy was getting rather over-dramatic lately, thought Flashjack.

_____

The Ghost of an Imago

Most weekdays it rained corpses, faceless, gurgling blood from slit throats. Flashjack would sit in the library, listening to the pounding on the roof, or stand to look out the floor-length windows and watch the bodies battering the jetty, falling out of the sky like ragdolls of flesh, slamming the wood and bouncing, slumping, rolling. He'd watch them splash into the water, sink and bob back up to float there, face-down, blood spreading out like dark ink until the sea itself was red. The troll under the jetty, who never showed himself these days, would be a dark shape in the water after the showers of death, grabbing the bodies and dragging them down into the depths; Flashjack had no idea what he was doing with them, wasn't sure he wanted to know.

The lake on the island was on fire. The island on the lake was choked with poisonous thorns. The castle on the island was in ruins. At the top of the beanstalk which was now a tower of jagged deadwood, bleached to the colour of bone, the giant sat in his castle, eyes and lips sewn shut, and bound into his throne by chickenwire and fish-hooks that cut and pierced his flesh. Flashjack had tried to free him, but every time he tried the wire grew back as fast as he could cut it. Flashjack wept at the giant's moans which he knew, even though they were wordless, were begging Flashjack to kill him; he just couldn't do it.

The worst were those that Flashjack *could* kill, the torture victims who were crucified, nailed to stripped and splintered branches, bodies dangling in the air, all the way up and down the thorny tower of the dead beanstalk. He recognised the faces he had seen through the window of Toby's eye, laughing in crowds, he knew that these were imagos of tormentors tormented, imagos of vengeance, and when he'd tried cutting them down they simply grabbed for him with madness and murder in their eyes; but he couldn't suffer their suffering, not in the Behold of the Eye, which was meant to be a place of beauty, and so he put them out of their misery with his knife as they appeared, most weekdays, one or two of them at a time, just after the rain of corpses.

When the body of the Voice manifested, it was that of Toby himself, or of a not-quite-Toby. Where Toby was dark-haired, not-quite-Toby was fair.

Where Toby was pale, not-quite-Toby was tanned. Where Toby was slight, not-quite-Toby was slim. Where Toby wore jeans and a tee-shirt, trainers and a baseball jacket that just didn't look right on him, not-quite-Toby wore exactly the same clothes except that on him they looked totally right. Where Toby moved with the gangling awkwardness of a growth-spurted adolescent not yet in full control of all his limbs, not-quite-Toby rose from the chair in the library's living-room with the limber grace of an athlete, an animal. He strolled up to Flashjack, where he stood at the entrance, one hand reaching out to lay the book he had been reading down on the countertop of the librarian's desk, the other reaching out to stroke the purring gryphon guard at Flashjack's side, in a fluid move that ended with an offered handshake.

"It's safe," he said.

"Why is it safe?" asked Flashjack, shaking his hand.

The ghost of an imago, the imago of a ghost of Toby looked up at him with a wry smile, a raised eyebrow. Something about the causal self-confidence was familiar to Flashjack—a hint of Toby's brother, Josh, maybe, or someone else he couldn't quite place.

"I'm not gay," said not-quite-Toby.

He laughed, patted Flashjack on the shoulder and turning, plucking his book back off the countertop, sauntered back to his chair, plumped down on it and put his feet up on the coffee-table.

"Hang on," said Flashjack, whose curiosity about the word Toby so furiously scrubbed from his school-bag had led him to some startling realisations. "I mean, I've seen what Toby looks at when he's wanking, mate. You've only got to look at his—"

It was then, as his hand raised to point and his head turned to look, that Flashjack noticed the statues in the Romance Section were all now draped in white sheets, and not-quite-Toby's smile was that of Josh when he'd bested his little brother easily in a sibling spat, of the tormentors after Flashjack had put his knife into their hearts, or of Toby, some days, when he just stood looking in the mirror for minutes at a time while corpses rained in the Behold of his Eye.

Fuzzy was smashing the statues with a crowbar that had been matted with blood and hair when it appeared in the Behold. With every statue that was smashed, the ghost of an imago, the imago of a ghost of Toby gave out a scream of blue murder and tried to curl himself into a tighter ball. With every statue that was smashed not-quite-Toby was less and less the easy, graceful, carefree straight boy that Toby wanted to be, more and more another version of the lad, another not-quite-Toby: one that was not just dark-haired but dark of eye and fingernail and tooth; one that was not just pale but corpse-white; one that was not just slight but skeletal; one that tore at his jeans and tee-shirt till they hung as rags; one that moved in twisted, warped, insectile articulations.

With every statue that was smashed, Flashjack just whispered, *no.*

"He's killing us," Fuzzy had snarled. "He's killing *himself. They're* killing him. *He's* killing *them.* Don't you get it, Flashjack? Don't you fucking get it? Can't you see what's being Beholden here every fucking day?"

He'd fought his way through a five-day hail of corpses that sunk his ship, hauled himself up onto the jetty with the troll's broken, bone-armoured body slung over his shoulders, hurled it through the doors of the library and stormed in, caught the defending gryphons by the throat, one in each hand, snapped their necks. Flashjack had roared to the attack, swashbuckling and heroic, a sword of fire whirling over his head, and been batted out of the air with a backhand slap.

Fuzzy had grabbed the crowbar from the coffee table, where Flashjack had been studying it, worried, and strode into the Romance Section, ripped the sheet off the first statue. Not-quite-Toby had run at him in a frenzy of rage, horror, fear, despair, but he'd not reached Fuzzy before the crowbar swung, connected with the white marble and shattered it utterly.

Now Fuzzy swung the crowbar for the last time, shattered the last marble statue and, as the thin shards of stone flew in every direction, the last beautiful corpse of Toby's stone-bound desire slumped to the library floor amid the dust of its thin shell. Fuzzy grabbed the stillborn imago by the hair and hauled it up so Flashjack could see and recognise the face, one of Toby's tormentors but, oh, such a good-looking one. Fuzzy turned on the wretch of a not-quite-Toby, pointing the crowbar at this thing now cowered in a corner, hissing, spitting madness at the revelation of its untruth.

"This is what Toby wants to be," he snarled. "Aren't you?"

"Fuck you, fuck you, fuck you, fuck you!"

"You're the imago made of his self-pity and self-loathing."

"Fuck you!"

"And just what is it that you are? Inside, beneath the lie? What do you *really* want to be? Tell him! Say it!"

The creature lunged, tears streaming down its face, clawed fingers out.

"I want to be *dead*!"

And the shadow that was Toby's Monster and the most loyal of all his imagos swung the crowbar in a wide arc, hard and fast, and brought it down with a sickening crunch upon the skull of not-quite-Toby.

"You can't do this, Flashjack. I can't let you."

"Was your solution any fucking better? Was it? You thought if you just shattered the lies, made him face the truth, that would make it all peachy? That it wouldn't be the final fucking straw?"

Around them the storm was raging through the Behold of the Eye, a fiery hail of planet-shards, stars falling from the heavens, smashing everything beneath it, burning everything it smashed, in an apocalypse of desire. The ruin of the library burned. The island itself burned. Every castle and kingdom, every city and savannah, forest and field, all the Beholden wonders of Toby's dreamscape burned. Only Flashjack and Fuzzy were able to stand against the scouring destruction, the one more fiery than the flame itself, the other darker than the blackest smoke, only them and the tiny broken piece of jetty that they stood on, Flashjack firing jets of ice-water into the sky like anti-aircraft fire, shattering the burning hail above them into sparks, and desperately trying, at the same time, to focus his concentration on the pile of bodies that he knelt over.

"I can do this," he said. "I can give him something to hold onto, something to want."

His fingers worked furiously on the flesh and bone, twirling and tweaking, squeezing and stretching, two skeletons into one bone, muscle woven around muscle around muscle then stitched into place.

"He doesn't *want* to want," snarled Fuzzy. "He *wants* to *not* want."

"I can make him want," said Flashjack.

At its core a heart that had once been not-quite-Toby, its body built of all the imagos of thwarted yearning, the boy would be beautiful when Flashjack was finished. He would be all Toby's desire-to-have and desire-to-be fused into one, and he would be irresistible, undeniable.

"I can't let you do that," said Fuzzy. "He *wants* me not to let you do that."

Flashjack looked up at the crowbar in the shadow's hand, then up at the empty darkness where the face should be. Had there been eyes, Flashjack would have stared straight into them with a fire the equal of the holocaust around them.

"Does he?" said Flashjack.

And as the shadow swung, a solid wall of ice smashed up through the wood between them, sparkling with the blue clarity of the sky but solid as a storm door, and though the shadow brought the crowbar down on it like a pick-axe, again and again and again, left a hairline crack and a smear of red blood, the wall did not break as Flashjack raised his finished creation up, cradling its head in his arms, and lowering his face to breathe himself into it with a kiss.

His Prison of Glass

Flashjack huddled in his prison of glass, watching the flames ravage the Behold of the Eye, engulfing everything, even boiling the very waters of the seas, setting fire to the coral and seaweed and dead fish of their dry beds. Soon there was nothing to be seen but the fire or, once in a while, a dark shape striding through the inferno, stopping to raise its arms, turning, revelling in the desolation. Flashjack watched this for a long time—he wasn't sure how long—arms wrapped round his tucked knees, missing his wings and his innocence. His strange new body was a work of art, but he wasn't exactly using it for what it was meant; he should be out there in the Behold, being shameless in his enjoyment of it, offering Toby an imago of desire unbound. But it wasn't safe. It just wasn't.

He waited, expecting Fuzzy to come back and try again to smash his way into the sanctuary and cage Flashjack had made for himself, turning water into ice, ice into glass. Fuzzy, however, was too busy with his new position as king of hell. So he waited, expecting the flames to burn themselves out any day now, any day, reasoning that once the broken dreams which fuelled the inferno were all stripped away to nothing, then the very lack of anything to care about would kill it; the fire would consume itself.

The fires of hell burned on.

Flashjack huddled in his prison of glass, watching the boy outside batter his fists against it. He buried his face in his crossed forearms, but it didn't really help; he couldn't hear the screams, which comforted him a little when he curled up in a ball at night and tried to sleep, but even when he closed his eyes he could see this new generation of tormentors tormented, each arriving naked and afraid, to be broken, mutilated, maimed for days, weeks, months, and then their skin stripped off, sewn to moon-bone structures speared into their shoulders until, eventually, they rose from the carnage of themselves, spread wide their ragged leather wings and joined the ranks of the tormentors to set upon the next new arrival.

Occasionally, something pretty, something beautiful would appear but it didn't last long; everything else almost immediately smashed and soiled by the demons, ruined and then burned, only those few imagos which had appeared inside Flashjack's glass prison had been spared destruction. There was the last remnants of the jetty, of course, now reshaped into a little palette bed of driftwood. On the floor was sand, soft and warm and golden, which had trickled down one day over his shoulder, as if through invisible fingers. There was a smooth pebble and a sea shell which Flashjack held now, one in each hand, wondering if in holding on to them, in being himself something to hold on to, he was only perpetuating the pain, if by letting the walls fall and walking out to let the demons tear apart the last vestiges of desire he could perhaps bring it all to an end. He couldn't do it.

Flashjack huddled in his prison of glass, his back turned to the horrors of the Behold, looking out the window of Toby's eye at the azure sky and golden sun. Then the vision shifted and there was a face, laughing but with warmth rather than cruelty, a friend mugging ridiculously, pushing his nose into a pig-snout with a finger. The boy's life was not bereft of happiness, kindness, joy; his world had autumn leaves, crisp winter snow, the buds of spring, and it had summer, hot and shimmering summer days like this when Flashjack would press his hands up to the glass and yearn to bring that sky and sun back into the cavernous waste of the Behold. Toby's friend mouthed something, listened to the response then laughed, went bug-eyed with his disbelief—*no fucking way, man*—and Flashjack wondered how his Beholder could be in a friend's good company, laughing and joking, and yet still so desolate of desire.

For the umpteenth time that afternoon, Flashjack lifted the little shard of mirror that had dropped into the sand in front of him a few mornings ago. He held it up as close to the glass as he could get it, angled it this way and that.

When you see someone with a twinkle in their eye, you must under-stand, often that twinkle is their faery flashing a little mirror to see if you too have a faery in your Behold, a little *how-do-you-do?* from one sprite to another. But sometimes what seems like a twinkle of whimsy might well be a glint of madness, the faery in the Behold of their Eye sending a desperate SOS in the hope that someone, anyone, will help.

For the umpteenth time that afternoon, there was no answer.

Flashjack woke with a start, and rubbed sleep from his face, ran his fingers through his hair. And felt the dampness of his fingers. And saw—

The Behold of the Eye was dark and empty, and he was wet from the drip-drip-drip of the ceiling of his prison of glass which had become a prison of ice and—as he clambered to his feet and reached out to touch the wall—now transformed again, losing its form completely and collapsing, in a rush of water, to soak into the sand beneath his feet and into the ash beyond. The window at his back, Flashjack peered into the gloom, but there was nothing, no fire, no demons, only darkness.

Yes, it's me, said the darkness, in a voice that Flashjack knew and that, for a second, frightened him, knowing as he did what Toby's Monster was capable of. Then he realised there was something different in its tone, something that was far more awful than the bitter, raging thing that had smashed the statues, far more terrible than the dark, despairing thing that had stood above him with a crowbar and with nothing where its eyes should have been. But he also knew, somehow, it wasn't a threat.

"You don't want to kill me," he said.

It doesn't matter any more. Nothing does.

The words sent a chill down Flashjack's spine.

"I don't understand."

The darkness said nothing, offered no explanation, but it seemed to coalesce a little, a vague shape, black upon black, that stood back a ways from Flashjack and off to one side, staring out the window. Slowly, Flashjack turned, not understanding what he was seeing at first, a cup of tea held in Toby's hands, the family dog sat in front of the armchair, looking up at him, people milling in the living-room—an aunt and uncle visiting, it seemed, and more—Toby's father in the kitchen at the phone, his mother getting up off the sofa to make more tea, wiping her eyes, his father dialling another number, and talking, then dialling another number, and talking, then dialling another number, and talking, and Toby was just watching him now, transfixed on him, though it seemed like he was saying the same thing over and over again, except now he wasn't saying it at all, just dropping the phone and burying his face in his hands, and Toby had turned to stare straight ahead at the TV set with the framed photograph on top, of Josh.

Then there were tears running down the window.

A Handful of Forevers

All through the funeral Flashjack worked. As the car drove them to the church, Toby looked out to one side, and suddenly there in the Behold was a shimmering image of the road the car was on, the spot they were passing, with Josh standing there, sun in his hair, hair in his eyes, about to step out but *not* stepping out, caught in an eternal moment. Flashjack grabbed the road and pinned one end to the window of Toby's eye, threw the other out into the ashen darkness as far as it would go, as far as Toby could want it to go, which was forever, and the fields unrolled from its verge as far as the eye could see, a moment transformed into eternity.

As the family sat in the church, oblivious of the minister's mute mouthings over the boy he'd never, as far as Flashjack was aware, had the slightest contact with, Flashjack took the frozen moment of a Josh-who-did-not-step and, grabbing every glint of a spark of a memory that appeared in the Behold, layered in the smiles and the strut and the style and the spats and the football trophies and the record collection and the David Bowie poster and all the vanity and cockiness and sheer shining brilliance that was Josh-before-he-stepped.

As the car pulled out of the driveway of the church and, out on the high street, an old man walking past came to a stop and took his hat from his head, then stood to attention with a sharp salute for the hearse of a total stranger, Flashjack grabbed the flood of unspoken gratitude, the tears of a Toby overwhelmed by the gesture, by wanting so much to respond, to say how much that simple silent respect said all that could or should be said in the face of death, and from the tears Flashjack made a sea, from the sea he made an azure sky, and into the sky, fashioned from the sunlight in the hair of the imago standing before him, Flashjack hurled a golden sun to light and warm Josh on his road into eternity.

As the coffin of polished mahogany slid slowly away through the red velvet curtain, Josh disappearing forever into the beyond of the crematorium, into the fire and the ash and the smoke, Flashjack grabbed the funeral pyre and the Viking longboat and the mausoleum and the torn lapels and the fistfuls of hair, the whole vast stupid spectacle of grief that Toby conjured in the Behold of his Eye, as if any monument or ritual could be sufficient, as if any monument or ritual could even begin to match the scale of his sorrow. And Flashjack turned the pyre into an autumn forest of yellow, red and orange leaves; he turned the longboat into a dragon that soared up into the sky, its sails now wings, to swoop and soar and turn and dive and bury itself deep in the earth, a vast reptilian power coiled within the land, *alive*; he turned the mausoleum into a palace, the palace into a city, the city into a hundred of them, each no larger than a grain of sand, a handful of forevers which he scattered out across the Behold to seed and grow; then, with the hair, he stitched the torn lapels together around his own body until he had a harlequin suit, not formed of elegant diamonds of black and white, but rather a rough thing of rags as rich a brown as the earth.

He turned to the imago of Josh-who-did-not-step, Josh-before-he-died, Josh-who-*did-not-die*, the Josh that Toby would now always and forever want so much and so unattainably with a desire that made all other desires seem as inconsequential as ash scattered to the wind; and Flashjack bowed, beckoning along the road with a twirl of his hand.

Epilogue

It should not be assumed that this ending, this new beginning was, for Toby, a moment of apotheosis which healed all wounds and banished all horrors. There were many bleak times in the years of Flashjack's journey with Josh into the wilds of the Behold, times when the old darkness would rise again in other forms, and fires would burn in the cities of the Behold. Although it was impossible for Toby to deny the crystal clarity of his yearning for an endless summer day of azure sky and golden sun and green fields in which his brother still lived, although from this imago whole fields of illusion sprang under Flashjack's dancing feet, filling the Behold of the Eye with new wonders, and although, somewhere along the long and winding road, it became clear that many of the imagos now popping into existence daily were clearly reflections of Toby's own appetence rather than grave goods for his lost brother (the shepherds fucking in the meadows were more than enough evidence of that, Flashjack thought), still, sometimes the wind would carry smoke and ash, and sometimes, when the storms rose, there would be a deep crimson tint to the clouds, a hint of blood and fire; and Flashjack would raise his eyes to the heavens, hoping not to see a falling corpse. It took Toby many years to learn to cherish life again.

But when he did, as he did, Flashjack was amazed at the vibrancy of the boy's reborn desire. It wasn't that the imagos it created were grand and exciting, wild worlds of adventure. If anything, many of them were so subtle that Flashjack nearly missed them: the swirl of grass in a field blown by the wind, the delicate streaks of stratocirrus in the sky; the way an orange streetlight on sandstone at night could give a building a rich solidity, like in some old master's oil painting. But all these imagos, Flashjack understood, spoke of an appetence that craved reality, that relished life, a passion for the fragile moments of beauty that might pass unnoticed if one were not, like Toby it seemed, all too aware of how ephemeral they were. So he knew that a change had taken place. It was only when Flashjack found the teddy bear lying in the field of long grass, however, that he truly realised how deep this change had been. The bear was smaller, and it didn't dance—didn't move at all—just a normal, everyday teddy bear, slightly tatty, but there was no mistaking this imago of an appetence out of lost childhood. There was no mistaking the bear, and there was no mistaking the darkness in his eyes, empty of rage now, empty of hate, not a darkness of lost hope but a darkness of quiet sorrow.

"I remember that," said Josh. "It was his. Fuzzy."

His tiny hand reached out to pluck the bear from Flashjack's grasp.

"I'll take it back to him," the little boy said.

He turned and began running across the field, head no higher than the grass. Flashjack took a step after the child, smiling to himself as he thought of the Grand Quest he could make of this, but a voice, low and resonant in his ear, brought him to a halt.

Let him go, said the wind in the grass, the emptiness that was, perhaps,

Flashjack thought, the real spirit of the Behold. *Let him go*, it said. *I'll look after him from here. He wants me to. Go home.*

Flashjack nodded, but he stood for a long while, watching the boy disappear into the grass, bear in hand, before he turned to leave.

It was years since he'd last stood looking out of the window of Toby's Eye, and with the healing of the boy's desire Flashjack was curious to see what new marvels he might find back where it had all begun. So what did he find there? Well, perhaps, in keeping with the most noticeable effect of that transformation, we should phrase it like this: What should he find there, but another faery! Why, there he was, sitting on the branch of an apple tree, sipping wine of the very richest red and smoking what can only be described as the Perfect Joint, rolled so straight and so smooth it seemed a veritable masterpiece. Batting his iridescent wings in the wind, picking dirt out from under his fingernails with his little kid-horns, or scratching and scruffling his green tousle of hair, he seemed quite at home

"Who the fuck are you?" said Flashjack. "Where did you come from?"

"A'right there," said the other faery. "I'm Puckerscruff. I'm a faery. You're a lust-object imago, right? Not bad, not bad at all. Taste *and* imagination; I knew I'd picked the right Beholder. Fancy a toke?"

"Wait a minute. *I'm* the bloody faery here," said Flashjack. "This is my Behold. Go find your own sodding Behold."

"Pull the other one, mate. Where's your wings?"

Flashjack's wings popped out on his back in a fit of pique as he crossed his arms. Puckerscruff looked surprised, then suspicious, then worried, then guilty.

"Look, mate, there wasn't a twinkle. I checked and there wasn't a twinkle. He was looking to Beholden someone, *itching* to, *bursting* to, and my hoary old tart was boring me towards self-lobotomy, so I was on the lookout for new digs, and this place seemed empty, see, so I thought, well, I can put on a little show just on the off-chance, while they're gazing into each other's eyes and doing the old tongue tango, right, and . . . and . . . hey, don't look at me like that. If he hadn't been *looking* for a faery, I wouldn't be here, would I? Seems to me like *someone* must have been neglecting his duties. Too busy making whoopee with the porn imagos, eh? Sorry, OK, OK, I take that back. I didn't mean it. It's just . . . please . . . don't make me go back. He's a fucking label queen, all fashion and no style, imagination of a seagull, does my fucking nut in. You and me, mate, you and me, we'll be a team, a twosome, a dynamic duo. I'll show you tricks you never dreamed of, mate."

All through this speech Flashjack had been gradually advancing on Puckerscruff who had been backing away, hands raised placatingly, but at this last sentence Flashjack stopped. Through the window, he could see, Toby was looking down over the sweep of his own chest and stomach towards the head bobbing up and down at his groin.

"What kind of tricks?" said Flashjack.

So Puckerscruff showed him.

It should not be assumed that this ending, this new beginning was, for any of the parties involved, a moment of cathartic release in which sexual identity was affirmed and all insecurity banished. For Toby it was by no means the first time and it was by no means the last step. For Flashjack it was one of the most spectacular experiences he'd ever known, but not quite, he claimed rather tactlessly, as good as when *he* did it. For Puckerscruff it was merely one in a long line of sexual adventures, and while Flashjack was a definite looker, he was a barely competent lover, clearly in need, Puckerscruff thought, of some good solid training.

So the Behold of the Eye was not transformed in an instant to utopian bliss. The rains of shattered albums, storms of semi-molten mixing decks and exploding glitterballs that followed most of Toby's explorations of the gay scene were, as far as Flashjack was concerned, a complete pain. He felt—and would say so loudly and repeatedly—that if Toby wanted to get laid so bad but found the clubs such a bloody agonising ordeal then Toby should just go to the bloody park at night and look tasty in the trees. In truth, he was worried—though he did not say this at all—that Toby didn't do the *cruising* thing because he was, on some level, still uncomfortable with his sexuality. Puckerscruff on the other hand, who had been horrified by his old Beholder's lack of musical taste, and who now revelled in Toby's imago of an ideal record collection, would bounce through these storms, fists flying, punching and head-butting the debris as it rained down, singing *Anarchy In The UK* at the top of his lungs.

It also has to be said that Flashjack and Puckerscruff were, as his laternal grandsister (adopted), Pebbleskip, had once warned Flashjack, not always the most tranquil of couples, with the result that more than a few arguments ended with the Behold divided in two as *your half* and *my half*. And what with two faeries in the Behold of his Eye rather than one, as Pebbleskip had also once warned, Toby's passions did at times tend to the intense, the glint in his eye more a fireworks display than a twinkle; Flashjack and Puckerscruff could see it in the way he drank and smoked, and partied and painted . . . and always with gusto. But Pebbleskip's talk of glory and truth, angels and demons was long since forgotten, so it was something of a surprise when the invasion came, though not *too* much of a surprise given the hallucinogen Toby had dropped a few hours before and the fact that Flashjack and Puckerscruff were now having a rare old time outside, whirling and twirling as they performed Flashjack's updated, two-man *Dance of the Killer Butterfly* to Toby's great amusement, his idea of the boundary between real and imagined being rather relaxed right now. It was Puckerscruff who noticed the demons crawling out of a corner of the room, first one, then another, then more, very soon a whole host of them, and angels too.

"Yeah, right," he said. "Not a chance, mate. You lot can just fuck off."

Then he and Flashjack began a variation of the *Dance of the Killer Butterfly*, this time aimed in the general direction of the angels and demons, with a little extra jazz hands. By the time it was over so was the invasion, the inventions of visionary rapture fluttering up into the air on their iridescent wings, every one of them reborn in a pirouette of pure whimsy.

"That's a damn sight better," said Toby.

LINKWORLDS
WILL McINTOSH

[*Strange Horizons*, March 17-24]

The world we were linked to was named Cyan, because of its color, blue-green with specks of yellow at the equator. It blotted out almost sixty percent of the blue and yellow sky. It looked like a gigantic curved wall, and it scared me because when I looked straight up part of Cyan was above me, and it felt like it could fall on me even though I knew that was impossible.

If I looked very closely, I could see roads and buildings on Cyan. There was movement in the sky between Allberry and Cyan: four to five thousand silver specks—a flock of flying puffer fish, migrating from Allberry to Cyan.

I did not want to live on Cyan, but Father said that passing a family name on to another world was a great thing, and that I should try my very best on the tests so I would be picked to live on Cyan, even though I would never see Father or Mother, or my sister Leela or my brother Hamn, or my uncle or my aunt, ever again.

When we were at the front of the line, an emigration staff member led us into the visitors' hall, which was a big empty room. The empty space made me feel dizzy and sick, so I sat on the floor and put my head between my legs.

The floor was made of shiny clear marble, and there were tiny skeletons of odd plants and animals embedded in it. Mother said I couldn't look at the floor now, maybe later, because they were waiting to give me my test, so I got up and held on to Mother with both hands and pushed my face into her shoulder so I wouldn't see all the empty space, but it still felt bad because I knew the empty space was there.

The testing room was smaller. The tester was a Cyanese woman. She was tall and thin, like she'd been stretched, and her eyes were set at angles instead of being horizontal. She told me to sit in the chair across the desk from her, then she told Mother to wait outside. I screamed when Mother let go of my hand, because I was completely surrounded by empty space, and she told me she'd be right outside, but that wasn't close enough, so when she closed the door I got up from the chair and tried to sit on the tester's lap. But she told me I had to sit in the chair across from her. So I did, but it felt very bad, so I wrapped my arms around myself and hummed the Yellow Bird song.

There was a big glass bowl on the tester's desk, and it was filled with about twenty-eight hundred marbles, painted to look like tiny worlds. I couldn't tell exactly how many marbles there were, because I didn't know the size of the bowl, but I recognized some of the worlds they were supposed to look like. I didn't like the way all the worlds were piled on top of each other, because that's not how the worlds are. Worlds have lots of space between them, and they whiz around, and they bounce off the edges of the universe and whiz back toward the middle, or they bounce off other worlds, only worlds don't collide much any more because people steer them with their singing.

"Kypo," I said, pointing to a black marble with a yellow stripe around its middle. I pointed at a green one; the green got darker toward the poles. "Cimsily."

"Yes, that's fine," the tester said. But she wasn't looking to see which marbles I was pointing at, so how did she know it was fine? She was fussing with a box of things behind her that I couldn't see, but I had seen it for a moment when I tried to sit in her lap.

She took out a booklet. "All right, Tweel. The first part of the test is about current events and issues on your world," she said. "What are the names of the six High Council members on Allberry?"

I said I didn't know.

"What is Semple Figsing?"

I said I didn't know.

She went on asking questions, and I went on saying I didn't know, until she put away her booklet and took out a box with 16 holes in the top. She told me that things would pop out of the holes, and I had to touch the blue and green ones, but not the red and yellow ones, before they went back into their holes. I didn't touch many blue and green ones. I saw what color they were very fast, but I have slow fingers.

More boxes and booklets came and went. Then the tester said, "The next part of the test is pattern acuity."

I sat up straighter in the chair. I liked patterns.

She held up a picture of gold-colored leaves connected by straight white lines. There were thirty-seven leaves and 162 lines in the picture.

"Which of the leaves disrupts the pattern?" she asked.

Disrupt meant misbehave, so I pointed to the bad leaf—the one that made me feel a little sick.

She held up another. "And in this one?"

I pointed.

Each picture had more and more leaves in it, which made it easier to find the disruptive leaf. The tester was looking at me now, and she was making an O with her mouth, and I wondered if I had done something that Polite People Don't Do, but all I was doing was pointing at leaves, so I decided that wasn't why she was looking at me. I decided she was looking at me because I was good at patterns.

She took out a new kind of picture, a swirl of nuts and berries and other fruits that looked as if I was looking down on them from above.

"Now, which single object does the pattern most hinge upon?" she asked.

"Hinge upon" sounded like a friendly thing to do, so I pointed at the friendliest one, a barberry toward the top left corner.

When I'd finished a bunch of "hinge upon"s, she came out with pictures of pretty colored stones, and asked, "Which, if removed, would cause the least shift in the existing pattern?" That would be the shyest, if it caused the least shift to the others, so I pointed out the shyest stone in each picture.

The tester stared at me, and I liked that, because the room didn't feel so empty when she stared at me. I still would have preferred to sit in her lap. She called out her instructions quicker and quicker as she went along, and the answers leaped at me before she even asked the questions, and I twisted my head sideways to catch a glimpse of the next picture as the tester was pulling it from the bag. The pictures came quicker; her voice seemed like it was filled with foreign sounds, pops and screeches, and my heart pounded with joy, and the empty space didn't matter any more because I was hugged by the puzzles that came from her bag. I laughed and was very, very happy.

Then, all at once, she stopped pulling pictures from her bag.

"Don't you have any more?" I asked.

The tester turned her palms up. "I'm sorry, that's all."

I cried, because I wanted to do more puzzles, but the tester came around her table and put her arm around my shoulder as she led me to the door, and that helped. And she said, "Tweel, I think you'll soon get to play with more patterns than you've ever dreamed of." And that helped even more, so I wiped my eyes on the sleeve of my shirt and sniffed to stop the dribble from my nose.

When I saw Mother I ran to her and hugged her hard and told her how many leaves were in each picture and how many nuts and berries and fruits and stones and how many marbles were on the tester's desk.

Father told me that I had scored very high on the test, and that Cyan would let me immigrate, and I would work as an Assistant Navigator. He was very proud, and so was Mother, and my sister Leela, and my brother Hamn, and my uncle and my aunt. I was sad, and scared, and that night I huddled close to my sister Leela and my brother Hamn and cried until I fell asleep with my face pressed against Hamn's damp nightshirt.

I didn't like the trip to Cyan. A Cyanese man put me in a harness and attached me to a very thick rope along with 47 other people who had been accepted for immigration. Then he turned a crank, and we were lifted into the air, and I was completely surrounded by empty space, and I screamed and hit myself because the pain made the empty space leave me alone. I went up, higher and higher, and the tugging on my harness got lighter, until I was almost floating, and I was still screaming, and it was hard to breathe, and I felt dizzy. Then I felt tugging on my head, and then my body flipped around and I was dropping toward Cyan, and the tugging from Cyan got stronger and stronger until my feet touched the ground.

I screamed and pulled at my harness until a man came and tried to take it off me. It took a long time, because I kept hugging him.

"Tweel! Who is Tweel?" a man shouted while I was still being unhooked. The man had a pointy white beard with a black streak in it, but no hair on his head. He was tall; he looked even more stretched than most Cyanese.

I raised my hands so he would know I was Tweel. He came right over and greeted me, and said his name was Mallowell, and that he was the chief of navigational science on Cyan, and I would be assisting him.

"You're a curious one," he said, while I wiped tears from my cheeks. "You're very good at some things, and very bad at others." He looked into the sky and made a *humph* sound, then he looked at me again. "Fortunately, all of the things we're responsible for are the things you're very good at!" Then he got very happy and he laughed, and patted me on the head, which I liked.

Cyan was nothing like Allberry. The ground was mostly silver stone instead of red clay, and there was almost no flat land at all; everywhere it was steep ups and steep downs. Steps were carved all over, leading in every direction, crisscrossing each other between buildings made out of the same silver stone and also transparent stone. Blue-green water raced through channels cut in the stone, and sometimes the stairs went over the channels. Because of all the running water, there was a hissing sound in the air that hugged you wherever you went. I liked that. I don't like silence.

Mallowell took me on a tour of my new home, the Science and Propulsion Center, and I stayed close to him, because there was so much open space and not many people. I didn't understand my home. We stopped in a room where people stood on pedestals of different heights and sang different notes while an old wrinkled Cyanese woman hopped around pointing a long forked stick at them. Another room had walls made of the transparent stone, and was filled with water. We didn't go into that room.

When it was time to go to sleep, Mallowell led me to a room that was as big as my whole house on Allberry, and told me it was my room, and showed me where my bed was, and where to store the stick I use to clean my teeth, and my satchel of spare clothing, and my softstone.

Then he left me all alone. As soon as he closed the door I screamed, because I had never been alone before. I heard Mallowell call through the door that there was nothing to be afraid of, that he was just next door.

There was no one at all to look at, only things, and none of the things were even moving, and I felt like I was falling down a deep hole. I ran to the window and looked into the sky so I could see worlds moving, and I recognized one of them, Spin, which I had last seen when I was nine years, 557 days old.

From the west, a giant world drifted into view, blotting out the edge of the sky. Though I had never seen this world in the sky, I knew it was

Allberry. Allberry was going away, and my family was going with it, and I might never see them again because worlds rarely link twice.

I watched Allberry as it moved east and shrunk at the same time. I pressed my cheek against the window pane, watching out the edge of the window until Allberry sank out of sight behind the trees to the east. Allberry was pink and red and yellow and orange, and I would watch the sky every day until I saw it pass again, and I would wave to my mother and father and sister Leela and brother Hamn and aunt and uncle.

I changed into my night clothes and went next door to Mallowell's room, and as quiet as I could so I wouldn't wake them, I climbed into bed between Mallowell and his wife, Seery, who I'd met at lunch.

Just as I was drifting off to sleep, the bed jerked, and Seery yelped and jumped out of the bed.

"Tweel? What are you doing?" Mallowell said. "You can't sleep here."

"Why not?" I asked.

"It's just not what people do," he said. I got up and went back to my own room, and got into my own bed and hugged my knees, and I couldn't stop shaking, but I finally fell asleep and then I probably did stop shaking, but I don't know because I was asleep.

My work place was Mallowell's laboratory. It was filled with big stone pots and circles made of transparent stone, and instruments with strings that might have made music but I didn't think so. There was a big hole scooped out of the ceiling and floor in the middle of the room, forming an open sphere, and in it thousands of marbles like the ones on the tester's desk hung suspended from strings. Light glowed from behind the ceiling and floor, just like the light that glowed in the sky.

"Mhyyrl," I said, pointing to a white marble with grey speckles. "Littleboom. Pellpinnin. Allberry!" I pointed to each one. I liked Mallowell, because he let me stay very close to him.

"Yes, very good!" Mallowell said. "We're not starting from scratch, then."

Then Mallowell started to talk. He called it a *lecture*. He told me all sorts of things about the worlds. Some of the things I already knew, but most of it I didn't know. I listened so hard I nearly forgot how empty the room was, and my heart pounded so I could hear it in my ears. When Mallowell told me something especially new, sometimes I cried, because it was so beautiful it made me happy and sad at the same time.

He told me the universe is shaped like a giant sphere, and when a world reaches near any edge of the universe, the edge pushes it back, toward the center. And that before people developed propulsion for their worlds, they would bounce off each other, and people would be crushed. That's why there are too many people on most of the worlds now, because no one is getting crushed. Mallowell estimated that Cyan had sixty thousand people on it (although he hadn't counted all of them to know this for sure), and that some worlds now had over one-hundred thousand.

But the most beautiful thing he told me was that the movement of the worlds makes music that we can't hear, and that the note each world sings as it moves depends on how far it is from the center of the universe. He showed me this on his model, by holding marbles tight so they didn't bob around, then plucking strings of different lengths. The strings made different notes when he plucked them. He said this was how propulsion works: we change the song our world sings by singing along with it, at just the right place, singing just the right songs, and this causes the world to move differently.

Mallowell said he wanted to map all the worlds in the universe, so he could understand it better, and predict how worlds moved in it. Then we would know where all the worlds were likely to be (unless they were using propulsion, which he called *error variance*) even when we couldn't see them. And best of all, my job was to help him!

"I want you to go outside once a day, always at midday, and draw a picture of where all the worlds are in the sky," he said.

"I can start yesterday," I said.

"Yesterday?" Mallowell said. "Don't you mean tomorrow?"

I shook my head, and picked up a softstone and sheet of parchment from Mallowell's work table, and sketched all the worlds that were in the sky when I looked at them midday yesterday. Then I pointed to the ones I knew and told him their names, and then I told him the worlds I'd seen before, and when I'd seen them.

Mallowell made an O with his mouth, just like the tester had done. He put his hand on my shoulder. "You—" he swallowed. "You can remember every world you've ever seen? And the date you saw them?"

I nodded.

Mallowell hugged me so hard that he squeezed a huff of air out of me. He spun around in a circle, and because he was hugging me I spun in a circle, too. He laughed and laughed, and said I was solid gold and a genius. I told him he was the genius, because he knew a lot more things than me. That night I got into my night clothes and waited until some time had passed, then I went down the hall and I wriggled into bed between Mallowell and Seery as quietly as I could.

But Seery still woke up, and huffed, and nudged Mallowell awake. He propped himself up on one elbow and looked at me, and I looked back at him and smiled.

He said "Now, Tweel, we've gone through this once. You can't sleep with us."

"Can I sleep near you?" I asked.

"How near?" he said. I pointed to the floor.

"Would that be acceptable, love?" Mallowell asked Seery.

"You're a lucky man to have me, Mallo," she said.

"I am indeed. Thank you, love."

Mallowell fetched me a big armful of quilts and weaves, and I made a nest at the foot of their bed.

"Till tomorrow, Tweel," Mallowell said, lying back down.

"Till tomorrow," I answered. "Till tomorrow, Seery."

She laughed. "Till tomorrow, Tweel. You'd better not snore."

I don't think I snored, because in the morning Seery didn't say that I did, but I don't know for sure because I was asleep.

A few days later, while I was making drawings of what worlds were in the sky when I lived on Allberry when I was four years and six days old, Mallowell told me that Cyan was going to link with a world called Ork in two days. Mallowell would meet with Ork's navigational scientists to exchange ideas, and he was going to bring me with him, because I was his assistant.

"Exchanging ideas is far more valuable than exchanging goods or people," Mallowell said later, while we were adding worlds and adjusting locations on his universe map. He was using his lecture voice. "We build on each others' ideas, and they spread. If the world that invented propulsion had not linked with other worlds and exchanged ideas, propulsion would not have spread, and we would still be living in constant fear of collisions."

"I think ideas are like the universe," Mallowell went on. He was holding his wooden angle-measure in one hand, and three marbles—which were new worlds to be added to the map—in the other. "Each thing we know is like a world, spinning about in our heads, and when two things we know collide, they see if they fit together in some interesting way. If they don't, they bounce away; but if they do, they cling together and change each other before bouncing away. And this is how ideas are formed."

I watched the three marbles in his hand, pressing against each other in a clump.

"Why not three?" I asked.

"Three what?"

"Why not three ideas colliding together at once, and seeing if they all fit together in some interesting way?"

"I suppose it could be three. Why not? Or four, or ten."

Mallowell opened his palm and chose one of the marbles, which represented Elto because it was grey on one hemisphere and silver on the other. I made the squeaking sound that I make when things shift in a way I don't like.

Mallowell looked at me. "What?"

"I want them to cling together. They're not done seeing if they fit together in some interesting way."

Mallowell looked at the marbles. They were shiny and smooth; his palm was rough and wrinkled. He looked at me.

"It doesn't have to be three at once. Two ideas can clump together, and then two different, and then the third two, and they will have passed on the same information as if they all three had clumped at once."

I shook my head no. I didn't know how to explain it, but I knew two, two, and two wasn't the same as all three at once. I could picture why in my head. I tried to explain.

"Two-idea links are lines. A three-idea link is a triangle. It's not the same as three straight lines."

Mallowell looked at me, thinking so hard some of the wrinkles on his face scrunched together.

"You're talking about worlds, aren't you? You're suggesting that linking three worlds at once to exchange ideas would advance knowledge faster than if they all linked separately?"

I nodded yes, because that was what I was suggesting. I liked science very much.

Mallowell thought some more, then he said, "*Humph*," and we went back to work.

That night I woke up in the deepest dark, and I missed my sister Leela and my brother Hamn very much, so I wiped my eyes on my nightshirt and crept into bed with Seery and Mallowell, taking care to be soft and quiet as a field marm. This time Seery did not wake up, and I fell right to sleep, happy and content.

My plan was to sneak from the bed before Seery and Mallowell woke, but when I opened my eyes, Mallowell was sitting up, looking at me. He laughed.

Seery woke and rolled over. She looked angry.

"It's what he's used to," Mallowell said to Seery. "He doesn't mean anything, you know, untoward, by it. Just until he adjusts?"

Seery looked at me and sighed. I smiled.

"He sleeps to your left, not between us," she said. "And *some nights* he cannot come to the room until high dark hour."

I nodded happily, though I didn't understand why I had to wait until high dark hour on *some nights*, or how many nights *some nights* might be. I hugged Seery, then I hugged Mallowell, then we rose, and I ran to fetch the stick I use to clean my teeth, and my satchel of spare clothing, and my softstone. Now I would sleep much better at night. There would still be too much open space during the day, so I would still shake and cry a lot during the day, but not at night.

Ork's navigational scientist was hairy and smelled bad, and he didn't care about our map. He only wanted to talk about propulsion. Ork already had sixty-four propulsion points compared to Cyan's sixteen. Mallowell asked him where they were in such a hurry to get to, then he laughed. But the Orkian scientist didn't laugh; he only rubbed his hairy chin, which made the muscles in his arm bunch up.

Before we had time to do much talking, the door of the meeting room flew open. It hit the wall and made a loud bang, and I screamed because I was startled. A big, hairy man with arms so thick they wouldn't lie straight at his sides came in. Three fat metal sticks dangled from his belt; they clanked together when he moved. He moved fast. He looked angry, and he was making loud breathing noises through his nose.

"We're leaving," he said to the Orkian navigational scientist without introducing himself. "Gather the rest of the science team and meet me at the bridge." Then he left without saying goodbye or even closing the door behind him.

The Orkian scientist got up from the conference table and ran out the door. He didn't even gather up his note papers first. I looked at Mallowell, and he shrugged.

Later, Mallowell told me why the man, who was the leader of Ork and was named Salyn, had been angry. Salyn wanted to trade a new thing he called "scrip" for Cyan's food and goods. "Scrip" was a piece of paper that said he would do a favor for Cyan later, or help if some other world tried to hurt Cyan. The Oldsters, who were the leaders of Cyan, and who Mallowell was one of, didn't like the idea, and that's why Salyn got angry and left.

I laughed when Mallowell explained what scrip was, because Cyan might not pass Ork again for years.

"Maybe that's why Ork is so interested in propulsion, so they can move more quickly and see the same worlds more often," Mallowell said.

It was an interesting idea.

When Mallowell suggested linking with more than one world at the same time to the other Oldsters, they didn't think it was a good idea. It would mean clearing a second linking point on Cyan, so people would have to move out of their houses, because their houses would be crushed. The other Oldsters didn't think it would add much, because we could link with as many worlds as we wanted, one at a time.

Mallowell told me this, then he told me he was like a spikefish—once he sunk his teeth into something meaty, he didn't let go.

Two hundred eighty-seven days later, Cyan linked with two worlds at once.

The other worlds were Gurpin and Ettentupan. We navigational scientists from the three worlds had a conference, and there was arguing and lots of people making lectures and asking questions and drawing with softstone. Some of the things that people knew stuck together with what other people knew, and soon everyone was talking about using glass to see things that are very far away, and all the scientists were excited by the time it was over.

The merchants were happy too, because linking with two worlds at once made trading easier.

Fifty-seven days after our three-way link, Mallowell and I were up in the observation tower. Mallowell was experimenting with holding special pieces of glass up to the sky to see far away, and he saw a remarkable thing: three worlds linked together. None of the three worlds were Gurpin or Ettentupan, the worlds we had triple-linked with.

"Your idea is taking flight, Tweel," Mallowell said. He put down the glass and rubbed my hair all around, which I liked. Sometimes Seery did it before we went to sleep.

"Tweel, I think I've spied an unrecorded world! Come take a look," Mallowell said.

I was watching the engineers install the sluices for Cyan's new waterway system. Soon we wouldn't have to empty piss buckets any more, and fresh water would come up to my room instead of me having to go down to get it.

I went over and looked into Mallowell's Longview.

"No, that's Ankari. We saw it once before." I told him when and where.

"Ah," Mallowell said.

I was about to pull my eye away from the Longview when something blotted out the world I was tracking. Just for a moment. Then it happened again. I changed the Longview's focus to short distance.

There were people in the sky!

"There are people in the sky!" I said.

"What?" Mallowell said. "What are you talking about? Let me see."

I let him see. I looked up with my naked eyes, and saw specks in the sky that I knew were people, because I'd just seen them close up.

"What in the universe . . . ," Mallowell said. "My goodness, they're corpses. Thousands of them."

"About eight thousand," I said.

"Cyan is plowing right through the middle of them, pulling them out of the sky!" Mallowell shouted at people in the streets to get inside as the specks got bigger and bigger, then the sky was filled with falling dead people. People screamed, and I saw a mother in a window across the way cover her child's eyes with her palm. Mallowell and I stood under an overhang and watched. One of the dead people landed on a spiral roof across the street with a loud thump. It was a lady in a pink dress. She was all cut up. I pushed my face into Mallowell's shirt because I didn't want to see her any more, and he put his arm around my head and led me inside.

Eight days later, we made an emergency-link with a world called Kokoru, because there was smoke coming from a lot of Kokoru's buildings, and they had spread a green signal, which means "help us." I didn't go to Kokoru, and I'm glad I didn't, because there were dead people there, too.

The people who weren't dead said that Salyn had linked with their world without permission, and taken things that didn't belong to him, and his army had killed lots and lots of people, and burned houses and shops.

If that wasn't bad enough, Salyn wasn't just the leader of Ork any more. He had linked seven other worlds with Ork all at once, in a big clump. Houses and people were crushed, because most worlds only have one linking spot cleared, and some of the worlds were squeezed in the middle. The crushing of things, and the killing, sounded very bad, but I thought that worlds squeezed together sounded very good, because if worlds were all hugged up together, and I lived in the middle of the hug, there would be much less open space, and my hands would stop shaking, and I wouldn't cry so much. I cried a lot.

The Oldsters decided that all us scientists should stop what we were doing and focus on what to do about Salyn, in case he ever passed near us again. Mallowell and I stopped working on our map, and tried to find out where Salyn was with the Longview, so we could avoid passing near him. But he must have been far away, because we couldn't find him.

Cyan signed an alliance with thirty-seven other worlds. We linked in clusters of two and three, and used propulsion to keep the clusters close together. Every day, the streets were filled with the thump of people marching in lines. Instead of baking blackcakes and making fabric birds that rode in the sky, everyone practiced killing invaders.

My job was to help Mallowell think of ways to run away from Salyn if he got too close. Propulsion. I wasn't good at propulsion. So I watched Mallowell. He was using our map to test propulsion models with different configurations of worlds linked together.

He tried linking a dozen worlds together in a line, then he set the whole line spinning very fast. I didn't think that was a good idea, because we would all get very dizzy if he tried that with real worlds.

The line of worlds formed a big, blurry circle as it spun, then suddenly the string that was holding it snapped, and it crashed to the bottom of the sphere of the universe and the line burst apart and the worlds bounced all over, then settled together at the lowest point in the sphere.

It scared me, but it wasn't the loud noise that scared me; it was something else that was in the back of my head where I couldn't get to it. I was so scared that my stomach hurt.

I told Mallowell I was sick, and I went to Seery and helped her sort peep nuts. She let me separate them into piles of 222, as long as I also removed the cracked ones while I was doing it, and this helped me not think about the spinning worlds so much, but I still saw them whenever I closed my eyes, so I tried not to close my eyes, but finally it was night and I had to go to sleep, and then I had to close my eyes.

I had a dream, that the spinning worlds didn't burst apart when they hit the bottom of the sphere. They just kept going, right through it, and Mallowell shouted, "What, what, what?" and stepped into the map, and he started to sink. His feet disappeared, then his knees, then his waist, until he was only a head. And his head said, "We're taking flight now, little Tweel, where the open spaces go on and on and on." Then his head sank too, and I was alone.

I woke screaming. Seery made a shush-shush-shush sound and rocked me, but I couldn't stop screaming for a long time. The empty space from my dream wouldn't go away; it was in my head, the back of my head felt like it had been opened up, and there was nothing back there but space— black, black space, going on and on.

And while I screamed, I saw a picture in my mind, of the angle that a line of linked, spinning planets would have to be at when it hit the edge of the universe, to break through it. And that made me scream even louder.

I cried out when I spotted Salyn's world-clump in the Longview. First it was a scared kind of cried out, but it turned into a wanting kind of cried out, because all the planets were hugging each other, and I wanted to climb inside and be hugged by all those planets so I would stop shaking and crying all the time.

It was a giant, lopsided ball, about 150 worlds linked together, rotating slowly end over end. I called Mallowell.

He didn't cry out; he just kept saying, "What, what, what"; and his hand shook when he adjusted the focus on the Longview.

The Oldsters signaled the rest of the alliance about the world-clump, and then the whole alliance ran. I went back to the map with Mallowell, and we figured out speeds and distances and evasive maneuvers as people poured into the streets, shouting and carrying pointed things.

"There's no way to escape him," Mallowell said while we lay in bed with the lights out. "Nowhere to run." He sounded very sad. Salyn's world-clump would catch up to our alliance in twenty-seven days and four hours.

There was nowhere to run. Nowhere that wasn't terrible; nowhere that wouldn't make me scream forever.

I was sorry Mallowell was sad, but I wanted us to live in Salyn's clump. I wanted Mallowell and Seery and me to huddle in bed with worlds and more worlds hugging us from the sky.

I heard Mallowell sniffle. "My Seery. What will become of us?" he said. I rolled over and put my fingers in my ears, but I could still hear him. "Our beautiful, beautiful Cyan."

He reached over and pushed his face into my neck and cried. I felt the wet from his tears on my neck, and the prickle of his beard.

"You've been a good assistant, Tweel. And a good friend."

Seery put her hand on my head and stroked my hair. She was crying.

I started to cry too, and shake, because I didn't want to tell them. But they let me sleep in their bed, and Mallowell told me science things, and they were sad, and I could stop them from being sad.

But if I did, I would be sad. And I would shake all the time.

I lay awake for a long time, with my heart pounding. Then I woke up Mallowell and Seery, and I told them about the open spaces that go on and on, and about how you get there.

For a long time Mallowell didn't understand what I meant. He kept asking, "Outside what? Outside where?" And I would answer, "Outside the universe." He asked how I could possibly know there was an outside to the universe, and I said, "Because it's a sphere."

I'd never seen Mallowell angry. I was very scared. I pressed my face against Seery's cloak and whispered the Yellow Bird song. I whispered because Rembagh, the man with the twisted stick who always sat in the tall chair in Oldster meetings, thumped his stick on the floor and told me to stop singing it out loud because it was distracting everybody.

"What choice do we have? Tell me! What choice do we have?" Mallowell screamed. His face was as red as the middle section of Gootang, which I'd last seen when it passed Allberry when I was twelve years and eleven days old.

"What you're suggesting is nonsense! Unmatched twaddle! Unbelievable bilge!" a pale-skinned woman from Gurpin said. I knew she was from Gurpin, because all of the alliance representatives wore robes that were the colors of their world, and she was wearing a yellow robe with zigzagged bolts of brown. "There is no outside. By definition there is no outside to the universe. We'll only waste precious time that we need to plan our defense."

"Our defense?" Mallowell said. "There's no defense against that abomination! It's gotten too big. It will eat us. It will eat everything. Our only hope is to go where it cannot follow."

"And where is that? Into your assistant's fantasy world?" the woman from Gurpin said.

"Let's be clear about what you're saying, Mallowell," the representative from Ettentupan said. "You want us to set our worlds spinning and head toward the edge of the universe while Salyn closes in, because your assistant assures you there is an outside of our universe, but he cannot explain why, nor can you?"

"He is an extraordinary boy—"

"Extraordinary?" the woman from Gurpin said. "It was his idea that caused this mess in the first place. Now you want us to trust him again?"

I stuck my fingers in my ears and sang the Yellow Bird song out loud. Seery took me out of the meeting, and I was glad. I don't like it when people are angry with me.

I didn't get dizzy when the line of worlds was spinning; it looked like it was the sky that was spinning. There was Salyn's clump, blotting out 35% of the sky, then it was gone, then it was back again, blotting out 36% of the sky.

I watched from the navigation plateau, which had walls, but no ceiling. Mallowell and Seery pressed against me on either side, but I still felt like I was falling into a deep hole.

When the chief navigator was not shouting directions to the signalers, he was shouting directions to the singers, who were standing on platforms of different sizes and singing into pipes of different circumference that led to Cyan's propulsion chambers. I had told him that the speed and angle had to be just right, or we would bounce off instead of going through. I wondered if he could get it just right. I didn't want him to, I wanted us to bounce off.

"Look!" Seery said, pointing at the sky.

The sky had gotten white and foamy, like the water at the bottom of a waterfall. There was a terrible boinging noise. I closed my eyes and pressed my hands over my ears, but I could still hear it and it made my stomach sick, so I shouted the Yellow Bird song, but that didn't help, and my stomach got worse. Mallowell and Seery were making unhappy sounds too. The boinging slid behind my eyeballs and it felt like it was going to push my eyes out onto the floor of the navigation plateau, and I thought about the woman from Gurpin who said I'd wrecked the universe, and I must have made another mistake, because this was not empty space, it was awful, awful pain.

Then, all of a sudden, it was gone. I opened my eyes.

The sky was huge, and black, and empty. Just like in my dream—empty space that went on and on, with no edges. I started to shake. I slid down between Mallowell and Seery until I reached the floor, then I hugged my knees, and I screamed.

"Ho, Tweel!" a man I didn't know said as I passed him in the great hall. He raised his fists in the air, which is how people on Cyan greeted Oldsters, but now also greeted me, which I liked.

"Hey-o, Tweel, and thank you!" a woman I didn't know said. She raised her fists as well.

A man I did know—Soothin, a singer—put his arm around me and pulled me close. "I'll be your comfort guard on this walk, Tweel. Where are you going?"

"To Mallowell's observation deck," I said as he walked with me. That's what they called it when people walked with me, my comfort guard. It was not as bad as I had thought, the endless black sky, because I had my comfort guard, and I got "ho"s and "hey-o"s from everyone I met. I liked the "ho"s even better than the comfort guard. It was like what I imagined living deep inside the planet clump would be, because the planets would have pressed around me even though they didn't actually touch me. The "ho"s and "goodly-met"s pressed against me the same way, even when there was empty space all around, and I did not shake and cry nearly as much. Maybe one day I would sleep in my own bed. But maybe not; I enjoyed sleeping with Seery and Mallowell.

Mallowell was looking into his Longview when I got to the observation deck.

"Go ahead, little Tweel, look," he said, wrapping his arm around my shoulder and motioning to the Longview.

I didn't want to look at the blackness through Mallowell's Longview. Even though Mallowell was smiling, I did not want to look. There were no planets there, and it had no edges. There was nothing but one glowing white ball that didn't give off enough light to light the black sky that went on forever.

Mallowell said, "Go on, you'll like this."

I looked. The Longview was focused on our universe, our home. I could see inside it, right through the sphere to the planets inside. I could see shadows of worlds—they looked like specks of dust, swirling inside. I wished the Longview was stronger, so I could find Allberry.

"Adjust the Longview seven degrees on the horizontal," Mallowell told me. So I did, and I saw . . .

I saw another universe, another sphere, with planets swirling inside.

"What, what, what?" I said.

Mallowell laughed. "Now five degrees horizontal, three vertical."

I adjusted again, and saw another sphere! It was more distant than the first two. I laughed. It was not so empty out here. That made me feel very happy, very hugged.

"Can we get into these spheres, just as we got out of ours?" Mallowell asked.

"Oh yes," I said. "Getting in would be much easier than out." In my mind, I could already see the angle that would allow us to break into the spheres from the outside.

"Ah. We are explorers then, not refugees," Mallowell said. He looked down at me. "We wanted an assistant navigator, and you ended up changing the universe." Then he reached over and rubbed my hair, which I liked.

THE GIRL-PRINCE
MERRIE HASKELL

[*Coyote Wild,* August]

Once upon a future time, in a spindle-tower held high by antigravity and the will of engineers, a woman slept, a poisoned trap for princes.

The tower's true meaning had been forgotten by even the most ancient of databanks, and all anyone knew was that the tower was a graveyard for the foolhardy, an unscaleable fable with no discernable prize at the top but the rumor of a woman no one remembered.

The galaxy's bravest and silliest boys threw themselves at the tower for centuries without stop, until one day, on an artificial planet circling an artificial star, a girl-prince came of age.

Finally allowed to access restricted databanks without parental oversight, the girl-prince stumbled across the story of the tower and was enthralled. She downloaded the information to show to her parents. "I can do this," she told them. "I can save the princess."

"Impossible," said her mother. "Not only does no one know the tower's location, seven thousand princes have lost their lives in quest of that princess."

"Just because others have died does not mean that I will lose my life."

Her father sighed, and said to her mother, "My darling, we have failed. I thought that by having a girl, we would avoid all of this."

"Girls have assailed the tower before, Father," the girl-prince pointed out.

"But we have spent your whole life ensuring your extreme hetero-normativity, daughter," said her mother. "My womb was flooded with all the right hormones, we gave you all the right toys, and we told you all the right fairy tales. You should have no desire to gallivant about the universe rescuing people!"

The girl-prince wondered why the desire to rescue things was considered a particularly masculine trait. And even if it weren't, she'd been raised in a galaxy full of strong women, a galaxy which included her own mother. Why had her parents thought she wouldn't notice these things?

She squared her shoulders, raised her chin, and said, "I am both girl and prince—one person, but not merely one thing."

Her father hmphed. "We should have locked *you* in a tower."

Her mother cried, "Oh, I know! We shall hold a ball, and when you look into the eyes of the right boy-prince, you'll fall in love and forget all about this silly quest."

"I don't want a ball," the girl-prince said. "I want to breach the tower."

Her mother buried her face in her hands, and could be heard muttering, "That damned tower. Have we made such a child that she would risk death on such an obviously Freudian symbol?"

Her parents sent her to her room with its pink-kitten wallpaper while they discussed the situation; whereupon the girl-prince packed her dresses, loaded all her favorite romantic horse novels on her small voidship's computer, and was gone before her parents could officially forbid the quest.

The girl-prince searched for the tower long and hard. She sought the counsel of historians and sneak-thieves, archaeologists and weapons experts, folklorists and physicists. She listened to every rumor of the tower's defenses, and prepared herself for each one, no matter how outlandish, spending a sidereal year of her home planet arming herself with skills and knowledge and equipment.

Eventually, the girl-prince found a gravitational cartographer who had discovered the tower from a safe distance, though he hadn't dared to publish its location. It was marked on all charts as a very boring black hole.

"And, truthfully, it is a black hole," the cartographer said, looking into the girl-prince's beautiful dark eyes. "The sort that traps souls instead of objects." The girl-prince wished she had six more beautiful dark eyes, so that she could roll them all at once to truly illustrate her contempt.

Sensing her discomfort but not the cause of it, the cartographer apologized. "Sorry. I didn't mean to get so deep, princess."

Rather than point out that people who announced their depth seldom had any, she just pointed out that she was a girl-prince, not a princess.

"What's the difference?" the cartographer asked.

"One is a sovereign, and the other is a commodity," the girl-prince said, which chagrined the cartographer and his very deep soul—so very deep that he had no trouble with the commercial enterprise of selling the tower's address for a handsome fee.

When the girl-prince found the tower, she was surprised to find it standing alone on an oblong asteroid tumbling alone, disbalanced by the artificial gravity of the tower. The asteroid was surrounded by the wreckage of hundreds of ships that had not been sufficiently cautious of the asteroid's eccentricities.

The girl-prince studied this situation for some time, and her vigilance revealed a long-held secret of the debris field: a one-person escape pod orbited among the smashed ships.

The girl-prince pulled back her ship, magnetized her hull, and lured a thick stream of debris away from the asteroid. Once away from the asteroid, she singled out the escape pod and brought it aboard her ship.

Inside the pod, which was of a design long out of date, the girl-prince found the hibernating body of a prince close to her own age. His clothing contained an unfathomably useless number of pockets. His head was shaved in the fashion of the third and most famous emperor of Lampur, an empire that had risen and fallen over a hundred life-spans ago. He was paler than the current human average, with dark lashes lying luxuriantly against his cheeks. The girl-prince sighed, and wondered if she had narrowly avoided falling in love by being unable to look into his eyes.

She was unable to revive the prince from his hibernation state. She thought that perhaps she should retreat to known space and find medical care for him, but she could not bring herself to give up the tower. It was like a physical compulsion. Hoping she was not caught in some unimaginable telepathic thrall, she resealed the escape pod, ejected it safely into space, placed a beacon on it for later retrieval, and went on her way.

She landed the voidship within view of the tower. Bleached bones piled high around the perimeter, looking like a white thorn brake from a distance; it was only as the girl-prince drew close that she saw them for what they were: human remains caught in transparent stickyfoam.

Staying well away from the perimeter of the stickyfoam graveyard, she circled the tower once, twice, three times, looking for a weakness in the defense, examining the bodies from afar. Mostly, there were skeletons, though a few bodies moldered in varying states of decomposition. The girl-prince marveled, wondering what sort of engineers had thought to introduce microbes or fungus or some such agent of decay into the tiny micro-environment of the tower. The same capricious engineers, she decided, who created a gravity pocket on an asteroid and then built a spindle-tower that needed anti-gravity to support it.

The local agents of decay were quite finicky, it appeared, eating voidsuits and clothing, human flesh and human hair, but they leaving alone the rock, the tower, and the bones. The girl-prince could think of no reason that they would not eat the bones as well, except perhaps that this barrier acted as a deterrent as well as a trap.

On her third circuit of the tower, a feeble wave from an unsecured hand alerted her that one of the bodies was still alive. She tried to address the hand's owner on every available frequency, but had no luck making contact. The hand fluttered and stopped, fluttered again and stopped, in a pattern that was neither random nor automated.

She fought back an urge to charge in, grapple hooks akimbo, and ascend up to rescue the prince. He had lived for some unknown amount of time in the stickyfoam. She had to assume that the universal forces of irony would not cause him to die when help was so close.

From her backpack, the girl-prince selected a small robot and sent it bounding off toward the stickyfoam perimeter. Two small nozzles sprouted from the tower's smooth surface and, shooting ropes of stickyfoam at the robot, brought it down with unfeeling efficiency. The robot kicked futilely until the foam hardened; then it kicked no more.

Noting the timing of these events, she sent two more robots after the first in quick succession. The first one was shot down just as before; the second darted close-but-not-too-close, snatched a stickyfoam sample before it hardened, and darted back to the girl-prince. She retreated with the robot and its sample to her voidship to run tests.

Her makeshift laboratory was up to the challenge of the stickyfoam, and in short order, she had a solution. She set some molecules to cook and some microbes to evolve while she dined on dull proteins from ship stores and slept on the voidship's narrow bunk. When the timer on her antistickyfoam concoctions buzzed, she called it a new day, and began afresh her assault on the tower.

The girl-prince dressed again in her heavy-duty miner's voidsuit before spraying a tank of her first potion over herself and her equipment. She strapped on a tank full of the second potion and advanced on the perimeter and the prince.

The tower sprouted its nozzles and aimed; stickyfoam rained over her and slid off, repelled by the structures of the molecules in her first potion. Puddles of stickyfoam hardened at her feet; she left them behind, climbing atop the pile of bones and foam until she reached the prince who might yet live. His free hand did not move at her approach, and she feared that he'd died after all. Nevertheless, she shot at him with her second potion, and watched with grim pleasure as her engineered bacteria dug into a delicious meal of stickyfoam.

Once released, the prince fell in a heap of others' princely bones towards the asteroid's surface; but the girl-prince was fleet of foot and accomplished with her gravity boots, and she was there to catch him.

The prince lived, though he was emaciated—nearly cadaverous, even— and did not regain consciousness when the girl-prince got him out of the voidsuit that had sustained his life. He'd managed to survive thanks to the ruthlessly efficient air and water recyclers in the suit, though he'd depleted his nutrient packs around the time that the girl-prince had been speaking to the depthless cartographer.

The girl-prince hooked the boy up to her voidship's medical system, but it was outclassed by the level of the boy's malnourishment and atrophy, and told her so. It would be best, the medical system said, to put the boy in stasis and get him to a hospital.

She knew the medical system was correct, though she was reluctant to shut the prince away. She liked the way his dark hair grew to a point at the center of his forehead. She wondered if she had again narrowly avoided falling in love by not being able to look into his eyes, either.

So the girl-prince took once more to the void, where she found the escape pod that she had rescued the day before. She lashed her own pod to the ancient one after placing the new prince in it, and left both princes safe and beaconed, beyond the grasp of the asteroid and the tower.

The stickyfoam was merely the first barrier. Though it had obviously proven effective over the years, the girl-prince could not have been the only one cautious and smart enough to breach it. So once she had cleared a path to the doorless entrance of the tower with her microbes, she employed the tactic for breaching the tower that she had developed during her investigation: she hooked herself into the previous room using the sort of timer-clip developed for asteroid mining slaves, and deployed one of her stock of small robots developed for derelict space ship exploration to go ahead of her and look around.

The robot was immediately defeated by an electromagnetic pulse. The girl-prince was prepared for this eventuality; EMPs were one of the most common security measures around, and only a fool wouldn't have prepared for one. The girl-prince hadn't known where in the lineup of traps a pulse might be employed, but both her ship and suit were hardened against EMPs, and the backpack that carried her robots and a few other necessities had been constructed to serve double duty as a Faraday cage.

Other princes had not been so wise; a few bodies were scattered inside the tower's door, lying in attitudes that suggested interesting electrical failures in their voidsuits. But these were all very old suit models; present-day voidsuits were all built to withstand coronal ejections and similar radioactive events.

The girl-prince's timer-clip ticked off the last seconds and released her, and she crept through the blank, white room, picking her way around the fallen princes—noting with interest that the local agents of decay were not active in this room—to the room's single feature: one staircase, leading up.

Once on the first stair, the girl-prince clipped herself again and deployed another robot. The robot climbed the stairs and stopped at the top to beckon her forward. She climbed to the end of her timer-clip tether and waited for it to release her, wondering if the timer-clip notion would ever prove to be useful to her.

When she finally drew even with the robot, she found another blank white room with another staircase leading up on the other side. The floor between the staircases was studded with an array of princely bodies held down by heavy nets. She urged her little robot onward. It had not traveled far before a heavy net shot from the ceiling and smashed the robot to the floor. Once the robot was down, small hooks emerged from the net's weights to dig into the floor.

This was a trap that could be gotten out of with brute strength or the proper equipment, as evidenced by shredded nets lying here and there around the room. But the greater majority of nets lay over silent, voidsuited lumps spread across the floor.

Just in case there was someone left alive here, the girl-prince tried all the frequencies at her disposal. No one answered. Perhaps there was a communication-jammer in the tower. She wished she had some device that monitored life-signs, but in all her planning, she had not considered the possibility of running into other princes yet alive. And yet she'd rescued two boy-princes. It didn't seem impossible that she would rescue more souls.

Fewer than a hundred bodies lay in the chamber, but from this distance she could see no signs of life. She would have to check each net.

The girl-prince had purchased a shadowsuit in the same system that had yielded the cartographer; she'd anticipated using it to achieve invisibility to a variety of sensors sooner or later in the confines of the tower, and so had carried it rolled in the bottom of her backpack. She slipped it on over her voidsuit and activated it. Holding her breath and a knife, she stepped forward into the room.

No nets came careening down onto her head immediately. She considered. If she attempted to move any of the bodies, either to turn them over to see through faceplates or to lift arms to check gauges, the movement would be targeted by the system.

The antiquity of most of the voidsuits made a detailed examination unnecessary. A cracked faceplate or a blown gasket told her everything she needed to know, and in most other cases, she could peer at the arm gauges. The few princes who had landed facedown atop their arm gauges numbered only six. The girl-prince gave a nervous glance at the smooth white ceiling, wondering where the nets came from and where the motion sensors were, then turned over the wrist of the first of these six.

The net flew much faster than she anticipated. She almost dodged, but one of the weighted grapples clipped her shoulder—hard enough even through the voidsuit's padding to bruise her. She sank to her haunches, breathing hard and rubbing her shoulder, grateful that the grapple hadn't torn the shadowsuit. When she caught her breath, she examined the prince's revealed gauges: empty. Long empty.

Hoping the first was the worst, she went on, but the fourth net caught her, managing to pin her left leg to the floor. Her knife was at the ready, however, and she sawed slowly through the net and continued on.

There were no victories in the net room, no lives to save. Somehow, given the effort she had put forth in checking, she expected more of a reward than the cold comfort of knowing she'd tried.

Once safely across the room, the girl-prince activated the timer-clip and deployed another of her diminishing stock of robots on the stairs. The robot climbed ahead of her for a long way and stopped at the top to whistle an all-clear. She climbed up after, waited for the timer-clip, and when she finally drew even with the robot, ordered it to scooted into the next blank, white room—where it promptly sank through the floor and disappeared from sight.

The girl-prince immediately attached the timer-clip again, this time setting it for a two-hour release. Then she crawled forward, poking the floor before her. In short order, solid floor gave way to liquid: slow ripples spread away from her finger.

She took a sample of the liquid and stowed it away, and sat back on her haunches to assess the situation. Was she meant to swim? There was no staircase on the other side of the room. Instead, a ladder hung down from the next level, far above the height that even the most athletic prince could reach by surging out of the liquid. And though the liquid was as opaque and as white as the walls of the room, she suspected that the utter absence of bodies here indicated not—as she had first hoped—that no one had died on this level, but that they had sunk to the presumably distant bottom of this bizarre swimming pool.

She lay down on the last step and put her hand out flat over the liquid, intending to see if she could touch the bottom of the pool. It wouldn't be typical of the tower's designers to use a nonlethal deterrent here, but there was always the possibility that the pool was only knee-deep. Wasn't there?

But she hesitated. Something seemed rotten. Was it stickyfoam redux? Did the liquid lure the unsuspecting in with the promise of easy wading, only to eat through their voidsuits, or to suck them under? Or were there Carapellian squid waiting beneath the surface?

The girl-prince held her hand above the surface so long that her arm trembled. In pulling it back, the palm of her glove smacked the surface of the liquid—and instead of rippling, the liquid held firm. The girl-prince jumped to her feet. Of course! It was a shear thickening fluid—a type of oobleck, which became more viscous when agitated, acting like a solid under impact. She could run right across the surface of this fluid, and as long as she didn't stop, she wouldn't sink.

Since she had some time to waste before her timer-clip released her, the girl-prince took off her shadowsuit so she wouldn't render it completely ineffective by covering it in goo, and spent some time feeling around in the oobleck, trying to see if she could reach bottom, or . . . But she could reach nothing with her arm, and though she had the timer-clip and its sturdy, space-rated tether, she knew that now was not the time to explore the oobleck. She tossed a beacon onto the liquid, watched as it first bounced around and then sank below the surface. She would use the beacon to orient her voidship's cannon beam, and blast a hole in the side of the tower to let out the fluid and discover what—and who—lay hidden beneath.

When the timer-clip released her, the girl-prince didn't pause to even think. She simply ran. And the oobleck held her up.

When she reached the ladder hanging down, she jumped once—twice—three times before reaching the bottom rung. She clung there for a long while, catching her breath, and then began the climb.

The cautious use of the timer-clip made the journey take forever, but also gave her time to ease her burning arms, for no configuration on her gravity boots gave her enough of a boost to ease the strain. The ladder passed through an increasingly small passage; occasionally, the lights went out, and the girl-prince had to continue on in the unwavering but tiny beam from her helmet. When she came to the trapdoor at the top, she almost didn't believe it. She had begun to think that she would just climb forever, that the tower was actually a wormhole, and an endless one at that.

The narrow passageway was not conducive to setting a robot to scout for her, so she simply set her timer-clip and opened the trapdoor, hoping that she wouldn't be pelted with lasers.

The room was the same blank whiteness as the other rooms of the tower—but for a splotch of color on a distant wall.

Against the wall was a couch. And on the couch, glowing like an ancient jewel, lay a beautiful woman. Her hair shone a rainbow of colors from blue to blonde, and her silky dress and smooth skin melded in a pattern of skin tones ranging from ebonywood to polar snow. The girl-prince felt monochromatic and plain of a sudden, and desired nothing more to possess this woman—no, to be this woman. She took an involuntary step up the ladder, then another, and another.

The rise and fall of the woman's perfect bosom was a testament to the atmosphere contained in the room. Almost—almost—the girl-prince reached for the snaps to unfasten her helmet, but something held her back. Unbidden, her feet climbed the last rungs of the ladder—and then she stopped, held back by the twined nanofilament ropes attaching her to the timer-clip. She looked down, away from the sleeping woman, and remembered her past actions as though they were in a fable from another land: *Oh, yes. I put that there, because this is a trap.*

Then the girl-prince was looking at the woman again, and for a long moment, she forgot everything about herself, from her name to her favorite novel. She longed only to reach the woman, to stroke her hair, to join her on the couch in tender sleep.

The girl-prince was spellbound.

When she came to herself again, the girl-prince realized she was half-bent over and walking in a comic parody of a dog running in place while straining against a leash. The woman was gone, and what was here instead amazed her.

At least two dozen princes stood still in a variety of senseless poses, as though frozen in time. Here one had an arm raised as though to dance. There, one was half-bent with lips pursed—as if kissing someone. Another was caught as though removing a ring from his finger. Most of the princes had taken off all or part of their voidsuits, the girl-prince realized—though a couple were still caught in the act of opening their helmets or removing a glove, and one stood stoic and fully dressed for hard vacuum, with an old-fashioned disc-nosed rayblaster aimed at the wall. Thirty princes, she counted, all frozen.

She checked her chronometer. Fifty minutes had passed while she strained, insensate, against the timer-clip. She felt the ache of that straining in her legs and shoulders. She had not managed to take a step beyond the trap-door.

And the timer-clip deserved the credit for why she was not frozen like the other princes. Clearly, whatever device did the freezing did not take effect until a prince was well and truly inside the room.

She had to leave. She really had to. But the timer-clip wouldn't allow her to. A frightening thought came to her: if the sleeping woman returned, would the girl-prince turn into a senseless zombie once more? And how long would the compulsion last this time? Quickly, before she could talk herself out of it, the girl-prince leaned down and added two more hours to the timer-clip.

There. That decision had been made. Now she sat down on the edge of the trap-door to think. There had to be a holographic projector at play. And an emotional resonator. Something that hijacked the brain as well as the eyes. She glanced around at the passion play staged around her. They were like a photo book shuffled out of order—the holographic projector probably moved the image around to avoid having princes bump into one another—but if one could mentally reshuffle them, the princes were arrayed like a series of *tableaux vivants*. There was the prince just come up the ladder, who first caught sight of the woman; then the prince took off his (or her, for there were several other girl-princes scattered around the room) voidsuit and approached the couch. He (or she) kissed the woman, embraced her—the princes stuck in the attitude of embracing a woman who was not actually there looked acutely uncomfortable—comforted her, knelt down, proposed marriage . . .

The only prince who didn't fit the pattern was the one aiming his rayblaster at the wall. The girl-prince squinted, and made out that his finger was on the trigger.

She didn't quite manage to think her next thought before the woman appeared again.

The girl-prince came to herself again, this time on the floor. She had once more been straining against the timer-clip, but she hadn't even been able to make it to her feet and had simply attempted to crawl to the woman on the couch.

The memory of the driving, urgent need to reach the woman faded quickly enough that the girl-prince just felt foolish for having fallen for the emotional resonator *again*. But there was no fighting that sort of bio-electrical stimulation for the duration of its attacks, she knew. She wondered which neurotransmitter it had exhausted to give her this temporary reprieve, and how long she'd have before it tried a new method of enchantment.

Seventy minutes had passed this time. She was terribly glad that she had reset the timer-clip, and now she reset it again. There was no telling what would happen next, and even though there had been a six-minute lapse between projections last time, a trap as complex as the tower wouldn't rely on a simple pattern.

It was time to perform some experiments. She could not head back to her voidship, thanks to the trusty timer-clip, but she still had one robot left in her pack. She let it loose in the room, and observing as it approached a prince, slowed, and then halted nearby, and its blinking tail lights stuck on solid amber. She wished she had another robot to verify, but time was acting strangely in this room, as though there were small instances of time dilation peppered throughout. The robot acted like it had approached an event horizon, rather than suffering from mechanical failure.

Using her helmet's internal cameras, she snapped still pictures for later comparison. Then she set the timer-clip to its maximum span, and hunkered down to wait and to think.

The princes were not frozen; they were just moving very slowly. Each had entered the tower's final room lifespans apart; each now lived out his moment of triumphant rescue in a private world. The ring-giving prince was blinking, about once every fifteen days, she estimated, and a tear coursed its slow, inevitable way down his left cheek with the speed of a glacier. A tear of joy? She wondered, but it didn't matter.

She wasn't yet certain what sort of device was holding the princes captive in time, and right now that didn't matter, either. She had to get free of the emotional resonator first. And she just didn't know how, other than to wait it out.

The girl-prince knew that she could survive—not healthily or happily, but she could *survive*—in her voidsuit for nearly forty days, just like the prince she'd rescued from the stickyfoam. It might take that long to hit the random point when her timer-clip would release her while she wasn't being manipulated by the tower. There was an equally good chance that the tower would win that game instead, but the girl-prince had been brought up to be an optimist.

In between bouts of mindless adoration of, and endless crawling toward, the illusory sleeping princess, the girl-prince had time to study the princes arrayed around her. They were not all handsome or beautiful, not all tall; in fact, some of them were clearly products of the random trait selection that came from natural conception. But there were not a few attractive specimens in the bunch, and the girl-prince surprised herself by not falling in love with a single one of them, even in the cases where she could see their eyes. The eyes, after all, were all that it would have taken to fall in love with the first two princes she'd rescued, or so she'd thought at the time. Now . . . now she didn't know.

She had come to the tower with mixed intentions. She'd been driven by a morbid curiosity combined with a daredevil streak, and the belief that, through sheer force of will she could change the universe for the better. And while she had considered the possibility of rescuing whatever princess might lie sleeping at the top of the tower—or that she would at least reveal that there was no such princess—she had not considered that she would actually save anyone's life.

She lost count of the number of times her senses had been assaulted by the hologram and the emotional resonator, but her chronometer informed her that three days had passed. She wondered if she was mad yet, trapped as she was; she did not have even the luxury of time-slowing, as the other princes did. Every time the projectors let up she dropped into exhausted sleep, and dreamed of the woman on the couch, of unclipping the timer-clip and slipping into her own private bubble of space-time.

She slipped all too easily from dream to false reality, coming to herself just long enough to remember who she was before everything was consumed once more by the need, the desperate need, to reach the princess. The girl-prince recognized it, and hated it, and found she was crying—and that she had been crying for days. She hadn't realized it before, between the manipulations of the emotional resonator and the water recycling action of her voidsuit.

Her misery came to an end when a flash of light turned the world to shimmering gold. The image of the beautiful woman on the couch disappeared abruptly. With a jolt, the girl-prince realized she was finally free of the emotional resonator.

The princes still stood in their spheres of slowness, but from the nose of the voidsuited prince's rayblaster, a continuous stream of light played, lovely and bright as it bored a slow hole in the wall.

The girl-prince sat down heavily and giggled with relief. She laughed until her voidsuit's oxygen rationing alert advised her to stop. She checked her gauges. New oxygen flow had decreased another five percent. Her suit's meager food supplies were gone, though enough nutrients remained in her water cycle to keep her alive for weeks. She took a sip of water and had to force herself to swallow it; in spite of the efficient recycling system, every sip held that faint taste of body matter and suit-oil.

With rationality restored, the girl-prince finally noticed that the hologram projector had been hiding. Each and every prince was trapped in a slow orbit around a tiny orb of light: Hochberg universes, just like she learned to make in physics class, along with atomic clocks and steam-powered rocket sleds and oobleck. Another Hochberg universe waited for her a few steps beyond the end of her timer-clip tether, between the trap-door and where the image of the sleeping woman had been projected for her.

It was a most diabolical trap.

The girl-prince had been prepared for any trap she could imagine, and one of the items in her supply kit included a can of sensorsol, used to identify archaic laserbeam traps. None of the advisors she had consulted could agree that it was a necessary tool, as laserbeam traps and the like were long out of fashion—if indeed they ever were in fashion, a point over which a number of historians liked to argue. Better overprepared than underprepared, though, and she had carried the can with her since entering this solar system.

She pulled out the can and dispersed its contents around the room, then waited for the manufactured fogbank to settle. The particles that entered each individual Hochberg universe slowed to a crawl, while the particles that stayed in the local time-space of the tower settled to the floor. When the local-time particles were out of the way, the influence of each Hochberg universe was perfectly delineated by a thin layer of particles trapped on the absolute horizon, and would be for some time. She now knew exactly how far the radius of each distortion extended.

She had nearly ten hours before her timer-clip would release, and that was ten hours to think through her next move. She could conceive of a way to free one prince in relatively short order, but she had no method to free them all—nothing in her backpack, nothing even in her voidship.

After modifying a few of the pieces of mining equipment that had come with her voidsuit, the girl-prince sat very still for another hour, waiting for the ping of her released timer-clip. Now it was time to brood. She might very well kill the prince with this plan—or all of the princes. She might kill herself. She might be overlooking some obvious solution to rescue everyone at once. But in the end, she had to go with the plan. There was no other way.

Her timer-clip released. She took the grapple-gun from her waistbelt and aimed carefully at the free Hochberg universe that had been meant for her. It was a very useful sort of grapple, known to have saved millions of lives in various void-related jobs, being made of a multifunctional substance that could be programmed to act like a magnet towards any one of a hundred generally solid substances—including the omnipresent element of carbon.

She fired the grapple, and waited.

The firing mechanism was powerful, the distance was short, and the grapple's attraction to the carbon of the tiny universe speeded it through the space-time bubble. It was nowhere as fast as the rayblaster's light beam, but once the grapple passed the absolute horizon, she figured she only had to wait a day or so for the universe to adhere to the grapple. She settled down to wait.

When the moment of contact was imminent, she steered the grapple filament towards one of the princes. She'd chosen the prince with the rayblaster; he had freed her, and she wished to free him in return. But it was more than a sense of parity and fairness; he was the only other prince who had sensed the trap, the only other prince who had not succumbed entirely to the emotional resonator and the holographic projector. He was perhaps the only prince who would, once freed, be able to help her free the rest of the trapped princes.

Finally, the Hochberg universe bobbed on the end of her filament like a tardigrade fish on a line—and then, still treating the apparatus like a fishing line, she whipped it along towards the blaster-prince's Hochberg universe. This balletic manipulation occurred in extreme slow motion, though once the absolute horizons of the two miniature universes meshed, things began to move faster. The universes jumped towards each other like magnets. Time shifted, sped and slowed then sped again—the blaster-prince was turning, was frozen, then was leaping. He jumped right at her, was knocking her down the trap-door chute and tumbling after. Behind them, an explosion sent a lick of fire down the chute, and the whole tower shuddered.

The girl-prince had enough time while falling to remember what waited at the bottom of the shaft. She was falling head first, and she rather had to; the shaft was too narrow for any sideways falling. Once clear of the shaft, she'd have to angle enough to get her shoulder down first: a good, rolling impact ought to be enough to keep from sinking into the oobleck below. She only hoped the prince behind her would be able to do the same.

The white surface of the pool was coming towards her, and she did manage to get in position for a roll. Her shoulder—her bruised one from the net room—absorbed a great deal of the impact and went immediately numb, in spite of the roll. She forced herself to continue rolling until she got up onto her feet, and then pelted across the chamber. When she reached the safety of the distant staircase, she was amazed that her body had been able to do what she asked.

She turned to look behind her for the blaster-prince, and he smacked into her again.

This time he didn't manage to tumble her down the stairs. Instead, they landed in a heap, with the top step pressed painfully into her spine and his boot jammed into her neck.

They disentangled, and spent the next few moments trying various frequencies for communication, and failing—certainly, her suspicions were correct, and the tower jammed all frequencies—in the end, they had to use helmet-to-helmet communication for their first conversation. Through their visors, she finally saw his eyes—a deep and luminous green that shone like lamps from his dark, lustrous skin.

It was inevitable. She fell in love. Just a little. But that turned out to be enough to last until she got to know him, and like him.

She explained only a little of how she had saved him and how he'd saved her before they retreated from the tower together. Once aboard her voidship, they shared a meal from her supplies, and where once the ship's stores had seemed humble and dull, they were now salted with hunger and the thrill of being alive. The blaster-prince ate well enough, but not with the same desperation as the girl-prince; he had spent only a day of his life traversing the perils of the tower, and only an hour of it in the room at the top.

The blaster-prince had the pierced earlobes of a race that had died off a three generations before; though it broke her heart, the girl-prince showed him this truth in the voidship's databanks. He read the entry of his people's conquest and disappearance several times in silence, before saying, "It is not the outcome I would have wished for, but when a prince embarks on a quest, he dies in the moment of departure. Does he not?"

The girl-prince didn't think so, but then, she was clearly a different sort of prince. She eyed her narrow bed longingly.

"You are tired," the blaster-prince said. "I will sit up here at your console and familiarize myself with the changes in the cosmos that I left behind so many years ago. You rest. And then . . . " He hesitated.

She yawned. "And then, we will rescue the rest of the princes?"

"Are you asking?"

"I am asking if you will join me. If you do not, I will rescue them alone."

She didn't know him well enough then to know, but the smile he gave her then meant that he had fallen in love with her in turn.

"Yes, I will join you," he said.

"And then we will destroy the tower?"

"Yes," he said. "That, too."

"You don't wish to find out who built the tower, and why?"

He shrugged. "If it was for some purpose beyond the trap it became, it does not matter. Perverted or intact, the tower's purpose will die with it."

"I am glad that you are practical," said the girl-prince, and fell asleep.

When she woke again, they found the remains of the blaster-prince's ship, which was well-equipped to blow a hole in the side of the tower. With the ship's engines, they created a controlled dark plasma field that drew all the Hochberg universes out of the tower, and rescued the princes thereby. Afterwards, they sifted in vain through the oobleck, hoping that some prince was alive in his or her voidsuit at the bottom, but they found only the dead.

In the end, the remaining princes tore down the tower and destroyed the asteroid that had housed it. The girl-prince and the blaster-prince returned the survivors to their homes, those that still had them, and incinerated the princes who had not survived.

The girl-prince brought the blaster-prince to her home, where they married. Together they became co-kings, once the girl-prince's parents forgave her for the crime of not waiting to be forbidden to do what she wanted.

The co-kings and the other living princes erected a monument to the tower's lost. Many came to see this monument, believing it to be a triumphal piece, but left disappointed by the simplicity of the statue and the words inscribed on the pedestal: *In memory of the princes we could not save.*

NOT ENOUGH STARS IN THE NIGHT
BRENDAN DUBOIS

[Cosmos]

It was 03:00 A.M. and chilly for October, but nobody by the shores of the lake seemed to mind what the temperature was. The weather report for once had been accurate, and the night sky was crisp and clear, the stars so bright it almost hurt to stare at them.

Ken Fletcher sat on a point of land that jutted out into the calm lake waters, sitting with the others who were fortunate enough to live here, listening to their laughs and whispers, waiting with them, waiting for them. A warbling cry from a loon out on the far shores made Fletcher shiver, and he pulled a blanket over his lap.

"Look!" came the voice of a young girl. "I saw one, right there!"

Fletcher tilted his head back, looked at the wide expanse of stars, and then . . .

"Right there!"

"Did you see it?"

"My God, it was like fireworks!"

Fletcher held his hands together, checked his illuminated watch. Right on time, and he sat with the group of people as the Leonid meteor showers kicked in, supposedly the best in a hundred years. Fletcher shifted his weight on the quilt he was sitting on, as the people around him stirred and laughed and pointed out the meteors streaking over head. One young boy—Jason, was that his name?—sat next to him and said, "Mister Fletcher?"

"Yes?"

"What's the difference between a meteor and a meteorite?"

"Well, Jason, a meteor is what you see when it burns through the Earth's atmosphere. A meteorite is when it doesn't burn all the way up and it lands on the ground."

"Oh. Thanks." And another voice in the darkness, "See, I told you he'd know. I told you."

More ooohs and aaaahs. He tilted his head back again, watched the streaks of the meteor trails overhead. Other meteors he had seen before, when he was younger, they were such a quicksilver flash, a blink of an eye and you were never sure if you had actually seen it. But the meteors churning their way through the atmosphere at this early hour, they were leaving thick, bright tails that dazzled the eyes.

He took a breath, smelled the lake water and the pine forests about them. There was no sound of traffic, no drone of overhead aircraft, no dome of orange light on the horizon that marked a mall or highway strip or housing stretch. Just the laughs and exclamations from the small collection of happy neighbours, watching the overhead sky show.

It looked perfect up there, the Milky Way stretching overhead, the gauzy wispiness making it look like some thin curtain of light had been stretched overhead. No aircraft, no satellites, no searchlights advertising God-knows-what.

There was movement about him, and somebody laughed. "Tucker! Sit down!"

An English springer spaniel dog dropped next to him, carrying a tennis ball in its mouth. The dog rolled over and Fletcher reached over and rubbed its belly. There was nothing there, just for a split second, and then the wiry sensation of the dog hair, the firmness of its skin. He scratched at its belly and there was another shriek from one of the children.

"There! Did you see that? Did you?"

A woman's voice, behind him. "Is Tucker bothering you?"

He turned and even in the dim light, could make out her long hair, stretching out over a down vest, worn over a cotton nightgown. Marie, he thought. That was her name.

"No, Marie, not at all," he said.

"Can I sit next to you?"

"Of course," he said.

Marie moved in next to him, and he lifted up the quilt so she could slide her long legs underneath. She shifted her weight so she was close to him, and he could smell her scent. A bit of vanilla in it, it seemed.

"Beautiful night," she said.

"God, you're right."

"Enjoying it?"

"Yes, yes, of course."

The children's voices were as excited as before, pointing out the streaks of lights. A few were so bright they reflected in the still waters of the lake. Marie leaned in. "I'm so glad you moved in this past summer. The people who lived in your place before . . . ugh."

He managed to smile. "Ugh?"

"Too many parties, too much noise at night, too much of everything. Nobody over there wanted to relax and blend in and enjoy the surroundings. Until you came along. Somebody who appreciated what it's like, living by a lake."

Cautiously he moved his right hand over to her, grazing her wrist, and then he travelled down and he touched the back of her hand. It was smooth and warm. It felt nice. He curled his fingers around and squeezed and she squeezed back, and she said nothing, just leaned into him, a wind coming up and some of her fine hair tickling his nose.

He breathed in her scent some more and then spotted something off to the west. A bright band of light, rectangular, just above the wooded horizon.

He looked at it and wondered if anyone else could see it, but everyone about him were still amazed at the light show overhead. He stared at the rectangular shape, stared and stared at it, and it didn't move, it didn't vary in intensity, it was just there. Damn it.

He took a breath and raised his voice: "Tango Charlie Charlie, end program twelve. End program twelve."

It all shifted. The laughter and the call of the loons and the scent of Marie's hair and the faint breeze from the lake and the stars and the trees and the reflection of the meteor trails on the water and the touch of Marie's hand in his . . . And faded out.

He took a breath.

The room he was in was small, the size of a one-person dome tent back when he had camped for a while, enjoying the solitude while growing up in a part of Montana that hadn't yet been subdivided. He blinked his eyes again as the tears rushed in, as they always did, when it felt for a moment as if he were a youngster, dreaming he'd won a million dollars, right up to the point when the alarm clock chimed in and shattered everything, just as you had the million dollars in your hand.

Behind him he could sense the noise and the lights and the chatter of the voices as the hatch slid open with a click, and Emerson leaned in and said, "You okay in there, traveller?"

"Yeah, give me a sec," he said, wiping at his eyes. The dream gone. Just like that. He moved around and started out. Hands reached to him, to lift him, and he tossed them off and blinked again in the harsh light of the testing room.

Workbenches, terminals, monitors, lots of chairs, a table for eating and drinking and dozing underneath. A large white board taking up an entire wall, filled with scribbles and diagrams. People looked at him, short-termers and full-timers, a couple of them with handhelds, pointing at him and sucking everything in, so he gave his quickie debrief, as good as he could: "Better but not quite there yet."

"Why the termination?" Emerson, a tall, lanky guy who was the group leader and still looked like a high school kid, trying to clear up his complexion and grow a beard.

"You were losing clarity on the western horizon. Looked like a damn window was opening up. Quite distracting."

"You could have kept on with the program," somebody said.

"Yeah, but why screw with it?" he said, irritation growing in his voice. "Everything starts chattering and falling apart. And there were two precursors that the program was collapsing. There was about a half-second delay in touching the dog's belly before I could feel anything. And there was something wrong with the woman's scent. The request was for cinnamon. I got vanilla."

"You sure?"

He walked over to one of the easy chairs, set up in the corner, which was his and his alone. He sat down and let his legs stretch out. "Yeah, I know the difference between vanilla and cinnamon. Jesus, leave me alone, will you?"

Somebody passed over a bottle of spring water, and he greedily drank. More comments were coming in from the crew, cascading over one another, as he sat there and decompressed and tried to take everything in.

It was always like this after a test session. Always. And even though he felt dehydrated and irritable and everything seemed too bright and too noisy, he knew he was one of the better testers, one of the more calm testers.

There were rumors on the Net about suicides and test facility shoot-ups from other testers, other competitors, who couldn't handle the quickie decompression from virtual reality to real reality, but the CorpNews uploaders always managed to squelch those stories. Most times.

He kept his eyes closed, as the chatter continued:

" . . . told you we needed another processor for that part of the horizon . . . "

" . . . it was a kludgy fix and you know it. Care to write the specs for something so confusing? Man, if you knew . . . "

" . . . I dunno, this scenario still seems too white bread for me . . . "

" . . . why a dog? I'd rather use my cat, he's better behaved . . . "

He opened his eyes, took in the test room. Off to the right was the sim module that he had just emerged from, with cables and output jackets coming off the top like some damn Medusa hair scare. A door leading to the rest of the building was off to the left, locked shut and tight, and with a sign pasted in the middle:

WHAT YOU SEE HERE . . .
WHAT YOU HEAR HERE . . .
WHAT YOU DO HERE . . .
WHEN YOU LEAVE HERE . . .
MAKE SURE IT STAYS HERE!

Just by the door, on both sides, were coat and helmet hangers. It was a warm day—evening by now?—so the coat hangers were empty. The helmet hangers were full up, with black mirrored V/R helmets hanging there, with the glove inputs dangling below. Another sign to the side of the racks: **V/R Helmets Are Not To Be Worn During Compensated Time!**

Workbenches lined three out of the four walls, with monitors and terminals of many sizes and shapes. He wasn't sure what they all did, and he didn't care. His job was to test, to evaluate, and he was glad to have a job so simple in such a time and place, even though he had been practically shanghaied at first.

He knew jokes were told at his expense, about the rural atavistic knuckle-dragger who didn't care or didn't do much with the wired world, but Fletcher didn't care. Well, he didn't care what they thought. He cared about a lot of things and most times, he couldn't talk to his co-workers about it.

He took another healthy sip of the water, then put the glass down and scratched at a mark on his forearm, where he'd been injected an hour earlier. The cocktail of drug goodies was what counted. The whole virtual reality industry had slammed up against the big brick wall of real reality years earlier, when the gamers and simulators and sexers wanted more than just sounds and images. They wanted the full tactile experience, from scent to touch and everything in between.

But always and always there were bugs, and this crew was hard at work, debugging their merry way along, while he got doped up and placed in the module, running this program over and over again.

They talked to each other in acronyms and phrases and short-hand language, spent hours working on the white board, scribbling and erasing, arguing and eating bad food and worse drink. And all the while he waited, sipping his spring water, eating simple and plain meals, as simple and plain as possible in this corporate cube, and then—like the members of some enthusiastic firing squad—they would turn and look at him and say, okay, Ken, time to get buttoned up and start tripping.

And luckily—oh sweet Jesus, the luck he had—the program was relatively simple and plain. White bread. Watching a meteor shower from the quiet and comfortable confines of a lake shore, with children and friends and a drooling dog, playing about, enjoying the quiet night, looking up into the fabulous night sky. Thank God it was so blessed simple.

Half the crew were now by the white board, the rest by a large monitor watching the events of the previous half hour. The monitor was split in two, a fuzzy display that showed the interior of the sim dome, while the other half was numbers and codes. That crew was trying to find the little burp that had caused him problems, while the crew at the white board was trying to guess what problem might crop up next.

Though the crews were supposedly equal, he could tell the difference between the full-timers and short-termers. The full-timers moved slow and true and smiled among themselves, knowing that They Had It Made. Stock options, 401(k), full med and dental, the whole circuit board. The short-termers—hired for specific tasks—were eager and quick to move, wanting to show that they'd do whatever it took to slide in and become a full-timer.

The door opened up and a slim guy walked in, looking like an over-sized bug, V/R helmet on his head. He took the helmet off and a couple of voices were raised up:

"Hey, Collins decided to join in!"

"Collins, what's new?"

Collins hung up his helmet, his short blond hair matted down with sweat. "Man, I almost got nailed in the parking lot. You'd think the pizza delivery boy-o's would know which end of the lot is the exit. Hey, I made the seventh level on Saturn's Rings. Finally!"

He ran his hands across his hair, wiped at his face. "Oh, one more thing. Got a NewsNet flash on the way over here. Saigon got nuked."

Emerson said, "No shit. What does it look like?"

"Suitcase job, what else? Near the Mekong so it could rain glowing water down on mama-san and papa-san. Nasty stuff."

"Credits?"

"Two so far. Both Islamic fundie branches. You bet it'll be a dozen by tomorrow."

A laugh. "And the new Hundred Year's War goes merrily along."

One of the short-termers said, "Saigon? I thought it was called Ho Chi Minh City."

"It was until Dell took over. One of the corporate officers had a dad who was a Viet War vet. Changed the name for sentimental reasons. They had bought naming rights when they set up their first assembly lines. Hey, anybody got stock in emerging Southeast Asia markets?"

Another laugh. "Those markets have been emerging for decades. You'd be an idiot to sock away some stuff in there. C'mon, back to work."

Fletcher finished his water. The new way of the world. Reality wasn't the huddled masses in the Third World and Second World, pressing out from their slums, their apartment high rises, the porous borders. Ships at sea and aircraft in the skies and buses on the ground being hijacked and commandeered by desperate people, trying to get someplace where the phones worked and the lights came on and men with guns didn't come into your home at night, blast you into bloody pieces over some ancient feud. All that didn't matter.

What did matter was the reality in the V/R helmets, the home theaters, the connected Sim Game networks spread across the world. That was the new reality. Everything else was markets and support and raw materials.

He stood up, stretched, felt the tendons and joints creak. He guessed he was raw material, in a way. He had grown up in one of the last wild stretches of Montana, dropping out of school, doing odd jobs here and there—mostly there, since who had money to pay for what passed as an odd job nowadays?—and hunting and fishing and trying to live like the old guys did, like Lewis and Clark. Reading book after book in the free libraries around the county.

Some adventure, until the Montana Highway Patrol picked him up one day, cited him for vagrancy. No real job, found himself on the welfare rolls—even though he had never asked for welfare a day in his life—and he found himself sucked into the Fed database for welfare recipients.

Rules were pretty clear—after assessment and testing, you had to go to where the jobs were, and that's how he found himself here, two years later, on the Left Coast, testbedding a new sim game, complete with everything you wanted in V/R. Hell of a ride. The aptitude tests and screening fitted him into this little slot, and he guess he was more fortunate than some, for he was considered a full-timer, not a short-termer. Which meant those extra goodies every two weeks and the fact that he could let loose every now and then.

Like right now.

Fletcher got up from his chair, tossed the plastic water bottle in a recycling bin. "Heading out," he announced to no one in particular. "Gotta go clear my head."

Most everyone ignored him, except Emerson, who said. "Going to take long?"

"Don't think so."

"'Kay. Make sure it's not more than fifteen minutes. Pager on?"

"Yeah."

He unlocked the door by waving his wrist chip at the bulky handle. It popped open and quickly closed behind him, ensuring there was no wasted time in having the door open for prying eyes, and to also make sure that other people didn't follow him out without scanning their own wrist chip. Tailgating.

He was in a long corridor, tiled floor nice and shiny, recessed lighting giving the same level of illumination if it was 11:00 A.M. or 11:00 P.M. The door he had just gone through was marked with a little plate—ROOM 19—all that identified what was going on behind there. Similar doors lined both sides of the corridor; he had no idea what in God's name was being devised behind those blank metal barriers.

He doubted more than a handful of people in the entire Corporation knew exactly what was going on in any of these rooms. One late night he had gone by a room—ROOM 31, he recalled—and was sure he could hear a woman screaming from behind the door. Maybe a sim, maybe reality, but it 'twernt his business none, so he kept walking.

Just like now. He headed down the corridor, to the red and yellow EXIT sign, and another quick flick of the wrist—the first wrist chips were worn on bands around one's wrist, but now they were surgical implants, and if you wanted to make a fuss about it, fine, you didn't get the job—and that door popped open as well, and he was out in the south parking lot.

Fletcher took a breath, and that was the damn thing about it all. The air was clean, the air wasn't choking, the air actually smelled OK. The new hydrogen economy was burbling along, there was an excess of power in most places in the First World, and the pollution and smog and the particulates in the air were slowly going away.

He took another deep breath, felt the cleanness of the air, even though traffic was humming along on the nearby four-laner. Progress laying its heavy hand. He walked out to the parking lot, his wrist trembling a bit. It was just an odd muscle reaction, that's all, for he knew that somewhere in the bowels of the Corporation, some Human Resources type was monitoring his movement. So what. Monitor away.

The parking lot was about half-full and he saw two people, walking away to another cube of a building. They both had V/R helmets on, and they looked like characters from some 1950s cheesy science fiction movie, stumbling around an alien landscape. What was alien, of course, was what was being seen in the V/R helmet.

There were little heads-up displays inside the helmet that allowed wearers to see where they were going in real-time, but NewsNet stories kept reporting V/R wearers walking into traffic, or going off the end of a pier, or falling off a mountain trail. Part of the experience.

Fletcher came to a little island of grass and two real trees in the centre of the lot, where a square brick building ran some sort of HVAC support for the complex.

He'd scoped out the place after he had first been hired—the only place in this part of the Corporation's archipelago that had trees—and at first found some moments of comfort there, decompressing after the first sim runs. Now it was a destination, a place to take some breaths and be away from people.

He ducked under the branches of the oak tree, and went around the brick building to a half-hidden area with a maintenance service ladder there. Keeping it easy, he climbed up two storeys, probably violating a half-dozen OSHA regs by climbing without proper gear, but so what. The roof was flat, except for some sort of bulky air intake system at the other end, and his feet crunched a bit on the roof covering as he stood up. He looked up at the night sky, shook his head, and went over to the air in take system. Under an overhang he pulled out a blanket roll—protected by a sheet of plastic—and he unrolled and lay down and stared up at the orange night sky.

Progress. Science fiction. A lot of the books he had read in those free libraries in Montana had been old science fiction tales from the 1950s and 1960s. Real hard science stuff, all predicting a world of science and progress, imagining cities in space and colonies on the Moon, Mars and Venus. He wasn't sure why, but those old tales had appealed to him, as he read them in the quiet reading rooms of the library, turning the brittle, yellowed pages. He had liked the old predictions, the old enthusiasms, about what science and progress would do.

He shifted his weight and folded his arms across his chest. Fletcher was no luddite, no anarchist, no flatearther. Hundreds of millions of people lived safe, secure, and healthy lives, all thanks to science and progress. That was the truth, and no amount of hand-wringing could change it. And yet . . . and yet . . .

Fletcher blinked his eyes, looked up at the night sky. A couple of lonely stars managed to blaze their way through the orange light of what passed for night. All those wonderful tales of progress had missed the boat. There were no cities on the Moon, Mars and Venus, and the only city in space was the decommissioned hulk of the old International Space Station, waiting to burn up in the atmosphere one of these days. A few probes had ambled their way through the solar system, but that had been it.

Science and progress had turned inward, creating new realities, creating entire new worlds, all within this old globe. And what was out there . . . Damn it, he'd seen the signs when he was younger, camping out by himself, seeing the glow on the horizon, the lights from the malls and the highways and the security zones and everything else, hounding away the night, making the day's hours stretch and stretch.

Astronomers had complained, and those complaints had been outdrowned and outnewsed by scandals, wars, and the latest V/R stats. So there you go.

But Fletcher remembered. He remembered those nights out in some woodland meadow, hearing a stream gurgle by, watching the great wheel of the night sky whirl about him, seeing lots of satellites and aircraft, sure, but also seeing the occasional meteor streak by. That had been a sight to see.

His pager started vibrating. Time go back to work, back to Room 19. For yet another night, there had been nothing up there. The orange sky and the few stars, and no shooting stars, no comets, nothing. Just the real reality, obscured by everything that helped support the new virtual reality.

Fletcher got up, rolled his bedroll and put it back in its hiding place, and went to the edge of the roof, knowing that in a few minutes, the drugs would enter his system and he would go to work, help create a program that simulated what it had once been, not so many years ago.

He took a breath, put his hands on the metal ladder, looked up again at the sky.

"Tango Charlie Charlie, end program twelve," he said, his voice soft. "End program twelve."

Nothing happened. The sky was still orange, the stars were still gone. His voice got louder, almost plaintive in its plea: "Tango Charlie Charlie, end program twelve. End program twelve."

Fletcher shook his head and started climbing back down.

No. It didn't work. It never worked.

But he always kept trying.

A BUYER'S GUIDE TO MAPS OF ANTARCTICA

CATHERYNNE M. VALENTE

[*Clarkesworld*, May]

Lot 657D
Topographical Map of the Ross Ice Shelf (The Seal Map)
Acuña, Nahuel, 1908
Minor tear, upper left corner. Moderate staining in left margin.

Landmass centered, Argentinean coast visible in the extreme upper quadrant. Latitude and longitude in sepia ink. Compass rose: a seal indicating north with her head, east and west with her flippers, south with the serrated ice floe on which the beast is situated. Legend in original handwriting. Ross Ice Shelf depicted with remarkable precision for the era, see Referent A (recent satellite imaging) for comparison.

The 1907 expedition to the Antarctic continent was doubly notable: it was on this virgin crossing that young Nahuel Acuña, barely free of university, lost his right foot to an Orca in estrus, and by simplest chance the good ship *Proximidad* employed an untested botanist by the name of Villalba Maldonado. Maldonado, himself a recent graduate of no less note than his illustrious shipmate, worked placidly as a cook to gain his passage, having no access to the funding that pursued Acuña through his career like a cheerful spaniel.

One may only imagine an unremarkable Saturday supper in the ice shadows and crystalline sun-prisms in which Villalba, his apron stained with penguin oil, his thinning black hair unkempt, his mustache frozen, laid a frost-scrimmed china plate before Acuña. Would he have removed his glasses before eating? Would they have exchanged words? Would he have looked up from his sextant and held the gaze of the mild-eyed Maldonado, even for a moment, before falling to? One hopes that he did; one hopes that the creaking of the *Proximidad* in one's mind is equal to its creaking in actuality.

Acuña's journal records only: *seal flank and claret for supper again. Cook insists on salads of red and white lichen. Not to my taste.*

The famous Seal Map, the first of the great Acuña Maps, offers a rare window into the early days of the rivalry, and has been assessed at $7500US.

Curator's Note: Whiskey stains date from approximately 1952.

Lot 689F
Topographical Map of the Ross Ice Shelf (The Sun Dog Map)
Maldonado, Villalba, 1908
Single owner, Immaculate condition.

Landmass low center, no other continents visible. Latitude and longitude in unidentified black ink. Compass rose: three-horned sea-goat, a barnacle-crusted tail indicating south, upturned muzzle designating north, vestigial fins pointing east and west. Sun shown centered, with rays embossed in gold extending all the way to the ice shelf. Parhelion is indicated, however, in the place of traditional concentric circles, two large dogs flank the orb of the sun, apparently Saint Bernards or similar, their fur streaming as if in a sudden wind, embossed in silver. Their jaws hang open, as if to devour the solar rays; their paws stand elbow-deep in the seawater, creating ripples that extend to the shoreline. The Map Legend explains that the pair of dogs, called Grell and Skell, may be found at coordinates *(redacted)* and that they require gifts of penguin feet and liverwort before they are willing to part with a cupful of the sun, which if carried at the end of a fishing pole and line before the intrepid polar *conquistador*, may burn with all the heat and pure light that he requires.

Offshore, a large, grinning Orca whale is visible, with a severed leg in her mouth.

When Maldonado returned from the *Proximidad* expedition, he arranged, presumably without knowledge of any competition, for the dissemination of his maps in parallel to Nahuel Acuña's own efforts. The printing of the Sun Dog Map, illustrated by Maldonado himself, was funded by the daughter of Alvaro Caceres, best described as a sheep and cattle magnate in the grace of whose shipping interests the *Proximidad* functioned. Pilar Caceres was delighted with the Maldonado sketches, and sold an ornate necklace of onyx and diamonds (Lot 331A) in order to finance this first map.

While the phenomenally precise Seal Map made Acuña's name and allowed him a wide choice of whalers and naturalists eager to avail themselves of his guidance, the Sun Dog Map stirred a mania for all things Antarctic in Buenos Aires. Nevertheless, Maldonado was not able to fund a second expedition until 1912, while Acuña booked passage on the *Immaculata* the following spring, confounded by the popularity of a clearly fraudulent document. He gave a lecture on the necessity of precision at the Asociación Cartographica Argentina in December of 1908, declaring it a ridiculous matter that he should be required to address such an obvious issue. He was, however, interrupted by vociferous requests for more exact descriptions of Grell and Skell.

Maldonado himself declined to appear before the Asociación despite three invitations, and published the Toothfish Map (Lot 8181Q) in early 1909 without their stamp.

This first and perhaps finest example of the cartography of Villalba Maldonado is one of only three remaining copies and has been assessed at $18500US.

Lot 699C
Map of the South Orkney Islands
Acuña, Nahuel, 1911
Sun damage throughout, fair condition.

Four large islands and sixteen smaller isles lie in the center of the map. Isla Coronación is the only named landmass. Latitude and longitude demarcated in Mediterranean octopus ink. Thirty-two point compass rose, crowned with military arrows wrapped in laurels, and bearing the archaic *Levante* designation on its eastern arm. See Referent B for satellite comparison.

The comparatively moderate climate of the South Orkney Islands (now the Orcadas) allowed Acuña to remain there throughout the war, returning his maps to the mainland via Jokkum Vabø, an illiterate sealer and loyal friend of the cartographer. The two men built the cabin in which Acuña worked and lived, and Vabø made certain that they smoked enough seal-meat in the summer months to keep his friend breathing, returning with costly inks and papers when migrations allowed. This was to prove the most prolific period of Nahuel's life.

From 1909 to 1918, Nahuel Acuña walked the length and breadth of the South Orkneys, polishing his teak prosthetic with the snow and grasses of the coast. He built a circular boat of sealskin and walrus-bones (Lot 009A), paddling from island to island with a gargantuan oar of leather and Orca-rib, a tool he must have found rich to use. He grew a long black beard that was said to glint gold in the sun, and never thereafter shaved it. He claimed later to have given Maldonado not the slightest thought during this hermitage, though Vabø would certainly have reported his rival's doings during his visits, and as the coyly titled Seal Pot Map details just this area, there is some dispute as to whether Maldonado might have actually managed landfall during his 1912 expedition aboard the *Perdita* and met cordially with Acuña. It is not possible to ascertain the authenticity of such rumors in either direction, but it is again sweet to imagine it, the two bearded mapmakers seated upon a snowy boulder, sharing lichen-tea and watching the twilight fall onto the scarlet flensing plains. It is a gentle pleasure to imagine that they had no enmity for one another in that moment, that their teapot steamed happily between them, and that they discussed, perhaps, the invention of longitude, or methods for slaughtering walrus.

First in the *Orcadas* series, this prime specimen of Acuña at his height has been assessed at $6200US.

Lot 705G
Map of the South Orkney Islands (The Seal Pot Map)
Maldonado, Villalba, 1914
Single owner, very slight water damage, lower right corner.

Five large islands and twenty-six smaller isles lie in the center of the map. All are named: Isla Concepción, Isla Immaculata, Isla Perdita, Isla Proximidad, Isla Gloriana, Isla Hibisco, Isla Sello Zafiro, Isla Pingüino Azul, Isla Cielo, Isla Pájaros del Musgo, Isla Valeroso, Isla Ermitaño, Isla Ocultado, Isla Graciento, Isla Mudanza, Isla del Leones Incansable, Isla

Sombras Blancas, Isla del Ballenas del Fantasma, Isla Zapato, Isla del Mar de Cristal, Isla del Morsas Calvas, Isla Rojo, Isla Ónice, Isla Embotado, Isla Mentira, Isla del Araña Verde, Isla Abejas, Isla del Pie de la Reina, Isla Acuña, Isla Pilar.

All ink sepia, compass is a seal's head peeking out of an iron pot, her flipper pointed south, the pot handles east and west, and her head, capped by the pot's lid, indicating north. Smaller versions of this creature dot the island chain, their faces intricately inscribed. The legend claims that these Footless Seals can be found on the sometimes-green shores of Isla Graciento, on the long Norwegian flensing plain that occupies most of the island: *When the Iron Try Pots left to render Seal Fat are left to boil until Moonrise, it occasionally Happens that a severed Seal Head which has a Certain blue Tinge to its whiskers will Blink and open its Eyes, and with Cunning Hop Away into the surf, carrying the Iron Try Pot with it as a new Body. If an Explorer is very clever, he will leave a few of his campfire Embers burning and pretend to Sleep. If he is an Excellent Feinter of Slumber, the Queen of the Seal Pots whose name is Huln will come to rest upon the dying Fire and warm Herself. If he has brought three Pearls as tribute, the Queen will allow him to dip his Spoon into the Pot and drink of her Broth, which is sweeter than dandelion honey, and will keep him Fed and Happy for a fortnight and more.* (translation: Furtado, 1971)

Unable to convince the skeptic Alvaro Caceres to fund a second expedition despite the popularity of his work, Villalba Maldonado contented himself with the attentions of Pilar Caceres. Portraits (Lots 114 & 115A-F) show a handsome, if severe woman, with a high widow's peak and narrow eyes. She continued to sell her jewelry to print his maps, but no amount of necklaces could equal a southbound vessel. However, she became an expert in the preparation of sheepskin parchment, and in this manner became all the more Maldonado's patroness. She wore red whenever she met with him, and allowed her thick hair to fall at least three times upon his arm. With the grudging consent of Alvaro, Villalba and Pilar were married in April of 1911. She wore no jewels, and her dress was black sealskin. She was soon pregnant, and their daughter Soledad was born shortly after Maldonado departed on the *Perdita* in 1912. Pilar arranged for him to stay on through 1915 as a nominal military service, and thus both cartographers walked the ice floes during the Great War, far from each other and as ignorant of the other's activities as of the rest of the world.

Six maps were printed and distributed between 1908 and 1912. Each was received with ravenous acclaim, and applications for passage to Antarctica tripled. "Paquetes" were sold at docks (Lots 441A-492L), wooden boxes containing "supplies" for a successful Antartic expedition: desiccated penguin feet, bundles of liverwort, fishing poles, sheets of music to be sung at the ice-grottos of the Dream-Stealing Toothfish, cheap copies of the six maps, and three small pearls. However, most enthusiasts found themselves ultimately unable to make such a perilous voyage, and thus Maldonado's reputation grew in the absence of Acuña or any definite rebuttal of Maldonado's wonderful maps.

Not to be confused with the plentiful copies included in the *paquetes*, this original Caceres-issue map has been assessed at $15900US.

Lot 718K
Map of Queen Maud's Land
Acuña, Nahuel, 1920
Single owner, immaculate condition.

Landmass right center, Chilean coast visible in top left quadrant. Latitude and longitude in iron gall ink. Compass rose is the top half of a young woman, her head tipped up toward north, her arms open wide to encompass east and west, her hair twisting southward into a point. See Referent C for satellite comparison, Points 1, 4, and 17 for major deviations.

Curator's Note: Obviously Queen Maud's Land was not the common appellation at the time of Acuña's map, however, his own term, Suyai's Plain, was never recognized by any government making a claim to the territory.

Upon returning from the South Orkneys in 1919, Acuña was horrified by the *paquetes* and Maldonado's celebrity. The sheer danger of packing penguin's feet instead of lamp oil made him ill, and he immediately scheduled a series of lectures condemning the cartographer, challenging him to produce either Grell or Skell (he did not state a preference) on a chain at the Asociación banquet, or Huln, if the dogs were recalcitrant.

Attendant at these lectures was a young woman by the name of Suyai Ledesma. In imitation of her idol, Suyai had begun to produce her own maps of the *pampas*, the vast Argentine interior where both she and Acuña had been born. She presented her research at the Asociación banquet in a modest brown suit, her voice barely audible. She concluded with a gentle reminder that "the cartographer's art relies on accuracy as the moon relies on the sun to shed her own light on the world. To turn our backs on the authentic universe, as it exists beneath and before us, is to plunge into darkness."

Though Ledesma and Acuña never married, they were not often separated thenceforward, and she accompanied him along with their two sons on the *Lethe* expedition to Iles Kerguelen in 1935.

However, until the 1935 expedition, Acuña felt it was his duty to remain in Buenos Aires, to struggle against Maldonadan Antarcticana and its perils, and to rail against his rival whenever he was given a podium and a crowd with more than two folk to rub together. These philippics were eventually assembled and published posthumously by Carrizo and Rivas under the title *On Authenticity* (1961). One copy remains outside of private collections. (Lot 112C)

Maldonado responded slowly, as was his habit in all things. In 1922, his sole rejoinder was a small package, immaculately wrapped, delivered to Acuña's home. Inside was long golden chain attached to a crystal dog's collar (Lot 559M) and a note (Lot 560M) reading: *As you see I do not, as I see, you disdain. It is big enough.*

But fate would have her way, and in the end the Antarctic was not quite big enough after all. In January of 1922, three young men were found frozen to their ship on the Shackleton Ice Shelf, still clutching their *paquetes*, in possession of neither a cup of sun nor the Queen of the Try Pots. In May, Acuña had Villalba Maldonado arrested for public endangerment.

This pristine map of Queen Maud's Land, produced at the height of conflict, has been assessed at $6700US.

Lot 781A
Map of the South Pole (The Petrel Map)
Maldonado, Villalba, 1925
Significant damage, burns in top center portion

Landmass center, eastern Antarctic coast visible. Latitude and longitude in walnut ink, black tea, and human blood. Compass rose: a snow petrel rampant, her claws demarcating southeast and southwest, her tail flared due south, her wings spread east and west, and her head fixed at true north. Beneath her is emblazoned: Seal of the Antarctic Postal Service—*Glacies Non Impedimenta*. (Ice Is No Impediment.) Alone of the Maldonado maps, color of indeterminate and probably morbid origin have been used to stain portions of the interior red, differentiating zones of "watermelon snow," fulminating plains of lichen grown bright and thick, bearing fruits which when cracked open are found to be full of fresh water, more and sweeter than any may ask. The red fields encircle a zone of blue ice, frozen rainwater enclosing a lake of brine. Upon this rainwater mantle, explains the map legend, sits the Magnetic Pole, which is a chair made of try pots and harpoon-blades. The Pole sits tall there, her hair encased in fresh, sweet water gone to ice, her eyes filmed. Her dress is black sealskin, her necklaces are all of bone and skulls. *Grell and Skell they are Her Playmates, Her Guardians Dire, and Huln she is Her Handmaid, but Never moves She, even Once.* (translation: Peralta, 1988.)

She is waiting, the notations go on to state, for the petrels which are her loyal envoys, to deliver a letter into her hands, written on sheepskin, whose ink is blood. What this letter will read and who it may be from, no whaler may say—it is for her alone, and she alone may touch it.

The Petrel Map was produced in Maldonado's third year in prison, delivered to the printer's by his bailiff and repaired there, as the original document was created using unorthodox methods, owing to Villalba's lack of access to plentiful inks. The viciousness and length of his incarceration and Acuña's uncommon success in enforcing the sentence may be credited to many things: the influence of the spurned Asociación, the corrupt bureaucracy which was prone to forgetting and misplacing whole cartographers, the persuasiveness of Acuña and the pregnant Suyai as to the menace of Maldonado and his clearly deliberate deceits. Nevertheless, the summer of 1925 saw the first map in three years, and a new rash of *paquetes* eagerly broke the docks, the Shackleton incident all but forgotten. Stamps of the Antarctic Postal Service were now included, along with stationary and "ice-proof" pencils.

The Petrel Map was completed from memory, according to Pilar, a testament to an extraordinary intellect bent on total and accurate recollection. Public outcry warred with the Asociación on the subject of Maldonado's release, and funds were mounted for a *Proximidad II* expedition, but there was no one to receive it, the Caceres-Maldonado accounts having been frozen, and the usual half-benign institutional fraud absorbed the money once more into the body of the state. Meanwhile, Acuña's tarnished star rose, and he was commissioned by the British Navy to deliver maps of the subcontinent.

By 1928 Maldonado was in complete isolation. He was not allowed visits from his wife, or perhaps more tellingly for our purposes, letters. Acuña was recorded as visiting once, in 1930, with his young son Raiquen. It is not for us to imagine this meeting, so far from the decks of the *Proximidad* and salads of lichen, far from claret and the green shadows of the *aurora australis*. However, after this incident, Acuña arranged for Maldonado to be moved to a special penitentiary in Ushuaia, on the southern tip of Argentina, with the shores of the South Shetlands in sight, on very clear days.

The Great Man looked up from his bread and held the eye of the Naval Cartographer. Their beards were both very long, but Acuña's was neatly cut and kept, while Maldonado's snarled and ran to the stone floor.

"I promised you, my friend," he said, his voice very rough, "that it was big enough. Big enough for us both to look on it and hold in our vision two separate countries, bound only by longitude."

"What's big enough?" little Raiquen asked, tugging on his father's hand, which had two gold rings upon it.

But Acuña did not answer. For my own part, my heart was filled with long plains of ice receding into eternity, and on those plains my prisoner walked with bare feet and a cup of gold.
—*Keeper of the Key: The Autobiography of a Prison Guard, Rafael Soto, 1949*

Villalba Maldonado died at Ushuaia on June 4th 1933. Acuña lived, feted and richly funded, until 1951, when he drowned off the shore of Isla Concepción. Suyai and her sons continued in residence on the islands, producing between them twelve maps of the area. (Lots 219-231H) Raiquen relocated in middle age to the mainland where he lives still in well-fed obscurity.

The Petrel Map was Maldonado's final work, and as such, has been assessed at $57000US.

Lot 994D
Captain's Logbook, the *Anamnesis*, disembarked from Ushuaia, 1934

Here is presented the logbook in which Soledad Maldonado signed her name and declared her cargo—an iron coffin lashed to a long sled. She left her ailing mother in Buenos Aires and sailed south as soon as tide and melt permitted, and Captain Godoy deposited her on the floes of the Weddell Sea per instructions. His full account of the voyage and Soledad's peculiar habits, studies, and intentions will be released only to the buyer, however, his notes conclude thus:

I watched the young lady amid her supplies, her sled, her eight bristling dogs, her father's long, cold coffin. She gave me a cool glance in farewell and turned southward, towards the interior ice. She waited for a long while, though I could not think what for. It was drawing on night, and there were many stars showing when it happened, and I must insist that I be believed and not ridiculed, no matter what I may now write.

Two great dogs strode out from the long plains of ice, enormous, thickly furred, something like Saint Bernards. They pressed their noses into her hands and she petted their heads, scratched behind their ears, let them lick her face slowly, methodically, with great care. The huge hounds allowed her to yoke them at the head of her team, and without a whip she directed them inward, onward, hoisting aloft as they flew a long fishing pole, at the end of which was an orb of impossible light, like a cup overturned and spilling out the sun.

The Log Book has been assessed at $10700US. Bidding begins at noon precisely.

THE THINGS THAT MAKE ME WEAK AND STRANGE GET ENGINEERED AWAY

CORY DOCTOROW

[Tor.com]

> *'Cause it's gonna be the future soon,*
> *And I won't always be this way,*
> *When the things that make me weak and strange get engineered away*
> —Jonathan Coulton, "The Future Soon"

Lawrence's cubicle was just the right place to chew on a thorny logfile problem: decorated with the votive fetishes of his monastic order, a thousand calming, clarifying mandalas and saints devoted to helping him think clearly.

From the nearby cubicles, Lawrence heard the ritualized muttering of a thousand brothers and sisters in the Order of Reflective Analytics, a susurration of harmonized, concentrated thought. On his display, he watched an instrument widget track the decibel level over time, the graph overlaid on a 3D curve of normal activity over time and space. He noted that the level was a little high, the room a little more anxious than usual.

He clicked and tapped and thought some more, massaging the logfile to see if he could make it snap into focus and make sense, but it stubbornly refused to be sensible. The data tracked the custody chain of the bitstream the Order munged for the Securitat, and somewhere in there, a file had grown by sixty-eight bytes, blowing its checksum and becoming An Anomaly.

Order lore was filled with Anomalies, loose threads in the fabric of reality—bugs to be squashed in the data-set that was the Order's universe.

Starting with the pre-Order sysadmin who'd tracked a $0.75 billing anomaly back to foreign spy-ring that was using his systems to hack his military, these morality tales were object lessons to the Order's monks: pick at the seams and the world will unravel in useful and interesting ways.

Lawrence had reached the end of his personal picking capacity, though. It was time to talk it over with Gerta.

He stood up and walked away from his cubicle, touching his belt to let his sensor array know that he remembered it was there. It counted his steps and his heartbeats and his EEG spikes as he made his way out into the compound.

It's not like Gerta was in charge—the Order worked in autonomous little units with rotating leadership, all coordinated by some groupware that let them keep the hierarchy nice and flat, the way that they all liked it. Authority sucked.

But once you instrument every keystroke, every click, every erg of productivity, it soon becomes apparent who knows her shit and who just doesn't. Gerta knew the shit cold.

"Question," he said, walking up to her. She liked it brusque. No nonsense.

She batted her handball against the court wall three more times, making long dives for it, sweaty grey hair whipping back and forth, body arcing in graceful flows. Then she caught the ball and tossed it into the basket by his feet. "Lester, huh? All right, surprise me."

"It's this," he said, and tossed the file at her pan. She caught it with the same fluid gesture and her computer gave it to her on the handball court wall, which was the closest display for which she controlled the lockfile. She peered at the data, spinning the graph this way and that, peering intently.

She pulled up some of her own instruments and replayed the bitstream, recalling the logfiles from many network taps from the moment at which the file grew by the anomalous sixty-eight bytes.

"You think it's an Anomaly, don't you?" She had a fine blond mustache that was beaded with sweat, but her breathing had slowed to normal and her hands were steady and sure as she gestured at the wall.

"I was kind of hoping, yeah. Good opportunity for personal growth, your Anomalies."

"Easy to say why you'd call it an Anomaly, but look at this." She pulled the checksum of the injected bytes, then showed him her network taps, which were playing the traffic back and forth for several minutes before and after the insertion. The checksummed block moved back through the routers, one hop, two hops, three hops, then to a terminal. The authentication data for the terminal told them who owned its lockfile then: Zbigniew Krotoski, login zbigkrot. Gerta grabbed his room number.

"Now, we don't have the actual payload, of course, because that gets flushed. But we have the checksum, we have the username, and look at this, we have him typing eighty-six unspecified bytes in a pattern consistent with his biometrics five minutes and eight seconds prior to the injection. So, let's go ask him what his sixty-eight characters were and why they got added to the Securitat's data-stream."

He led the way, because he knew the corner of the campus where zbigkrot worked pretty well, having lived there for five years when he first joined the Order. Zbigkrot was probably a relatively recent inductee, if he was still in that block.

His belt gave him a reassuring buzz to let him know he was being logged as he entered the building, softer haptic feedback coming as he was logged to each floor as they went up the clean-swept wooden stairs. Once, he'd had the work-detail of re-staining those stairs, stripping the ancient wood, sanding it baby-skin smooth, applying ten coats of varnish, polishing it to a high gloss. The work had been incredible, painful and rewarding, and seeing the stairs still shining gave him a tangible sense of satisfaction.

He knocked at zbigkrot's door twice before entering. Technically, any brother or sister was allowed to enter any room on the campus, though there were norms of privacy and decorum that were far stronger than any law or rule.

The room was bare, every last trace of its occupant removed. A fine dust covered every surface, swirling in clouds as they took a few steps in. They both coughed explosively and stepped back, slamming the door.

"Skin," Gerta croaked. "Collected from the ventilation filters. DNA for every person on campus, in a nice, even, Gaussian distribution. Means we can't use biometrics to figure out who was in this room before it was cleaned out."

Lawrence tasted the dust in his mouth and swallowed his gag reflex. Technically, he knew that he was always inhaling and ingesting other peoples' dead skin-cells, but not by the mouthful.

"All right," Gerta said. "Now you've got an Anomaly. Congrats, Lawrence. Personal growth awaits you."

The campus only had one entrance to the wall that surrounded it. "Isn't that a fire-hazard?" Lawrence asked the guard who sat in the pillbox at the gate.

"Naw," the man said. He was old, with the serene air of someone who'd been in the Order for decades. His beard was combed and shining, plaited into a thick braid that hung to his belly, which had only the merest hint of a little pot. "Comes a fire, we hit the panic button, reverse the magnets lining the walls, and the foundations destabilize at twenty sections. The whole thing'd come down in seconds. But no one's going to sneak in or out that way."

"I did *not* know that," Lawrence said.

"Public record, of course. But pretty obscure. Too tempting to a certain prankster mindset."

Lawrence shook his head. "Learn something new every day."

The guard made a gesture that caused something to depressurize in the gateway. A primed *hum* vibrated through the floorboards. "We keep the inside of the vestibule at ten atmospheres, and it opens inward from outside. No one can force that door open without us knowing about it in a pretty dramatic way."

"But it must take forever to re-pressurize?"

"Not many people go in and out. Just data."

Lawrence patted himself down.

"You got everything?"

"Do I seem nervous to you?"

The old timer picked up his tea and sipped at it. "You'd be an idiot if you weren't. How long since you've been out?"

"Not since I came in. Sixteen years ago. I was twenty one."

"Yeah," the old timer said. "Yeah, you'd be an idiot if you weren't nervous. You follow politics?"

"Not my thing," Lawrence said. "I know it's been getting worse out there—"

The old timer barked a laugh. "Not your thing? It's probably time you got out into the wide world, son. You might ignore politics, but it won't ignore *you*."

"Is it dangerous?"

"You going armed?"

"I didn't know that was an option."

"Always an option. But not a smart one. Any weapon you don't know how to use belongs to your enemy. Just be circumspect. Listen before you talk. Watch before you act. They're good people out there, but they're in a bad, bad situation."

Lawrence shuffled his feet and shifted the straps of his bindle. "You're not making me very comfortable with all this, you know."

"Why are you going out anyway?"

"It's an Anomaly. My first. I've been waiting sixteen years for this. Someone poisoned the Securitat's data and left the campus. I'm going to go ask him why he did it."

The old man blew the gate. The heavy door lurched open, revealing the vestibule. "Sounds like an Anomaly all right." He turned away and Lawrence forced himself to move toward the vestibule. The man held his hand out before he reached it. "You haven't been outside in fifteen years, it's going to be a surprise. Just remember, we're a noble species, all appearances to the contrary notwithstanding."

Then he gave Lawrence a little shove that sent him into the vestibule. The door slammed behind him. The vestibule smelled like machine oil and rubber, gaskety smells. It was dimly lit by rows of white LEDs that marched up the walls like drunken ants. Lawrence barely had time to register this before he heard a loud *thunk* from the outer door and it swung away.

Lawrence walked down the quiet street, staring up at the same sky he'd lived under, breathing the same air he'd always breathed, but marveling at how *different* it all was. His heartbeat and respiration were up—the tips of the first two fingers on his right hand itched slightly under his feedback gloves—and his thoughts were doing that race-condition thing where every time he tried to concentrate on something he thought about how he was trying to concentrate on something and should stop thinking about how he was concentrating and just concentrate.

This was how it had been sixteen years before, when he'd gone into the Order. He'd been so *angry* all the time then. Sitting in front of his keyboard, looking at the world through the lens of the network, suffering all the fools with poor grace. He'd been a bright fourteen-year-old, a genius at sixteen, a rising star at eighteen, and a failure by twenty-one. He was depressed all the time, his weight had ballooned to nearly three hundred pounds, and he had been fired three times in two years.

One day he stood up from his desk at work—he'd just been hired at a company that was selling learning, trainable vision-systems for analyzing images, who liked him because he'd retained his security clearance when he'd been fired from his previous job—and walked out of the building. It had been a blowing, wet, grey day, and the streets of New York were as empty as they ever got.

Standing on Sixth Avenue, looking north from midtown, staring at the buildings the cars and the buses and the people and the tallwalkers, that's when he had his realization: *He was not meant to be in this world.*

It just didn't suit him. He could *see* its workings, see how its politics and policies were flawed, see how the system needed debugging, see what made its people work, but he couldn't touch it. Every time he reached in to adjust its settings, he got mangled by its gears. He couldn't convince his bosses that he knew what they were doing wrong. He couldn't convince his colleagues that he knew best. Nothing he did succeeded—every attempt he made to right the wrongs of the world made him miserable and made everyone else angry.

Lawrence knew about humans, so he knew about this: this was the exact profile of the people in the Order. Normally he would have taken the subway home. It was forty blocks to his place, and he didn't get around so well anymore. Plus there was the rain and the wind.

But today, he walked, huffing and limping, using his cane more and more as he got further and further uptown, his knee complaining with each step. He got to his apartment and found that the elevator was out of service—second time that month—and so he took the stairs. He arrived at his apartment so out of breath he felt like he might vomit.

He stood in the doorway, clutching the frame, looking at his sofa and table, the piles of books, the dirty dishes from that morning's breakfast in the little sink. He'd watched a series of short videos about the Order once, and he'd been struck by the little monastic cells each member occupied, so neat, so tidy, everything in its perfect place, serene and thoughtful.

So unlike his place.

He didn't bother to lock the door behind him when he left. They said New York was the burglary capital of the developed world, but he didn't know anyone who'd been burgled. If the burglars came, they were welcome to everything they could carry away and the landlord could take the rest. He was not meant to be in this world.

He walked back out into the rain and, what the hell, hailed a cab, and, hail mary, one stopped when he put his hand out. The cabbie grunted when he said he was going to Staten Island, but, what the hell, he pulled three twenties out of his wallet and slid them through the glass partition. The cabbie put the pedal down. The rain sliced through the Manhattan canyons and battered the windows and they went over the Verrazano Bridge and he said goodbye to his life and the outside world forever, seeking a world he could be a part of.

Or at least, that's how he felt, as his heart swelled with the drama of it all. But the truth was much less glamorous. The brothers who admitted him at the gate were cheerful and a little weird, like his co-workers, and he didn't get a nice clean cell to begin with, but a bunk in a shared room and a detail helping to build more quarters. And they didn't leave his stuff for the burglars—someone from the Order went and cleaned out his place and put his stuff in a storage locker on campus, made good with his landlord and so on. By the time it was all over, it all felt a little . . . ordinary. But in a good way, Ordinary was good. It had been a long time since he'd felt ordinary. Order, ordinary. They went together. He needed ordinary.

The Securitat van played a cheerful engine-tone as it zipped down the street towards him. It looked like a children's drawing—a perfect little electrical box with two seats in front and a meshed-in lockup in the rear. It accelerated smoothly down the street towards him, then braked perfectly at his toes, rocking slightly on its suspension as its doors gull-winged up.

"Cool!" he said, involuntarily, stepping back to admire the smart little car. He reached for the lifelogger around his neck and aimed it at the two Securitat officers who were debarking, moving with stiff grace in their armor. As he raised the lifelogger, the officer closest to him reached out with serpentine speed and snatched it out of his hands, power-assisted fingers coming together on it with a loud, plasticky *crunk* as the device shattered into a rain of fragments. Just as quickly, the other officer had come around the vehicle and seized Lawrence's wrists, bringing them together in a painful, machine-assisted grip.

The one who had crushed his lifelogger passed his palms over Lawrence's chest, arms and legs, holding them a few millimeters away from him. Lawrence's pan went nuts, intrusion detection sensors reporting multiple hostile reads of his identifiers, millimeter-wave radar scans, HERF attacks, and assorted shenanigans. All his feedback systems went to full alert, going from itchy, back-of-the-neck liminal sensations into high intensity pinches, prods and buzzes. It was a deeply alarming sensation, like his internal organs were under attack.

He choked out an incoherent syllable, and the Securitat man who was hand-wanding him raised a warning finger, holding it so close to his nose he went cross-eyed. He fell silent while the man continued to wand him, twitching a little to let his pan know that it was all OK.

"From the cult, then, are you?" the Securitat man said, after he'd kicked Lawrence's ankles apart and spread his hands on the side of the truck.

"That's right," Lawrence said. "From the Order." He jerked his head toward the gates, just a few tantalizing meters away. "I'm out—"

"You people are really something, you know that? You could have been *killed*. Let me tell you a few things about how the world works: when you are approached by the Securitat, you stand still with your hands stretched straight out to either side. You do *not* raise unidentified devices and point them at the officers. Not unless you're trying to commit suicide by cop. Is that what you're trying to do?"

"No," Lawrence said. "No, of course not. I was just taking a picture for—"

"And you do *not* photograph or log our security procedures. There's a war on, you know." The man's forehead bunched together. "Oh, for shit's sake. We should take you in now, you know it? Tie up a dozen people's day, just to process you through the system. You could end up in a cell for, oh, I don't know, a month. You want that?"

"Of course not," Lawrence said. "I didn't realize—"

"You didn't, but you *should have*. If you're going to come walking around here where the real people are, you have to learn how to behave like a real person in the real world."

The other man, who had been impassively holding Lawrence's wrists in a crushing grip, eased up. "Let him go?" he said.

The first officer shook his head. "If I were you, I would turn right around, walk through those gates, and never come out again. Do I make myself clear?"

Lawrence wasn't clear at all. Was the cop ordering him to go back? Or just giving him advice? Would he be arrested if he didn't go back in? It had been a long time since Lawrence had dealt with authority and the feeling wasn't a good one. His chest heaved, and sweat ran down his back, pooling around his ass, then moving in rivulets down the backs of his legs.

"I understand," he said. Thinking: *I understand that asking questions now would not be a good idea.*

The subway was more or less as he remembered it, though the long line of people waiting to get through the turnstiles turned out to be a line to go through a security checkpoint, complete with bag-search and X-ray. But the New Yorkers were the same—no one made eye contact with anyone else, but if they did, everyone shared a kind of bitter shrug, as if to say, *Ain't it the fuckin' truth?*

But the smell was the same—oil and damp and bleach and the indefinable, human smell of a place where millions had passed for decades, where millions would pass for decades to come. He found himself standing before a subway map, looking at it, comparing it to the one in his memory to find the changes, the new stations that must have sprung up during his hiatus from reality.

But there weren't new stations. In fact, it seemed to him that there were a lot *fewer* stations—hadn't there been one at Bleecker Street, and another at Cathedral Parkway? Yes, there had been—but look now, they were gone, and . . . and there were stickers, white stickers over the places where the stations had been. He reached up and touched the one over Bleecker Street.

"I still can't get used to it, either," said a voice at his side. "I used to change for the F Train there every day when I was a kid." It was a woman, about the same age as Gerta, but more beaten down by the years, deeper creases in her face, a stoop in her stance. But her face was kind, her eyes soft.

"What happened to it?"

She took a half-step back from him. "Bleecker Street," she said. "You know, Bleecker Street? Like 9/11? Bleecker Street?" Like the name of the station was an incantation.

It rang a bell. It wasn't like he didn't ever read the news, but it had a way of sliding off of you when you were on campus, as though it was some historical event in a book, not something happening right there, on the other side of the wall.

"I'm sorry," he said. "I've been away. Bleecker Street, yes, of course."

She gave him a squinty stare. "You must have been *very* far away."

He tried out a sheepish grin. "I'm a monk," he said. "From the Order of Reflective Analytics. I've been out of the world for sixteen years. Until today, in fact. My name is Lawrence." He stuck his hand out and she shook it like it was made of china.

"A monk," she said. "That's very interesting. Well, you enjoy your little vacation." She turned on her heel and walked quickly down the platform. He watched her for a moment, then turned back to the map, counting the missing stations.

When the train ground to a halt in the tunnel between 42nd and 50th street, the entire car let out a collective groan. When the lights flickered and went out, they groaned louder. The emergency lights came on in sickly green and an incomprehensible announcement played over the loudspeakers. Evidently, it was an order to evacuate, because the press of people began to struggle through the door at the front of the car, then further and further. Lawrence let the press of bodies move him too.

Once they reached the front of the train, they stepped down onto the tracks, each passenger turning silently to help the next, again with that *Ain't it the fuckin' truth?* look. Lawrence turned to help the person behind him and saw that it was the woman who'd spoken to him on the platform. She smiled a little smile at him and turned with practiced ease to help the person behind her.

They walked single file on a narrow walkway beside the railings. Securitat officers were strung out at regular intervals, wearing night scopes and high, rubberized boots. They played flashlights over the walkers as they evacuated.

"Does this happen often?" Lawrence said over his shoulder. His words were absorbed by the dead subterranean air and he thought that she might not have heard him but then she sighed.

"Only every time there's an anomaly in the head-count—when the system says there's too many or too few people in the trains. Maybe once a week." He could feel her staring at the back of his head. He looked back at her and saw her shaking her head. He stumbled and went down on one knee, clanging his head against the stone walls made soft by a fur of condensed train exhaust, cobwebs and dust.

She helped him to his feet. "You don't seem like a snitch, Lawrence. But you're a monk. Are you going to turn me in for being suspicious?"

He took a second to parse this out. "I don't work for the Securitat," he said. It seemed like the best way to answer.

She snorted. "That's not what we hear. Come on, they're going to start shouting at us if we don't move."

They walked the rest of the way to an emergency staircase together, and emerged out of a sidewalk grating, blinking in the remains of the autumn sunlight, a bloody color on the glass of the highrises. She looked at him and made a face. "You're filthy, Lawrence." She thumped at his sleeves and great dirty clouds rose off them. He looked down at the knees of his pants and saw that they were hung with boogers of dust.

The New Yorkers who streamed past them ducked to avoid the dirty clouds. "Where can I clean up?" he said.

"Where are you staying?"

"I was thinking I'd see about getting a room at the Y or a backpacker's hostel, somewhere to stay until I'm done."

"Done?"

"I'm on a complicated errand. Trying to locate someone who used to be in the Order."

Her face grew hard again. "No one gets out alive, huh?"

He felt himself blushing. "It's not like that. Wow, you've got strange ideas about us. I want to find this guy because he disappeared under mysterious circumstances and I want to—" How to explain Anomalies to an outsider? "It's a thing we do. Unravel mysteries. It makes us better people."

"Better people?" She snorted again. "Better than what? Don't answer. Come on, I live near here. You can wash up at my place and be on your way. You're not going to get into any backpacker's hostel looking like you just crawled out of a sewer—you're more likely to get detained for being an 'indigent of suspicious character.' "

He let her steer him a few yards uptown. "You think that I work for the Securitat but you're inviting me into your home?"

She shook her head and led him around a corner, along a long cross-town block, and then turned back uptown. "No," she said. "I think you're a confused stranger who is apt to get himself into some trouble if someone doesn't take you in hand and help you get smart, fast. It doesn't cost me anything to lend a hand, and you don't seem like the kind of guy who'd mug, rape and kill an old lady."

"The discipline," he said, "is all about keeping track of the way that the world is, and comparing it to your internal perceptions, all the time. When I entered the Order, I was really big. Fat, I mean. The discipline made me log every bit of food I ate, and I discovered a few important things: first, I was eating about twenty times a day, just grazing on whatever happened to be around. Second, that I was consuming about four thousand calories a day, mostly in industrial sugars like high-fructose corn syrup. Just *knowing* how I ate made a gigantic difference. I felt like I ate sensibly, always ordering a salad with lunch and dinner, but I missed the fact that I was glooping on half a cup of sweetened, high-fat dressing, and having a cookie or two every hour between lunch and dinner, and a half-pint of ice-cream before bed most nights.

"But it wasn't just food—in the Order, we keep track of *everything*; our typing patterns, our sleeping patterns, our moods, our reading habits. I discovered that I read faster when I've been sleeping more, so now, when I need to really get through a lot of reading, I make sure I sleep more. Used to be I'd try to stay up all night with pots of coffee to get the reading done. Of course, the more sleep-deprived I was, the slower I read; and the slower I read the more I needed to stay up to catch up with the reading. No wonder college was such a blur.

"So that's why I've stayed. It's empiricism, it's as old as Newton, as the Enlightenment." He took another sip of his water, which tasted like New York tap water had always tasted (pretty good, in fact), and which he hadn't tasted for sixteen years. The woman was called Posy, and her old leather sofa was worn but well-loved, and smelled of saddle soap. She was watching him from a kitchen chair she'd brought around to the living room of the tiny apartment, rubbing her stockinged feet over the good wool carpet that showed a few old stains hiding beneath strategically placed furnishings and knick-knacks.

He had to tell her the rest, of course. You couldn't understand the Order unless you understood the rest. "I'm a screwup, Posy. Or at least, I was. We all were. Smart and motivated and promising, but just a wretched person to be around. Angry, bitter, all those smarts turned on biting the heads off of the people who were dumb enough to care about me or employ me. And so smart that I could talk myself into believing that it was all everyone else's fault, the idiots. It took instrumentation, empiricism, to get me to understand the patterns of my own life, to master my life, to become the person I wanted to be."

"Well, you seem like a perfectly nice young man now," Posy said.

That was clearly his cue to go, and he'd changed into a fresh set of trousers, but he couldn't go, not until he'd picked apart something she'd said earlier. "Why did you think I was a snitch?"

"I think you know that very well, Lawrence," she said. "I can't imagine someone who's so into measuring and understanding the world could possibly have missed it."

Now he knew what she was talking about. "We just do contract work for the Securitat. It's just one of the ways the Order sustains itself." The founders had gone into business refilling toner cartridges, which was like the 21st century equivalent of keeping bees or brewing dark, thick beer. They'd branched out into remote IT administration, then into data-mining and security, which was a natural for people with Order training. "But it's all anonymized. We don't snitch on people. We report on anomalous events. We do it for lots of different companies, too—not just the Securitat."

Posy walked over to the window behind her small dining room table, rolling away a couple of handsome old chairs on castors to reach it. She looked down over the billion lights of Manhattan, stretching all the way downtown to Brooklyn. She motioned to him to come over, and he squeezed in beside her. They were on the twenty-third floor, and it had been many years since he'd stood this high and looked down. The world is different from high up.

"There," she said, pointing at an apartment building across the way. "There, you see it? With the broken windows?" He saw it, the windows covered in cardboard. "They took them away last week. I don't know why. You never know why. You become a person of interest and they take you away and then later, they always find a reason to keep you away."

Lawrence's hackles were coming up. He found stuff that didn't belong in the data—he didn't arrest people. "So if they always find a reason to keep you away, doesn't that mean—"

She looked like she wanted to slap him and he took a step back. "We're all guilty of something, Lawrence. That's how the game is rigged. Look closely at anyone's life and you'll find, what, a little black-marketeering, a copyright infringement, some cash economy business with unreported income, something obscene in your Internet use, something in your bloodstream that shouldn't be there. I bought that sofa from a *cop*, Lawrence, bought it ten years ago when he was leaving the building. He didn't give me a receipt and didn't collect tax, and technically that makes us offenders." She slapped the radiator. "I overrode the governor on this ten minutes after they installed it. Everyone does it. They make it easy—you just stick a penny between two contacts and hey presto, the city can't turn your heat down anymore. They wouldn't make it so easy if they didn't expect everyone to do it—and once everyone's done it, we're all guilty.

"The people across the street, they were Pakistani or maybe Sri Lankan or Bangladeshi. I'd see the wife at the service laundry. Nice professional lady, always lugging around a couple kids on their way to or from day-care. She—" Posy broke off and stared again. "I once saw her reach for her change and her sleeve rode up and there was a number tattooed there, there on her wrist." Posy shuddered. "When they took her and her husband and their kids, she stood at the window and pounded at it and screamed for help. You could hear her from here."

"That's terrible," Lawrence said. "But what does it have to do with the Order?"

She sat back down. "For someone who is supposed to know himself, you're not very good at connecting the dots."

Lawrence stood up. He felt an obscure need to apologize. Instead, he thanked her and put his glass in the sink. She shook his hand solemnly.

"Take care out there," she said. "Good luck finding your escapee."

Here's what Lawrence knew about Zbigniew Krotoski. He had been inducted into the Order four years earlier. He was a native-born New Yorker. He had spent his first two years in the Order trying to coax some of the elders into a variety of pointless flamewars about the ethics of working for the Securitat, and then had settled into being a very productive member. He spent his 20 percent time—the time when each monk had to pursue non-work-related projects—building aerial photography rigs out of box-kites and tiny cameras that the Monks installed on their systems to help them monitor their body mechanics and ergonomic posture.

Zbigkrot performed in the eighty-fifth percentile of the Order, which was respectable enough. Lawrence had started there and had crept up and down as low as seventy and as high as eighty-eight, depending on how he was doing in the rest of his life. Zbigkrot was active in the gardens, both the big ones where they grew their produce and a little allotment garden where he indulged in baroque cross-breeding experiments, which were in vogue among the monks then.

The Securitat stream to which he'd added sixty-eight bytes was long gone, but it was the kind of thing that the Order handled on a routine basis: given the timing and other characteristics, Lawrence thought it was probably a stream of purchase data from hardware and grocery stores, to be inspected for unusual patterns that might indicate someone buying bomb ingredients. Zbigkrot had worked on this kind of data thousands of times before, six times just that day. He'd added the sixty-eight bytes and then left, invoking his right to do so at the lone gate. The gatekeeper on duty remembered him carrying a little rucksack, and mentioning that he was going to see his sister in New York.

Zbigkrot once had a sister in New York—that much could be ascertained. Anja Krotoski had lived on 23rd Street in a co-op near Lexington. But that had been four years previous, when he'd joined the Order, and she wasn't there anymore. Her numbers all rang dead.

The apartment building had once been a pleasant, middle-class sort of place, with a red awning and a niche for a doorman. Now it had become more run down, the awning's edges frayed, one pane of lobby glass broken out and replaced with a sheet of cardboard. The doorman was long gone.

It seemed to Lawrence that this fate had befallen many of the City's buildings. They reminded him of the buildings he'd seen in Belgrade one time, when he'd been sent out to brief a gang of outsource programmers his boss had hired—neglected for years, indifferently patched by residents who had limited access to materials.

It was the dinner hour, and a steady trickle of people were letting themselves into Anja's old building. Lawrence watched a couple of them enter the building and noticed something wonderful and sad: as they approached the building, their faces were the hard masks of city-dwellers, not meeting anyone's eye, clipping along at a fast pace that said, "Don't screw with me." But once they passed the threshold of their building and the door closed behind them, their whole affect changed. They slumped, they smiled at one another, they leaned against the mailboxes and set down their bags and took off their hats and fluffed their hair and turned back into people.

He remembered that feeling from his life before, the sense of having two faces: the one he showed to the world and the one that he reserved for home. In the Order, he only wore one face, one that he knew in exquisite detail.

He approached the door now, and his pan started to throb ominously, letting him know that he was enduring hostile probes. The building wanted to know who he was and what business he had there, and it was attempting to fingerprint everything about him from his pan to his gait to his face.

He took up a position by the door and dialed back the pan's response to a dull pulse. He waited for a few minutes until one of the residents came down: a middle-aged man with a dog, a little sickly-looking schnauzer with grey in its muzzle.

"Can I help you?" the man said, from the other side of the security door, not unlatching it.

"I'm looking for Anja Krotoski," he said. "I'm trying to track down her brother."

The man looked him up and down. "Please step away from the door."

He took a few steps back. "Does Ms. Krotoski still live here?"

The man considered. "I'm sorry, sir, I can't help you." He waited for Lawrence to react.

"You don't know, or you can't help me?"

"Don't wait under this awning. The police come if anyone waits under this awning for more than three minutes."

The man opened the door and walked away with his dog.

His phone rang before the next resident arrived. He cocked his head to answer it, then remembered that his lifelogger was dead and dug in his jacket for a mic. There was one at his wrist pulse-points used by the health array. He unvelcroed it and held it to his mouth.

"Hello?"

"It's Gerta, boyo. Wanted to know how your Anomaly was going."

"Not good," he said. "I'm at the sister's place and they don't want to talk to me."

"You're walking up to strangers and asking them about one of their neighbors, huh?"

He winced. "Put it that way, yeah, OK, I understand why this doesn't work. But Gerta, I feel like Rip Van Winkle here. I keep putting my foot in it. It's so different."

"People are people, Lawrence. Every bad behavior and every good one lurks within us. They were all there when you were in the world—in different proportion, with different triggers. But all there. You know yourself very well. Can you observe the people around you with the same keen attention?"

He felt slightly put upon. "That's what I'm trying—"

"Then you'll get there eventually. What, you're in a hurry?"

Well, no. He didn't have any kind of timeline. Some people chased Anomalies for *years*. But truth be told, he wanted to get out of the City and back onto campus. "I'm thinking of coming back to Campus to sleep."

Gerta clucked. "Don't give in to the agoraphobia, Lawrence. Hang in there. You haven't even heard my news yet, and you're already ready to give up?"

"What news? And I'm not giving up, just want to sleep in my own bed—"

"The entry checkpoints, Lawrence. You cannot do this job if you're going to spend four hours a day in security queues. Anyway, the news.

"It wasn't the first time he did it. I've been running the logs back three years and I've found at least a dozen streams that he tampered with. Each time he used a different technique. This was the first time we caught him. Used some pretty subtle tripwires when he did it, so he'd know if anyone ever caught on. Must have spent his whole life living on edge, waiting for that moment, waiting to bug out. Must have been a hard life."

"What was he doing? Spying?"

"Most assuredly," Gerta said. "But for whom? For the enemy? The Securitat?"

They'd considered going to the Securitat with the information, but why bother? The Order did business with the Securitat, but tried never to interact with them on any other terms. The Securitat and the Order had an implicit understanding: so long as the Order was performing excellent data-analysis, it didn't have to fret the kind of overt scrutiny that prevailed in the real world. Undoubtedly, the Securitat kept satellite eyes, data-snoopers, wiretaps, millimeter radar and every other conceivable surveillance trained on each Campus in the world, but at the end of the day, they were just badly socialized geeks who'd left the world, and useful geeks at that. The Securitat treated the Order the way that Lawrence's old bosses treated the company sysadmins: expendable geeks who no one cared about—so long as nothing went wrong.

No, there was no sense in telling the Securitat about the sixty-eight bytes.

"Why would the Securitat poison its own data-streams?"

"You know that when the Soviets pulled out of Finland, they found forty *kilometers* of wire-tapping wire in KGB headquarters? The building was only twelve stories tall! Spying begets spying. The worst, most dangerous enemy the Securitat has is the Securitat."

There were Securitat vans on the street around him, going past every now and again, eerily silent engines, playing their cheerful music. He stepped back into shadow, then thought better of it and stood under a pool of light.

"OK, so it was a habit. How do I find him? No one in the sister's building will talk to me."

"You need to put them at their ease. Tell them the truth, that often works."

"You know how people feel about the Order out here?" He thought of Posy. "I don't know if the truth is going to work here."

"You've been in the order for sixteen years. You're not just some fumble-tongued outcast anymore. Go talk to them."

"But—"

"Go, Lawrence. Go. You're a smart guy, you'll figure it out."

He went. Residents were coming home every few minutes now, carrying grocery bags, walking dogs, or dragging their tired feet. He almost approached a young woman, then figured that she wouldn't want to talk to a strange man on the street at night. He picked a guy in his thirties, wearing jeans and a huge old vintage coat that looked like it had come off the eastern front.

" 'Scuse me," he said. "I'm trying to find someone who used to live here."

The guy stopped and looked Lawrence up and down. He had a handsome sweater on underneath his coat, design-y and cosmopolitan, the kind of thing that made Lawrence think of Milan or Paris. Lawrence was keenly aware of his generic Order-issued suit, a brown, rumpled, ill-fitting thing, topped with a polymer coat that, while warm, hardly flattered.

"Good luck with that," he said, then started to move past.

"Please," Lawrence said. "I'm—I'm not used to how things are around here. There's probably some way I could ask you this that would put you at your ease, but I don't know what it is. I'm not good with people. But I really need to find this person, she used to live here."

The man stopped, looked at him again. He seemed to recognize something in Lawrence, or maybe it was that he was disarmed by Lawrence's honesty.

"Why would you want to do that?"

"It's a long story," he said. "Basically, though: I'm a monk from the Order of Reflective Analytics and one of our guys has disappeared. His sister used to live here—maybe she still does—and I wanted to ask her if she knew where I could find him."

"Let me guess, none of my neighbors wanted to help you."

"You're only the second guy I've asked, but yeah, pretty much."

"Out here in the real world, we don't really talk about each other to strangers. Too much like being a snitch. Lucky for you, my sister's in the Order, out in Oregon, so I know you're not all a bunch of snoops and stoolies. Who're you looking for?"

Lawrence felt a rush of gratitude for this man. "Anja Krotosky, number 11-J?"

"Oh," the man said. "Well, yeah, I can see why you'd have a hard time with the neighbors when it comes to old Anja. She was well-liked around here, before she went."

"Where'd she go? When?"

"What's your name, friend?"

"Lawrence."

"Lawrence, Anja *went*. Middle of the night kind of thing. No one heard a thing. The CCTVs stopped working that night. Nothing on the drive the next day. No footage at all."

"Like she skipped out?"

"They stopped delivering flyers to her door. There's only one power stronger than direct marketing."

"The Securitat took her?"

"That's what we figured. Nothing left in her place. Not a stick of furniture. We don't talk about it much. Not the thing that it pays to take an interest in."

"How long ago?"

"Two years ago," he said. A few more residents pushed past them. "Listen, I approve of what you people do in there, more or less. It's good that there's a place for the people who don't—you know, who don't have a place out here. But the way you make your living. I told my sister about this, the last time she visited, and she got very angry with me. She didn't see the difference between watching yourself and being watched."

Lawrence nodded. "Well, that's true enough. We don't draw a really sharp distinction. We all get to see one another's stats. It keeps us honest."

"That's fine, if you have the choice. But—" He broke off, looking self-conscious. Lawrence reminded himself that they were on a public street, the cameras on them, people passing by. Was one of them a snitch? The Securitat had talked about putting him away for a month, just for logging them. They could watch him all they wanted, but he couldn't look at them.

"I see the point." He sighed. He was cold and it was full autumn dark now. He still didn't have a room for the night and he didn't have any idea how he'd find Anja, much less zbigkrot. He began to understand why Anomalies were such a big deal.

He'd walked 18,453 steps that day, about triple what he did on campus. His heart rate had spiked several times, but not from exertion. Stress. He could feel it in his muscles now. He should really do some biofeedback, try to calm down, then run back his lifelogger and make some notes on how he'd reacted to people through the day.

But the lifelogger was gone and he barely managed twenty-two seconds his first time on the biofeedback. His next ten scores were much worse.

It was the hotel room. It had once been an office, and before that, it had been half a hotel-room. There were still scuff-marks on the floor from where the wheeled office chair had dug into the scratched lino. The false wall that divided the room in half was thin as paper and Lawrence could hear every snuffle from the other side. The door to Lawrence's room had been rudely hacked in, and weak light shone through an irregular crack over the jamb.

The old New Yorker Hotel had seen better days, but it was what he could afford, and it was central, and he could hear New York outside the window—he'd gotten the half of the hotel room with the window in it. The lights twinkled just as he remembered them, and he still got a swimmy, vertiginous feeling when he looked down from the great height.

The clerk had taken his photo and biometrics and had handed him a tracker-key that his pan was monitoring with tangible suspicion. It radiated his identity every few yards, and in the elevator. It even seemed to track which part of the minuscule room he was in. What the hell did the hotel do with all this information?

Oh, right—it shipped it off to the Securitat, who shipped it to the Order, where it was processed for suspicious anomalies. No wonder there was so much work for them on campus. Multiply the New Yorker times a hundred thousand hotels, two hundred thousand schools, a million cabs across the nation—there was no danger of the Order running out of work.

The hotel's network tried to keep him from establishing a secure connection back to the Order's network, but the Order's countermeasures were better than the half-assed ones at the hotel. It took a lot of tunneling and wrapping, but in short measure he had a strong private line back to the Campus—albeit a slow line, what with all the jiggery-pokery he had to go through.

Gerta had left him with her file on zbigkrot and his activities on the network. He had several known associates on Campus, people he ate with or playing on intramural teams with, or did a little extreme programming with. Gerta had bulk-messaged them all with an oblique query about his personal life and had forwarded the responses to Lawrence. There was a mountain of them, and he started to plow through them.

He started by compiling stats on them—length, vocabulary, number of paragraphs—and then started with the outliers. The shortest ones were polite shrugs, apologies, don't have anything to say. The long ones—whew! They sorted into two categories: general whining, mostly from noobs who were still getting accustomed to the way of the Order; and protracted complaints from old hands who'd worked with zbigkrot long enough to decide that he was incorrigible. Lawrence sorted these quickly, then took a glance at the median responses and confirmed that they appeared to be largely unhelpful generalizations of the sort that you might produce on a co-worker evaluation form—a proliferation of null adjectives like "satisfactory," "pleasant," "fine."

Somewhere in this haystack—Lawrence did a quick word-count and came back with 140,000 words, about two good novels' worth of reading—was a needle, a clue that would show him the way to unravel the Anomaly. It would take him a couple days at least to sort through it all in depth. He ducked downstairs and bought some groceries at an all-night grocery store in Penn Station and went back to his room, ready to settle in and get the work done. He could use a few days' holiday from New York, anyway.

> About time Zee Big Noob did a runner. He never had a moment's happiness here, and I never figured out why he'd bother hanging around when he hated it all so much.

> Ever meet the kind of guy who wanted to tell you just how much you shouldn't be enjoying the things you enjoy? The kind of guy who could explain, in detail, *exactly* why your passions were stupid? That was him.

> "Brother Antony, why are you wasting your time collecting tin toys? They're badly made, unlovely, and represent, at best, a history of slave labor, starting with your cherished 'Made in Occupied Japan,' tanks. Christ, why not collect rape-camp macrame while you're at it?" He had choice words for all of us about our passions, but I was singled out because I liked to extreme program in my room, which I'd spent a lot of time decorating. (See pic, below, and yes, I built and sanded and mounted every one of those shelves by hand) (See magnification shot for detail on the joinery. Couldn't even drive a nail when I got here) (Not that there are any

nails in there, it's all precision-fitted tongue and groove) (holy moley, lasers totally rock)

> But he reserved his worst criticism for the Order itself. You know the litany: we're a cult, we're brainwashed, we're dupes of the Securitat. He was convinced that every instrument in the place was feeding up to the Securitat itself. He'd mutter about this constantly, whenever we got a new stream to work on "Is this your lifelog, Brother Antony? Mine? The number of flushes per shitter in the west wing of campus?"

> And it was no good trying to reason with him. He just didn't acknowledge the benefit of introspection. "It's no different from them," he'd say, jerking his thumb up at the ceiling, as though there was a Securitat mic and camera hidden there. "You're just flooding yourself with useless information, trying to find the useful parts. Why not make some predictions about which part of your life you need to pay attention to, rather than spying on every process? You're a spy in your own body."

> So why did I work with him? I'll tell you: first, he was a shit-hot programmer. I know his stats say he was way down in the 78th percentile, but he could make every line of code that *I* wrote smarter. We just don't have a way of measuring that kind of effect (yes, someone should write one; I've been noodling with a framework for it for months now).

> Second, there was something dreadfully fun about listening him light into *other* people, *their* ridiculous passions and interests. He

could be incredibly funny, and he was incisive if not insightful. It's shameful, but there you have it. I am imperfect.

> Finally, when he wasn't being a dick, he was a good guy to have in your corner. He was our rugby team's fullback, the baseball team's shortstop, the tank on our MMOG raids. You could rely on him.

> So I'm going to miss him, weirdly. If he's gone for good. I wouldn't put it past him to stroll back onto campus someday and say, "What, what? I just took a little French Leave. Jesus, overreact much?"

Plenty of the notes ran in this direction, but this was the most articulate. Lawrence read it through three times before adding it to the file of useful stuff. It was a small pile. Still, Gerta kept forwarding him responses. The late responders had some useful things to say:

> He mentioned a sister. Only once. A whole bunch of us were talking about how our families were really supportive of our coming to the Order, and after it had gone round the whole circle, he just kind of looked at the sky and said, "My sister thought I was an idiot to go inside. I asked her what she thought I should do and she said, 'If I was you, kid, I'd just disappear before someone disappeared me.' " Naturally we all wanted to know what he meant by that. "I'm not very good at bullshitting, and that's a vital skill in today's world. She was better at it than me, when she worked at it, but she was the kind of person who'd let her guard slip every now and then."

Lawrence noted that zbigkrot had used the past-tense to describe his sister. He'd have known about her being disappeared then.

He stared at the walls of his hotel room. The room next door was occupied by at least four people and he couldn't even imagine how you'd get that many people inside—he didn't know how four people could all *stand* in the room, let alone lie down and sleep. But there were definitely four voices from next door, talking in Chinese.

New York was outside the window and far below, and the sun had come up far enough that everything was bright and reflective, the cars and the buildings and the glints from sunglasses far below. He wasn't getting anywhere with the docs, the sister, the datastreams. And there was New York, just outside the window.

He dug under the bed and excavated his boots, recoiling from soft, dust-furred old socks and worse underneath the mattress.

The Securitat man pointed to Lawrence as he walked past Penn Station. Lawrence stopped and pointed at himself in a who-me? gesture. The Securitat man pointed again, then pointed to his alcove next to the entrance.

Lawrence's pan didn't like the Securitat man's incursions and tried to wipe itself.

"Sir," he said. "My pan is going nuts. May I put down my arms so I can tell it to let you in?"

The Securitat man acted as though he hadn't heard, just continued to wave his hands slowly over Lawrence's body.

"Come with me," the Securitat man said, pointing to the door on the other side of the alcove that led into a narrow corridor, into the bowels of Penn Station. The door let out onto the concourse, thronged with people shoving past each other, disgorged by train after train. Though none made eye contact with them or each other, they parted magically before them, leaving them with a clear path.

Lawrence's pan was not helping him. Every inch of his body itched as it nagged at him about the depredations it was facing from the station and the Securitat man. This put him seriously on edge and made his heart and breathing go crazy, triggering another round of warnings from his pan, which wanted him to calm down, but wouldn't help. This was a bad failure mode, one he'd never experienced before. He'd have to file a bug report.

Some day.

The Securitat's outpost in Penn Station was as clean as a dentist's office, but with mesh-reinforced windows and locks that made three distinct clicks and a soft hiss when the door closed. The Securitat man impersonally shackled Lawrence to a plastic chair that was bolted into the floor and then went off to a check-in kiosk that he whispered into and prodded at. There was no one else in evidence, but there were huge CCTV cameras, so big that they seemed to be throwbacks to an earlier era, some paleolithic ancestor of the modern camera. These cameras were so big because they were meant to be seen, meant to let you know that you were being watched.

The Securitat man took him away again, stood him in an interview room where the cameras were once again in voluble evidence.

"Explain everything," the Securitat man said. He rolled up his mask so that Lawrence could see his face, young and hard. He'd been in diapers when Lawrence went into the Order.

And so Lawrence began to explain, but he didn't want to explain everything. Telling this man about zbigkrot tampering with Securitat data-streams would not be good; telling him about the disappearance of Anja Krotoski would be even worse. So—he lied. He was already so stressed out that there was no way the lies would register as extraordinary to the sensors that were doubtless trained on him.

He told the Securitat man that he was in the world to find an Order member who'd taken his leave, because the Order wanted to talk to him about coming back. He told the man that he'd been trying to locate zbigkrot by following up on his old contacts. He told the Securitat man that he expected to find zbigkrot within a day or two and would be going back to the Order. He implied that he was crucial to the Order and that he worked for the Securitat all the time, that he and the Securitat man were on the same fundamental mission, on the same team.

The Securitat man's face remained an impassive mask throughout. He touched an earbead from time to time, cocking his head slightly to listen. Someone else was listening to Lawrence's testimony and feeding him more material.

The Securitat man scooted his chair closer to Lawrence, leaned in close, searching his face. "We don't have any record of this Krotoski person," he said. "I advise you to go home and forget about him."

The words were said without any inflection at all, and that was scariest of all—Lawrence had no doubt about what this meant. There were no records because Zbigniew Krotoski was erased.

Lawrence wondered what he was supposed to say to this armed child now. Did he lay his finger alongside of his nose and wink? Apologize for wasting his time? Everyone told him to listen before he spoke here. Should he just wait?

"Thank you for telling me so," he said. "I appreciate the advice." He hoped it didn't sound sarcastic.

The Securitat man nodded. "You need to adjust the settings on your pan. It reads like it's got something to hide. Here in the world, it has to accede to lawful read attempts without hesitation. Will you configure it?"

Lawrence nodded vigorously. While he'd recounted his story, he'd imagined spending a month in a cell while the Securitat looked into his deeds and history. Now it seemed like he might be on the streets in a matter of minutes.

"Thank you for your cooperation." The man didn't say it. It was a recording, played by hidden speakers, triggered by some unseen agency, and on hearing it, the Securitat man stood and opened the door, waiting for the three distinct clicks and the hiss before tugging at the handle.

They stood before the door to the guard's niche in front of Penn Station and the man rolled up his mask again. This time he was smiling an easy smile and the hardness had melted a little from around his eyes. "You want a tip, buddy?"

"Sure."

"Look, this is New York. We all just want to get along here. There's a lot of bad guys out there. They got some kind of beef. They want to fuck with us. We don't want to let them do that. You want to be safe here, you got to show New York that you're not a bad guy. That you're not here to fuck with us. We're the city's protectors, and we can spot someone who doesn't belong here the way your body can spot a cold-germ. The way you're walking around here, looking around, acting—I could tell you didn't belong from a hundred yards. You want to avoid trouble, you get less strange, fast. You get me?"

"I get you," he said. "Thank you, sir." Before the Securitat man could say any more, Lawrence was on his way.

_____

The man from Anja's building had a different sweater on, but the new one—bulky wool the color of good chocolate—was every bit as handsome as the one he'd had on before. He was wearing some kind of citrusy cologne and his hair fell around his ears in little waves that looked so natural they had to be fake. Lawrence saw him across the Starbucks and had a crazy urge to duck away and change into better clothes, just so he wouldn't look like such a fucking hayseed next to this guy. *I'm a New Yorker,* he thought, *or at least I was. I belong here.*

"Hey, Lawrence, fancy meeting you here!" He shook Lawrence's hand and gave him a wry, you-and-me-in-it-together smile. "How's the vision quest coming?"

"Huh?"

"The Anomaly—that's what you're chasing, aren't you? It's your little rite of passage. My sister had one last year. Figured out that some guy who travelled from Fort Worth to Portland, Oregon every week was actually a fictional construct invented by cargo smugglers who used his seat to plant a series of mules running heroin and cash. She was so proud afterwards that I couldn't get her to shut up about it. You had the holy fire the other night when I saw you."

Lawrence felt himself blushing. "It's not really 'holy'—all that religious stuff, it's just a metaphor. We're not really spiritual."

"Oh, the distinction between the spiritual and the material is pretty arbitrary anyway. Don't worry, I don't think you're a cultist or anything. No more than any of us, anyway. So, how's it going?"

"I think it's over," he said. "Dead end. Maybe I'll get an easier Anomaly next time."

"Sounds awful! I didn't think you were allowed to give up on Anomalies?"

Lawrence looked around to see if anyone was listening to them. "This one leads to the Securitat," he said. "In a sense, you could say that I've solved it. I think the guy I'm looking for ended up with his sister."

The man's expression froze, not moving one iota. "You must be disappointed," he said, in neutral tones. "Oh well." He leaned over the condiment bar to get a napkin and wrestled with the dispenser for a moment. It didn't cooperate, and he ended up holding fifty napkins. He made a disgusted noise and said, "Can you help me get these back into the dispenser?"

Lawrence pushed at the dispenser and let the man feed it his excess napkins, arranging them neatly. While he did this, he contrived to hand Lawrence a card, which Lawrence cupped in his palm and then ditched into his inside jacket pocket under the pretense of reaching in to adjust his pan.

"Thanks," the man said. "Well, I guess you'll be going back to your campus now?"

"In the morning," Lawrence said. "I figured I'd see some New York first. Play tourist, catch a Broadway show."

The man laughed. "All right then—you enjoy it." He did nothing significant as he shook Lawrence's hand and left, holding his paper cup. He did nothing to indicate that he'd just brought Lawrence into some kind of illegal conspiracy.

Lawrence read the note later, on a bench in Bryant Park, holding a paper bag of roasted chestnuts and fastidiously piling the husks next to him as he peeled them away. It was a neatly cut rectangle of card sliced from a health-food cereal box. Lettered on the back of it in pencil were two short lines:

Wednesdays 8:30PM
Half Moon Café 164 2nd Ave

The address was on the Lower East Side, a neighborhood that had been scorchingly trendy the last time Lawrence had been there. More importantly: it was Wednesday.

The Half Moon Café turned out to be one of those New York places that are so incredibly hip they don't have a sign or any outward indication of their existence. Number 164 was a frosted glass door between a dry-cleaner's and a Pakistani grocery store, propped open with a squashed Mountain Dew can. Lawrence opened the door, heart pounding, and slipped inside. A long, dark corridor stretched away before him, with a single door at the end, open a crack, dim light spilling out of it. He walked quickly down the corridor, sure that there were cameras observing him.

The door at the end of the hallway had a sheet of paper on it, with HALF MOON CAFÉ laser-printed in its center. Good food smells came from behind it, and the clink of cutlery, and soft conversation. He nudged it open and found himself in a dim, flickering room lit by candles and draped with gathered curtains that turned the walls into the proscenia of a grand and ancient stage. There were four or five small tables and a long one at the back of the room, crowded with people, with wine in ice-buckets at either end.

A very pretty girl stood at the podium before him, dressed in a conservative suit, but with her hair shaved into a half-inch brush of electric blue. She lifted an eyebrow at him as though she was sharing a joke with him and said, "Welcome to the Half Moon. Do you have a reservation?"

Lawrence had carefully shredded the bit of cardboard and dropped its tatters in six different trash cans, feeling like a real spy as he did so (and realizing at the same time that going to all these different cans was probably anomalous enough in itself to draw suspicion).

"A friend told me he'd meet me here," he said.

"What was your friend's name?"

Lawrence stuck his chin in the top of his coat to tell his pan to stop warning him that he was breathing too shallowly. "I don't know," he said. He craned his neck to look behind her at the tables. He couldn't see the man, but it was so dark in the restaurant—

"You made it, huh?" The man had yet another fantastic sweater on, this one with a tight herringbone weave and ribbing down the sleeves. He caught Lawrence sizing him up and grinned. "My weakness—the world's wool farmers would starve if it wasn't for me." He patted the greeter on the hand. "He's at our table." She gave Lawrence a knowing smile and the tiniest hint of a wink.

"Nice of you to come," he said as they threaded their way slowly through the crowded tables, past couples having murmured conversations over candlelight, intense business dinners, an old couple eating in silence with evident relish. "Especially as it's your last night in the city."

"What kind of restaurant is this?"

"Oh, it's not any kind of restaurant at all. Private kitchen. Ormund, he owns the place and cooks like a wizard. He runs this little place off the books for his friends to eat in. We come every Wednesday. That's his vegan night. You'd be amazed with what that guy can do with some greens and a sweet potato. And the cacao nib and avocado chili chocolate is something else."

The large table was crowded with men and women in their thirties, people who had the look of belonging. They dressed well in fabrics that draped or clung like someone had thought about it, with jewelry that combined old pieces of brass with modern plastics and heavy clay beads that clicked like pool-balls. The women were beautiful or at least handsome—one woman with cheekbones like snowplows and a jawline as long as a ski-slope was possibly the most striking person he'd ever seen up close. The men were handsome or at least craggy, with three-day beards or neat, full mustaches. They were talking in twos and threes, passing around overflowing dishes of steaming greens and oranges and browns, chatting and forking by turns.

"Everyone, I'd like you to meet my guest for the evening." The man gestured at Lawrence. Lawrence hadn't told the man his name yet, but he made it seem like he was being gracious and letting Lawrence introduce himself.

"Lawrence," he said, giving a little wave. "Just in New York for one more night," he said, still waving. He stopped waving. The closest people—including the striking woman with the cheekbones—waved back, smiling. The furthest people stopped talking and tipped their forks at him or at least cocked their heads.

"Sara," the cheekbones woman said, pronouncing the first "a" long, "Sah-rah," and making it sound unpretentious. The low-key buzzing from Lawrence's pan warned him that he was still overwrought, breathing badly, heart thudding. Who were these people?

"And I'm Randy," the man said. "Sorry, I should have said that sooner."

The food was passed down to his end. It was delicious, almost as good as the food at the campus, which was saying something—there was a dedicated cadre of cooks there who made gastronomy their 20 percent projects, using elaborate computational models to create dishes that were always different and always delicious.

The big difference was the company. These people didn't have to retreat to belong, they belonged right here. Sara told him about her job managing a specialist antiquarian bookstore and there were a hundred stories about her customers and their funny ways. Randy worked at an architectural design firm and he had done some work at Sara's bookstore. Down the table there were actors and waiters and an insurance person and someone who did something in city government, and they all ate and talked and made him feel like he was a different kind of man, the kind of man who could live on the outside.

The coals of the conversation banked over port and coffees as they drifted away in twos and threes. Sara was the last to leave and she gave him a little hug and a kiss on the cheek. "Safe travels, Lawrence." Her perfume was like an orange on Christmas morning, something from his childhood. He hadn't thought of his childhood in decades.

Randy and he looked at each other over the litter on the table. The server brought a check over on a small silver tray and Randy took a quick look at it. He drew a wad of twenties in a bulldog clip out of his inside coat pocket and counted off a large stack, then handed the tray to the server, all before Lawrence could even dig in his pocket.

"Please let me contribute," he managed, just as the server disappeared.

"Not necessary," Randy said, setting the clip down on the table. There was still a rather thick wad of money there. Lawrence hadn't been much of a cash user before he went into the Order and he'd seen hardly any spent since he came back out into the world. It seemed rather antiquarian, with its elaborate engraving. But the notes were crisp, as though freshly minted. The government still pressed the notes, even if they were hardly used any longer. "I can afford it."

"It was a very fine dinner. You have interesting friends."

"Sara is lovely," he said. "She and I—well, we had a thing once. She's a remarkable person. Of course, you're a remarkable person, too, Lawrence."

Lawrence's pan reminded him again that he was getting edgy. He shushed it.

"You're smart, we know that. 88th percentile. Looks like you could go higher, judging from the work we've evaluated for you. I can't say your performance as a private eye is very good, though. If I hadn't intervened, you'd still be standing outside Anja's apartment building harassing her neighbors."

His pan was ready to call for an ambulance. Lawrence looked down and saw his hands clenched into fists. "You're Securitat," he said.

"Let me put it this way," the man said, leaning back. "I'm not one of Anja's neighbors."

"You're Securitat," Lawrence said again. "I haven't done anything wrong—"

"You came here," Randy said. "You had every reason to believe that you were taking part in something illegal. You lied to the Securitat man at Penn Station today—"

Lawrence switched his pan's feedback mechanisms off altogether. Posy, at her window, a penny stuck in the governor of her radiator, rose in his mind.

"Everyone was treating me like a criminal—from the minute I stepped out of the Order, you all treated me like a criminal. That made me act like one—everyone has to act like a criminal here. That's the hypocrisy of the world, that honest people end up acting like crooks because the world treats them like crooks."

"Maybe we treat them like crooks because they act so crooked."

"You've got it all backwards," Lawrence said. "The causal arrow runs the other direction. You treat us like criminals and the only way to get by is to act criminal. If I'd told the Securitat man in Penn Station the truth—"

"You build a wall around the Order, don't you? To keep us out, because we're barbarians? To keep you in, because you're too fragile? What does that treatment do, Lawrence?"

Lawrence slapped his hand on the table and the crystal rang, but no one in the restaurant noticed. They were all studiously ignoring them. "It's to keep *you* out! All of you, who treated us—"

Randy stood up from the table. Bulky figures stepped out of the shadows behind them. Behind their armor, the Securitat people could have been white or black, old or young. Lawrence could only treat them as Securitat. He rose slowly from his chair and put his arms out, as though surrendering. As soon as the Securitat officers relaxed by a tiny hair—treating him as someone who was surrendering—he dropped backwards over the chair behind him, knocking over a little two-seat table and whacking his head on the floor so hard it rang like a gong. He scrambled to his feet and charged pell-mell for the door, sweeping the empty tables out of the way as he ran.

He caught a glimpse of the pretty waitress standing by her podium at the front of the restaurant as he banged out the door, her eyes wide and her hands up as though to ward off a blow. He caromed off the wall of the dark corridor and ran for the glass door that led out to Second Avenue, where cars hissed by in the night.

He made it onto the sidewalk, crashed into a burly man in a Mets cap, bounced off him, and ran downtown, the people on the sidewalk leaping clear of him. He made it two whole storefronts—all the running around on the Campus handball courts had given him a pretty good pace and wind—before someone tackled him from behind.

He scrambled and squirmed and turned around. It was the guy in the Mets hat. His breath smelled of onions and he was panting, his lips pulled back. "Watch where you're going—" he said, and then he was lifted free, jerked to his feet.

The blood sang in Lawrence's ears and he had just enough time to register that the big guy had been lifted by two blank, armored Securitat officers before he flipped over onto his knees and used the posture like a runner's crouch to take off again. He got maybe ten feet before he was clobbered by a bolt of lightning that made every muscle in his body lock into rigid agony. He pitched forward face-first, not feeling anything except the terrible electric fire from the taser-bolt in his back. His pan died with a sizzle up and down every haptic point in his suit, and between that and the electricity, he flung his arms and legs out in an agonized X while his neck thrashed, grating his face over the sidewalk. Something went horribly *crunch* in his nose.

The room had the same kind of locks as the Securitat room in Penn Station. He'd awakened in the corner of the room, his face taped up and aching. There was no toilet, but there was a chair, bolted to the floor, and three prominent video cameras.

They left him there for some time, alone with his thoughts and the deepening throb from his face, his knees, the palms of his hands. His hands and knees had been sanded raw and there was grit and glass and bits of pebble embedded under the skin, which oozed blood.

His thoughts wanted to return to the predicament. They wanted to fill him with despair for his situation. They wanted to make him panic and weep with the anticipation of the cells, the confession, the life he'd had and the life he would get.

He didn't let them. He had spent sixteen years mastering his thoughts and he would master them now. He breathed deeply, noticing the places where his body was tight and trembling, thinking each muscle into tranquillity, even his aching face, letting his jaw drop open.

Every time his thoughts went back to the predicament, he scrawled their anxious message on a streamer of mental ribbon which he allowed to slip through his mental fingers and sail away.

Sixteen years of doing this had made him an expert, and even so, it was not easy. The worries rose and streamed away as fast as his mind's hand could write them. But as always, he was finally able to master his mind, to find relaxation and calm at the bottom of the thrashing, churning vat of despair.

When Randy came in, Lawrence heard each bolt click and the hiss of air as from a great distance, and he surfaced from his calm, watching Randy cross the floor bearing his own chair.

"Innocent people don't run, Lawrence."

"That's a rather self-serving hypothesis," Lawrence said. The cool ribbons of worry slithered through his mind like satin, floating off into the ether around them. "You appear to have made up your mind, though. I wonder at you—you don't seem like an idiot. How've you managed to convince yourself that this—" he gestured around at the room "—is a good idea? I mean, this is just—"

Randy waved him silent. "The interrogation in this room flows in one direction, Lawrence. This is not a dialogue."

"Have you ever noticed that when you're uncomfortable with something, you talk louder and lean forward a little? A lot of people have that tell."

"Do you work with Securitat data streams, Lawrence?"

"I work with large amounts of data, including a lot of material from the Securitat. It's rarely in cleartext, though. Mostly I'm doing sigint—signals intelligence. I analyze the timing, frequency and length of different kinds of data to see if I can spot anomalies. That's with a lower-case 'a', by the way." He was warming up to the subject now. His face hurt when he talked, but when he thought about what to say, the hurt went away, as did the vision of the cell where he would go next. "It's the kind of thing that works best when you don't know what's in the payload of the data you're looking at. That would just distract me. It's like a magician's trick with a rabbit or a glass of water. You focus on the rabbit or on the water and what you expect of them, and are flummoxed when the magician does something unexpected. If he used pebbles, though, it might seem absolutely ordinary."

"Do you know what Zbigniew Krotoski was working on?"

"No, there's no way for me to know that. The streams are enciphered at the router with his public key, and rescrambled after he's done with them. It's all zero-knowledge."

"But you don't have zero knowledge, do you?"

Lawrence found himself grinning, which hurt a lot, and which caused a little more blood to leak out of his nose and over his lips in a hot trickle. "Well, signals intelligence being what it is, I was able to discover that it was a Securitat stream, and that it wasn't the first one he'd worked on, nor the first one he'd altered."

"He altered a stream?"

Lawrence lost his smile. "I hadn't told you that part yet, had I?"

"No." Randy leaned forward. "But you will now."

The blue silk ribbons slid through Lawrence's mental fingers as he sat in his cell, which was barely lit and tiny and padded and utterly devoid of furniture. High above him, a ring of glittering red LEDs cast no visible light. They would be infrared lights, the better for the hidden cameras to see him. It was dark, so he saw nothing, but for the infrared cameras, it might as well have been broad daylight. The asymmetry was one of the things he inscribed on a blue ribbon and floated away.

The cell wasn't perfectly soundproof. There was a gaseous hiss that reverberated through it every forty six to fifty three breaths, which he assumed was the regular opening and shutting of the heavy door that led to the cell-block deep within the Securitat building. That would be a patrol, or a regular report, or someone with a weak bladder.

There was a softer, regular grinding that he felt more than heard—a subway train, running very regular. That was the New York rumble, and it felt a little like his pan's reassuring purring.

There was his breathing, deep and oceanic, and there was the sound in his mind's ear, the sound of the streamers hissing away into the ether.

He'd gone out in the world and now he'd gone back into a cell. He supposed that it was meant to sweat him, to make him mad, to make him make mistakes. But he had been trained by sixteen years in the Order and this was not sweating him at all.

"Come along then." The door opened with a cotton-soft sound from its balanced hinges, letting light into the room and giving him the squints.

"I wondered about your friends," Lawrence said. "All those people at the restaurant."

"Oh," Randy said. He was a black silhouette in the doorway. "Well, you know. Honor among thieves. Rank hath its privileges."

"They were caught," he said.

"Everyone gets caught," Randy said.

"I suppose it's easy when everybody is guilty." He thought of Posy. "You just pick a skillset, find someone with those skills, and then figure out what that person is guilty of. Recruiting made simple."

"Not so simple as all that," Randy said. "You'd be amazed at the difficulties we face."

"Zbigniew Krotoski was one of yours."

Randy's silhouette—now resolving into features, clothes (another sweater, this one with a high collar and squared-off shoulders)—made a little movement that Lawrence knew meant yes. Randy was all tells, no matter how suave and collected he seemed. He must have been really up to something when they caught him.

"Come along," Randy said again, and extended a hand to him. He allowed himself to be lifted. The scabs at his knees made crackling noises and there was the hot wet feeling of fresh blood on his calves.

"Do you withhold medical attention until I give you what you want? Is that it?"

Randy put an affectionate hand on his shoulder. "You seem to have it all figured out, don't you?"

"Not all of it. I don't know why you haven't told me what it is you want yet. That would have been simpler, I think."

"I guess you could say that we're just looking for the right way to ask you."

"The way to ask me a question that I can't say no to. Was it the sister? Is that what you had on him?"

"He was useful because he was so eager to prove that he was smarter than everyone else."

"You needed him to edit your own data-streams?"

Randy just looked at him calmly. Why would the Securitat need to change its own streams? Why couldn't they just arrest whomever they wanted on whatever pretext they wanted? Who'd be immune to—

Then he realized who'd be immune to the Securitat: the Securitat would be.

"You used him to nail other Securitat officers?"

Randy's blank look didn't change.

Lawrence realized that he would never leave this building. Even if his body left, now he would be tied to it forever. He breathed. He tried for that oceanic quality of breath, the susurration of the blue silk ribbons inscribed with his worries. It wouldn't come.

"Come along now," Randy said, and pulled him down the corridor to the main door. It hissed as it opened and behind it was an old Securitat man, legs crossed painfully. Weak bladder, Lawrence knew.

"Here's the thing," Randy said. "The system isn't going to go away, no matter what we do. The Securitat's here forever. We've treated everyone like a criminal for too long now—everyone's really a criminal now. If we dismantled tomorrow, there'd be chaos, bombings, murder sprees. We're not going anywhere."

Randy's office was comfortable. He had some beautiful vintage circus posters—the bearded lady, the sword swallower, the hoochie-coochie girl—framed on the wall, and a cracked leather sofa that made amiable exhalations of good tobacco smell mixed with years of saddle soap when he settled into it. Randy reached onto a tall mahogany bookcase and handed him down a first-aid kit. There was a bottle of alcohol in it and a lot of gauze pads. Gingerly, Lawrence began to clean out the wounds on his legs and hands, then started in on his face. The blood ran down and dripped onto the slate tiled floor, almost invisible. Randy handed him a waste-paper bin and it slowly filled with the bloody gauze.

"Looks painful," Randy said.

"Just skinned. I have a vicious headache, though."

"That's the taser hangover. It goes away. There's some codeine tablets in the pill-case. Take it easy on them, they'll put you to sleep."

While Lawrence taped large pieces of gauze over the cleaned-out corrugations in his skin, Randy tapped idly at a screen on his desk. It felt almost as though he'd dropped in on someone's hot-desk back at the Order. Lawrence felt a sharp knife of homesickness and wondered if Gerta was OK.

"Do you really have a sister?"

"I do. In Oregon, in the Order."

"Does she work for you?"

Randy snorted. "Of course not. I wouldn't do that to her. But the people who run me, they know that they can get to me through her. So in a sense, we both work for them."

"And I work for you?"

"That's the general idea. Zbigkrot spooked when you got onto him, so he's long gone."

"Long gone as in—"

"This is one of those things where we don't say. Maybe he disappeared and got away clean, took his sister with him. Maybe he disappeared into our . . . operations. Not knowing is the kind of thing that keeps our other workers on their game."

"And I'm one of your workers."

"Like I said, the system isn't going anywhere. You met the gang tonight. We've all been caught at one time or another. Our little cozy club manages to make the best of things. You saw us—it's not a bad life at all. And we think that all things considered, we make the world a better place. Someone would be doing our job, might as well be us. At least we manage to weed out the real retarded sadists." He sipped a little coffee from a thermos cup on his desk. "That's where Zbigkrot came in."

"He helped you with 'retarded sadists'?"

"For the most part. Power corrupts, of course, but it attracts the corrupt, too. There's a certain kind of person who grows up wanting to be a Securitat officer."

"And me?"

"You?"

"I would do this too?"

"You catch on fast."

The outside wall of Campus was imposing. Tall, sheathed in seamless metal painted uniform grey. Nothing grew for several yards around it, as though the world was shrinking back from it.

How did Zbigkrot get off campus?

That's a question that should have occurred to him when he left the campus. He was embarrassed that it took him this long to come up with it. But it was a damned good question. Trying to force the gate—what was it the old Brother on the gate had said? Pressurized, blowouts, the walls rigged to come down in an instant.

If Zbigkrot had left, he'd walked out, the normal way, while someone at the gate watched him go. And he'd left no record of it. Someone, working on Campus, had altered the stream of data fountaining off the front gate to remove the record of it. There was more than one forger there—it hadn't just been zbigkrot working for the Securitat.

He'd *belonged* in the Order. He'd learned how to know himself, how to see himself with the scalding, objective logic that he'd normally reserved for everyone else. The Anomaly had seemed like such a bit of fun, like he was leveling up to the next stage of his progress.

He called Greta. They'd given him a new pan, one that had a shunt that delivered a copy of all his data to the Securitat. Since he'd first booted it, it had felt strange and invasive, every buzz and warning coming with the haunted feeling, the *watched* feeling.

"You, huh?"

"It's very good to hear your voice," he said. He meant it. He wondered if she knew about the Securitat's campus snitches. He wondered if she was one. But it was good to hear her voice. His pan let him know that whatever he was doing was making him feel great. He didn't need his pan to tell him that, though.

"I worried when you didn't check in for a couple days."

"Well, about that."

"Yes?"

If he told her, she'd be in it too—if she wasn't already. If he told her, they'd figure out what they could get on her. He should just tell her nothing. Just go on inside and twist the occasional data-stream. He could be better at it than zbigkrot. No one would ever make an Anomaly out of him. Besides, so what if they did? It would be a few hours, days, months or years that he could live on Campus.

And if it wasn't him, it would be someone else.

It would be someone else.

"I just wanted to say good bye, and thanks. I suspect I'm not going to see you again."

Off in the distance now, the sound of the Securitat van's happy little song. His pan let him know that he was breathing quickly and shallowly and he slowed his breathing down until it let up on him.

"Lawrence?"

He hung up. The Securitat van was visible now, streaking toward the Campus wall.

He closed his eyes and watched the blue satin ribbons tumble, like silky water licking over a waterfall. He could get to the place that Campus took him to anywhere. That was all that mattered.

ABOUT THE AUTHORS

BETH BERNOBICH fell into a fantasy world years ago and discovered she likes it there just fine. Her short stories have appeared in *Asimov's, Interzone,* and *Postscripts,* among other places. Her first novel is forthcoming from Tor Books in 2010.

Several of **MERCURIO D. RIVERA**'s stories have appeared in *Interzone,* including the acclaimed "Longing for Langalana," which won the magazine's annual readers' poll for favorite story of 2006 and can be heard at TransmissionsFromBeyond.com. His upcoming story in *Electric Velocipede* titled "Dear Annabehls" is set in the same universe as "Snatch Me Another." Mercurio's fiction can also be found in *Abyss and Apex, Aoife's Kiss, Sybil's Garage, Otherworlds Anthology, Northwest Passages: A Cascadian Anthology, Sounds of the Night* and elsewhere.

NANCY KRESS is the author of twenty-six books: three fantasy novels, twelve SF novels, three thrillers, four collections of short stories, one YA novel, and three books on writing fiction. She is perhaps best known for the "Sleepless" trilogy that began with *Beggars in Spain.* The novel was based on a Nebula- and Hugo-winning novella of the same name. Kress has also won three additional Nebulas, a Sturgeon, and the 2003 John W. Campbell Award (for *Probability Space*). Her most recent books are a collection of short stories, *Nano Comes to Clifford Falls and Other Stories* (Golden Gryphon Press, 2008); a bio-thriller, *Dogs* (Tachyon Press, 2008); and an SF novel, *Steal Across the Sky* (Tor, 2009).

Kress's fiction has been translated into twenty languages. She is a monthly columnist for the Chinese magazine *Science Fiction World.* Kress lives in Rochester, New York, with the world's most spoiled toy poodle.

TINA CONNOLLY is a writer and face painter who lives with her husband in Portland, OR. Her stories have appeared in *Strange Horizons, GUD, Heliotrope*, and the anthology *The End of an AEon*. She is a graduate of Clarion West 2006 and has a website at http://tinaconnolly.com.

REBECCA EPSTEIN is twenty-seven years old, blonde, then brunette, then blonde again. Then brunette. She grew up in New York and is now getting her fiction MFA in Tucson, Arizona—a very dry, very warm, very languid sort of place. She lives with one parrot, one female dog who lifts her leg to pee, and one male dog who does not. She also has this old guy with enormous wings who hangs out in the chicken coop in her backyard, and sometimes she throws rocks at him. She has been published in *The Sycamore Review* and *Arts & Letters*, won the 2006 Silent Voices Short Story Award, the University of Arizona's Beverly Rogers Fellowship, and last year was nominated by her MFA program for the Best New American Voices award.

JASON STODDARD is an evil marketer, metaverse developer, and proponent of positive science fiction (though he has been known to enjoy a dystopia or two—shh.) He's a Theodore Sturgeon Memorial Award and Sidewise Award finalist, and editors at *Futurismic, Sci Fiction, Interzone, Strange Horizons*, and other publications have been crazy enough to buy his stories. He has two novels, *Winning Mars*, and *Eternal Franchise*, forthcoming from Prime Books in 2010. He lives in Los Angeles, CA, with his wife and eight reptiles. Feel free to email jason@strangeandhappy.com.

PETER S. BEAGLE was born in New York City in 1939 and raised in the borough of that city known as the Bronx. He originally proclaimed he would be a writer when ten years old: subsequent events have proven him either prescient or even more stubborn than hitherto suspected. Today, thanks to classic works such as *A Fine and Private Place, The Last Unicorn* (plus its award-winning sequel, "Two Hearts"), *Tamsin*, and *The Innkeeper's Song*, his dazzling storytelling has earned him millions of fans around the world.

In addition to stories and novels Peter has written numerous teleplays and screenplays, including the animated versions of *The Lord of the Rings* and *The Last Unicorn*, plus the fan-favorite "Sarek" episode of *Star Trek: The Next Generation*. His nonfiction book *I See By My Outfit*, which recounts a 1963 journey across America on motor scooter, is considered a classic of American travel writing; and he is also a gifted poet, lyricist, and singer/songwriter.

For more information on Peter and his works, see www.peterbeagle.com or www.conlanpress.com.

DAVID DUMITRU was born in a time when children rode in station wagons, unbuckled, often hanging from the steering wheel like spider monkeys while some lady who may or may not have been one's mother sped along the two-lane blacktop smiling an oddly iridescent valium smile. David survived. The simple and wholly puzzling fact of his survival imbued David with an internal wanderlust that would later impel him to seek the horizon, eventually rendering him profoundly unreliable and not a little lacking in social graces. Thus exiled from the bosom of humanity, David took up with the likes of *The Martian Chronicles* and *Dandelion Wine*, *The Illustrated Man*, and *I, Robot*. David, happily, has never returned from exile. David's good friend Theo, the theophagous monkey, says, "They are indeed coming for us and there is nothing we can do about it. Therefore, scratch what itches before it's too late."

HAL DUNCAN was born in 1971, brought up in a small town in Ayrshire, and now lives in the West End of Glasgow. A member of the Glasgow SF Writers Circle, his first novel, *Vellum*, won the Spectrum Award and was nominated for the Crawford, the BFS Award and the World Fantasy Award. As well as the sequel, *Ink*, he has published a poetry collection, *Sonnets for Orpheus*, a stand-alone novella, *Escape from Hell!*, and various short stories in magazines such as *Fantasy, Strange Horizons* and *Interzone* or anthologies such as *Nova Scotia, Logorrhea*, and *Paper Cities*. He also collaborated with Scottish band Aereogramme on the song "If You Love Me, You'd Destroy Me" for the *Ballads of the Book* album from Chemikal Underground.

WILL McINTOSH has published stories in *Science Fiction: Best of the Year, Asimov's, Strange Horizons, Interzone, Postscripts*, and others. He is currently at work on two novels, one a baseball fantasy, the other concerns dating during an apocalypse. By day he is a psychology professor in the Southeastern U.S.

MERRIE HASKELL lives in southeastern Michigan. Her work has appeared in *Asimov's, Strange Horizons*, and other magazines, both online and off. Further trivia is available at http://www.merriehaskell.com.

BRENDAN DUBOIS is an award-winning author of eleven novels, two anthologies, and nearly one hundred short stories. His short fiction has appeared in *Playboy, Ellery Queen's Mystery Magazine, Alfred Hitchcock's Mystery Magazine* and other publications. A lifelong resident of New Hampshire, please visit his website at www.BrendanDuBois.com.

Born in the Pacific Northwest in 1979, **CATHERYNNE M. VALENTE** is the author of the Orphan's Tales series, as well as *The Labyrinth, Yume no Hon: The Book of Dreams, The Grass-Cutting Sword, Palimpsest* and five books of poetry. She is the winner of the Tiptree Award, the Mythopoeic Award, the Rhysling Award, and the Million Writers Award and has been nominated for the Pushcart Prize, shortlisted for the Spectrum Award was a World Fantasy Award finalist in 2007 and 2009. She currently lives on an island off the coast of Maine with her partner and two dogs.

CORY DOCTOROW lives in London, where he writes novels (the most recent being the YA bestseller *Little Brother*) and coedits the popular blog Boing Boing (boingboing.net). He is the former European Director of the Electronic Frontier Foundation and remains a fellow of the organization, as well as working with the UK Open Rights Group.

HONORABLE MENTIONS

Erik Amundsen, "Turnipseed" (*Fantasy*)

Charlie Anders, "Suicide Drive" (*Helix*)

Elizabeth Bear, "Overkill" (*Shadow Unit*)

Naomi Bloch, "Same Old Story" (*Strange Horizons*)

Michael Blumlein, "The Big One" (*Flurb*)

Sarah Rees Brennan, "An Old-Fashioned Unicorn's Guide to Courtship"
    (*Coyote Wild*)

John Brown, "From the Clay of His Heart" (*IGMS*)

Alan Campbell, "The Gadgey" (*Strange Horizons*)

Deborah Coates, "How to Hide a Heart" (*Strange Horizons*)

Hal Duncan, "The Toymaker's Grief" (*Lone Star Stories*)

Charles Coleman Finlay, "The Rapeworm" (*Noctem Aeturnus*)

Merrie Haskell, "The Wedding Dress Parties of 2443" (*Quantum Kiss*)

Paul Jessup, "A World Without Ghosts" (*Fantasy*)

Alaya Dawn Johnson, "Down the Well" (*Strange Horizons*)

Alice Sola Kim, "We Love Deena" (*Strange Horizons*)

Nicole Kornher-Stace, "Yell Alley" (*Fantasy*)

Bill Kte'pi, "The End of Tin" (*Strange Horizons*)

Jay Lake, "The Sky that Wraps the World Round" (*Clarkesworld*)

Jay Lake, "A Water Matter" (*Tor.com*)

Ann Leckie, "The God of Au" (*Helix*)

Yoon Ha Lee, "Architectural Constants" (*Beneath Ceaseless Skies*)

Rose Lemberg, "Geddarien" (*Fantasy*)

James Maxey, "Silent as Dust" (*IGMS*)

Bruce McAllister, "Hit" (*Aeon*)

Meghan McCarron, "The Magician's House" (*Strange Horizons*)

Holly Messinger, "End of the Line" (*Baen's Universe*)

Silvia Moreno-Garcia, "Enchantment" (*Reflection's Edge*)

Richard Parks, "On the Wheel" (*Hub*)

RECOMMENDED MARKETS

Abyss and Apex
www.abyssandapex.com

Aeon Magazine
www.aeonmagazine.com

Apex Magazine
www.apexbookcompany.com/apex-online/

Baen's Universe
baens-universe.com

Beneath Ceaseless Skies
www.beneath-ceaseless-skies.com

Cabinet Des Fees
www.cabinet-des-fees.com

Chiaroscuro
www.chizine.com

Clarkesworld Magazine
www.clarkesworldmagazine.com

Cosmos Magazine
www.cosmosmagazine.com

Coyote Wild
coyotewildmag.com

Fantasy Magazine
www.fantasy-magazine.com

Farrago's Wainscot
www.farragoswainscot.com

Flurb
www.flurb.net

Futurismic
futurismic.com

Helix
www.helixsf.com

Hub
www.hub-mag.co.uk

InterGalactic Medicine Show
www.intergalacticmedicineshow.com

Lone Star Stories
www.lonestarstories.com

Quantum Kiss
www.quantumkiss.com

Reflection's Edge
www.reflectionsedge.com

Shadow Unit
shadowunit.org

Shiny
shinymag.blogspot.com

Strange Horizons
www.strangehorizons.com

Subterranean
subterraneanpress.com/magazine

Tor
www.tor.com

ABOUT THE EDITOR

RICH HORTON is a software engineer in St. Louis. He is a contributing editor to *Locus*, for which he does short fiction reviews and occasional book reviews; and to *Black Gate*, for which he does a continuing series of essays about SF history. He also contributes book reviews to *Fantasy Magazine*, and to many other publications.